THE DEATHBREW AFFAIR
THE LETHAL WEBS #1

NANCY NORTHCOTT

The Deathbrew Affair

ISBN-10: 1-944570-91-8
ISBN-13: 978-1-944570-91-0

Production team:
Cover by Lyndsey Lewellen, Llewellen Designs
Copyedits by Ann Wicker, Eastoak Media
Formatting and interior design by Libris in CAPS

Published by Rickety Bookshelf Press
For more information, contact info@ricketybookshelfpress.com

For Mark & Gavin
They're not Anglophiles, but they know how to live with one.

CHAPTER ONE

Crouching under a desk wasn't the best way to see Italy, but I hadn't come as a tourist. I glanced at my watch, clearly visible in the dark through my night vision eyepatch.

Eleven seventeen.

Fooling the scanners so I could break into this office had taken too much time. Only thirteen minutes left to see what was in the concealed safe and return to my job in the warehouse ten floors below, or I'd blow my cover.

Rumor had it the desk's owner, JJD Industrials magnate Jasper Jones-Demerest, was dealing black market arms to rogue nations. My real employer, the international intelligence agency Arachnid, had picked up chatter about an important meeting here. They'd sent me, Katherine "Casey" Billings, to find out how deep in the muck Jones-Demerest waded now.

I scowled at the safe. Paranoia's a survival skill in the black market arms business, but putting a safe inside the kneehole of the desk had to take some kind of prize. My neck already had a twinge that warned of a crick forming.

My watch vibrated, and I yanked the chair in close to me to keep its displacement from showing on the overhead security camera.

Every three minutes, it did a five-second sweep, long enough to register those present but not long enough for even a lip-reader to decipher a secret deal. I had twelve minutes before I needed to resume my shift, but no room to open the safe.

The elaborately carved, mahogany desk was roughly the size of India but still had little space under it for five feet, eight inches of me. Then there was the bulk under my green JJD Industrials coverall from my Walther PPK and the pack that held my extra ammo and tools flush against my stomach. And the big chair.

All that made an already small space downright cramped. Good thing I wouldn't be here long.

My watch vibrated again, signaling an end to the camera sweep. I elbowed the chair out of my way. I had a camera jammer, which I'd used to reach the office, but it unfortunately worked for only two minutes at a time. On top of that, repeated use at such close intervals would cause a flicker in the feed. Better not to risk it unless time ran too short.

We'd obtained a print of Jones-Demerest's index finger, and our scientists had incorporated it into a small sheath, sort of like a tiny condom, to fool the safe's scanner.

I shoved my finger into the sheath, but the latex twisted. It went on at an angle that yielded a lumpy fit. Hell. I yanked it off and tried again. This time it slid smoothly over my fingertip. Only eleven more minutes left on my break.

I pressed my fake-printed index finger to the scanner. With a barely audible click, the safe popped open a quarter inch. At last!

Opening the door, I checked the arrangement of the contents. Just files stacked neatly, no objects I'd have to replace with care. I grabbed the top file and flipped it open. Swiss bank account numbers. Nice but not what I'd come for, and I had no time to spend on it. I traded it for the next one.

Project Utopia, the top sheet read, with a list of tactical weapons below the title. I ran my microscanner down the pages to copy it. The scanner's internal light source didn't affect my eyepatch, so I skimmed as the scanner recorded.

Jones-Demerest had purchased farmland in Yorkshire. Odd. Lab supplies, too. I frowned. That stuff wasn't in his usual line. Neither were the mass orders for eggs on the next page.

Eggs with weaponry? Uh-oh.

When I turned the page, a phrase jumped out at me, *LD-50*.
Shit.

I flipped to the next page, and something worse jumped out, *Bacillus anthracis*. Anthrax. That explained the eggs. They were incubators. Hell in a handbasket.

Below, I read *Salmonella typhimurium*, Latin for salmonella, *Salmonella typhi*, typhoid fever, and *poena summa*, the Latin for *highest punishment*? That had to stand for something vile.

Coupled with the reference to LD-50, the term for the dosage needed to kill fifty percent of the test population, this information could mean only one thing. Jones-Demerest, that bastard, had graduated from bullets to biowarfare.

I cursed him silently as I scanned the rest of the file. When I finished, my watch read eleven twenty-four, giving me six minutes before my break ended.

The other three files in the safe, labeled *Annual Report*, *Ledger*, and *Quarterly Returns*, appeared related to his cover business. I didn't have time to scan them, and stealing them would tip him off that someone had penetrated his security.

I couldn't risk that, especially given what I now knew. I stacked all the files and shut the door.

The timer signaled another sweep, so I pulled the chair in again. While I waited, I replaced my tools—except for the jammer—in the flat pack under my clothes and sealed the seams.

The timer vibrated again. All clear. Four whole minutes to make it downstairs, when I needed at least five. Crap.

I pushed the chair away, climbed out, and replaced it. I dashed across the antique Persian carpet and out of Jones-Demerest's palatial office, through the smaller one for his personal assistant and across the still-smaller reception room for visitors. This guy had as much status space between his sanctum and the world as the monarchs of old. Probably an ego to match.

Soon, none of that would matter. Arachnid would jump all over this.

Anyone putting bioweapons into the world deserved the worst possible punishment, and I'd see that Jones-Demerest reaped exponentially more than he'd meant to sow. But I shelved the terrifying image his intentions evoked. I could worry about that later. Now I had to escape without being discovered.

At the door, I paused to straighten my caramel-brown wig and green ball cap, which working in cramped quarters had pushed askew. I didn't hear anyone in the hallway.

Holding the jammer down to fool the security camera across from the door, I slipped out into the hall. All clear.

My heart beating fast but my feet silent on the burgundy carpet, I hurried toward the elevator. Offices lined the walnut-paneled corridor, including those for the chief operating officer and chief financial officer.

Nice little enclave they had up here, serving the King of Slime. Whether or not they knew about his side businesses, they benefited from the tainted income.

Bringing home the evidence I carried might save thousands of lives. It would also spur Arachnid to move against Jones-Demerest. My late partner, David Rhys, had been killed while we were investigating a gun-smuggling ring tied to the rat-bastard.

David. My throat tightened, and my chest ached. He and his wife had treated me like family. He'd been gone sixteen months, and I still had occasional nightmares about his death. Still wrestled with guilt and second-guessing.

If Arachnid went after Jones-Demerest, I wanted the point position.

At the corner, I activated the jammer to send the security camera into an internal replay while I jogged past. The elevator waited where I'd left it. I had to bet security wouldn't notice the elevator grid if the video screens stayed clear.

I hit the jammer again to foil the camera inside and used my counterfeit key—required for the penthouse level—to send the cab down to floor seven. The elevators from the warehouse went only that far, to the domain of low-level management. As the doors opened there, I squeezed out.

I ran down the hall to the warehouse elevator and pushed the button. Nothing. Oh, hell, someone must've used it.

Checking my watch, I wheeled toward the stairs. Eleven twenty-seven. Three minutes left before I'd have to test my creative excuse.

Behind me, a door clicked open. "What are you doing up here?" a man's voice asked in suspicion-tinged Italian.

So much for my three minutes.

I pasted on a smile, summoned my own Italian, and turned. "I was looking for the lounge. I'm new."

Approaching, he frowned. He was about five nine and pudgy. I could take him if I had to. His eyes dropped to read the ID badge clipped on my chest pocket.

4

"Maybe you can help me," I suggested, though his frown implied he felt more apt to call security. I gauged the distance as he closed. If he came within reach—

"The lounge is on the warehouse level, by the lavatories." He stopped just outside my kicking range.

"The door was shut." I gave him my best Clueless Babe impression. "One of the men told me there was another one up here. Isn't there?"

"You can discuss that with Signor Abruzzi." Reaching for my arm, he stepped forward.

I'd never survive a chat with the shift supervisor. When Signor Suspicious gripped my right arm, I socked him in the belly with a hard left. Shock broke his grip. With a groan, he crumpled into my rising knee.

Something dinged behind me. Pivoting, I slammed my right elbow down at the base of his skull, and he collapsed. With me facing the open elevator doors.

And the elevator camera.

Shit.

Swallowing against panic, I pressed the button on my watch to signal Petunia McIntosh, my backup, to move in 'cause my butt was in a sling.

I had no time to tie up my new friend. Jumping over his sprawled form, I bolted for the stairs.

There were security cameras on each floor in the stairwell, but I still had the jammer. Holding the button down, I lunged through the door. A leap and a knee-jarring landing, and I reached the turn. Another leap brought me to the next floor.

I'd just hit the next landing when the klaxons shrieked, a bone-rattling clamor filling the office floors. The stairway lights blinked red. My heartbeat went into adrenaline surge overdrive. Damn. But I'd known Jones-Demerest wouldn't have dolts watching the security monitors.

The elevator camera had probably torpedoed my cover, but using the jammer should keep them from knowing exactly where I was. I hoped.

I ripped a few orange gumballs out of my pack. The midget smoke bombs, which resembled nickel gum, might come in handy. As backup, I also pulled out a jawbreaker. It looked like a rough-textured, yellow gumball but packed a hellacious flash/bang combination.

Holding the jammer down, I frog-jumped down to the warehouse level. The guards might know I was trouble, but as long as they didn't know where, they couldn't overwhelm me. The fire door was one floor down, with an alarm. Since that would alert them to my route, I'd try evasion first.

Removing my wig revealed my hair's true, dark brown color. I tossed the wig and cap down the stairs to lay a false trail, then unzipped my coverall partway so I could draw my Walther from its shoulder holster more easily if I needed it.

Gulping in a deep breath to brace myself, I slipped out of the stairwell. Just as alarms sounded in the warehouse.

A wooden pallet stacked high with boxes of ball bearings blocked my view of the warehouse but not of the loading bay door. It stood about a dozen yards past the pallets, open to the balmy night. With a screech, the metal hatch started downward to cut off my exit route.

"Hey!" someone behind me yelled in Italian. "You, stop!"

Crap. I flung a gumball in his direction. It smashed on the concrete as I drew the Walther. Acrid black smoke erupted. The guy coughed, a deep, racking, sick sound. That should slow him down.

I hurled the flashbang toward the opposite side of the room. It detonated with a blinding flare, and I flung the other two gumballs in different directions. The more false trails, the better.

Through the flare of light and the ear-splitting din of shouts and coughs and klaxons and banging, I ran flat-out for the loading bay. Maybe there'd be a boat I could steal at the end of the dock to carry me downriver to meet Petunia. The Tiber River was the weak chink in the plant's armor. Everything on land was fenced, guarded with electricity and dogs.

A couple of guys by the loading bay wheeled toward the din I'd created. I never lose sleep over killing agents of chaos, but I try to avoid whacking some dupe who's just doing his seemingly innocent job. I threw my last gumball and plunged at the door. I half skidded, half rolled under the metal panel an instant before it thudded into its floor slot behind me.

That bought me a few minutes. Ignoring my scraped, stinging hands, I jumped off the loading platform and sprinted thirty yards across the empty freight yard for the dock. I didn't bother with the jammer. The outside cameras would pick me up, but I'd lost any hope of secrecy anyway.

Fear tightened my throat. I swallowed to clear it. I'd survived worse scrapes than this.

A faint scent of motor oil hung in the air. Across the broad, moon-silvered river lay other companies' warehouses, now deserted.

Tall stacks of crates awaiting tomorrow morning's barge pickup took up most of the dock. At least I'd have some cover. Heart racing, I darted behind them.

No boat.

Shit. I hoped that didn't mean I'd used my quota of luck for tonight. Personal reasons aside, I had to let Arachnid know what I'd found. Just thinking of the deaths an effective bioweapon could cause in a single release made me ill.

I'd have to swim downriver—and conceal myself underwater before the guards caught up to me. Which could be any minute.

But I couldn't let haste or anxiety lure me into a stupid mistake. Jaw set, I ducked behind the crates, set the Walther down and shucked the coverall and pack. That left me with a tank suit and sneakers.

Loud, male voices came from the direction of the building. I didn't have much time. From the body pack, I drew a waterproof pouch containing the scanner, the fingerprint sheath, the night vision eyepatch and my two spare magazines for the Walther. I'd take them and my weapon. The ordinary, unremarkable tools I hadn't needed to use, I'd leave in the pack and fling it into the river. The splash would draw attention to that spot while I swam away in a different direction.

I hoped.

Footsteps hit the metal dock, fast and angry. They stopped abruptly.

Uh-huh, sneaking up on me. A little late for caution, though. Also a little soon for my needs.

Silently, I set the waterproof pouch down and gripped the Walther. I held my breath, crouching, and listened.

Two people, by the sound of their muffled but heavy footsteps. One on my left and one on the right. A flanking maneuver, but *divide and conquer* could serve me as well as them.

The one on the right sounded closer. But the crate on the left stood only waist high, while the ones on the right rose about six feet.

I'd have to go left. It's hard to explode into action around something. "Over" works much better, especially with an assist from gravity.

I set my hands cautiously on top of the low crate, waiting. With the gun in my right hand, I'd have to put most of my weight on my left. The right-hand guy reached the corner. I surged upward, vaulting over the crate and twisting to slam my feet into his dark-clad companion.

He had a lineman's blocky build, but I hit him squarely and hard. He toppled backward with a grunt. His gun barked, and a bullet zinged past my ear.

I landed, spinning toward the second guy as he rushed toward me. Just as I'd figured, only two of them. This doofus didn't even have his gun drawn. I took a step forward to meet him and pivoted on my left foot for a right roundhouse kick to the ribs. He swatted at my leg, an amateur move.

My toe stuck—some kind of crap on the dock—but my leg was already swinging. The kick drove his arm aside and struck him in the ribs, not as hard as it should've.

White-hot pain blossomed in my left knee. At least it didn't collapse, but I couldn't run on it. I had to finish this quickly.

The guard staggered. Righted himself to lunge at me. I set my weight on my right foot, blocked his punch with my left forearm, and hit his temple with the butt of my Walther. He dropped silently.

His buddy stirred. A squad of men in guard uniforms, about a dozen, charged from the reopened warehouse gate.

I rolled across the crates. When I landed, my left leg screamed blue murder and crumpled.

Stifling a groan, I knelt to jerk the mermaid mask out of my pack. I sealed the waterproof pouch with the things I was taking, then hurled my pack low and hard off the dock. It hit the water with a satisfying splash about eight feet out, in a spot where I might've dived.

Holding the pouch, the mask, and my gun, I slid into the water. Damn, but it was cold. I swallowed a gasp.

I surfaced under the dock to the sounds of gunfire and Italian curses and the dank, oily stink of polluted river. Bullets ripped knife-like splashes where my pack had sunk.

At least my leg worked well enough to tread water, though every kick sent fire up my thigh. I could swim, more or less, and probably hadn't torn the ligaments completely. Maybe luck hadn't deserted me after all.

I fitted the mask over my face and pulled the straps tight. If the filter didn't work in this nasty water, I wasn't out of the swamp yet. Cautiously, I submerged the lower half of my face and inhaled. The mask drew air from the water. Not as much as I'd've liked but enough to sustain me until I reached the rendezvous downstream.

The guards were shooting into the river at random now. I sank under the water and used my arms to push myself down a meter, two, then three. Now the water would not only conceal me but slow any stray bullets that came my way.

I set my lips in a line behind the mask and, ignoring my screaming knee, kicked out into the current. Next up, ending the twisted career of Jasper Jones-Demerest.

#

Three hours later, I perched on the edge of a leather seat in an Arachnid jet racing north over the Italian Alps. Settling back, I spared a moment's gratitude for the convenience. I still carried enough of Hartner Falls, North Carolina, my textile-mill hometown, with me to see private cars and jets as privileges not to be taken for granted.

The small plane didn't have a shower, but it did stock a limited selection of track pants and t-shirts for agents who, like me, had suffered recent wardrobe losses. I might still have gunky hair, but I did have clean, if baggy, clothes.

Petunia wrapped a pressure bandage around my swollen knee. Brows knitted below her spiky blonde hair, she stared at the bandage, then popped a huge, purple gum bubble. "You know, Casey," she said with her Scots lilt, "for a roundhouse kick, you pivot on your toes."

"Tell that to the guy who didn't clean the dock."

"I don't think you tore anything, but you'll have to stay off it for a bit." She spoke from both paramedic training and long experience with field operatives.

"I don't have time to rest. We have to nail this guy."

"*We* need not include either of us, you know. Arachnid has scores of operatives."

"Yeah, but I discovered this plot. We should have first crack at breaking it."

We'd transmitted my data ahead on a scrambled channel. By the time we reached London headquarters, the analysts there would have as clear a picture of Jones-Demerest's bioweapons scheme as my information could supply.

Petunia—probably not her real name, but that was her business—looked skeptical. "I'd like to be a fly on the wall when you try convincing the Spider Lady of that."

"You could probably sell tickets." Going by the title Arachne, as all regional directors did, our boss made Hitler look as determined as a marshmallow man. "Don't bet against me, though. I thrive on uphill battles."

I'd had to, to escape Hartner Falls.

"Everyone in Arachnid knows you do." Petunia grinned. "It's a couple of hours to London. Take an anti-inflammatory and rest."

"Maybe later."

Petunia rolled her eyes as though she'd expected that reply. "Suit yourself, but I'm dozing." She belted herself into the seat across from mine.

I slid down in my seat to practice controlled breathing. It did little to dull the pain. Resting made sense, but drugs would fog my brain for the coming argument.

I have first dibs would cut no ice with Arachne, but telling her my real reason for wanting this gig so badly would get me scratched from it for sure.

Lack of objectivity, she'd say. She'd be right about that but wrong about personal reasons always being a hindrance.

I owed David and his family. For his funeral, his petite, blond wife, Amelia, had worn green and dressed their two sad, bewildered little girls in floral prints, the outfits David loved best on them. Not even the bright spring dresses could bring the sparkle back to those young faces.

The memory stabbed into my heart. As it always did. One way or another, I would keep the promise I'd made Amelia that day. I would bring Jones-Demerest down.

I'd fight for this case if I had to.

Abuse of power was personal to me. The mill town where I grew up ran on the old model, with the mill owner controlling everything from the schools to the churches to the grocery store. Nobody sneezed without begging "Mr. Jim" Hartner's pardon. No kid dared win a game from any of his sons. Or defy a Hartner's orders, no matter how petty or unfair.

I'd learned that the hard way when I was eight, when "Jimbo" Hartner, the youngest, ruined what turned out to be my last evening with my grandfather. Ever since, I'd fought for what I wanted. Sheer determination let me escape the grinding mill town life that so easily squelched any hope of something better.

I'd read everything I could get my hands on in high school, busted my ass putting myself through college, even changed my speech patterns to fit into a less rural world. From my cover as a business consultant to my covert work for an agency named after a spider, I'd built a life that suited me.

In Greek mythology, Arachne was a weaver turned into a spider by Athena. At Arachnid, we spun webs to nail people like Jones-Demerest and keep the world safe.

Jones-Demerest had money and power, and he was abusing them to get more of both—wanted more badly enough to create and likely sell a plague that would kill hundreds, maybe thousands, of people who'd never done anything to injure him.

Son of a bitch was too mild a term for him. Also unfair to female dogs. *Devil spawn* came closer.

Terminated would be even better. Especially if I could convince my perceptive, iron-willed, always-the-job-first boss that I was up to taking care of him.

CHAPTER TWO

Petunia and I disembarked at London Gatwick's corporate section as dawn turned the sky pink. We breezed through Customs, thanks to our diplomatic credentials, and out to Arachnid's waiting car and driver, a perk only the urgency of our mission warranted.

The car zipped north on the M23, then slowed to merge with the lorries—trucks, to us Americans—and cars heading into London on the A23 to start the day. Weary and sore as I was, my spirits rose at the bustle. I loved the city's cosmopolitan nature as much as I did the simple decency of my former neighbors in Hartner Falls. For their sake and that of all the simple, decent places around the world, Arachnid had to stop Jones-Demerest.

Petunia dozed in her corner, but I had too much on my mind to nap. I've never mastered the trick of instant sleep to instant wake. Besides, David's dead, contorted face haunted me, along with the pain thinking of him always brought.

I knew in my bones that the weapons ring he'd died investigating was linked to JJD Industrials. I just couldn't prove it, and my guilt over his death, which everyone had insisted wasn't my fault, had put me on a *watch for imminent crackup* list for a couple of months.

Any mention of his name would trigger all sorts of psych unit alerts. So I had to convince Arachne some other way. Racking my brain for a persuasive argument, I watched the buildings and the traffic grow more dense as we neared London.

I still hadn't come up with anything convincing when we arrived at Arachnid's headquarters, a discreet office building in South Wimbledon. The proprietors of the tailor shop, florist, estate agency, and tea room in our block didn't know about the acres of labs and workshops, not to mention secret escape routes and storage bays, Arachnid maintained underground.

Our neighborhood of clunky post-war buildings lacked the charming ambience of Wimbledon High Street with its two-story and three-story Victorian and Georgian shops, but it also drew less curious foot traffic.

I took the elevator down to level one, the most secure facility. Petunia left me at the workshops, level four, with a bright "Cheers, and best of luck."

I needed all she could wish me, seeing as how no decent arguments had come to mind. *I found out about it, so it's mine* sounded a tad too childish to sway Arachne. I had to hope my training and my work on the case so far would suffice.

From the elevator to Arachne's office, I limped maybe a score of steps over unremarkable, British blue carpeting, the indoor/outdoor type because people occasionally bled on it, to a steel door with a faux oak finish. Our money went into operations and security, not indulgence.

When I opened the door, Lucy, the matronly receptionist, nodded to me. "She's expecting you."

It wasn't yet eight a.m., but that figured. We'd all long suspected the Spider Lady lived either here or very close by.

Her assistant, Martin, gave me a curt nod from his corner cubicle. His blond good looks—of the geeky, gold-rimmed-glasses variety, but still quite nice—were wasted on his rigid personality. I'd often wished Arachne went in for the flirty, cheerful type of assistant so common in spy movies. Someone like that would probably drive her no-nonsense self nuts, though.

Despite the early hour, someone else waited to see her. An open, raised copy of London's *The Times* newspaper hid the visitor's face. Judging by the big hands gripping the sheets, the long, sturdy legs clad in neat gray trousers, and the large, shiny black Oxfords, he was male. The tabloid-sized sheets also obscured his upper body except for neatly combed black hair and admirably broad shoulders.

Whoever he was, I had priority. I tapped on the office door, and Arachne's well-bred, upper-crust, British alto called, "Come in, Miss Billings." No too-modern *Ms.* business for her.

Trying not to limp, I marched into her office. I kept my voice brisk and businesslike. "Good morning, Arachne."

Short, gray-haired, and immaculately attired in a dark green, silk pantsuit, she regarded me over half-moon glasses. "Sit down before you fall down. I've heard all about your knee."

Petunia was too thorough sometimes. "It isn't as bad as we first thought." I stifled a wince as I bent it to sit.

"Mmhm."

The dry acknowledgement boded ill. In her immaculate office and her stylish presence, I felt even grubbier. I tried for a casual expression and hoped I didn't look sappy.

Papers littered her desk, most likely intel from around the world. She folded her hands on top of them. The look in her eyes was almost kind, and that made me uneasy. *Brisk* was more her style. "Our analysts concur with your assessment and Miss McIntosh's," she said. "We believe Jones-Demerest is developing bioweapons. Unfortunately, important though your information is, it isn't proof that will stand up in court."

What? My mouth dropped open. I couldn't breathe. Who cared about prosecuting him? I just wanted him dead. I swallowed, groping for words, but she didn't give me a chance to speak.

Still with that appalling, kind expression on her face, she said, "Studying these diseases isn't illegal. Even working with them, if one has the correct permits, is allowed."

"We don't need that level of proof," I managed. "Not if we terminate the rat-bastard. Arachne—"

"No." She held up a hand to stop me. "I understand what you want, Miss Billings. I share your sentiments, but Jones-Demerest is too prominent and well connected for that to be a viable option. Especially if we can prosecute him instead."

"We've had so much luck with that," I muttered, for once undaunted by the raised eyebrow that probably signaled her dislike of sarcasm.

"That may be about to change."

As I sat straighter, she continued, "Apparently, Jones-Demerest has opened a private community in Yorkshire. Under the cover of research laboratories he supports, he has also bought everything he needs for a bioweapons factory. We plan to investigate that."

"I hate bioweapons." Only slightly more than I hate having my partner's guts blown out because I didn't arrive in time.

The silence lengthened, but I set my jaw. Better not to push too soon. Let her be the first to speak.

"You're one of six field agents, only two of whom are female, with the proper training to read the relevant lab reports."

A concession? Did that mean—?

"You're also the right age, if your knee recovers in time."

"The right age?"

"To work with the MI5 officer assigned to this problem." She pressed a button on her telephone. "Martin, send in Lord Bainbridge."

I had the job. Hooray, but...lord? MI5? "Uh, not to look gift horses in the mouth or anything, but I prefer to work alone."

I especially didn't need some effete, spoiled Lord Whoever in my hip pocket. I'd had enough of to-the-manor-born princelings by the time I finished elementary school. Which Arachne knew. Nor did I need anyone to watch out for again. I try to learn from my tragic mistakes.

"This is MI5's patch, Miss Billings. We include them, or they'll try to exclude us. I've no time for interagency squabbling." Her stern expression warned me not to argue.

I'm stubborn but not crazy, so I shut up. Maybe I could still work this to my advantage.

Someone tapped on the door. She called, "Come in," and I stood politely to greet my new colleague.

He had to be the guy from the outer office. Tall, broad-shouldered and rugged, he could've been a pirate in spite of the fine suit and navy silk tie with narrow, pale blue stripes. A visitor badge dangled from a lanyard around his neck.

I recognized the level *I am the boss* look in his gray eyes from my mirror. It made me suddenly conscious that my hair reeked of L'Air de River Muck and my clothes didn't come close to fitting.

Nothing about him said *effete*, for sure, but I didn't feel any better about this pairing. Me and Lord Pirate working together would be like two guys waltzing, both trying to lead.

Still, I pasted on a smile and stuck out my right hand. "I'm Casey Billings. Pleased to meet you."

We clasped hands. My pulse did a funny little hop before it settled. Too briefly for me to read, something glinted in his eyes.

"Miss Billings." He had a firm, fast handshake, with none of that silly *I can break your fingers* garbage. His glance noted my scuzzy appearance, but he didn't comment.

He took the seat Arachne indicated, in the armchair next to mine. I caught an appealing whiff of cedar as he sat.

"Arachne, good morning," he said, his deep voice damnably smooth and warming, like good brandy going down. "Just so we're all clear, Her Majesty's government has directed me to head this operation."

He wasn't one to waste time. Despite wishing him off my case, I had to admire that. But why the hell did I feel so...conscious of him?

My boss's smile would've chilled a tarantula's blood. "Having spoken to the home secretary, I'm certain we'll have no difficulty working together. That's why you're here."

"That's settled, then." He nodded as though he'd expected as much. Could MI5 really pull our strings that easily?

She ignored the gesture. "You'll be working with Miss Billings. As you are, she's rather an independent sort."

To put it mildly. I gave His High-Horse Lordship my Prom Queen smile. The one that shows lots of teeth. "I'm sure we'll get along famously."

If I had to label his answering smile, I'd call it Courtier Patronizing. "I've no doubt," he said. He glanced at Arachne, then cocked an eyebrow at me. "If you can restrain your impulsive tendencies and follow my lead, you'll make an ideal wife for me."

CHAPTER THREE

In your dreams, I almost blurted. I stopped myself just in time. Arachne thought blurters had poor impulse control, so I substituted, "If you're up to the challenge."

He had the gall to look amused. "I don't anticipate any difficulty."

Annoyed, I glanced at Arachne. She watched the interplay impassively, as usual, assessing it while giving away nothing.

Still, I had the assignment—even though Himself came with it. I could afford to press a bit. "I assume his lordship is referring to some plan you and MI5 hatched while I was flying home. Maybe someone could fill me in."

"It's quite simple." Arachne folded her hands on the desk. "Jones-Demerest's private community is marketed to busy couples seeking a respite. He calls it the Simply Yorkshire Farm and Brewery. You and Lord Bainbridge will pretend to be such a couple, infiltrate the compound, and raid and destroy the bioweapons laboratory we believe he's hiding on an adjacent tract. Unfortunately, the medical research he supports gives his purchases cover, and his social connections also limit our options, as I said."

She made it sound as routine as picking up eggs and a quart of milk on the way home. "Why are we sure he's making the weapons there? Isn't that a little close to him for comfort?"

Arachne nodded at His Lordship. He turned toward me. "We believe he assumed that risk in order to supervise closely. We were already watching him because several laboratories he supports purchased large quantities of live bacteria. Traffic between the compound and those laboratories has picked up in recent days, an ominous change in light of your findings.

"A nice piece of work, by the way." Despite his matter-of-fact tone, he gave me a brief nod, as though in salute.

I swallowed my surprise at the compliment and mustered a smile. "Thanks. I assume someone has worked out cover identities for us—wait a minute. If you're a lord, you must've gone to all the best schools. Eton, Cambridge, whatever. If we're mingling with moneyed people, won't someone recognize you?" I didn't care for those people, but he came from that set.

He shrugged. "Can't be helped. My unfortunate reputation for reckless self-indulgence will bolster the image. Sorry, but you're to be a brash American gold digger."

His wry tone took the bite out of the idea. Maybe he wasn't as stiff as I'd first thought. I replied, "I've always wanted to enjoy the lifestyles of the rich and famous."

"Don't grow too comfortable," Arachne said. "Neither Arachnid nor MI5 can afford to subsidize this operation forever."

Good grief, she was smiling. Teasing. This was quite a contrast to her earlier coolness. She must really respect His Lordship.

There was another wrinkle to this, though. "If I'm to be your wife, Lord Bainbridge, how will you explain being single again when the mission ends?"

"Alas," he responded dryly, "consumed by passion, I neglected to check public records, which revealed your prior marriage. In view of my careless image, no one will doubt the tale."

I frowned, surprisingly concerned for him. "How do you stand that reputation when you have a dangerous, demanding job?" Not my business, but I couldn't help asking.

His face went stony. "It's for queen and country."

He might pretend not to mind, but his stark expression said otherwise. I nodded acknowledgement, which he seemed not to see.

Though the circumstances differed, I knew how it felt to be judged as something you weren't. Mill workers' kids weren't expected to become anything that mattered. Even now, people back home, including some of my family, assumed my supposed job as a business consultant couldn't be very important or pay very much.

Arachne said, "Miss Billings, pick up a briefing notebook today.

You'll also see the doctor. If all goes well, you'll leave for Yorkshire by the end of next week."

If it didn't go well, another agent, who probably already had the same material I'd receive, would get the job.

I flexed my knee. *Ow*, but it'd just have to heal. I couldn't lose this shot at Jones-Demerest.

"We'll use my Yorkshire estate as a base," Bainbridge informed me. "After setting our cover stories straight and so forth."

"Of course." I had a feeling the *and so forth* could mean trouble, but I'd have plenty of time to deal with that.

"That's all, then." Arachne stood. "Good day to you both."

Lord Bainbridge stood, gesturing that I should precede him to the door. Rising, I stared up at him. "Do you have a first name? Other than Lord? Since we're going to be married, I probably should know it."

A spark that might have been amusement or surprise lit his eyes, then vanished. Deadpan, he answered, "Richard Henry Arthur John Basingstoke, sixteenth Earl of Bainbridge, twelfth Viscount Wilsham and eighth Baron of Leaford, at your service." Still deadpan, he sketched a slight bow. "My friends call me Jack, so my wife would also."

Oh, would she? Role or no role, I wasn't taking orders. I grinned at him. "I'm sure I can come up with something better. Sweetie-pie."

Definitely surprise in his gray eyes this time, and wariness. Good. He needed to know what kind of partner he was getting. So did I. I'd spend our *settling into our roles* time finding his buttons and taking his measure.

Since he seemed to care about chivalry, I humored him by going through the door first. I'd bet earls generally take precedence over spies, though.

In the outer office, I turned to face him. "Too bad we have to skip the wedding. Arachne could throw quite a party."

"I'm sure." He sounded as though he'd bitten something sour. Extending his hand to shake, he said, "I'll be in touch over the next sennight or so."

Had he chosen the antiquated term for a week to rattle me? Two could play that game.

Holding onto his hand, I smiled and tried to ignore the warmth in my palm and, even worse, in the depths of my body at the contact. I really hoped I wasn't blushing. "It's Casey. Darling Casey to my husband."

Lucy, the receptionist, ignored the byplay, but Martin made a sound a lot like a snort. Judging from the prickle between my shoulder blades, he'd directed his glower there.

Lord Jack raised an eyebrow as his face resumed its Courtier Patronizing expression. "I believe Claire suits you better. Darling." He touched two fingers to his brow in parting salute. "Au revoir."

I felt like raising a hand in a fencer's salute to acknowledge a hit. He knew my real name, which I hate.

Katherine Claire fit my mother's idea of elegance. She figured such a name belonged on the "right" side of the tracks, where she aspired for our family to live someday. Because she loaded the name with frilly images, it became my byword for prissy.

The door closed behind Bainbridge. I shot Martin a glare. "Did you give him my file?"

"He's MI-Bloody-Five. Likely doesn't need our file on you." He sniffed. "You're free to ask Arachne about that." Still typing—how did he do that and talk, too?—he added, "If I were you, I wouldn't do it smelling of river water."

I wouldn't do it at all, as he well knew. Arachne told you what she wanted you to know. In her view, that was plenty. Besides, she valued our secrecy too much to give out anyone's info unless absolutely necessary. Snapping at Martin, no matter how tempting the prospect, wouldn't change anything.

Meanwhile, I had a briefing book to claim and the doctor to see. Not to mention an overdue shower to take. Resolved not to limp in Martin's presence, I stalked painfully out of the office.

#

An hour later, after a shower and a visit to the infirmary, I soaked my knee in the whirlpool. I had the women's locker room to myself, so I also brooded.

I should've remembered the old adage about being careful what you wished for. I'd gotten my wish, but it unfortunately came with a partner. Even worse, that partner had a take-charge personality and a patrician background. And the usual MI5, stick-up-the-butt attitude.

Scowling, I slid deeper into the water. Arachne knew all that about me, and she'd given me this assignment anyway. I had to justify her trust. I'd be switched and blistered before I gave MI5 an excuse to shut us out of this case. I had my share of organizational loyalty as well as my debt to David.

Besides, I had no reason to assume His Interloping Lordship was a snob. I'd stay on my guard about that until I knew for sure, though.

The locker room's automatic door *shushed* open and shut. I looked up, straight into Petunia's cocky grin. She strolled down the row of lockers toward me.

"Congrats. I'm in as well." She patted the paperbound briefing book under her arm. "Your Yankee charm must've done it for you."

"More like age, gender, and training in bioweapons." I sighed heavily but didn't manage to expel any frustration.

She plopped onto a bench, far enough from the whirlpool to escape its surrounding humidity. "You've landed the jammiest assignment to come along in years, and you're moping. Why?"

"It's..." I couldn't explain in a way she'd understand. "Not important."

"Right." But she stayed where she was, frowning at me.

Too bad I couldn't just sink under the water and vanish. Petunia pursuing an idea was a bulldog hanging onto a bone.

"It's your lordly new partner, isn't it?" she said. "I know you like taking the lead, but you should read the briefing. Between the lines, it all but calls him a legend."

Was that awe in her voice?

Yes. Crap. That boded ill for my ability to manage him.

"You have info on His High-Horseness?" I straightened with a slosh. "Let's see."

"And risk you splashing on it? I don't think so. Had to pledge everything up to my hypothetical firstborn for this."

"I won't touch it. Hold it where I can see it. Please."

She rolled her eyes but obliged, standing just close enough for me to read the pages. Someday I'd get her for that so-patient look on her face, but I had to read fast before she tired of playing mannequin.

I skimmed over background—Eton and Cambridge, as predicted. Also MIT in biochemistry under an alias, and—"The George Cross?"

I tried to scale down my undignified yelp. That decoration was the highest accolade for civilian bravery in the UK. "Is he a freaking Knight of the Garter, too?"

Geez, I hated being impressed with my unwelcome partner. With an award like that, he might be sufficiently impressed with himself, and with reason, to make my life even harder.

Petunia snapped the notebook shut. "No Garter. The GC was awarded in secret, known only to a handful of people in the government."

"That info has to be wrong. The George Cross is approved by a committee, not given in secret."

"D'you really think Her Majesty's government—any government, come to that—can't secretly do pretty much anything it wishes?" she asked.

I couldn't argue with that, just wrinkled my nose.

"Thought so." She blew and popped a pink bubble, looking smug. "I'd bet we're not s'posed to know."

"Score one for our side, then."

Arachnid and the security forces of its supporting nations existed in an uneasy alliance. We got money they didn't, and we stood outside the rules that constrained them. Yet they had respectability. Even worse from our perspective, they sometimes got credit for our deeds that our secrecy prevented us from claiming.

I tried my version of winsome on Petunia. "Open that again, huh?"

"Not with you in a shrieking mood. You're getting a copy."

"Which I'm..." I glanced at the clock. "...still half an hour from claiming. Are you saying there's more shrieking material in there?"

"Let's just say we all have our crosses to bear."

"And His Lordship is mine," I concluded glumly.

She retreated to the bench again. "If you must have a partner, you could do far worse," she noted.

"I guess so. It's the *if I must have* bit that's the rub."

"I've worked with you enough to grasp that, but why?"

Because I hate being the one who comes back.

The thought was bleak. Painful. Hovering on the edge of Dreaded Personal Revelation Land, I readjusted my knee while I looked for a way out. Nothing presented itself, and Petunia sat with the patient stillness of a marble statue.

Or a predator.

"Partners let you down," I managed awkwardly. Just as I'd let David down, no matter how many people thought there was nothing I could've done. There should have been something.

"Well, I like that." She glared at me. "Who pulled your arse out of the river a few hours back?"

"I didn't mean you, and you know it. You're top-grade, but a backup and a partner...it's different."

"Especially the decision-making," she noted, mollified.

Damn, she was shrewd. "Yeah."

Her expression softened into thoughtfulness. "So who let you down, Casey?"

Emily Graham, who was supposed to study hard and flee Hartner Falls with me but married the quarterback-turned-plant-nursery-owner and stayed. At least the mill closing hadn't put them out of business.

Then there was Trey, my ex-fiancé, who declared me the love of his life until I decided to attend the FBI Academy. Having a wife who was a "glorified cop" didn't fit his graciously wealthy social image. Unfortunate, since my acceptance at Quantico crystallized my previously vague desire to protect and serve somehow. To stand between those who wanted to live decent lives in peace and those who would prey on them, whether of the white collar or the switchblade variety. I'd given back Trey's ring, to the dismay of my family and the delight of his.

Finally there was the Bureau, which found me too much of a free thinker for its hallowed ranks, though that had worked out okay because I'd landed here four years ago, at age twenty-five. Until then, I'd never felt that I truly fit in anywhere. I still couldn't believe how lucky I was to be here.

None of which Petunia needed to know. She waited patiently, watching me think.

"You want a list?" I cocked an eyebrow at her, a sign I wanted the subject closed.

"Not enough to fight you for it." She grinned again, undaunted.

That's the trouble with letting people get to know you. They become harder to intimidate.

"It's not only that, I think," she continued. "Do you have a problem with Lord Jack?"

"Well, there's the MI5 issue, but mainly it's the lord thing." Not to mention my personal baggage about patriarchies. "Makes me think of stiff collars, Scotch whisky, and riding to hounds."

She frowned at me. "I can see all that, but they don't just give you the GC. If he has it at his age—thirty-three, if you're curious—and with his job, he likely did something dirty and dangerous that was also extremely important."

"There's that, I guess." It actually was some comfort. "Bainbridge can probably carry his own weight."

"You'll find more goodies in the book." She actually smirked at me. "Speaking of your new partner, you do know Bainbridge is his title, not his surname?"

"He's my partner. I assume I can call him what I want." If he was going to call me Claire, I for-damned-sure would. "Besides, I've read letters in novels, ones where lords sign themselves by first name and title —like Joe GrandPoohBah or whatever."

"Yes, but that's the custom for signing letters."

I didn't mean to be rude, but I was determined to stand on equal footing with Himself, as I would with any other partner. "So they treat their titles like last names. I call people I work with by their last names a lot. You know that."

Her eyes narrowed, but her mouth twitched up at the corners. "You're being deliberately impertinent."

"Absolutely." Partly in honor of the whole *Claire* business. "Besides, I come from a non-peerage country. So what else is in that book?"

"You'll see. I'm off to start setting up. See you in Yorkshire." She bounced off the bench, heading for the door with an enviably healthy stride.

"Y'know, his people trounced your Scots ancestors a couple hundred years back. Are you in his corner?"

"No, in my own." At the door, she tossed me a cocky look. "I'm stuck with you both."

I wrinkled my nose at her but called, "Safe trip," as the door slid open.

"You, too, and best of luck with the knee," she called back through the closing door.

With Petunia watching my back in her guise as my personal assistant, I had a greater margin for error in case my lordly partner screwed up. Or worse, I did.

Silence settled on the empty locker room. I swished a hand in the water, making little waves. What is it the Chinese say? *May you live in interesting times*? I've heard they mean it as a curse. It felt like one.

When I next met my new partner, I'd better have everything about this mission down pat. Including a nervy nickname for him, of course.

I glanced at the clock. Twenty minutes left to soak. If I couldn't come up with something by the time I climbed out of here, I was slipping.

#

There's no luxury better than a few hours' sleep in my own bed. I put the water on for tea and took the lift down to pick up my mail.

I'd been gone three weeks, so the front desk was holding it for me. I had a nice little one-bedroom flat in Southwark near the Imperial War Museum, which sat on land formerly occupied by Bethlem Hospital for the Criminally Insane, better known as Bedlam. Which all struck me as highly appropriate.

I liked to jog past the museum, across Westminster Bridge with a nod to the statue of the Iceni warrior queen Boadicea, and around Parliament Square, where I tipped my water bottle to Churchill's and Abe Lincoln's statues before I came home. But I needed two working knees for that.

The doorman and front desk crew were extra security provided by Arachnid since a bunch of us lived in the building. They didn't waste time on chit-chat, so I had my mail in nothing flat.

Riding back up in the lift, I sorted. Bills, ads, and three copies of *Time Out*, the weekly magazine listing current entertainment and dining options. I shifted the latest issue to the top to check tonight's offerings.

A square envelope of heavy, cream-colored paper fell out of the stack. Careful of my knee, I stooped to pick it up. A gold-embossed crest adorned the back, a boar standing on crossed swords. *Uh-oh.* I knew only one nobleman.

I flipped the envelope. On the front were my name and address written in strong, bold script. The address looked like black fountain pen ink. No stamp. It must have been hand-delivered, which implied lackeys. I couldn't see Lord Jack dropping by himself.

I opened my door in time to hear the kettle whistle. My British friends mostly used electric kettles with automatic shut-offs, but I liked the whistle. On my way to the kitchen, I dropped the rest of the mail on the couch next to my briefing book and the transcriptions of my scans from Jones-Demerest's safe.

While the tea brewed, I ripped open the fine vellum and tugged out a square note sheet bearing the same gold crest. Was this part of the plan? I doubted it. The note read, "Lord Bainbridge requests the honour of Miss Billings' company for tea on Tuesday, June 10, at four PM." That was four days from now.

Lord Bainbridge? Miss Billings? Good grief, this was old-school formality of the highest order.

I tapped the invitation against my fingertips. Someone had written this, and someone had delivered it. I could call up the front surveillance camera and see who'd brought it. I'd bet my tea, though, that I wouldn't recognize the person.

Either Lord Take Charge was lax about security, which seemed unlikely, or the people around him had high clearance. If they didn't, writing an invitation to someone he'd introduce in a week as his wife was a stupid risk.

I carried the pot and a mug into the living room and sat on the couch with a couple of cushions under my knee. Although I flipped through *Time Out*, I couldn't focus.

What in blazes was he doing? We'd see each other at work. Why tea? And what did a person wear to tea these days? I was pretty sure jeans and a hoodie didn't cut it.

Why did I care, anyway? I was better with guns than teacups, which was how I liked it. Yet I wanted to make a good impression. On him.

Of course, we'd work better together if I did. That was why. Wasn't it?

After a moment, I shook my head, banishing the worry. I couldn't let this partnership mess with my brain. Someone at Arachnid would tell me what to wear, and I'd comply.

I turned on the television news for background noise and picked up the briefing book. I'd already read the general, mostly common-sense plan Bainbridge and I would follow in Yorkshire. Half listening to the news, I skimmed over the part on bioweapons and on down to section about Jones-Demerest's new compound.

The Simply Yorkshire community provided meal service in a dining hall, maid service in the one-or-two-bedroom cottages, and make-work jobs for those with some sort of weird desire to feel like they were "pulling together to run the community." Riding and golf were available through arrangements with area businesses.

Maybe it was a simple life to people who lived in mansions with giant staffs. To me, it looked pretty cushy. I skipped to Jones-Demerest's charity work.

"The financial world is buzzing today," the BBC announcer said, "over rumors that Hawkshead Shipping, a family-held concern for nearly two centuries, may accept industrialist Jasper Jones-Demerest as an investor. Negotiations are rumored to be occurring. Jones-Demerest was seen in close conversation with Hawkshead's Chief Executive Officer at the Birmingham AIDS gala last night."

I looked up in time to see a picture of the slimy rat-bastard talking to a younger, dark-haired man, both of them wearing tuxes. The younger man looked vaguely familiar. I scowled at Jones-Demerest, but the Hawkshead Shipping name niggled my brain. Where had I seen it?

The answer hit me like a smack over the ear. I grabbed my briefing book and flipped it open. Maybe I was wrong. I had to be wrong.

But the name popped out again, this time from Bainbridge's bio. Hawkshead Shipping was his family business, which they'd entered as investors in the reign of Charles II, becoming full owners under Victoria.

Funny, how he hadn't thought to mention a business relationship with our target.

Someone at Arachnid should have caught it, but the transcriptions weren't done by the same analysts who prepared mission briefs. Making the connection might take them a day or two.

I dug the scrambled phone out of my purse and speed-dialed Martin's direct line. When he answered, I said, "I need Arachne. Now."

CHAPTER FOUR

Nothing works off my frustration like blowing holes in something. Two hours after talking to Arachne, I obtained medical permission to take my braced knee and my weapon to the Arachnid firing range, under a public garden. I had time and irritation to kill before meeting with Arachne and Bainbridge.

Our analysts had noted the Hawkshead Shipping connection about the time I phoned Arachne. Less than an hour later, she'd summoned me for the discussion Bainbridge demanded.

Not that I thought we needed to confer. Either Hawkshead Shipping and Bainbridge were clean or they weren't. Establishing which didn't require face time. Maybe wanting it was a lord-of-the-manor thing.

I sighted on the man-shaped target.

The Walther's comforting crack barked faintly through my headphones. Fighting the recoil kick required me to focus, and the holes appearing in the target gave me a certain savage satisfaction. This was probably the most I'd get until I blew Jones-Demerest's lab.

Preferably without the involvement of Lord Dubious Loyalty.

The middle of the target looked pretty well shredded. I set the gun down and slapped the button to bring the target in. It slid down the wire toward me. Yep, shredded. I gave myself a nod of approval.

Way down to my left and behind me, the door squeaked open. My skin prickled, usually a warning sign. I glanced through the glass dividers to the doorway.

Bainbridge strode toward me, his face set in grim lines. *Down*, I told my weirdly fluttering pulse. I was in no way scared of him and certainly not glad to see him. George Cross or not, the man had to prove we should trust him.

"You're early," I noted. Briskly but neutrally, I hoped.

"They told me you were here." He stared hard at me. "The next time you have questions about my integrity, raise them with me first."

I took my time removing my safety glasses and protective headphones and laid them and the Walther on the ledge in front of me before turning to face him. "You expect there to be a next time?"

"There had better not be." Steel edged his voice and glinted in his eyes.

"We'll see. As for coming to you, procedures bar my doing so. Besides, taking that approach might've ensured no one else noted the connection for a while."

His eyes narrowed. "Think carefully before you stand on that insinuation."

"I don't need to, and you know it." If threatening looks had deterred me, I'd never have left Hartner Falls. "Trusting a dirty operative tends to be a person's last mistake."

His curt nod seemed to grant the point. "If you feel that way, you and your illicit colleagues needn't take part in this operation."

Give up my chance at Jones-Demerest? Forget avenging David?

When snowmen guarded the gates of Hell.

I didn't say that, though, because his word choice struck me. "My *illicit* colleagues? Tell me, is it Arachnid in general you don't trust or me in particular?"

"I don't trust anything governed by a secret committee."

"That lets me off the hook, then. I pay very little attention to our oversight committee."

"Nor do you pay much heed to anyone else, apparently."

That hit too close to my personal business. "We're not here about me. So what's the deal with Hawkshead Shipping and Jones-Demerest?"

"My younger brother runs the shipping line." Standing with his shoulders rigidly square, he ground the words out as though they hurt his jaw. "His talks with Jones-Demerest are a recent development but unimportant. I own enough shares to keep the company clean."

"You could've demonstrated that by messenger." Someone from Arachnid would go over Hawkshead Shipping's articles of association to make sure he was right, but saying that would only antagonize him further, maybe for nothing.

"When someone challenges my honor, Miss Billings, I address the issue in person." *As men do* hung, unsaid, in the air.

"Which brings you down here to see me."

"My colleagues at the Security Service are satisfied," he stated, using the other name for MI5. "I trust that Arachne will be also. What about you?"

Assuming all that was true, I could be either satisfied or off the case. "If my boss is happy, I will be, too. For now." Because I had no other acceptable choice. "Next time, let me in on these little secrets."

"I would have." More ground-out words. "If I'd known."

He inclined his head in a curt nod and pivoted to leave. Tension still vibrated in the air. That last admission, again assuming its truth, must've cost him a lot.

If we were going to work together, someone had to make amends, and the man stalking toward the door didn't seem inclined to. That left me, damn it.

I forced a warmer tone. "I got your invitation to tea."

He stopped and glanced over his shoulder at me. "And?"

"Why tea?"

Turning to face me, he said, "It's a civilized way to start a mission and brief you on my family and our various homes."

"Various?" As in, more than one or two?

"We own Bainbridge House here in London, which the company primarily uses, a cottage in Cornwall, a shooting box in Scotland, and the manor in Yorkshire. We'll be using the manor for this mission. I have a flat in Green Park Lane as well. Finally, there's Bainbridge Park, the ancestral seat. Hawkshead Shipping runs it as an ancillary enterprise."

"Really." All that was quite a step up from my folks' shotgun cottage in the mill village. I pushed aside a jab of envy. "That gives me some insight into the gold-digger mentality."

The taut line of his shoulders relaxed. "They sound grand, but the rambling old things cost a fortune to heat."

"Just like any other house, but more?" I asked.

His practical comment lit a spark of kindred feeling in me. I squelched it. His mansions and my folks' house had nothing in common but the fact that people lived in them.

"Precisely." His balance shifted as though he meant to leave. "How's your knee?"

"Better. Should be in fine shape in a few days."

"Good." He nodded but said nothing else, as though he'd abruptly run out of words.

I'd used my store of ideas, too. An awkward silence fell.

His glance drifted to my target. "Nice shooting." He sounded sincere.

"Thanks. Uh—you want to have a go?" If I was stuck with a partner, I wanted to know as much as possible about him. Like, could he keep pace with me?

He looked surprised, but only for an instant. "All right."

While I reloaded, he changed the target. I reached around the partition to snag headphones and safety glasses from the next booth.

He donned them and accepted the Walther. "I prefer the Glock 9, but I've used one of these."

When he faced the target, I slid my headphones and glasses on. His arm swung up in a smooth arc that leveled off at his shoulder. He squeezed the trigger in rapid, evenly spaced bursts. Recoil would've made my hand buck between rounds. He controlled it with the barest flicker of motion.

He looked good doing it, too. Strong, solid, and reliable. I admire competence, and I had a momentary flash of a Lancelot in the age of firearms. I shrugged the image aside. Romanticizing my partner served no good purpose.

He lowered his arm and hit the target recall button. The middle of the target, the bull's-eye, showed only four holes. I didn't see light through any of the outer rings. But my briefing book said he had terrific marksmanship scores. Which fit if he was doing what I suspected.

He took the target off the clip and held it to the light. Without comment, he passed it to me.

Up close, I could see that each hole was too big for a single round to have made. I'd guessed right. He'd put more than one—several, most likely—through each hole. Shooting that precise more than justified the scores in our dossier on him. It also put him way ahead of me.

"Great job," I managed. I hated to have him outdo me. And with my own weapon. One he didn't even like.

"Thanks." He raised an eyebrow, stealing my best commanding look.

"What about tea?"

If Arachne passed him, as he seemed certain she would, I'd have to accept his offer in the interest of teamwork. I might as well pretend things were settled. For now. "Tea sounds good. I'll send you a note this afternoon."

"No need. I'll expect you Tuesday." He'd gone back into his stiff, formal mode.

"Right." I'd send the note anyway. He already looked down on us *illicit* agents. I wasn't going have him add a lapse in manners to his reasons for disapproving of us.

He glanced at the door. "We're due at our meeting."

"You go ahead. I need to put things away here." Besides, I didn't want to look too much like an ally until I actually had Arachne's confirmation of his story.

#

Unfortunately for me, Arachne accepted Bainbridge's explanation. Which meant I had an appointment for tea on Tuesday.

I knew I was in trouble when he opened the door of his flat. Our eyes met, and his, surprisingly, warmed to smoky gray. No one who disapproved of me and Arachnid should look so welcoming. That annoying awareness of him prickled over my skin again, too. As though that weren't bad enough, his hand at the small of my back as he ushered me into his parlor set off all kinds of tingly feelings I really could do without.

We had nothing in common. This was hormones. Which meant all these irritating responses would fade.

I told my hormones to get over themselves and focused on my surroundings. He'd furnished the room in the hard-surface, right-angle, dark-wood-or-leather style guys tend to favor. Books lining the walls gave the square room a cozy feel despite the dark furniture. Double doors, closed now, marked one side wall.

The broadsword hanging point-down over the mantel seemed the perfect companion to the antique globe in the corner and the smell of old leather bindings in the air. I'd never seen a broadsword outside a museum. I managed not to stare.

One glance at my host's Tattersall shirt and gray wool trousers reassured me about the sky-blue, silk twin set and tan slacks I'd chosen, though nothing could dress up the garish, purple-red hair color I'd acquired for this mission.

One possible social error avoided, thousands to go.

In between avoiding gaffes, I intended to find out more about my partner. Briefing books don't tell you little things like how to deal with a person.

When his assistant, Simon Pennington, brought in a tea tray, I recognized his sturdy build, unremarkable features, and light brown hair from the security recording at my building. The video had not, however, caught the keen intelligence in his level gaze, a sign that he might be called an assistant but likely ranked much higher.

Bainbridge introduced us. Simon also had a brisk, businesslike handshake. All in all, I felt good about his helping Petunia watch our backs.

"I'll leave you, then," he said. With a glance at Bainbridge, he added, "You're not available, I assume."

"Not today." Bainbridge nodded to him.

Simon glided out, his balanced, economical movements consistent with advanced martial arts training.

I sank into an overstuffed leather armchair, the movement easier because I'd been able to ditch the knee brace. "So is he really your personal assistant or just pretending to be?"

"Pretending," Bainbridge replied. "A useful cover at times." He poured tea and offered me a delicate china cup in pale blue.

Gold-rimmed, I noticed. I added sugar and stirred with a spoon that, judging by its weight, had to be silver. That same crest of a boar and crossed swords adorned the handle's tip.

Those details underlined the wealth he probably took for granted. "Tell me about the Yorkshire manor," I said.

"It's a small Palladian house, built about 1780 with ill-gotten gains from the American wars. Seventeen rooms, eighty-seven acres."

According to my research on him, the Palladian house had supplanted a Georgian manor with original landscaping by the famous Capability Brown. Interesting that Bainbridge didn't brag about that.

He continued, "Incidentally, it's about thirty kilometers from Jones-

Demerest's new community."

The nearness would simplify logistical support. "If seventeen rooms make a small house, what's a large one?"

Amusement warmed his eyes. My stomach fluttered, probably from surprise at his relaxed attitude.

"Bainbridge Park is large," he answered, "with twenty-two bedrooms, a ballroom, four parlors, master and mistress suites, a library...Shall I go on?"

"No, I've got it. Anything I should find extra impressive, or will general awe do?"

"We take pride in the chess set in the blue parlor. The ninth earl played a game on it with the Duke of Wellington."

"Before or after Waterloo?" I asked to avoid showing how impressed I really, if reluctantly, was.

"I'm not sure." He stiffened, as though listening. "Hang on."

Now I heard it, too. A woman's voice alternating with a man's, coming nearer.

I shot a glance at my host, who'd said he wasn't available. "I take it you aren't expecting whoever that is."

"No, but it must be a relative, to be so insistent."

"I can take the tea tray in there, if it isn't a closet." I jerked my head toward the double doors. "Unless this could be an opportunity to make an impression—"

"No. We'll follow the plan." As he spoke, he loaded the creamer, the pot, and his cup onto the tray. "Hurry."

Now I could make out words, a firm contralto insisting, "Now look here, Pennington. You know he won't turn me away. Move aside, man."

I put my cup and the sugar bowl on the tray, slung my purse over my shoulder, and grabbed the tray. Bainbridge sprang to open the double doors. I scurried through them, into a bedroom full of more dark furniture.

"It's my aunt," he said. "Wait here. I'll send her away quickly."

It pays to obey a native guide, so I nodded.

He jerked the bedroom doors shut just before the parlor door's faint click heralded his visitor. I set the tray on a rattan bench at the foot of an enormous, canopied bed. With a crested headboard and huge, ornately carved posts that conveyed an impression of bygone eras, it contrasted with the squared, modern dresser, clothes press, bedside tables, and lamps.

The bed linens and draperies, in red, gold and brown prints, reminded me of India. Definite guy ambience.

"My boy! Pennington claimed you were not at home, but Robin said he'd spoken to you a short while ago. Are we interrupting you with a guest?" came through the doors in that commanding contralto.

"No, but I'm rather busy."

"This won't take long. I believe you know Jasper Jones-Demerest. He's keen to meet with you."

I caught my breath. Jones-Demerest? Here? My fists balled. Oh, what a fabulous opportunity!

"Afternoon, Jones-Demerest." Only an idiot would think Bainbridge sounded welcoming. "This isn't a convenient time."

"I don't mean to intrude, of course." Jones-Demerest's baritone sounded too smooth, almost oily. "Your brother mentioned something about your not wanting an investor. When your aunt said she was coming to see you, I naturally thought we might discuss the matter. We had hoped Sir Percival might join us, but he had a previous engagement."

Sir Percival...That must be the great-uncle who ran Hawkshead Shipping before Bainbridge's brother took over. The one who'd worked on the World War II Enigma project, breaking Germany's codes, as a teen prodigy. And who might—or might not—have been part of MI5 in its early days. Surely he wouldn't associate with a scuzz like Jones-Demerest.

"Some other time, perhaps," Bainbridge said.

How could he not want to seize this moment? Our plan, which he considered so unalterable, called for us to make a splashy appearance in Yorkshire, but now his aunt, whom we could scandalize, had unexpectedly arrived with our target, whom we could impress.

It was too good an opportunity to let slip.

Could I make him see that? If we were going to work together, I'd better. We had a choice here and couldn't consult.

I decided to trust my hunch.

Shucking off my outer clothes, I padded to his closet. A dress shirt would serve my purpose. He had a neat rack of them, mostly blue or white but a few with subtle stripes. Their faint sheen denoted fine cotton, and the exclusive Jermyn Street labels proclaimed hand tailoring. It figured. I grabbed the nearest one, white with blue stripes, and pulled it on over my underwear.

It smelled faintly of cedar. It also swallowed me. I'd seen that he was a big guy, standing about six two, but I hadn't realized how broad in the shoulder he was. Dwarfed in his shirt, I felt feminine and sexy. Warm.

No. I shook my head. No warm little rushes. Not about him. They'd only complicate things.

The voices beyond the door had fallen to a muted rumble. I buttoned part of the shirt front and checked the full-length cheval mirror by the closet. No good unless I wanted to flash our audience, and I much preferred not to. We wanted his aunt to talk about us, not have a stroke on the spot.

My cleavage has never been of the lush variety that spills over necklines. It's more the kind you can sort of spot if you take a close look in the right light. As a result, it left the top of the shirt gaping.

I sighed and fastened the button nearest the bosom. Okay, better. Besides, given Bainbridge's party boy reputation, which his bio fully supported—I mean, he'd dated so many models, starlets, and jet-set heiresses that he seemed to be going for a record—I could probably go full-out ditz. That should shock his aunt enough to compensate for not exposing so much skin.

At least I'd worn silk underwear today, in honor of not being in the field. It looked suitably racy where the shirt hung open at the bottom.

On second thought, with Jones-Demerest on hand, I buttoned another button and hid it. I'll let the bad guy see my undies, and more, if it helps me nail him—but only if necessary.

Leaning over so my hair hung, I ran my fingers through it at cross-angles. When I straightened, it looked wildly disarranged. As though I'd just had tempestuous sex.

As if. That'd been so long ago, I could barely remember. That long drought was probably behind my baffling attraction to my temporary partner.

I threw my discarded clothes around, peeled back the bed's covers, and scattered the pillows. That should do it.

Yet I hesitated. If I went through with this, I couldn't turn back, and there might be hell to pay with Bainbridge.

David would have thought this idea hilarious. I caught my breath at a sudden, sharp pain in my chest. With Bainbridge, it was fifty-fifty that he'd even go along with it. Surely, though, he would see my improvisation's value.

I tiptoed to the doors. "I've a great deal to do today, Aunt Beatrice," Bainbridge said with a touch of impatience.

"I must say, Jack, you're very abrupt," the woman said. "Unless you do have a guest?"

That sounded like my cue. I shoved the doors open, leaned on one with my arm stretched up it, and bumped my hips out to the other side. "Bainsiekins, sweet buns, let's finish our matinee."

I'd expected someone like Her Majesty the Queen, well beyond middle-age and going a little stout. This woman had the hairstyle, but she was hatchet-faced, with a little bow mouth that put me in mind of medieval portraits. Thin and wiry-looking, she wore an elegant, lilac suit —with a skirt, not slacks—in nubby silk.

"Oops." I hunched my shoulders and clapped a hand over my mouth. Behind it, I said, "I didn't know we had company."

Her nostrils flared. "Jack—"

Seated where I had been, Jones-Demerest ogled my legs. I wanted to punch his fleshy jaw.

Bainbridge faced me. Hot anger flashed through his eyes before they went blank, then became doltish and adoring. He held out a hand to me.

"Aunt Beatrice, this will come as a bit of a surprise, I'm afraid, but I'd like you to meet my wife. Darling, this is my aunt, Lady Beatrice Devereaux, and that is Mr. Jasper Jones-Demerest. Aunt Beatrice, Jones-Demerest, this is Claire. Lady Bainbridge."

Despite his harsh tone, Bainbridge had made the introductions smoothly. I flashed my biggest, brightest smile at everyone. "Hey, Bernice. Jasper." I flapped a hand at them. "You don't need to bow or curtsey or any of that."

I hadn't thought she could stiffen more, but she did. "You may call me Lady Beatrice. Claire...was it?"

"Like 'Claire de Moon,' that song." Hips swinging, I glided over to Bainbridge. Since my normal pace was a long, fast stride, that sashaying thing felt weird.

He drew me tightly to his side. Very tightly. "That's 'Clair de Lune,' darling."

"Yeah, right." In that position, I could tell he kept himself in shape. Really, really good shape, and I liked the way he felt against me far too much. I beamed at him, though, giving him points for picking up on the song. "Whatever."

With a moony look at me, he said, "You're adorable."

I giggled. I was out of practice, but I managed.

Lady Beatrice directed a laser look at me. "This seems rather sudden, Jack."

"When it's right, it's right." He planted a quick kiss on my mouth.

The kiss shivered all the way down to my toes. I tightened my hold on him in reflex, glancing up at him. His eyes echoed my surprise and desire, but only for a moment. In the next instant, he resumed his goofy expression.

He stroked my waist, generating another shiver, drat it. I'd been celibate longer than I realized.

"I met Claire at a nightclub," he continued in the vein of our cover story. "She's a fitness trainer from New York."

"But I'm originally from Richmond," I said in my best too-perky manner. "That's in Virginia."

I patted his waistline, which was enticingly rock solid. I let my hand rest there but kept it still. With an effort. "Bainsiekins doesn't need a trainer, of course." Not by a long shot. "We just hit it off great."

"Indeed." Ice encased the word. "Young woman, I require a private word with my nephew. Jasper, please excuse us."

"Of course." He rose and made a slight bow in our direction. "Lord Bainbridge, Lady Bainbridge, so sorry to have intruded." As he turned away, his glance ran over me from head to toe. Lecher.

As the door shut behind him, Lady Beatrice said, "You, too, Claire, if you please."

I cast Bainbridge a doubtful look. Giving me calf eyes, he stroked down to my shirt-covered rear and gently squeezed it. Electric current ripped up and down from his fingers.

I gasped, and my nipples hardened. *Crap.* This assignment was going to be serious trouble. Sneaking a glance, I found a reassuring bulge at his zipper. At least I wasn't the only one affected.

"We don't have time, I'm afraid, Aunt Beatrice," he said firmly.

"Darling, if we're going to Asprey this afternoon, we must hurry."

The mention of the famous jeweler turned Lady Beatrice ashen and impressed me with his willingness to go all in for this mission.

"You should become better acquainted before you make extravagant purchases," she said faintly.

"Oh, I know what I like," I assured her. "Rubies. Rubies and emeralds."

The vision of such expensive gems in my hands seemed to silence her. I fingered the neckline of Bainbridge's shirt and beamed at him. "Do we have to go right this minute, Bainsiekins?"

"We can delay a bit." He smiled down at me. "Aunt Beatrice, good day. We're off to Yorkshire to start our honeymoon, then to Paris and wherever else we feel inclined to go."

"But Jack," she protested, "we can't accept Jasper's investment without your signature."

"I've already made my feelings plain. I won't change my mind. Now you must excuse us. I'll give you a ring when we return."

He ushered me into the bedroom before she had a chance to marshal a counter-attack. He closed the doors behind us, but his warning look said he wasn't sure she'd surrender so easily.

We stood by the doors, listening. After a few moments, the parlor door squeaked open and clicked shut.

Bainbridge turned a white-hot glare on me. "You're off this case."

CHAPTER FIVE

I kept my eyes locked on Bainbridge's stormy gray ones and my tone even. "You just introduced me as your wife. I'm in up to my teeth."

"I'll find another way."

"Before you go all self-righteous and lordly—"

"Don't call me that." Stone-faced, he made his tone icy.

So I'd hit a nerve. Nice to know he had one. "No offense intended, but look at this a minute. Jones-Demerest thinks you're distractible and I'm an idiot, and your aunt will talk about this to everyone she knows. Won't she?"

The *yes* lit his eyes before they hardened. "We had a plan. I told you to stick to it."

"I would've consulted you if there had been time."

"That isn't the issue."

"Sure it is, but don't you see that we need to seize the moment when a chance arises?"

"That sort of thinking lured Richard III to his death at Bosworth Field," he snapped.

"Failure to adapt the battle plan got Pickett's men butchered at Gettysburg."

We glared at each other. I might not have been right, but I hadn't been so very wrong. "Why can't you admit this is a good development?"

And why the blazing hell was awareness of him still generating bubbling heat deep inside me?

"Dress and get out." He scooped my sleeveless shell off the bed and handed it to me. "I'll tell Arachne the Security Service will go it alone."

"The hell you will." I yanked the borrowed shirt off.

The flash of heat in his gaze did nothing to dim his scowl.

Swallowing my *hah!* reaction, I pulled on my top. "I just moved us a giant step down the road."

"With insubordination, which I won't tolerate. No, Miss Billings. We're finished." His hard eyes underlined the words.

I shoved my legs into my slacks and tried not to think about Arachne's warning that we had to make nice with MI5 because Britain was their patch.

"You think you can just come up with a new plan, presto-chango? You're nuts. Bonkers. Also conceited as the day is long. You try to dump me, and Arachne will have your hide."

"You'll be lucky if I don't have yours."

"You and what army?" I shoved my feet into my shoes and grabbed my cardigan. Unfortunately, I couldn't yield to my urge to storm out. There was too much at stake for such bratty bickering.

I blew out a hard breath, trying to moderate my tone. "Bainbridge. Jack. Look—"

The hard anger in his eyes softened a little, but a beep came from his dresser before I could finish. At the same time, a *pip-pip* sound came from my purse. Eying each other warily, we reached for our respective phones.

Arachne's voice came over mine, with the tinny sound of scrambling. "Miss Billings. Where are you?"

"At Lord Bainbridge's."

"Excellent. He's receiving a transmission. Watch it with him. We're moving your timetable up." A click ended the conversation. I glanced over at Bainbridge, who was opening a panel in his wall while holding his phone to his ear.

Behind the panel hung a flat television screen. Numbers flashed on it, counting down from five. The numbers ended, and a man's square-jawed, weary face appeared. I didn't recognize him. He must be MI5.

"Paris authorities report fifteen confirmed cases of this mysterious illness," he said in a clipped Oxbridge accent. "All were riders in a particular car on the Metro last Wednesday at noon. Symptoms include high fever, muscle aches, and increasing chest congestion with shortness of breath. Culture samples do not respond to antibiotics. The disease appears to be a new strain of the influenza virus."

Bainbridge and I glanced at each other in shared alarm, our anger drained by the news.

The man on the screen continued. "Our best guess is an aerosol infectant, something odorless that spread more efficiently than any currently known form of weaponized virus or bacillus."

Oh, crap. My stomach churned with imagining the havoc something like that could wreak. I stared at the screen, where my efforts to wish this away had no impact.

"Will report further developments," the man said.

The screen went dark. Into his phone, Bainbridge said, "Yes. Straight away."

He snapped the phone off, directing a hard stare at me. "We leave for Yorkshire tomorrow afternoon, so understand one thing. In American terms, screw with me again and I'll have your ass."

I'd pushed him far enough already, so I let that crack go. "See you tomorrow." Good thing my knee was healing so fast.

"Tomorrow." He made the word sound like a threat.

#

We headed to Yorkshire in a state of armed truce. The day was bright and the scenery bucolic, both at odds with the tension between us. Neither of us said anything, aside from the minimal greetings courtesy required, for the first hour.

I'm okay with the silence people share when they're comfortable with each other. I hate the tense kind that comes with guarded tongues and limited trust, especially between supposed allies. Maybe he didn't figure we started working together until we reached Yorkshire, but I like to dive on in.

Bainbridge sped up the motorway, joining in the general disregard of the seventy miles per hour national speed limit. He also drove with ease and—thanks to his dark green Triumph Spitfire convertible—style, though I was surprised someone so tall could fit in the small car.

"Nice ride," I said. "Very smooth."

Even with the top down, my newly spiked hair didn't do that annoying flap-in-my-face bit. The smell of freshly mown grass, probably from one of the fields bordering the road, teased my nose.

"Ta." Uttering the shorthand version of *thanks* absently, he passed a lorry and fell back into his Heathcliff brooding mode.

"Any special reason you chose it?" I became especially persistent when facing lack of cooperation.

"No."

Not only brooding but stubborn. If he wouldn't respond to polite gambits, what would he do with a more personal one? "I just wondered. Seems I remember reading that your grandfather flew a Spitfire in the Battle of Britain."

He cocked that eyebrow at me again. "I like the car."

I smiled. "That was more than one word. Great! So let's discuss the weather."

An answering smile slowly, as if reluctantly, curved his mouth. His eyes crinkled at the corners, and my stomach did its new and annoying flutter again.

"If you wanted to talk," he told me, "you only had to say so."

"I'm saying so. Although the weather's nice, I'd rather talk about the dark cloud, Jones-Demerest. Have you thought any more about yesterday's news?"

"A good bit. I don't like coincidences."

"Me neither. If he isn't behind this, I don't know who could be."

"Which doesn't mean someone else isn't."

"No." I frowned at the field of bright yellow rape flowers by the motorway. "Yet there was no reference to any kind of flu in the file I found. And the mystery disease is in Paris, not here."

He shrugged. "We don't know that list was comprehensive, and Paris is a fast trip by Channel tunnel. Given what you did find, Jones-Demerest merits a closer look anyway."

"Um. You know, he literally could fill a room with gold coins and roll in them if he wanted. So why go into something like bioweapons that're physically dangerous to handle and carry terrible penalties if you're caught?"

"No one expects to be caught. And some people never have enough." With smooth, efficient motions, Bainbridge passed a couple of law-abiding cars and swung back into his lane. "Perhaps that's it."

"Maybe. Doesn't feel like it to me, though. Besides, there's that file name, *poena summa*. For whom or what does he want the 'highest punishment?' And why?"

Bainbridge's left hand rested on the gear shift, long fingers drumming as he thought, and I flashed on the memory of him squeezing my rear. My lower body clenched.

Biting my lip, I looked out the window to hide my reaction. Our cover as newlyweds required us to share a bed from here out, a circumstance best handled dispassionately. I didn't seem to be doing well with that.

"His file says he's ethnic Romany," Bainbridge noted, "a fact he never discusses except to say his family fled here to escape the Nazis in 1943. They changed the family name soon afterward."

"They arrived with nothing and became rich in two generations. He should be grateful to Britain."

"*Should be* and *is* don't always match."

"Tell me about it."

Bainbridge had gone back to brooding, staring at the road ahead. Lord Heathcliff and I needed to be completely on our game for this mission. That meant we needed to feel like a team instead of like two people dancing around each other, and as soon as possible. "So do you have any other ideas about Jones-Demerest, Jack? Even shaky ideas?"

He frowned at the road. "The motive must be something substantial. The news from Paris has spread around the world. That sort of fanfare usually leads to a very big bang."

"Let's hope not." I drummed my fingers on my thigh, thinking. "Despite the threatening message, the only additional outbreaks have been cases seemingly related to the originals. I wonder why."

Wind whipped his inky hair into his face, and he shoved it back. "Rather like waiting for the other shoe to drop."

"Yes, and I wish I knew how long we have before it does."

"That may not matter. The genie has escaped the bottle."

He passed a slow-moving sedan with a frustrated-sounding roar of his engine. I caught a brief whiff of motor oil.

I stared down at the large diamond and emerald ring adorning my left hand for the mission. He was right about the genie. The plague had entered the population.

France's GIGN internal security unit had been unable to detect any sign of a weapon on the subway. Too bad that didn't guarantee there hadn't been one.

Meanwhile, Jones-Demerest had increased his security, probably due to my Italian incursion, and the World Health Organization declared a level three pandemic alert. A few cases with human-to-human transmission sufficed for that, so it wasn't as bad as it sounded. Except catching everyone who had contact with a carrier didn't seem likely.

Which brought me back to why all this was happening. "I think it's personal. He's risking everything, if it really is him, and people don't do that just for money."

"Perhaps," Bainbridge said. "At least the contagion is localized."

"For now." Pandemics had six phases. Going to level four would mean the virus could pass easily between humans. "Infected carriers might already be moving across the world."

"Let's hope not. As for Jones-Demerest, the motive's a knotty problem."

I sighed, lifting my face into the wind. His word choice reminded me of my college history class. "Yeah. Too bad we're not Alexander."

He shot me a sideways glance. "Pardon?"

"Alexander the Great. The Gordian knot." I mimed chopping through something. "Instead of struggling to untie it, he—"

"Drew his sword and cut it," Bainbridge said in a dry tone. "I know. I did attend Cambridge."

"I figured you'd get it. Anyway, now we have to find our sword. Figuratively speaking."

"Indeed."

"Why do you think he wants to invest in your family company? More to the point, why do you think your brother's interested if the company's as solid as it looks?" He already hated this subject, but the answer could be important.

"It's solid. As for Jones-Demerest, perhaps he has contraband to move. Could be disease or conventional arms."

We shared a grim look. Port security—cargo security in general—could use some improvement.

Bainbridge turned his attention back to the road. For now, I'd let him evade my question about his brother. He might've ignored it because he didn't like admitting ignorance, or the answer might be something he didn't want to share with me.

Either way, pressing him could endanger our fragile truce. I put that on my list of things to find out by other means.

#

Four hours out of London, Bainbridge turned off the motorway, heading for his house and the official start of our mission. He took a hard left at the top of the M-1 exit ramp and then veered onto the first of several breathtakingly narrow, twisty lanes that qualified as roads only by virtue of being paved. The British generally drive them with hell-for-leather assurance that seems to invite collisions, so I didn't think he was trying to intimidate or impress me by doing the same.

I gritted my teeth and endured the three interminable miles to the entrance of Bainbridge Manor. A discreet plaque on one of the two gray stone pillars flanking the entrance read, "Private Residence."

We swung onto the long, gravel drive. Bainbridge flicked his eyes at me. "Ready?"

"Game on." In preparation for greeting the staff, I loaded a wad of gum.

We swept around a curve, and the house came into view. Gray stone, Palladian style, as promised. Sunlight glinted off clean windowpanes all across the building's front.

"Looks very nice," I said. Far above anything Hartner Falls had to offer. The only place in North Carolina that could top it was the Biltmore estate. "I'll watch for the chess set."

"Right. I'll give you a tour later."

He parked in a wide gravel space in front of the house. We left the car and mounted an impressive flight of wide stone stairs to a terrace.

The door swung open as we approached, revealing a short, stout man in a dark suit. He bowed. "Lord Bainbridge. Madam. Welcome home."

"Hey." I popped a bubble.

Unperturbed, for which I gave him a point, the man replied, "Good day, madam."

"Claire, this is Mathers, our butler."

"Charmed," I said.

"I assume you've prepared the master suite," Bainbridge continued. "My wife can meet the staff before dinner, informally."

"As you wish, sir. Madam, on behalf of all the staff, welcome to the manor."

Taken by surprise, I managed to remain a little airy as I thanked him.

"Someone will bring in our bags," Bainbridge said, "and see to the car."

He escorted me into a high-ceilinged foyer with a floor of black and white marble squares. A staircase with heavy, ornately carved banisters rose from one side and turned at a right angle above an inner doorway before winding upward. Below a gold-framed Baroque mirror on a side wall sat a small table with carved legs and trim. It held a silver salver stacked with envelopes.

"This is beautiful," I said as Mathers walked past us. He exited through the door below the stairs.

This place was like something out of a book. Or *Architectural Digest*. Or history. I'd done surveillance or passed information in such places, in both France and Britain, but I'd never had to live in one. If I had to, I could pretend I actually belonged here, at least for a while, but my engagement to Trey had demonstrated how badly the real me fit among the people who lived in such places.

Bainbridge looked right at home despite his casual, Lord Country Squire yellow pullover sweater, brown corduroy pants, and suede oxfords. My low-riders, purple cross-trainers, and cropped, red hoodie, on the other hand, looked garishly out of place, which probably meant I'd made the right impression walking in.

Sorting through the heavy, square envelopes on the silver salver, he said, "Aunt Beatrice has served us well. These are invitations."

I locked eyes with him. "In other words, our little display served us well."

He stiffened but kept his level gaze on mine. "This time," he said curtly. "We should accept some of these, for appearances' sake at least."

"How will that help us find an excuse to move to Jones-Demerest's cushy little joint?"

"Planting gossip, of course. It'll give us an excuse for moving into Simply Yorkshire." He shot me an amused look. "I hope a bit of deceit doesn't offend you."

"Ha. Funny."

He ripped open the envelope in his hand, glancing at the contents.

"From the local Master of the Hunt. We're invited to join a pleasure ride on Monday to welcome our new neighbor, Jones-Demerest."

Riding? Horses? I gulped harder and forgot my irritation with my partner. "Fox hunting's illegal now, isn't it?"

"We don't hunt live foxes but follow a scent laid down by the huntsman." His hand at my waist urged me toward the stairs. "In any event, the season doesn't open until the fall. This will be a group ride with a picnic at the end."

"Uh, will everyone be riding, or will some people be just hanging out? Maybe drinking and gossiping?" I had to find a way to make this hunting gig work. "I could hang out, see what I can pick up."

"Everyone rides." He shot a quizzical glance at me. "Claire, you do ride?"

"Well, no. That is, I've been on a horse, but jumping might be a bit of challenge. Stone fences, ditches, things like that, I mean."

"So I gathered." He smiled.

If he laughed, I'd have to punch him.

"I'll teach you," he decided.

Bad to worse. "It's not a skill I need much."

He shrugged. "I don't mind doing the investigating if you'd rather stay here."

I wouldn't, and I'd have bet my favorite field knife he knew it.

We rounded a corner, heading upward. According to the floor plan I'd received, there were four floors to this house.

"How many stripes on your black belt?" he asked.

I frowned at him. "Like you don't know."

"Humor me."

"Two," I said warily. Each denoted a degree, or step up, in rank. "What does that have to do with anything?"

"Anyone with two stripes on her belt—" His expression shifted abruptly from kind to adoring. "And this is the main residential level. Don't be intimidated, darling. You'll learn your way around."

A second later, my head cleared the top stair, and I spotted the approaching staff member who'd caused Bainbridge's fast shift. The sturdily built, brown-haired man nodded. "Welcome home, sir, madam."

"Thank you, Thomas."

As Bainbridge replied, Thomas opened a section of wall and stepped through it. The wall swung to behind him.

I stared at the Lord of the Manor. "Is he afraid of me?"

"The staff try to be unobtrusive when I'm home. A habit left from the days when my aunt ran the household."

What days? That wasn't in his file. Though I could well believe Her Important Ladyship would like to keep staff in the background.

I'd known that was the old—very old, even antiquated—custom, of course, but now that I confronted living with the idea, it felt weird. And creepy. But I wasn't there to reform the aristocracy, only to tolerate it as needed to get my job done. That included him.

Before I could comment, he continued, "As I was saying, anyone who earns a second-degree black belt has superb balance, the main skill necessary to become a proficient rider. You're also very fit, which gives you an advantage."

"I'll manage the horse thing." I smiled to keep from gritting my teeth. I couldn't shirk half the work, nor could I let him go without backup. I also didn't trust him to seize any opportunities that might arise, plan-bound as he was. "When should we start?"

"After tea. That will give us time to check our messages, go over these invitations, and settle in. And here we are. This is the countess's room." He opened a paneled door, walnut by the look of it, and stepped aside for me.

Beyond the doorway lay a large, high-ceilinged room. Panels of fabric in a green, floral print hung from the ceiling halfway down the paneled walls, and matching draperies framed the windows with their vista of the dale below the house. The four-poster also had matching curtains. Walking into that room felt like diving into a sea of green. At least the carpet provided relief from green, if not from flowers—these recognizable as pink and yellow roses.

A delicate yellow-on-green floral satin loveseat and matching armchairs completed the appalling décor.

"It's nice," I lied. "Someone likes green." Someone who had to be colorblind not to find it overwhelming.

"My mother chose it," he said. "Rather green for my taste, but the next countess can redo it as she chooses."

That'd be his wife, who would share his bed for real. And about whom I had no business having pangs. They must've been due to all that green.

He followed me inside, where a middle-aged woman was closing a large, elaborately carved cabinet in light oak. Smiling, the woman said, "Welcome home, sir, madam."

Bainbridge thanked her by name—Mrs. Bolton, which I gave him a point for knowing—and introduced me to our housekeeper. We exchanged greetings. She then hurried into an adjacent room.

"Shouldn't I meet everyone?" I asked.

"We'll greet them before dinner. Besides Mathers and Mrs. Bolton, there's the head groundskeeper, who's currently on holiday, a household assistant, Thomas, whom we met in the corridor, and two women from the village who help with the cleaning. And my steward, Alex Grey. We also have a full-time groom and a part-time one for the horses."

Far fewer than I'd expected. But I got my ideas of British household staff from period dramas on TV, not exactly the most reliable guides for modern life.

He nodded toward the door Mrs. Bolton had used. "That leads to our adjoining dressing rooms, and my room's beyond. We'll use that one. The bed's larger."

Thank goodness for that, on multiple counts. I wanted some space between me and his unfortunately tempting bod at night. Adjoining rooms made sense, but adjoining *dressing* rooms? Major overkill. Maybe this was how little Spielberg-type aliens felt when they saw us wearing clothes, bewildered about why we'd see the need.

Someone tapped on the corridor door. It opened, and I wheeled toward the sound.

A woman strode across the carpet, her brown hair pulled sleekly back, her black suit, hose and heels immaculate. Discreet, black-framed glasses balanced on her nose. "Welcome home, sir, madam."

I blinked and finally recognized her. I'd never seen Petunia in a suit. Or glasses. Or with sleek, as opposed to semi-orderly, hair.

"Miss McIntosh," I finally managed. "Any news?"

"I'm afraid so." She took a step closer before saying, her voice low, "The disease, which appears to be a new strain of avian flu but transmissible between humans, is spreading. One of the cases from Paris has died, and the World Health Organization has declared pandemic alert level four."

#

Petunia's news made me forget about the oddness of the rich and aristocratic. The virus had reached sustained person-to-person transmission very quickly.

Perched on the dainty green chairs, Bainbridge and I sipped tea while scanning the latest updates on encrypted tablets. If anyone tried to break the encryption, the hard drives would self-destruct. At last, I realized I'd flipped through these lab reports and interviews three times. I set the tablet onto the tea table. "I get zip. Also zero, zilch, and *nada*."

"Not especially eloquent but all too accurate." He laid his tablet on the table, too.

"You know," I said, "I keep worrying that, bad as Jones-Demerest is, someone else is doing this and we're on the wrong track."

"That's always possible. We must be certain before eliminating him as a suspect, however, and if we can catch him in any of his other illegal dealings, so much the better."

"Good point. So what can we do from here?" Charging over to Paris came to mind, as did taking out Jones-Demerest on sight.

He cocked an eyebrow at me. "Our job, of course."

If he'd been anything like David, I could have made a joke about speeding things along with my Walther, but Himself probably wouldn't think it was funny.

"Meanwhile," he continued, "let's put you in a saddle and start your lessons. I'll order a mare brought to the paddock."

"If we must, but socializing feels like a waste of investigating time. I'd rather move into that commune and dive in."

"We must set our cover first. You know that." Frowning, he stood and rubbed the back of his neck as though it ached. "You might want to put on boots."

"I only have my work boots, lace-up ones with steel-reinforced toes and special cushioned soles for sneaking." Such as I'd rather be doing, but his frown hinted that he shared my impatience, so I smiled at him. "They're my favorites."

"Good God, they probably are," he muttered. He might've intended that forced-looking smile to reassure me. Instead, it made him appear to be fighting indigestion. "Any sturdy shoes will do. And put on some clothes you can move in. I'll fetch my boots and meet you in the entry hall when you're ready."

"Right." I gave him a bright, cheery I Am Not Scared look that probably didn't fool him a bit. "Actually, everything I have is like this. I'll just have to muddle along as I am."

His glance took in my low-riders—in which my sitting on a horse would give the world a great view of what I euphemistically called anatomical detailing—*oh, hell!*—and heat kindled in his eyes. But he said only, "I'll just put on my boots, then."

He headed for the adjoining room. Missing David's wry humor, I stifled a sigh. At least dressing inappropriately would fit the plan. Besides, I'd have pranced naked along the runway at New York Fashion Week if it brought Jones-Demerest down.

#

Bainbridge and I strolled down the hill in front of the house. At the bottom lay a wide meadow and, beyond it, a stand of trees that had to be several acres on each side.

"Nice forest," I commented, nodding at it. Such large stands of trees aren't common in Yorkshire, with much of the land given over to sheep. Or, occasionally, horses.

"The home wood," he replied. "It's all that remains of a much larger wood that was enclosed as a deer park. As sheep grew more profitable, the wood gave way to grazing."

"You raise sheep?"

He shook his head. "We lease the land to those who do."

In the meadow, a ring of white wooden fencing enclosed a grassy space. A stocky groom who looked to be in his late twenties stood inside it, patting the neck of a sleek, reddish horse. A chestnut, if I remembered my scant store of horse trivia correctly.

The horse didn't look as big as I'd feared it might. Bainbridge, on the other hand, looked even taller. Maybe that came from the whole horse thing and my discomfort with it.

A chill wind blew across the lawn, bringing the scents of grass, trees, and horse, and raised bumps on my exposed midriff. Cursing silently, I pretended not to notice. If the groom noticed, he also pretended not to.

I leaned into Bainbridge's arm. "It's a very big horse, Bainsiekins. I don't know about getting up there."

I wasn't really afraid of horses so much as uncertain how to approach them. In my limited experience, they had no interest in human logic.

"You'll love Calypso, darling." He introduced me to the groom before saying, "Thank you, Stafford. I'll take it from here."

Passing the reins over, Stafford said, "Catherine did quite well this year, sir." He paused, then blurted, "I can't thank you enough. The tuition—"

"Helping your sister was my pleasure." Bainbridge's firm tone closed the subject.

The groom nodded slightly and stepped back.

Bainbridge had paid tuition for his groom's sister? That indicated a generosity I hadn't seen so far. Maybe even a kind heart.

"This side, darling." The Horse Lord beckoned me around to the beast's left. "You mount from here."

I was about to ask, only half kidding, why a dinky, leather placemat sat where the saddle should be when a flicker of light to my left caught my eye. I glanced toward it. There it came again, through the trees flanking the drive. Like sunlight glinting off metal.

I looked at Bainbridge but didn't need to get his attention. He stood focused on that flicker, his back to the groom. His eyes met mine in grim warning. Someone was watching us.

CHAPTER SIX

Over his shoulder, Bainbridge said, "We've changed our minds, Stafford. Perhaps tomorrow."

"Yes, sir." With another touch to his hat brim, the groom led the horse away.

Bainbridge stared at the road. The flash of light came again, from the same area, and a dark blue Jaguar emerged from the screening trees. "It's my brother's," he said.

The car's metal could have caused that flash of light, with emphasis on *could*. But maybe not. The flashes had been stationary, but the car was moving along the drive. Now that it had cleared the trees, its occupants would have a clear view of us until they'd almost reached the house.

With warning in his eyes, he bent his head. "I'll give you some time to work up to your riding lesson, darling." On the last word, his mouth slammed down on mine.

My brain crashed like a computer with a power surge, and the current roared down to my toes, curling them and melting my knees. When my head cleared, his tongue was in my mouth, fencing with mine. His stroked like velvet one moment and plunged hard and fast the next. Each movement sent ripples of heat deep into my body. Kissing him felt surprisingly right, and I moaned around the exquisite mouthful.

Not to be outdone, I sucked his tongue. He growled and yanked me even closer, something I wouldn't have thought possible. A hard bulge that hadn't been there a few minutes ago jabbed my belly. It stirred heat and craving a little lower. Rocking against it, I jammed my hand into his back pocket and squeezed.

He turned up the heat on his kiss, another surprise that trumped mine. My head fogged again.

The world came back at last with the news that he was kissing my neck. Using his tongue, which shot delight into my taut nipples and on down.

"Jack," I gasped, fighting for sanity. If we didn't stop, we might well end up naked in the middle of this ring.

I'd never felt so wanted and challenged and turned on, all at the same time, in a man's arms. The combination was intoxicating. Both my hands had found their way into his back pockets, reveling in the hard, sculpted contours under his pants. One of his hands made delicious little circles under the back of my cropped top while the other cupped my butt, its thumb stroking the very low back waistline of my jeans.

"Jack." I slid a hand into his hair and tugged with a bit of force. "Jack—Bainsiekins, sweet-buns—" I had to gulp in air to finish "—people can see."

That caught his attention, and he froze. A couple of heartbeats later, he raised his head. Except for his harsh breathing, he looked entirely composed. I knew better, thanks to the proof pressed into my belly, and the knowledge saved me from ego damage because my heart was pounding.

He kissed me again, fast and hard. "Let's go inside, darling."

"Right away," I agreed. In a lower voice, I added, "What if the car didn't cause those flashes of light from the trees?"

His eyes hardened momentarily. "The people we're supposed to be wouldn't think of that, and we have too few staff to search the grounds. Besides, they aren't trained to confront intruders."

We started across the lawn toward the house. He kept his arm around my waist, and our hips bumped with every step. With someone whose bones I actually meant to jump, the contact would've been sexy. Instead, it felt awkward, but I welcomed the distraction from the warm pressure of his hand at my waist, between the cropped top and the low-riders.

"My brother must've seen us," he said, "but it's a long drive. We'll hurry upstairs before he reaches the house."

Then we would presumably make him wait to talk to us and further solidify our image as lust-maddened newlyweds. Groping each other along the way, we stumbled inside and up the stairs.

Bainbridge opened a door for me, entered the room on my heels, and banged the door shut behind us with the nicely defensible thud of heavy wood hitting the jamb.

The air held faint traces of his cedar scent, and I suddenly realized we weren't in the Land of Cheesy Green. This must be his room. It had the same type of dark guy furniture and India-print hangings as his London bedroom. Bad taste apparently didn't pass through the genes.

"Nice room." I refrained from asking if he'd swap. He probably wouldn't find that amusing. "By the way, nice improvisation down in the paddock. You gave us good cover."

He shot a sour look at me. "I don't improvise."

"You planned that in advance?" The idea certainly took some of the bloom off the rosy moment.

"I knew that, at some point, we might unexpectedly come into the view of someone we wanted to impress. I didn't know whether we'd ever use the strategy."

I stared at him. I'd anticipated that someone might spy on us or watch us, but I hadn't gone so far as to decide *if spied upon, make out* or anything similar.

"What if the circumstances hadn't been right for kissing?" A mild term for what we'd done, but anything more accurate felt like dangerous ground.

"I had an alternative strategy, of course."

"Right. Uh, how many plans do you have?"

"Enough to cover all contingencies." He frowned at me, apparently not liking my skeptical expression. "I'll lay it out for you if you like."

"You're kidding me. Nobody makes a plan for the spur of the moment." And no plan could ever mandate a kiss that personal and intense. "Besides, putting it in writing—"

"I'm not that foolish," he snapped, crossing his arms. "It's in an encrypted file. Sit down, and I'll explain the contingencies to you."

"You know, it's okay. I believe you." I also needed a new adjective. Anal retentive didn't begin to describe him.

He directed a stern look at me. "A proper plan addresses all possibilities. Failure to do so demonstrates inadequate forethought."

"That's...illuminating."

We stared at each other, worlds apart in mindset. At least this little exchange had killed whatever remained of my recent hormonal surge.

Good. I'd remember this moment the next time our roles sent us into lip-lock.

Someone tapped on the door. "Sir?"

"In the bed," he urged me and jerked off his sweater. I yanked the covers down, dived under them, and pushed my hoodie off my exposed shoulders. Behind me, he said, "Come in."

The corridor door opened. A male voice said, "Sir, Mister Basingstoke and Lady Beatrice have come to call. Are you available?"

"Show them to the blue parlor, Thomas, and tell them we'll see them shortly. Thank you."

"Yes, sir."

When a quiet thud signaled the door closing, I slid out of bed and fixed my clothes. "You know, the flash of light off the car doesn't explain why I really felt like we were being watched outside. That, plus your family's arrival, raises a question. They wouldn't hire someone to spy us, would they?"

"Unlikely." Bainbridge had transformed himself into Lord Disheveled, his shirt unbuttoned halfway down and the tail hanging out on one side. An enticing patch of dark, silky-looking hair covered the center of his chest.

"Robin, my brother, would consider that unsporting. Aunt Beatrice might hire a detective, but she'd use one too good for us to spot so easily."

"I'm that popular, huh?" I grinned at him.

Unbuttoning the rest of his shirt front, he frowned. "You're overdressed. Do you have a negligee?"

So much for fun banter. "Yes."

"Put it on. We'll let them cool their heels for a bit."

"After which we'll distract them from pursuing this Jones-Demerest deal, I assume. That's why they came, isn't it?"

"Probably. We might also learn something." He tossed a pillow onto the floor. "Go on. I have this in hand."

I didn't like being dismissed, but I reminded myself to make nice with MI5.

I'd reached his dressing room when he said, "Claire."

He waited until I poked my head back into his now-disarranged room. "Robin is sensitive about being the business head but not the controlling shareholder." His face softened, at odds with his stiff tone. "I don't want him hurt."

I nodded. "I'll be right back."

So Lord Control Freak, like Dorothy's poor Tin Man, had a heart behind his rigid facade. I made a mental note to cut his brother some slack.

Lady Beatrice, though, was fair game. I had a hunch she was the real force behind this investment plan. Before she left today, I meant to find out.

#

We let the family cool their heels for half an hour while we gargled cognac and finished setting our stage. To reinforce our scandalous image, we would see them in his bedroom instead of the parlor.

Bainbridge sent for a cheese tray, and we munched on the contents in a careless way that scattered crumbs on the low table. And on us.

He mussed his hair and unbuttoned his shirt the rest of the way. While one of the staff summoned his relatives, we arranged ourselves on the leather sofa. He lounged across it with his head on an arm and me draped over him.

I wouldn't have suspected him of lounging, a posture too relaxed for someone with his hidebound, old-school brain. But a very sharp brain.

His encircling arm held me to his chest and side. The cedar scent of his clothes, now mixed with cognac, and the feel of his strong, toned physique along my torso made me uncomfortably warm. My pink, silk baby-doll negligee did nothing to filter out his body heat.

In keeping with my role, I slid my arm around his waist, under his shirt, bare skin to bare skin. His chest hair narrowed at the base of his sternum, and a thin line led down over the ripped abs under my forearm. I swallowed a sigh of pleasure and, hoping he hadn't noticed, glanced up at him.

He pressed his face into my spiky hair. However, I thought—hoped—I saw a muscle work in his jaw. My celibate misery would definitely love to have his for company.

Footsteps came down the hall. Keen with warning, his gaze met mine. We were about to be on. Instantly, I focused. Only to have his eyes go smoky gray as he said, "Kiss me, Claire."

If he was willing to greet his family that way, I wouldn't balk. I brushed his mouth with mine, tasting cognac and Stilton cheese, but didn't linger for fear of going up in a blaze that would crash my brain again. Instead, I trailed slow, light kisses along his jaw. And felt the muscle work under my lips.

I couldn't resist nestling closer to him. His hand tightened on my shoulder. Stroked down to my hip. My lower body clenched on a sudden rush of heat. For one deluded moment, I felt as though I really belonged right where I was.

Focus, I told myself sternly. Any second now—

A tap on the door heralded the guests. Their guide stepped aside for them to enter and closed the door behind them.

Lady Beatrice sailed in first, only to pull up short, nostrils dilating and eyes wide, when she spotted us.

The man behind her almost bumped into her. "Jack—"

I looked up from nuzzling Bainbridge's cheek and flashed our guests a big smile. "Oh, hey, Bernice. It's great to see you again. Can you stay to supper?"

"Good idea, darling." Bainbridge smiled at me in a silly, lopsided way. Without looking away from me, he said, "Aunt Beatrice, Robin, what can we do for you?"

"You can—you can—sit up and receive your guests properly," she sputtered. She dropped into one of the two chairs opposite us as if she couldn't stand up any longer.

I put on a pout. "Well, shit, Bernice—"

"Language, darling." Bainbridge tapped my lips gently. "Robin, sit down."

Robert Basingstoke, whom I'd seen on TV back in London, also plopped into his chair, but he was gamely trying to smile. "You haven't introduced me to your wife, Jack. I gather this may not be the best time to visit."

"It may not," Bainbridge agreed amiably. "Nevertheless, Claire, this is your brother-in-law, Robert Basingstoke. We call him Robin. Robin, meet Claire."

"It's a pleasure." I twinkled at him as best I could. I'm never sure how well I pull off things like that. "I always wanted a brother."

Actually, I had one, but it seemed the thing to say.

The flicker around Robin's eyes might have stopped a wince. "Welcome to the family, Claire."

"Thanks, Robin." I beamed at him.

He directed a hesitant look at his brother. "Jack, we need to discuss the business. Perhaps Claire could excuse us."

Bainbridge sat up. His movement necessarily put me upright, too. I leaned into his solid shoulder and reminded my quivery hormones he took *control freak* to new levels.

He laced his fingers through mine. "I have no secrets from Claire. What is it?" Despite his mild expression, his steely tone warned against argument.

His brother apparently read the code. "We need to take this chance with Jones-Demerest, Jack. He can bring us other business, and carrying his products will give us a steady revenue stream."

He continued in that vein, detailing the financial advantages to having an industrial partner. Lady Beatrice fixed me with a steely stare, so I snuggled closer to Bainbridge, getting a view of his six-pack that made my fingers itch. I wrapped my free hand around the open edge of his shirt to still the itch and studied his brother under cover of his chin.

In any other company, Robert Basingstoke would've been an attractive man. He and Bainbridge shared a family resemblance, though Robin's general demeanor was milder.

Next to his brother, however, he just looked like...less. Less height, less breadth to his shoulders, less strength to his jaw, less interesting features. None of which he could do anything to change. No wonder he chafed at running the company while his supposedly ne'er-do-well elder brother held the reins.

Holding the family title still counted for a lot in the Basingstokes' circles. Being the heir still beat being the "spare," to put it in their parlance. Maybe he saw this deal as a way to step out of his brother's shadow, a chance to win some acclaim. To be the main brother for once?

My instincts said, *right on*. My brain said to tread carefully raising the issue with Bainbridge, but I had to mention it. It could be important. Besides, like it or not, he was my partner.

Robin at last wound down. "You should trust my judgment," he finished. "I know the daily operations down to the last penny on the balance sheet. We need something like this."

Bainbridge's thumb rubbed the back of my hand, creating a feeling of tenderness I almost wished was real. With a glance at his brother, he said, "Look around at the world, Robin. Taking on a partner now brings more risk than benefit."

"What does that mean?"

"There's a flu outbreak in France, in case you haven't noticed. Judging by the news, it promises to be as bad as avian flu, if not worse. Remember what happened to international travel and trade when that flared up in Asia."

"You should remember that turned out to be overblown."

"I remember the world was damn lucky."

Bainbridge was right. In a flu pandemic, as much as half the population faced infection, and a quarter of those developed complications like pneumonia that were often fatal. This was nothing to dismiss so lightly, and part of me wanted to shake the knowledge into his brother.

Lady Beatrice leaned forward. "Robin. Jack. Instead of speculating about possible disease outbreaks, let us focus on more predictable factors. Jones-Demerest isn't our sort, but he has a demonstrated flair for making money."

"What d'you mean, not our sort?" I asked.

"He's a gypsy, Claire," she said. "Couldn't you tell?"

I longed for my gum, something I could chomp into. Not having it, I gave her a blank look. "Why would I care?"

"You needn't," she said. "Nor should Jack discount the man's ability because of his origins."

"I don't," he said curtly. "Nor do I care to discuss this when I've already made my decision. We're on our honeymoon. I don't want business intruding."

Robin snorted. "You never want business intruding, but this time it must. We can't keep an investor hanging."

"This isn't the time to take on potential liability or assume any duty toward anyone else."

"We can write the contracts to cover liability," Robin insisted. "South Pacific shipping grows more dangerous daily because of piracy. We could use an infusion of funds." Eying his brother, he added, "It's not like you to interfere, Jack. Or to take such an interest."

Although Bainbridge stiffened beside me, he answered calmly. "Aunt Beatrice has urged me for years to take a more active role in the family. And you know I'm always aware of the company's status. Hawkshead is a family concern. There's no good reason to bring in an outsider."

"Dammit, Jack!" Basingstoke shot to his feet. "If you want to talk of responsibility, let's. The company is my responsibility. Spending the earnings and, now, popping in to interfere seem to be yours. I won't have it. Bloody hell, you owe me this!"

Bainbridge rose slowly to face his brother. He released my hand, but I stood with him. My partner doesn't fight in any manner while I just sit by.

He kept his eyes locked on his brother's angry face. "Claire, Aunt Beatrice, please excuse us." She frowned, and he added, "Now."

CHAPTER SEVEN

Lady Beatrice reluctantly stood. I guessed an order from head of the family must carry some weight with her.

As she headed for the door, Bainbridge turned to me, his eyes granite. "You, too, darling."

I hated to leave him. His brother meant to give him hell, all in keeping with Bainbridge's cover, and Bainbridge meant to stand there and take it because the truth was an Official Secret. Yeah, that was the job, but it still bit. At least my family was always in my corner, even when they didn't agree with my choices. Or know about my real job.

But I had to do as he'd said. Unable to offer more meaningful support, I stretched up to plant a quick kiss on his cheek. "I'll change for dinner."

He nodded. I padded from the room.

When I reached my dressing room, I hesitated. I'd have bet my Arachnid ID that Bainbridge wouldn't tell me what his brother said, exactly. I also had a nasty feeling I might need to know.

Eavesdropping on the bad guys is part of the job. Eavesdropping on my partner bites, but I did it anyway.

"I earn the money," Robin snapped. "All you do is spend it. And I don't care what goes in the family trust. When you retain sole discretion and control, it's the same as keeping it yourself."

"I didn't realize you found your dividends and salary inadequate," Jack said coldly.

"Sod that. I got a first in business economics at Oxford, and I'm in the office every day. You were sent down from Cambridge and have never taken more than a passing interest in the company."

Being sent down meant expulsion. Bainbridge was a brilliant scholar but had the public record of a nincompoop. He'd chosen that path, which said a lot about him. It still had to burn at times, though.

Robin continued, "Then there were your drunken episodes in clubs that made the tabloids, the cheap women you ran with, habits you still haven't given up entirely. Now you spend your time traveling and...in a nightclub, was it, where you met her?"

"Don't tread that path, Robin." Bainbridge's words fell like chipped stone.

Of course he would defend any woman he married. He was that kind of guy. And we weren't actually a couple. But I still got a quick brush of warmth over my heart.

"Sorry. But you must listen to me on this, Jack."

"Just wait," Bainbridge said, "until this flu subsides. I'll take another look then."

"Have you taken the first one?" Challenge rang in the words.

"I do read what you send me." The dry tone took the sting out of Bainbridge's words. "I'm open to revisiting this, Robin."

"If Jones-Demerest doesn't find another partner."

"If he could, he wouldn't go to a small company like Hawkshead. He'll be there when we're ready."

"I'm ready now," Robin said. After a moment, he added, "I shan't let this go, Jack. I've emailed the other shareholders."

Well, that sucked. Arachnid's analysts had noted a provision in the Hawkshead Shipping bylaws that would allow other shareholders to overrule the earl despite his holding the majority of the shares.

The silence lasted several beats before Bainbridge said, "If you must, but I won't change my mind." He paused. "I know I'm a trial, Robin, but I do stock good cognac."

"You do." Bainbridge must've handed him a glass because he added, "Thanks, Jack."

I could feel the tension ebb. Brotherly silence fell, and I put one foot silently behind the other, preparing for a tactical withdrawal.

"Oh, by the way," Bainbridge said casually, "I'm teaching Claire to ride. Thought I saw someone on the hill above the paddock. Did you see anyone when you drove in?"

Nice. He'd managed to follow up in a way that wouldn't look

suspicious.

"Perhaps it was a tourist come to gawk at the house," Robin said. You do have a 'private residence' sign at the gate. You're sure you saw someone?"

"Not certain, no. Have some Stilton."

A pause, then some crunching.

"Mmm," Robin said. "Delicious." He paused. "Claire seems very friendly."

"Yes, she is. She's settling in nicely."

"Not much like Mum." Robin sounded cautious.

"No, thank God."

What had been wrong with their mother? Did it matter?

"Right." Robin's caution yielded to relief. "To Claire, the first fun Countess of Bainbridge in three hundred years."

"To Claire."

Crystal clinked. I backed away. Either Robin really liked the new me or he was covering his bases, playing up to his majority shareholder in case the others didn't come through for him. Regardless, I might be able to draw him out.

#

A few minutes later, I was considering the just-barely-decent cocktail dresses in my armoire. Someone knocked on the dressing room door. "Come in," I said.

Bainbridge opened the door. He leaned on the frame, his eyes shadowed and weary.

I checked my movement toward him. "Are you okay?"

"Of course." He straightened, standing upright. "Why?"

Because lines of strain were carved in his face, an answer he wouldn't appreciate and another sign that his cover sometimes bothered him. "That couldn't have been fun."

He grimaced. "It's about to become less so. Aunt Beatrice is staying over for a few days, and Jones-Demerest is coming to dinner tomorrow."

"Since when? I welcome the chance at him, but I don't like surprises unless I create them."

Rolling his shoulders, he replied, "Robin admitted Aunt Beatrice invited Jones-Demerest before they left London."

Closing the antique oak armoire, I took great care not to slam the door. "Does she do things like this all the time, barging into your flat, dropping in to stay, inviting people to your house? Suppose we'd had plans?"

"She grew up here, and my father gave her the run of the place. After Mum died, she spent a great deal of time with us."

"So she thinks this is her house." I shook my head. Why didn't he seem more concerned? We'd agreed on the ride north that I would irritate her when I saw her again—which we hadn't expected to be so soon—and see what I could get her to let slip. But that was before she'd barged in here, with Robin for reinforcements. "You know, Jack, she could really screw things up with this butting in."

"If she does, I'll deal with it."

"Why not just send her back to London?"

He shook his head. "More effort than it's worth. Don't worry, Claire. I have matters in hand."

It looked more like Aunt Steel Magnolia had matters in hand, but maybe he'd spent too much time fighting her to care anymore. I cared, but she was his family, and thus his problem. Not mine.

"Okay." I just hoped he was right.

He nodded. "Since I'm here, there are some things I must attend to. I'll see you at dinner." I nodded agreement, and he withdrew into his own quarters.

I tugged the negligee off and pulled on a pair of low-riders and a bright purple, cashmere hoodie. The more I thought about his aunt, though, the madder I got. The lives of hundreds, maybe thousands, of people rode on this mission. Which she was screwing with.

Frowning, I wandered into the Green Zone and plopped onto the couch. His family dynamic wasn't my problem. Yet I couldn't stop gnawing at it, maybe because I liked the guy. I didn't especially want to, and I could really do without that annoying little hum of attraction that seemed to be a constant, but I tended to like people who were smart and dedicated and kind.

Not to mention hot.

Gak! Sitting around wasn't doing me any good. Maybe a walk in the sunshine would help. The house had extensive gardens, including a walled, Elizabethan knot garden. Whatever that was. This was as good a time as any to find out.

Heading down the stairs, through a narrow corridor, and out onto the rear terrace, I thought about Lady Beatrice. Irritating her would be easy. But maybe sucking up to her would have a better effect.

After all we'd done to make her think I was an idiot, not to mention her readiness to believe that, I doubted she would be open to overtures from me. Unless maybe she thought I could bring Jack around to her side about Jones-Demerest.

Yeah. Right.

But it was worth considering.

Mulling the possibilities, I wandered into the garden to the right of the house. The roses—mostly white, that being the emblem of Yorkshire —were blooming, and brick-bordered beds of bright red and blue and purple and yellow flowers I couldn't name offered a riot of cheerful color.

The knot garden lay at the rear, enclosed by a six-foot-high, brick wall. The red brick looked weathered and chipped, as though it were very old.

I'd almost reached the gate when a *beep-beep* came from inside the garden. Was that a ringtone?

"Yes, Robin?" Lady Beatrice's voice said. "Yes, I'm alone. I'm sitting in the knot garden. Your brother and that woman are in the house."

So much for a relaxing stroll among the flowers. Could I turn her presence to my advantage somehow? And why did it matter whether she was alone?

This might be none of my business, but that bit about being alone sounded suspicious. Stepping carefully and silently on the gravel path, I moved closer to the wall. Her ladyship's voice sounded far enough inside the garden that I should have time to cross the fifteen feet to the corner and hide before she could reach the gate.

"I don't want to invoke that clause any more than you do," she announced.

What clause? Did she mean the one that let the other shareholders overrule the earl despite his majority ownership? That was the most likely option.

She was coming closer, footsteps crunching on the gravel. As I slipped toward the corner, she added, "I imagine Jack has forgotten that small detail, but we must reserve it as a last resort....I agree."

Considering that he had a lightning brain and a superb memory, I would bet he hadn't forgotten whatever it was she was holding in reserve.

But he might not have thought about it lately.

I reached the corner and slid around the wall. Hinges squeaked. Lady Beatrice must've opened the gate. "I'll give you a ring if anything changes. Otherwise, I'll see you tomorrow."

Hmmm. While the rasp of her footsteps on gravel receded, I worked my way around the garden and across the back lawn to a side door. I needed to return to the house but not be obvious about coming from the same direction she had.

Inside, I hurried up the stairs and checked my partner's room. Empty. Whatever estate business he was doing probably still had him occupied.

I used the connecting doors—and connecting dressing rooms, *geez!* —to wander into the Green Nightmare. Thinking, I crossed my arms and leaned on the bedpost.

Arachne had privately instructed me to monitor Jones-Demerest's efforts to gain a share of Hawkshead. Access to shipping he could control would be just too handy for his illegal weapons business. Whether or not he was responsible for this flu plague.

Bainbridge seemed certain about his control of the family company. But Arachne was heavily into the *smile but maintain vigilance* school of thought. On top of that, Lady Beatrice and Robin were getting ready to overrule him.

Maybe I should do a little recon. Rattle her cage, if need be, and see what popped out. I grabbed a couple of sticks of gum, chomped down on them, and strolled out into the hall.

Bainbridge wouldn't like my not clearing this with him. Still, as long as he was my partner, I had his back. Against any kind of foe.

Only when I had reached the corridor did I realize I had no idea where the foe was quartered, nor did I know how to find out from anyone but Bainbridge. That left me with old-fashioned reconnaissance. I checked every room until I found one with the door closed. I knocked on the dark paneling.

After a couple of seconds, Bainbridge's aunt called, "Well? What is it?"

Bingo. Got it on the first try.

I jerked the door open and sauntered through. "It's me, Bernice." I let the door bang behind me.

Through her teeth, she said, "My name, Claire, is Lady Beatrice. Not...ever...Bernice. I would appreciate it if you would remember that."

"Sorry." I smiled. "Listen, I wanted to ask you about this deal Bainsiekins isn't so hot on. Why do you think it's so great?"

Her eyes narrowed, and suspicion rolled off her in waves. "Why do you ask?"

"Well, gee, me and him are a team now, y'know. If this is good for us, I want to help."

Lips pursed, she studied me. I tried to look sweet, not my usual mode.

After a moment, she shook her head. "You wouldn't understand."

"Why not?" I summoned my best hurt expression.

She probably intended that smile to be kind, but it screamed condescension. "I doubt your background as a trainer extended to international finance."

"Yeah? Well, that doesn't make me stupid." I stood with my hip bumped out to one side and looked her up and down. "Since we're being honest and all, I'd appreciate it if you didn't invite company to supper without Honeykins and me saying it's okay. It's our house. Y'know?" I smacked my gum.

She actually shuddered before drawing herself up like a ramrod. "This is my family home, young woman. I shall invite whom I please. As I always have."

"Yeah. I got that, Bernice—"

"It's Be-ah-trice, you stupid tart." Bright spots of color blazed in her cheeks, and her eyes glowed laser-hot.

There was my opening. In one stride, I moved into her space and stood right in her face. "Well, get this, Be-ah-trice. This is my family home now. I'm the countess. I say who comes to dinner."

I dropped the ditzy airhead routine and looked right at her, the same *don't screw with me* look I give people when I'll kill them if they move. Blanching, she took a step backward.

I took a step forward. "Got that?" I asked softly.

She rallied with a calculating look in her eye. "Jack would toss you out on your taut little rump if he heard you speaking to me in that disrespectful way. Don't push me, Claire, for he wouldn't appreciate it."

He for-damned-sure wouldn't, but I'd chosen my course. "I'll take my chances." Smirking, I tacked on, "I'm really, really good at cheering him up."

"Get out," she ordered, livid.

"Yeah, I'm done here. But don't mess with me, Auntie Bea, or your visits to the family home are history."

Her chest puffed up, probably in indignation. "Jack is a brilliant man who wastes his natural gifts. If you truly cared about him, you would encourage him to reach his potential, not indulge his worst habits."

I smiled. "Deal with it." I sashayed out the door. Maybe I'd made her think twice, maybe not, but I couldn't let her interference go without trying to win my partner some peace.

Yet her words stuck with me. Maybe she really did care about him, and if she did, that made his need to hide what he was that much worse for both of them.

Still, she'd better not muck around with the new, if temporary, Countess of Bainbridge. My noble partner and I had enough to worry about without his family yanking his chain.

I strolled back to "my" room. As soon as I opened the door, my smug satisfaction evaporated. Bainbridge sat in one of the chairs, facing the door with an expression about as satisfied as a thunderhead.

CHAPTER EIGHT

"Hi," I said. "Did you need something?" Just in case, I pushed the door shut.

He looked at me for a long moment, during which I fought a strong urge to squirm.

"What the bloody hell was that?" he demanded. "I told you I had the situation in hand."

He must've walked by and heard us, which was very bad luck for me. "With all due respect, Jack, you were evading the issue. You like for us to stick to your plan, but she's a loose cannon come to blow it up. If we don't bring her under control, she could wreck this."

"I won't allow that to happen." He stood slowly.

"Neither," I said deliberately, "will I."

Our eyes locked, his expression as stubborn as I knew mine must be.

He crossed toward me with a smooth, predatory stride. "I warned you about insubordination."

"We agreed I'd get her to hate me so we could see what spewed out. I'm doing that."

He was still coming. I stifled the impulse to back up. If I gave ground on this, Lady Beatrice would run roughshod over us both. "So what I did fits the plan."

He looked coldly pissed. If he believed a word of what I'd said, I'd eat my low-riders. He didn't stop until his chest brushed my breasts, generating a tingle I seriously did not welcome. When he put his hands on the wall on either side of my head, I realized I'd never made it fully into the room.

Looming over me, he said, "I repeat. I am in charge here. You will take no action I have not approved."

He looked pretty scary, like a nightmare inquisitor, but I couldn't afford to break eye contact and thus seem to concede. I balled a fist and touched it gently to his side. "If you're trying to intimidate me, you shouldn't leave yourself open. I've put bigger guys than you on stretchers."

"I'll take my chances. Meanwhile, stay out of my family business."

I opened my mouth for a smart retort about Jones-Demerest and his family business, but what came out was, "You deserve better."

He looked as startled as I felt. His eyes softened, the anger fading. Regret flickered through them, turning them smoky gray, and then desire darkened them.

My heartbeat gathered speed. I suddenly realized I'd grown to like his cedary scent. Remembered that he tasted of brandy and felt like power personified.

His head lowered. My chin rose.

Control freak, I reminded myself frantically. I ducked under his arm and spun away.

He lowered his arms and pivoted to face me, his expression a stony mask. "Leave Aunt Beatrice to me."

I took a deep, steadying breath. "I'll try. That's the most I can promise. So what would you suggest for tonight?"

"Let's go to York for dinner." His posture lost its stiffness. "Have a getaway meal before the fun starts. Away from the house, we can talk without risk of interruption. I know a pub that's by a bridge. The traffic crossing it is noisy enough to cover a quiet conversation."

"I'm up for it." Even if his most likely motive was keeping me out of Aunt Ramrod's face.

"As for tomorrow, call Miss McIntosh. If we're having an impromptu dinner party, we'll invite some neighbors and have a real one."

"And cut off the chance for private talk. Nice. Um…you'll have to show me how to call her."

Surprise flickered in his eyes before he masked it. He walked to the bed and fingered a long, narrow strip of embroidered linen hanging beside it. "Pull this. Someone will come to see what you want, and you can have that person summon Miss McIntosh."

"Doesn't Petunia have a phone extension I can use or something easy like that?"

He grinned, making me feel annoyingly hot and quivery inside. "Actually, yes. I was having you on. Pick up the phone and ring forty-three."

I rolled my eyes, but I suspected there were people in his set for whom embroidered bell pulls and go-betweens were still the norm.

Yes, indeed, welcome to Circusville, Casey, and you'd better not forget your partner's the ringmaster. Jones-Demerest's determination to join the shipping company raised interesting questions, and Bainbridge seemed oblivious. He was too smart not to see it, so what else was going on?

#

Seated at a picnic table by the Ouse River a few hours later, I poked at the last of my shepherd's pie. Glad as I was to get my partner away from his interfering relatives, I also felt as though we were proverbial fiddlers in a burning Rome. We should be working this case, not sitting here.

Once a flu strain became fully contagious, its global spread was inevitable. Border controls and travel restrictions could only delay it. Every continent would probably have outbreaks in three months.

"Something in the food?" Bainbridge asked.

"Visions of dead people." I looked grimly at him.

We sat on opposite sides of the table in front of the Royal Arms pub. Other customers sat or stood around us on the patio with their drinks or meals of choice, unconcerned about the danger spreading in the shadows.

Bainbridge pushed away the last of his classic steak and kidney pie. "We need to speed this along," he said. "Move into that compound without delay. Tomorrow night's dinner should give us an opportunity. It just can't look—"

"As though we're angling for it. I know." I blew out a breath of frustration and lowered my voice. "A normal virus spreads fast enough. An engineered, planted one makes me feel like I'm in a race. One I'm currently losing."

His expression hardened. "This is a chess game, not a sprint." The stern expression gave way to a wry one. "I realize you'd feel better if we could blow up something and solve the problem. For what it's worth, so would I."

I acknowledged his teasing with a quick smile. "This dinner party might as well be useful. What if we stage a fight in front of everyone and I demand we go there?"

"That could work. With the right setup." Flicking a glance at me, he said, "I have a plan I can show you."

I sighed. "I was afraid you might."

The corners of his eyes crinkled in a half smile, but he didn't reply. I suddenly realized I'd somehow become comfortable with him at last. If he could tease me, he must also feel settled into our partnership.

Sipping lager, I leaned one elbow on the table and looked around. The Ouse River flowed some six feet below the cobblestones. An excursion boat drifted past, its lights not yet on though it was early evening. Summer twilight lingers in Britain, and more so in the North.

Behind me, traffic rolled across the Ouse Bridge, as he'd predicted. The pub sat below street level, with a steep flight of stone stairs leading up to the road.

Across the river, new condos or apartments blocked any view of the ancient city walls. I glanced at Bainbridge. His gaze roamed idly over the scenery, his face as relaxed as his posture. He wasn't scoping out an unfamiliar scene, as I did. He was looking at things he knew, as if he belonged among them. As, of course, he did.

As Jasper Jones-Demerest never, in this land of hereditary peerages that dated back centuries, truly would. As I never could among what passed for *society* in Hartner Falls. I'd never cared much about that, but I found myself envying Bainbridge. He might be keeping secrets and taking flak within his family, but he seemed at ease in the wider world where he'd grown up.

Did Jones-Demerest share that envy but to a lethal degree?

Bainbridge glanced at me. "You're looking at me as though I fell from the clouds."

"Sprang from the soil, more like. I was thinking about belonging. You look as if you do, while some rich, respected, philanthropic people never really will."

His expression sobered. "It can't be that simple."

Choosing my words because we were in public, I added, "I'm not even sure what 'it,' meaning the end purpose, could be."

"Indeed." He sipped his beer from its sleek pint glass. After a moment, he gestured with it toward a point over my shoulder. "See that stone wall down there, the one with the tall windows?"

I turned to look, ducking a little to peer under the bridge. "What about it?"

"That's the Guildhall, where the city council would've met with Richard III on his visits to York."

Richard III. That's why the pub sign looked familiar. I'd seen a similar image in the National Portrait Gallery.

"You're thinking about the prototype Wicked Uncle and looking content?" I asked.

Come to think of it, he'd also thrown Richard III at me during our dispute in London. And on our walk through Abbey Museum Park on the way here, he'd pointed out the ruins of St. Mary's Abbey and informed me that Richard III, then Duke of Gloucester, had probably visited there when he came to the city.

"Are you a fan or something?" The man was only accused of stealing his throne from his nephew and then murdering the boy, which hardly seemed like behavior someone of Bainbridge's character would condone, let alone admire.

He said, "I wouldn't go that far, but I don't believe the charges against him have been proven."

Now I was intrigued. I'm not much for history, but I do like mysteries. I come from the state where Sir Walter Raleigh lost his colony, after all.

Bainbridge cast a casual glance around us. Though his posture stayed relaxed, his gaze sharpened as it swung back to me. He cupped my cheek as the moony look came over his face. "You're so beautiful sitting there. I want a photo, darling. Smile."

Since he had no reason to take a photo of me, he must be photographing something behind me. Obliging him, I cocked my head and smiled while he aimed his phone at me.

"Send it to me, Honeykins."

"Doing it now."

My phone chimed. I pulled it out and looked at it. He'd sent me the photo, all right. He'd also copied his agency and included the message *Identify?* The photo showed two burly guys at the table by the stairs leading up to the street. One wore a leather jacket, the other denim.

Both had plain, inconspicuous features and wide shoulders and seemed focused in our direction.

Raising an eyebrow at him, I murmured, "Are they watching us?"

"Seem to be. Better safe than sorry," he replied. "Do you know them?"

"No," I whispered. In a louder voice, I said, "Ooh, Honeykins, I'm sending it to my friend Ceelie. She'll be so jealous!" Giggling, I forwarded the photo to Arachnid's urgent intel line.

Bainbridge gave me another dimwitted smile and folded his hand around mine. Playing along, I laced my fingers through his and tried not to notice how good that felt. Role-playing could carry a person away, but I wouldn't have expected that with him. We were too incompatible.

We nursed our beer for a few minutes. Both our agencies responded that they didn't have anything on these guys.

We looked at each other. "So whose are they?" I asked.

He shrugged. "At a guess, Jones-Demerest's, but they aren't sufficiently trained to be inconspicuous."

"Points to us, then."

"Let's see how determined they are," he suggested softly, still with the silly, brainless smile.

"By all means." I swung my legs over the bench and stood.

When he reached my side, he draped an arm over my shoulders. Leaning close, he murmured, "We'll head for the museum."

His breath on my ear generated hot, happy quivers between my legs. Ignoring the rush, I slid my arm around his lean waist and again noticed how firm it was. Obviously, I handled these roles much better with a married partner my brain filed as off limits.

As we strolled toward the bridge and Low Ousegate Street, I glanced at the table by the stairs. The two guys still sat there. The one facing us stared through me. Each nursed a glass of something, but they sat upright, tense and not lounging.

I squeezed Bainbridge's waist twice, quickly, to let him know I'd pegged them. Now we would see whether they followed. If someone was having us watched, we needed to know who.

We climbed the short flight of steps to Low Ousegate, then turned right. We'd left the car on the far side of the museum grounds, which meant we had a bit of a walk to get to it.

"If these guys were following us," I murmured, "do they know where the car is? If I were them and I knew, I'd have someone lying in wait."

"We'll deal with that if we must."

At a leisurely pace, we turned left to stroll down Spurriergate. A few people wandered the neighborhood, but the light was failing fast now. The restaurants and pubs were open, with all the shops now closed.

"We need some maneuvering room," Bainbridge said softly. "Away from all these people. Then we'll see what happens."

"Lead on." I smiled up at him and glimpsed the two men from the pub trailing us at a discreet distance.

Bainbridge flicked a glance over his shoulder. His eyes gleamed with the same anticipation humming through me. For the first time, I felt completely in tune with him.

"So far, so good," he murmured.

He let his steps weave just a bit. I followed suit, and we bumped each other. I even giggled.

"Two of them, two of us," I whispered. "I'm willing to bet we're better than they are."

"Bound to be. The museum grounds should be closed now. Whether these two follow us inside will tell us a great deal."

I dropped my head briefly to his shoulder in agreement. The quick, affectionate kiss he pressed onto my hair shouldn't have made my heart skip. Must be the excitement of the chase.

The street name changed a couple of times as we walked, and I figured this must've been a warren in medieval times. Our two shadows followed, never too close but never far enough back that we could shake them easily.

After a few minutes, we reached the Lendal Street gate for the museum, the one we'd walked out of a couple of hours earlier. The tall, iron gates were locked now, as he'd predicted. To the right were the stone ruins of the medieval hospital—St. Leonard's, he'd said—a blockish, one-story structure of gray stone and, beyond it, the adjoining, ghostly shell of a two-story building. One wall jutted upward beyond the tall, iron fence at the far side, its roofline pointed and its empty upper-story window arches spooky in the moonlight.

Bainbridge halted, and his arm around my waist made me stop, too. "Before Henry VIII dissolved the monasteries, this was St. Mary's Abbey, darling. When Richard III was Duke of Gloucester, he and his wife often came to York. He would've known this place."

"You are a fan," I whispered. In a louder voice, I said, "You said that already. Who cares about some dead king, Bainsiekins?" I leaned into him and shifted my body to peek at the two men.

They stood on the opposite side of the street, a few feet back from the corner and facing the ruins. One of them lit a cigarette. Farther up Lendal, York Minster loomed in the twilight, its pale stone gleaming in the deepening gloom. Half a dozen people stood out in front of it, chatting and taking photos.

From the pub behind us, light and voices spilled. Lots of people there.

"We must draw them away from all these bystanders," Bainbridge murmured. "This way."

He tugged me to the left, onto a narrow, cobbled lane that sloped downward to the river. The crenellated, stone walls of the museum ran parallel to it on our right, with Lendal Bridge on our left.

In a louder voice, feigning absorption in his subject, he proclaimed, "As Duke of Gloucester, the future Richard III administered the North for his brother, King Edward IV, in a just and fair manner. He was beloved here but unfortunately didn't understand the southern power base. There are Roman ruins, too, and what remains of St. Leonard's Hospital."

I sighed loudly. "Yeah, whatever."

"Come on, darling. There's a low spot in the walls down here. We'll just nip in for a quick look."

"They're closed. Besides, it's just a bunch of old rocks," I whined, following him.

"Fascinating ones, you'll see. We won't hurt anything, and no one at the museum will care. I'm one of its benefactors. Come along."

He led me about halfway down the lane, well below street level now, and with shrubbery filling the space between the crenellated stone wall and the walkway. Tugging me off the path, he said, "Just through here."

As we turned, I glanced back. Our pursuers had moved to the top of the lane. No one else was in sight, though voices approaching below us meant there were people on the river walk that fronted the museum grounds.

Bainbridge and I pushed our way between the bushes to reach the wall. The branches rasped over our clothes. Good thing I was wearing a canvas jacket and jeans. Sure enough, there was an old gateway in the stonework, with an opening of about a foot between it and the arch's top. Boosting up on the top of the gate, we were able to shinny over the wall.

More bushes awaited, slapping at our clothes as we dropped down amid them. We pushed through and found ourselves on the museum's lawn.

Uphill on the lawn to our right lay the curved wall of the old Roman ruins and, by the street, the one-story part of the ruined medieval hospital. Between them and the remains of the old abbey's nave stood the museum, its neoclassical portico of yellow stone illuminated by spotlights. The abbey ruin was only one long wall, a couple of arches, and fragments of columns with one illuminated archway in the high wall creating a ghostly, beautiful effect I didn't have time to appreciate just now.

Not much cover there, and another high, iron fence blocked us from the area between the hospital and the Roman ruin. The lamps illuminating the walkway through the grounds weren't helpful either.

Rustling in the bushes behind us implied we needed to make a plan fast.

Between the abbey ruin and the river stood a two-story, stone and half-timbered building, one of the old abbey's support facilities. We could hide behind it but would be instantly exposed to anyone who came around behind it. Only one big bush stood near it for concealment.

The rustling behind us had given way to voices. We had to hurry.

There was one other structure on the grounds. I eyed the squatty, octagonal building on a rise between the museum and the river. An old observatory, it was surrounded by trees and a terraced garden.

Even as I decided it was a good place to lurk, Bainbridge headed toward it. Great minds, et cetera.

"Now what?" I asked, resisting the urge to point out that we were improvising by the moment.

Bainbridge's grin flashed briefly, making my insides stupidly squishy. "We draw them in," he replied.

For comfort, I'd worn running shoes, ones with glittery yellow trim applied so they fit Claire's love of glitz. That was probably a good thing, despite the way the trim caught the scant light available. The spike heels on my other Claire shoes were not as reliable for walking on grass.

We ran up the rise. Despite the lights on the grounds, the trees around the observatory cast a deep well of shadow. And the eight sides provided plenty of angles.

"We must take them out quickly but quietly," Bainbridge muttered. "We need answers, but we don't want a security guard coming into the middle of this."

"Oooh, Honeykins," I giggled, loud enough for someone on the grounds to hear me but not to carry as far as any guard shack. I hoped. "You're so smokin' hot."

We cocked our heads, listening. Footsteps came rapidly over the grass toward us.

"Not only observing, then," Bainbridge said softly.

We stepped onto the pavement around the observatory and slipped to the far side of the building. He faced right, and I faced left.

One of the men crept around the building on my partner's side. I glanced over. Jack's left arm flashed upward to block a punch. His right fist slammed into his attacker's face.

He could handle this, so I looked toward my side of the building. A moment later, the back of my neck twitched. I wheeled toward Jack again, turning directly into a bear-hug grab that pinned my right arm between my chest and my captor's.

CHAPTER NINE

I curled my free hand's fingers back to strike with the heel of my hand but didn't have the distance to power the blow. I could reach the Walther under my jacket, but a shot would draw attention we didn't want and, if it went astray, endanger any civilians nearby.

The guy grabbed for my wrist. I stamped on his instep—oh, to have those spike heels now!—twisted my arm under his rising one and slammed my fist into his ribs.

"Bitch," he wheezed, then grabbed for my arm again, but I was already turning, taking advantage of his one-armed grip to draw enough space for that hand-heel strike. It slammed into his nose. Cartilage broke with a sickening *crunch*, and blood spurted.

His grip loosened. I pivoted to slam my locked fists into his temple. Holding his nose, he couldn't block. A roundhouse kick would've been better but also too professional for ditzy Claire. He staggered into the wall. Dropped to his knees.

I snap-kicked him upside the head, and he collapsed. I shot a glance over my shoulder.

Bainbridge took a blow to the gut, but he dropped into a crouch and swept his opponent's legs out from under him. He hadn't drawn his Glock, probably sharing my desire not to attract inconvenient attention.

I looked back at my guy. Still down for the count, so I spun to help my partner. He didn't need it, though, not holding the guy on his knees with one arm twisted behind his back. He banged the assailant's head into the stone wall.

Breathing hard, Bainbridge looked at me. A quick nod of approval, and he said, "We'll have to bring one around."

"Mine maybe—Wait." A stray sound caught my attention. More footsteps. Multiple sets. Coming from the far side of the grounds, off Marygate.

"I heard it," he informed me softly. We melted into the trees. Four guys hurried toward us from the opposite side of the gardens. They were making a beeline for the observatory. Their buds must've clued them in.

In the dim light, Bainbridge's lips tightened. "We can't start a brawl here," he decided. He waved at the two-story, half-timbered building near the river. "That will block their view in a moment. We'll go then."

I nodded. We would have to time this right for the lines of sight to work in our favor.

"Go," he breathed.

Muffling our footsteps as best we could, we darted down the hill to the big bush at the corner of the half-timbered structure. Now the guys were softly calling to their comrades. As they crossed in front of the building, we sped behind it, toward the museum park's far wall.

A curse came from the observatory area, then, "There they go!"

We hadn't reached cover fast enough.

"Sod it," Jack muttered.

We ran flat-out. The noise of our footsteps would betray our position, but that couldn't be helped. Feet pounded behind us but didn't gain.

The wall at the far end was stone and about six feet high but no problem for people who regularly ran obstacle courses. We were over it in seconds and dashing up Marygate to reach the car park.

#

There was no one lying in wait by the car. "I'm guessing whoever was watching the car came to help at the gardens," I said as Bainbridge started his Triumph.

"Very likely." He backed out of the parking space and headed into the street.

"We're lucky they didn't have guns," I commented. "Or else were afraid they'd draw too much attention." They couldn't be ordinary muggers, never having tried for our money.

"A suppressor would take care of that." Bainbridge's eyes flicked to his mirror.

"Anyone back there?"

"Not so far, but it won't be difficult to guess what route we'll take home." His smile had a definite wolfish cast. "Perhaps we'll get another crack at them."

"Preferably with better odds and no civilians around."

We cleared the city walls and headed into the countryside. No lights showed in the mirror. Since Bainbridge drove with his usual relaxed daring, I figured no one was following without headlights, either. Few houses bordered this road, which meandered over the countryside and into Wensleydale.

"How's your knee after all that?" he asked.

"A little sore but hardly enough to mention. It should be fine in a couple of days."

"That's good."

I shifted in my seat to see him better. "Suppose something happened to you, maybe a fatal something. What happens to your shares in Hawkshead Shipping then?"

"If there is a regularly scheduled shareholder meeting in progress— Hell." His lips tightened. In the glow from the dashboard instruments, his face turned grim. He down-shifted and stepped on the gas.

I twisted in my seat to look behind us. Too far back for the lights to hit ours, a low-slung coupe trailed us. "It could be nothing."

"It came out of the lane for a cottage that's stood empty for a year. Didn't use the lights until they turned onto the road."

The car could hold two kids who'd been necking and just forgotten about the headlights at first, but I liked coincidence no better than Bainbridge did. Now the car gained rapidly. Swell.

"I have only one magazine for the Walther on me," I informed him.

"Open the glove box." He roared into a turn that flung me into the passenger door. "Press your thumb to the inside of the latch."

When I complied, the back of the glove compartment, with the usual assortment of maps, a tidy one unlike my jumbled desk drawer, rolled forward. Rolling up behind it came a compartment with a Walther PPK, a suppressor, and four magazines strapped into place. I grabbed everything but the gun and stuffed the mags into my pockets. Then I drew my Walther and screwed the suppressor, or silencer, onto it.

"You think of everything, your lordship."

"We try."

He did something I couldn't see to his armrest. It dropped downward to reveal another tight little compartment with a Glock, a silencer, and magazines strapped into it.

Driving one-handed at a speed that had the tires squealing on curves, he extracted the magazines and passed them to me. The suppressor followed. "Hold these, would you?"

"My pleasure." I laid his gear in my lap while I chambered a round in my weapon. "I assume you have a plan."

I did, but it involved shooting the pursuer through the rear windshield. He might have something more subtle in mind.

"It's called turnabout." The car fishtailed out of a turn, and he yanked it back on course. "There's a farm lane about a kilometer ahead. If we can reach it unobserved."

"Hide? I'd rather take the fight to the enemy."

"Right, but with the element of surprise."

"I could go with surprise." I hung on as he wound along the narrow, twisting lane. The other car had dropped back a little.

"Driver's not used to this road," he said, "so we have an advantage. On the other side of this hill, it straightens out. They could overtake us then."

"You know every turn, though." Even if he was screeching around them at a dangerous rate. "You've got great tires."

"I've driven this road since I earned my license." He glanced in the mirror. "No sign of them. Good."

He slowed, stomped on the brake, and backed into the roadside darkness. I held my breath, hoping the low chassis wouldn't snag on something. As soon as the tires left the pavement, he killed the lights. A few more yards, and he stopped. "Out," he said, grabbing his stuff from my lap.

Since the ragtop had no dome light, we didn't have to worry about it betraying our position. I bailed into a grassy field about thirty feet from the road, up a slight rise, and grabbed my gear. With only moonlight to break the darkness, I had trouble seeing landscape details.

I eased my door shut and quietly said, "Now what?"

A car flashed by. I ducked, but it didn't slow.

"Back here, in the grass." Screwing the suppressor onto his Glock, he ran about twenty yards down the rutted lane and waved me into the grass. "Take that side. They'll miss us when they reach the hilltop and can see along the road. When they return, we'll try, as you Americans like to say, to get the drop on them."

"I like it. I assume we're not going to kill them since we could use some information."

"Not if we can help it. Wait for my signal to come out."

Headlights appeared on the road. A few seconds later, a car rolled slowly into view. We ducked into the grass. He disappeared, but I could see the car pass. It looked like the one that had followed us and moved slowly, as though its occupants searched for something.

The glow of its taillights vanished around the curve. The occupants must mean to approach us from the side.

A chilly breeze swished the grass into my face. Somewhere nearby, an owl hooted. Off to our left, beyond the copse of trees that bordered this field, a horse whinnied. Even I know they're not prone to making noise at night. I glanced that way. Tall grass makes silent movement difficult, but anyone with training and practice can manage it.

Another faint sound from the left, like branches brushing against something, broke the stillness. I peered toward it. A man's ghostly shape broke from the trees, moving slowly. Then another. And—*oh, crap!*—another.

No problem if we wanted to shoot them all, except we didn't.

As they neared the lane, I could make out their faces. They weren't the guys who'd jumped us in York, though they had similar stocky builds and nondescript features.

Moonlight glinting on their guns' barrels added another complication. They inched forward, spreading out a little. Circling toward the car.

Their course would bring them between us and the car, which was to our benefit because we'd be behind them. They were taking their time but not crouched or spread far apart. As though they didn't consider us dangerous.

Maybe they thought we'd stopped for a quickie.

They positioned themselves with one on each door and one at the back on the driver's side. The two at the sides inched forward. In the darkness, they probably couldn't see the interior. I sighted on the one by the passenger door.

The one by the driver's door lunged for it, gun ready, and yanked it open. He straightened as if in shock.

In that moment, Bainbridge sprang from the grass and pressed his silencer to the neck of the other man on that side of the car. "Don't move."

I had to give him points. His approach had made no betraying noise, and he'd executed his attack so fast I'd barely seen it.

"Easy, mate." The man by the driver's door raised his hand, with the gun still in it. "No need for all that. We just want a word with you and your lady."

"Drop the guns. All of you." Menace rang in Bainbridge's voice. "Then kick them away."

Having my partner face three armed men alone, even holding a gun to one, made my stomach queasy. Before David died, it wouldn't have. I itched to jump out beside Jack, but he'd told me he would cue me. If I let fear rule my thinking, I was finished. I blotted my clammy left palm on my jeans.

The man Bainbridge held hostage dropped his weapon and kicked it under the Triumph. The other two exchanged glances.

"My wife," Bainbridge said amiably, "is one of those gun-crazy Americans, and she doesn't like being followed. Drop your weapons or she'll open fire."

"Now, mate, let's just have a word, and we'll leave." The leader stooped slowly, as though to set down his weapon.

I kept my focus on the other guy. With his gun still in the air, he eyed Bainbridge a bit too intently. Suddenly, his gun barrel shifted, coming to bear on my partner. I fired two quick shots.

The bullets struck the guy high in the right shoulder. He dropped his weapon. With a cry, he staggered against the car and slid to the ground. Staying down, I edged toward that side to keep him in my sights. If he tried for his gun, I'd have to kill him.

The leader's gun barrel whipped upward, but Bainbridge fired across his prisoner's shoulder. A black splotch blossomed in the leader's forehead. Spinning backward, he fell on his face.

Bainbridge's prisoner had the sense to stand still.

"Bollocks, I'm shot." My target clutched his shoulder.

"Don't give her cause to do it again," Bainbridge said. "Now we'll have that word. Who sent you, and why?"

"Some bloke in London," his prisoner said. "Don't know his name."

That might or might not be true. I glanced toward the trees. No one had appeared, so these guys must not have had backup. Either that, or the backup had fled.

"Come out, darling," Bainbridge called. He must also have been waiting to see if backup arrived.

I rose slowly, keeping the Walther trained on our new friends. "Oooh, Hubbypoo! That was awesome!"

"Ta, darling. Good shooting."

"Thanks." I sauntered to his side, my eyes wide. "I never shot anybody before. Oooh, is he dead?"

"Need—doctor," the man I'd shot groaned.

"All in good time," Bainbridge said. "Yes, darling, that fellow's dead. His friends won't tell us who sent them."

"I heard." I pretended to consider. "Can I shoot another one?"

"She's crazy!" Bainbridge's prisoner said.

"Nah, just pissed off." I waved the gun at him. "Tell you what, you tell us what you know, and we'll call the doctor." We wouldn't actually let them bleed to death, but admitting that now would be bad strategy.

"I don't know," Bainbridge's prisoner insisted. "I swear. Some bloke in London wanted us to see Lord Bainbridge put in hospital, cautioned to mind his own business. That's all."

"All," Bainbridge repeated in a dry voice. He glanced at me. "Call the police, Claire."

I pretended to, but the call really went to Simon, not to the North Yorkshire Police. MI5 could sort out the jurisdictional issues. For all we knew, this attack had nothing to do with Jones-Demerest, but the timing, so soon after Bainbridge's disagreement with his brother, stank.

After that, I called Petunia, who would notify Arachnid. I tucked my phone away. "I know a little first aid," I said. "If nobody tries anything funny."

"We'll tie this one up first," Bainbridge said. "I've a length of rope in the boot."

Once the guy was restrained, we set about patching up his friend. We couldn't talk, but I didn't doubt we puzzled over the same question. Who wanted Bainbridge out of the way, and why?

#

"I would've just shot you," I said as Bainbridge drove back to his estate. We'd left an Arachnid crew in charge of cleaning up the bad guys, hauling them in to find out what they knew.

"Ta, darling." He flicked me a wry glance.

"No, seriously. If you're in my way and I'm a person who doesn't balk at supplying weapons to bad guys or developing a bioweapon, why wouldn't I just have someone take you out?"

"Apparently that question arose during the Crimean War."

"Crimean—oh, right. 1850s somewhere around the Black Sea."

He nodded. "Best known for the charge of the Light Brigade and, on a cheerier note, Florence Nightingale's pioneering nursing care."

"Right. Got it."

"As I was saying before that little interlude, the ninth earl had a provision written into the governing articles to the effect that the death of the majority shareowner—"

"Himself, in other words."

Bainbridge nodded. "The company's business would be frozen for one year if the earl died under suspicious circumstances. No assets might be sold, no changes made to the governing structure."

"Which would include taking in an investor."

Another nod. I frowned out at the darkness. "But if you were in the hospital, maybe in a coma, and Robin called a meeting…Who votes your shares?"

"Robin," Bainbridge replied, his voice as dry as a desert in July.

CHAPTER TEN

The next evening, I girded for battle, otherwise known as dinner with the enemy, in a dark blue, satin cocktail dress. Strapless and equipped with a pushup bra, it also boasted a skirt gathered at mid-thigh on the left side.

In the interests of partnership, not really because I was curious about his reaction to the hot dress, I decided to let Bainbridge approve my outfit. I knocked on his dressing room door.

We still had no answers as to who wanted him incapacitated. Yet he'd gone into control freak mode, refusing to discuss any connection to the Hawkshead Shipping issue beyond the obvious concession that the attack was probably related to it. I missed the harmony, the sense of being in sync, I'd felt last night.

I hadn't told him about Arachne's call this afternoon, just before my surprisingly smooth riding lesson. No matter how worried he was or was not about the family company, I had my private instructions. Jones-Demerest was not to gain a foothold in international shipping.

Damn it, I hated keeping secrets from my partner, but he left me no choice. He was a control freak in everything else. Why not with his family?

He opened his door, his crisp, white cotton shirt partly open above dark gray trousers. A dark crimson tie hung loose around his neck, and my heart beat suddenly, stupidly faster.

Swallowing, I told my hormones to cut it out. "I thought I'd give you a veto on the dress if you wanted it."

His gaze dropped to my augmented and largely exposed bosom, and the sudden warmth in his eyes generated heat deep inside me. He took his time scanning down my bare legs to the stiletto heels on my feet and back up.

Trying for calm, I took a deep breath as his glance reached my chest. He set his jaw and inhaled audibly before he averted his eyes.

After a moment, he said, "That's a nice choice."

His husky tone sent new ripples of heat through me.

He cleared his throat. "But your neck's a bit bare," he added in his usual bland tone. He reached to the side and claimed a flat box off a chest of drawers. "I pulled this out for you earlier."

Snapping the box open, he revealed a choker-length necklace of rubies, each the size of my first thumb joint and surrounded by small diamonds. A matching pendant dangled from the center.

I didn't need lapidary training to know the stones were real. "This looks like an heirloom. Are you sure I should wear it?"

"The Countess of Bainbridge doesn't dine in company without jewels. It would look odd if you didn't wear something from the collection. Turn around."

He fastened the necklace around my neck. Just knowing I had a valuable antique on my person took my breath away, and the touch of his fingers on my nape created more annoying tingles.

"I thought this would look well on you," he said.

Stunned that he'd cared about that, I turned to face him. "It's gorgeous." And probably one of the most expensive pieces in that collection.

He directed a critical eye at my neck. "Yes, excellent." He cleared his throat again. "You look lovely."

Our gazes locked, his smoky gray and warm in a way that made me feel as though I had to step much closer or a lot farther back. Insanely, I wanted to touch him.

"Thanks," I managed. Trying to take us back to normal, I asked, "They're okay with the purple hair?"

"Indeed." He smiled, and the tension between us eased. "I'll be ready in a few minutes."

I stepped back so he could close his door. The dressing room's cheval mirror drew me like a magnet. The stones glittered in the overhead light, flattering my bolstered bosom. Despite the weird, spiky hairdo, I did look elegant.

"Good enough to jump the tracks," I told my reflection.

Whoa. Where had that come from?

My mind flew back to my senior year in high school. I'd been nominated for a Morehead Scholarship, a prestigious full ride offered by UNC-Chapel Hill. The counselor had warned me my extra-curriculars, consisting of a drone job at a local store and one sport, basketball, probably weren't enough for a win, but I'd made the finals. Planning to leave school for the interview, I changed into my best dress and a lacy, white cardigan after gym class.

In the hall outside the locker room, I met "Jimbo" Hartner, Mister Jim's grandson and the mill's future owner. His friends surrounded me, standing in my personal space.

Fingering my sweater, he sneered, "You might look good enough to jump the tracks, but the committee'll see you're just a linthead bitch made for tendin' looms and droppin' brats."

I couldn't breathe. Rumor had it he'd applied for the Morehead but hadn't made the first cut, but saying so would cost my daddy his job. Jimbo was probably pissed that he couldn't wreck this chance for me to escape from Hartner Falls.

"We'll see," I said through my tight throat.

He smacked my shoulder with his open palm, a quick, hard shove. I stumbled back against the locker room door as he and his pals strolled away. I'd stood there, clutching my books so hard the edges hurt my fingers, wishing I could take him apart.

I'd never been sure Jimbo's daddy hadn't tried to pull strings on the selection committee. Because of the counselor's warning, I'd figured I wouldn't get the scholarship anyway, but that kernel of doubt, of fear of the Hartners' power, had eaten at me.

Staring at my wide-eyed, tense reflection, I drew a steadying breath. I'd grown up on the wrong side of the tracks, but neither side figured in my life anymore. I could take guys like Jimbo apart now.

Bainbridge's arrogance didn't carry a bully's taint. I was free of all that. Why was I remembering this now?

Bainbridge tapped on the door as he entered. "Ready?"

"Ready." I accepted his offered arm and felt unusually conscious of its firm bulk beneath his sleeve. Not that it mattered in the long run, but I liked the fact that he was still taller than I was, even though I wore those spike heels.

Together, we walked down the carpeted hall—Axminster carpeting, Petunia had said, very expensive—down the stairs and into the foyer. I directed a questioning glance at him. I'd studied the house's layout, but I didn't know where the guests waited.

"They're in the blue parlor." He steered me that way, and we paused on the threshold.

At the far end of the room stood Jones-Demerest, talking amiably to Robin. Each held a drink. Seated on the delicate, Regency sofa's royal blue cushions, Lady Beatrice chatted with a younger, blond woman. The rest of Bainbridge's invited neighbors, a middle-aged couple and a pair who looked as though they were in their mid-sixties, sat on spindly, matching armchairs.

When we entered, conversation died. Everyone turned polite, expectant faces toward us. The sixtyish woman looked appalled for a heartbeat before mastering her face.

I smiled, but adrenaline hummed in my veins. We'd seated Jones-Demerest and Robin next to me at dinner. After I promised not to shoot Jones-Demerest under the table. I wasn't entirely sure Bainbridge was kidding when he extracted that promise.

If he wasn't, he should've known better. I wouldn't kill the evil genie until we had the information on his bioweapons.

Sucking in a deep breath, I said, "Hey, everybody! Wow, Bainsiekins —what a quiet crowd! Put on some music, and let's liven it up."

He winced to just the perfect degree before smiling at me. "Perhaps later, darling. First let's meet everyone."

As we started toward the nearest woman, a dowager in black silk accessorized with a pinched smile, I twinkled and repressed a sigh. Bainbridge had described our assignment as a chess match, and the evening loomed ahead as long and painfully as one.

#

The two hired waiters hovering around the dinner table gave the back of my neck a compulsive itch. I'd known dining with the aristocracy wouldn't be a simple, pass-the-potatoes kind of meal, and at least I was okay with the snowy Irish linen tablecloth and napkins, the Royal

Doulton dishes, and the Waterford crystal. In fact, I liked the elegant ambience.

The clink of silver cutlery on china and the murmur of voices created a relaxed mood. Over the fish course, I turned to Robin. "Why do you like this investment so much?"

Surprise flickered across his face. "I didn't know business interested you, Claire."

"Well, you just met me." I gave him the big, wide smile I called Bright and Clueless. I'd been using it so much tonight that my face was starting to hurt. "I was self-employed before I married Bainsiekins. I had to keep my own books. You know, Form 1040, Schedule C, quarterlies. All that."

Robin raised his brows in a gesture startlingly like his brother's. "He lets you call him Bainsiekins in public?"

"What else would I call him?" I furrowed my brow to simulate bewilderment, but I didn't like the condescension in his tone.

"What, indeed?" Robin directed an amused glance at Jones-Demerest, as though they shared a secret.

Not good. Really not good. "Anyway, why this deal?" I persisted.

After another glance across the table, Robin said, "We need to diversify. Jasper's cargo would provide a steady revenue stream and compensate for some of our south Pacific losses. Pirates grow bolder every week."

Which reinforced Bainbridge's point about risk, but I didn't say so. Instead, I turned to Jones-Demerest, who was staring at my enhanced bust. I leaned forward to give him a better view and, maybe, distract him. "What do you get out of the deal?"

He wrenched his gaze from my chest to my Clueless Babe face. "It's simple. I gain a dependable carrier and more control over my cargo's movements."

As we'd suspected. I smiled. "So you don't think this Paris flu or bird bug, or whatever, will be a problem? Honeykins's real worried about it."

"Jack worries only when he chooses to focus," Robin said. "When this blows over, he'll have forgotten he cared so much."

I tucked my left foot, the one near him, behind the right so I couldn't kick him. He was mocking a man who'd put his neck on the line for this country more than once. A man who, regardless of all else, was still his brother, damn it.

Restraining the glare he deserved, I gave him a pouty look. "You don't seem to like Jack much."

"Lord Bainbridge is a man of wide-ranging interests," Jones-Demerest said. "Well respected, of course, but not heavily involved in the business community."

"Jack's my brother," Robin said. "I'm entitled to be annoyed with him."

But not to lay bare his perceived faults this way. "Why are you, though? He's only doing his job." Digging for the nerve, I added, "You know, as head of the family. He explained it to me."

"Then he didn't explain it very well," Robin said stiffly.

Pay dirt. I'd hit that nerve, that dislike of being in Jack's shadow. I probed for it again. "Doesn't he have final responsibility? Isn't that why he gets such a big vote on things?" It sure as hell was. "And even I can tell he's really smart, even if he didn't graduate from college."

Robin's lips tightened briefly. "Claire, you don't understand."

"I think I do." I damn well knew I did. I glanced down the table at Bainbridge and caught him watching me. A slow smile curved his mouth and warmed my insides.

I gave him a genuine smile, not a ditzy one, in return. As his partner, I stood with him, even if no one else here did. Our gazes held, and his softened. My heart did a quick hop-skip.

Jones-Demerest cleared his throat and waited until I looked at him. "The thing is, Lady Bainbridge, your brother-in-law manages the company's daily affairs. He therefore knows its precise situation on any given day."

His gaze drifted back to my chest. Ugh. It really was too bad that I couldn't punch him. But maybe this boob fixation was a weakness we could use somehow.

I opened my eyes wide at him. "So you think Bainsiekins should listen to him more."

"Christ, yes." Robin stabbed at his salmon even though cutting the tender, flaky stuff didn't require a knife.

"I think having Lord Bainbridge reconsider would be to all of our advantages," Jones-Demerest said tactfully. "It would also avoid a family dispute I understand may turn nasty."

Just how much had Robin told him about the family conflict? And how cozy were he and Robin? Did they have any financial ties? I'd have Petunia check on that.

For now, I'd learned what I mainly wanted to know, which was that Bainbridge's brother deeply hated being number two and would go to great lengths to get his way.

CHAPTER ELEVEN

I let my gaze drift down to Bainbridge's end of the table. Though I'd never say so to him, he looked like sexiness personified in his tailored jacket. I was glad the length of the table lay between us, helping keep temptation at bay.

Four people sat on each side. His aunt and the youngish blonde, Lady Daphne Something, flanked him. The middle-aged and seniorish couples from the town held the center seats. On his right, the elegant Lady Daphne leaned slightly toward him, and they appeared to be deep in conversation.

They also looked very good together. Very comfortable, which I had no right to feel miffed about.

I pushed the corners of my mouth down a bit and leaned toward Robin. "Who's that talking to Honeykins? I can't remember her name."

Robin leaned forward to look. "That's Lady Daphne Archibald. She and Jack have known each other forever."

Bainbridge smiled at her, a relaxed, intimate smile I couldn't help envying. I frowned more deeply. "He's talking to her an awful lot."

"He's the host." Robin took a bite of fish.

Lady Beatrice leaned forward to direct an approving smile at Lady Daphne. I sipped wine, watching them and aware Jones-Demerest was watching me.

Since Robin had no discretion about family matters, why not let them think I also had none? "Your aunt doesn't like me," I informed Robin.

He smiled. "She'd like you better if you remembered her name. Don't worry, Claire. She'll come round. It's good for Jack to have someone who shares his love of fun. Neither you nor he need worry about Hawkshead. I manage it well."

His smile turned smug, and another flash of insight pinged me. He wanted his brother to marry a party girl. A wife such as I pretended to be would provide a disincentive for Bainbridge to take a closer hand in the business.

I continued to stare down the table. Bainbridge flashed me a warm look before his aunt claimed his attention.

"Who made this stupid sitting rule, anyway? I like sitting next to my Hubbypoo." I sighed and pulled up my opening salvo for Jones-Demerest. "No offense, Robin, but we haven't had much time alone since we got to England. It's always something. And there are always people coming and going. We don't have any privacy around here."

Jones-Demerest turned a concerned look on me. "If that continues to trouble you, madam, you might find my newest little business of interest. It's a community where couples can live a simple life, working in the brewery or tending the sheep or helping administer the community. Or simply relax. Our residents have plenty of privacy."

"Do they really? That sounds fun." Getting him to say that had been way easier than expected. I assumed a thoughtful expression. "I don't think Honeykins would agree, though."

"You and Lord Bainbridge should try it out." Jones-Demerest glanced at Robin before adding, "It would be a nice refuge from any family turmoil."

It would also keep Bainbridge from addressing the Hawkshead shareholders, I'd bet. Damn, but he really did deserve better than the family he had.

#

As the party moved to the parlor for after-dinner drinks, Bainbridge glanced at me. My smile told him I'd laid the groundwork for our plan. He strolled off to join the men.

I watched him out of the corner of my eye. No harm in watching, right? His tailored jacket emphasized the lean lines of his torso and the breadth of his shoulders.

Accepting a glass of brandy from one of the hired waiters, I drifted toward the women. This party felt too much like Hartner Falls gatherings, men standing in one clump by the hearth, women seated in another by the terrace doors, and the food more or less in between.

Petunia had suggested that we serve dessert at the table, but we'd opted for the less formal option to keep people circulating.

"So we jaunted to New York for a long weekend," the elegantly coiffed, dyed-blonde-to-cover-gray woman on my right said. "Tiberino had some interesting new bags, but I didn't find much worth bothering about in the boutiques."

Tiberino bags? We had something in common after all.

"I prefer the Rome salon," an older woman across from her said. "Best to go to the source."

"I like Cartier," I volunteered, carefully mispronouncing it as Cartee-er. "They have such gorgeous, sparkly window displays."

"One would never guess." The older woman smiled, her expression taut. Her glance swept from my purple-red hair to my bright red toenails.

She could only have meant it as a slur, but I smiled. "I'm learning to be subtle."

She winced. "Lord Bainbridge's aunt, Lady Beatrice, and I were at Lady Margaret Hall together. Perhaps you've heard of it?"

"Gosh, no." I widened my eyes at her. "Is that, like, community college?"

She shot me a frosty look. "It's one of the colleges of Oxford University."

"Bainsiekins went to Cambridge College."

"Cambridge University," she corrected in steely tones. "He attended Kings College, Cambridge."

"Whatever." I suddenly need to escape the condescension I'd invited. "Anybody want cheese? Dessert?"

The women around me shook their heads, and I backed out of the circle. Having established my ditziness with them, I could move to phase two of Bainbridge's plan.

Brooding, I sailed toward the dessert table. They were treating me as my behavior had urged them to, so why did I resent them? I'd circulated among the rich and privileged before, several times, without having this overwhelming urge to stick it to them. So why now?

I chose a fluffy, finger-sized Napoleon and glanced over at

Bainbridge. Nope, I was not jealous. At least, not enough to matter. So what was eating at me?

Was it the ease of their lives, compared to my family's? Or, following that thought, was it the belonging thing again, the fact they'd found their niche and part of me wanted to fit there, too?

Because it was Bainbridge's niche?

I froze on the thought. Was I more jealous than I knew?

"Charlotte," Lady Beatrice said to one of the other women, "I hear you're supporting Daphne's Paki charity."

I stiffened at the ethnic slur, but Lady Daphne quietly said, "Pakistani, Lady Beatrice, if you please." She had steel in her voice.

I turned to watch.

"Yes," the middle-aged woman said, "I'm supporting Daphne's Manchester after-school center. Helping these young people gain an education helps us all in the end." Over her sherry, she tossed Lady Beatrice a defiant look.

Bainbridge's aunt snorted. "Waste of time. They're likely future jihadis anyway. Just ask Jasper about the ones he hired." An emphatic nod emphasized the words.

Lady Daphne replied, "Every group has its troublesome members. I prefer to work for change, Lady Beatrice."

For that, I had to give her points. And Charlotte, too. Maybe there was more to these women—and to some of the ones in Hartner Falls—than I'd been willing to admit.

But I'd worry about that later. Now I had a job to do. I drifted toward the men around the fireplace. Their conversation centered on markets and futures. Odd, how no one talked about the flu. Maybe they felt safe from it. If so, they were making a big mistake.

I sidled up to Bainbridge. "...downturn can't last," he commented.

"Easy for you to say," one of the older men replied. "You've a shipping line. Everyone needs cargo moved."

"Not just now," Bainbridge said.

The expressions of the men around him went from smiles to, variously, frowns and grimaces. Jones-Demerest shook his head sadly. Next he'd probably weep crocodile tears.

When I leaned into Bainbridge's shoulder, he put an arm around me but didn't look my way. I'd arrived to start our fight. Since the flu had come up, though, it might be worth waiting to see who said what.

"It's probably nothing," Jones-Demerest said, "though of course it's a tragedy for those affected."

Yep, crocodile sympathy.

He continued, "I'm sure the authorities will contain it. It'll probably amount to no more than that avian flu, a dramatic scare with relatively confined damage."

"I wouldn't call what's happening confined." Charlotte's short, stubby husband frowned from his spot opposite Jack.

"Relatively speaking, of course," Jones-Demerest agreed with a solemn nod.

Relatively, my ass. But I gave him a wide-eyed nod. "Let's hope so."

"Well, not much use in our brooding on it," the other man, John Harbottle, said. "Anyone want a refill?" Everyone declined, and he headed for the bar.

I burrowed into Bainbridge's shoulder.

He frowned down at me. "Did you want something, darling?"

"Let's get some air."

"Aren't you feeling well?"

"Not right now." I pouted at him. "C'mon, Honeykins. Come with me." I took his drink from him and set it on a table. "'Scuse us, y'all."

They looked a bit bemused. Jones-Demerest gave us a patronizing smile. A couple of the others exchanged a knowing glance. Knowing, hah! They had no idea.

Bainbridge glowered but followed me through the double doors and out to the terrace. "That's far enough. What is it, Claire?" He pitched his curt tone perfectly, just loud enough to carry indoors.

"I'm bored." I set my plate on a table so I could put both arms around his neck. "Come upstairs and entertain me." I kissed his jaw.

Catching my wrists, he pulled my arms away from him. "This isn't the time. You should become better acquainted with our neighbors."

"They don't like me." I bumped my hips into his and got a zap-like tingle, not to mention an ego boost, when I brushed his erection. "I don't know the people they talk about."

"Listen and learn. You'll meet everyone soon enough."

"Do I have to?" I let a little whine creep into my voice.

"Claire, we discussed this." He met whining with impatience. "The position of Lady Bainbridge carries certain expectations. Socializing with our neighbors is a minor one."

"I'd rather socialize with you."

He gripped my shoulders, holding me away from him. "Claire—"

"This is our damn honeymoon," I snapped. "You promised me Paris. Italy. Jamaica. But what do I get? A brother-in-law and a stuffy old harpy of an aunt! That's no honeymoon. What happened to fucking each other's brains out, huh?"

"You had no complaints last night," he fired back.

"Yeah, well, since then, zippo!"

I had to give him major points. Living this down would be a huge embarrassment, but he was damning the torpedoes, sailing full speed ahead. Sympathy brought the tears I needed—I'm not as good as I'd like to be at summoning them—and I tried to match his style.

"I want the honeymoon you promised me, Jack. Now!"

"That would be rude," he said between his teeth. "And you might consider my wish to renew old friendships." He ran his hands gently down my arms, giving me goose pimples all over. "I want to show off my wonderful bride."

He kissed me lightly, then slid his arms around my waist to tug me into his arms. The goose pimples became serious excitement bumps, but I broke free.

"They're rude to me, and they look down on me, and your awful aunt has turned them against me." My frustration over his tolerance of Lady Beatrice gave me the final boost into outright tearful fury. "If you loved me, you'd want to be alone with me."

Tears streaming, I ran into the house, no mean trick in stiletto heels.

"Claire," he called. "Bloody hell."

He didn't follow me. We had to appear seriously on the outs. Maybe Jones-Demerest would even try to make peace?

CHAPTER TWELVE

Sobbing loudly, I flounced into a wide corridor adjacent to the parlor. I plopped onto a dainty sofa covered in green damask and buried my face in my hands.

The tears slowed to a trickle. I needed to keep them going. I thought of David, of Jones-Demerest's smug lies a few minutes ago, and outrage came to my rescue.

"What the bloody hell do you want?" Thanks to Bainbridge's lapel mike, his voice hummed faintly in my earring.

"Jack, you know I don't like to intrude."

Oh, hell, it was Lady Daphne, not Jones-Demerest. *Go away*, I thought-beamed at her.

"Not now, Daph," my partner said. The nickname hit me like a punch.

"Forgive me, but it's obvious your wife is upset."

Clearly, my thought-beaming didn't work. Where the hell was Jones-Demerest? Had he even noticed our quarrel, or had we wasted that big display?

"We can be a tough bunch to crack," dear Daph said. "Perhaps this is a bit much to expect of a young bride."

"It's her new world," Jack said. "She'll be fine."

"In time, of course. For now, make it easier if you can. Who ever did that for any of us?"

Brooding silence.

I sneaked a peek between my fingers. Lady Daphne stood by Jack, their backs to me, her hand on his shoulder.

"You waited a long time," she said softly. "She's different. Perhaps that's why you chose her. It's also why she'll have a rough go of it at first."

"She'll manage."

"All the faster if you reassure her tonight. Now."

A new tension permeated the air. They stood a little farther apart.

"Reassure her," he repeated quietly. "As I failed to reassure you."

Her chin rose. "I didn't say that."

"No. You didn't."

"She asks for what she wants, Jack. You won't have to guess, only listen."

He took a step back from her. "Right, then." He sounded rueful. I couldn't see his face in the shadows. "Excuse me, Daph."

The terrace lights showed a wistful smile on her face. "I'll tell them not to expect you until breakfast."

Bainbridge strode across the terrace toward me, and I went back to crying. Not only had nosy *Daph* involved herself way too much in our fictional marriage, but she'd probably precluded Jones-Demerest's intervention.

Hell in a handbasket. I wanted to choke her.

I could hear Bainbridge's footsteps now. To be sure everyone heard what we said, I had to meet him outside the parlor. Wiping my eyes, I hurried toward him.

He opened his arms. "Darling."

I flung himself into his embrace. "Bainsiekins, I'm sorry, I—"

"Hush." He pressed his index finger to my lips with an apology in his eyes. "You're right, darling," he said in a low, husky voice. "Today hasn't been a honeymoon. I'm going to make that up to you now."

His head swooped down in one of those brain-crashing kisses. My brain duly crashed, my body sang, and I leaned into his hard, strong front to wallow in the sensory ocean.

He nudged my chin back, and my head de-fogged for a moment.

Pressing my lips to his ear, I whispered, "At dinner. He suggested it."

"Good," Bainbridge murmured. Then he kissed my neck, a long, slow, tongue-flicking kiss created bubbling heat deep inside me. "I'll— follow up."

"Now?" I couldn't let him completely take charge. I twisted my head aside and returned the neck kiss. When I nibbled his neck, at the base of his jaw, he made a strangled sound and crushed me against him.

He caught my mouth again. His hand cupped my breast, and a full-body solar flare turned my knees to wax. Fighting for clarity, I arched into him. His hand slid to my butt and his mouth to my ear.

"Upstairs," he whispered, and his breath in my ear gave me eager shivers. "It's expected of us."

We sort of stumbled up the carpeted stairs with our hands all over each other. Our horny newlyweds bit should've earned us an acting award, except that natural lust boosted it a lot. I noticed that climbing the stairs made intriguing ripples in the muscles of his ass under my fingers.

At the first landing, he scooped me up in his arms without losing a step. I had a purely hormonal rush of pleasure, a primitive, ingrained response to caveman power, before his mouth caught mine again and my brain stopped working.

When it reactivated, he was striding down the upstairs corridor. I pulled my mouth free to suck the pulse point under his jaw. He groaned and staggered into his room, kicking the door shut behind us.

His hot, silver eyes held my gaze riveted as he slowly lowered his arm so my legs slid downward. The change in position rubbed my body along his until my feet touched the floor. We were still in full-body contact, and I wanted nothing more than to hook my leg around his hip and bring him even closer to my aching crotch.

Swallowing hard, I leaned reluctantly away from him. His hand on my butt tugged me back, and the sudden contact with his erection shot lightning all the way to my breasts.

His mouth covered mine, tongue probing. His hand kneaded my breasts. Awash in hot, greedy sensation, I moaned. Found his hard cock through his trousers and gripped it.

He growled into my mouth. His hips jerked forward, and he shucked his jacket.

A new wave of dizziness, awareness of wanting and being wanted, roared through me. Damn, but he felt good. Physically good. Mentally good.

Too good.

I held him tighter. Slid my hand into the back waistband of his trousers. Groaning, he licked my ear. His mouth covered mine again as we stumbled into the room. We fell onto the bed. Rolled together.

We should stop. I knew it. I didn't care.

His hot, soft mouth traveled down my neck. Over the bare swell of my breast. Whimpering, I arched up to him as he palmed my right breast. I didn't remember opening his shirt or tie, but my hands were inside, one cupping his neck under his collar, the other roaming the hard, warm planes of his chest with its silky mat of hair.

When he rolled above me, his legs tangled with mine. His big, warm hand slid into my skirt slit and caressed its way up to my thong-bared rump. Cupping it, he squeezed.

I gasped and jerked up, my hips bumping his hard crotch. What was left of my brain screamed red alert. We were at the brink of not turning back.

As though he also realized it, Bainbridge groaned again. His hand slipped out of my dress and up to fist on the pillow by my head. He rested his forehead on mine. His harsh, ragged breathing sounded loud in the room. Breathless myself, I gently gripped his hard, bunched biceps to tell him I agreed.

Giving in to an attraction so volcanic would blur the line between playing our roles and indulging ourselves, and we simply couldn't risk that. Besides, we were extremely incompatible. This was hormones, nothing more.

"We can't do this," he said in a rough voice.

Not wanting to say the word *no*, I shook my head. I sucked in air but didn't try to keep my honest regret from my voice. "I don't sleep with my partner."

The question had never arisen between me and the very married David, but I had a feeling sex with Bainbridge would be a game-changing act—though whether for good or ill, I had no idea. In addition to a distraction we couldn't afford.

"Neither have I," he said, in the wry voice I'd come to recognize as a good sign, "so far."

With a sigh, he rolled onto his back. He tugged me to him, his arm encircling my shoulders. Moving away seemed like a good idea, putting some distance between me and his warm, solid frame, the cedar scent of his clothes, the faint, sandalwood scent of the man himself. But I didn't want to.

I drew the edges of his shirt together, slid an arm around his neck, and forced my breathing to slow, as his did, and my pulse to settle.

Gradually, desire faded. Behind it came cozy warmth. Security.

False security, I reminded myself. Temporary. Yet our ability to bring ourselves under control and lie together this way proved, if nothing else, that we could trust each other. I could trust myself with him.

I glanced at the opposite wall. Framed together, a photo and certificate hung on the paneled surface. In the photo, a younger Bainbridge smiled broadly as he held the reins of a large, brown horse. He wore a black coat, buff pants, and a black, domed hat with a strap hanging loose under his chin and a bill over his brow. I frowned at it.

"What?" Following the direction of my gaze, he said, "That was taken the day Galahad and I won the Middleham Meet in Three-Day Eventing."

"Which is what, and why are you wearing a funny hat?"

"It's a riding helmet. The competition is dressage, or form and style, cross-country riding, and show jumping." His face softened. "Galahad was a wonderful horse. He died last year."

"And you're how old in that picture?" This peek into his past, at the happy, relaxed youth so different from the controlled man beside me, fascinated me.

"Seventeen." Ruefully, he said, "I loved eventing, but I no longer have time for it."

"Me and basketball." Remembering my folks cheering their heads off in the high school gym, I added, "Your parents must've been very proud."

"So they said." His voice lost its warmth. He kissed the top of my head and sat up, withdrawing his arm and pulling into himself. "We might as well turn in."

"Okay." I seemed to have said something wrong, but I didn't know how to fix it. His earlier exchange with Robin about their mom popped into my mind. Not my business, though.

Admiring the broad, straight line of his shoulders and his long, pantherish stride, I watched him walk to his dressing room. At least we had separate stripping areas.

He glanced at me, and the heat in his eyes made me aware my skimpy skirt was up to my ass and my push-up top barely covered the essentials. Yet I felt like a sex goddess. Knowing I affected him the same way he did me gave me a heady sense of power.

He wrenched his gaze away. "Back in a bit," he said, and stalked out the door.

Biting my lip, urging my hormones to take a seat, I slid off the bed. The sooner we got back to business as usual, the better.

#

Sometime in the night, I woke to solid warmth along my back and a warm, heavy weight over my waist. Bainbridge's arm around me, I realized dimly. He'd spooned me. Judging by his slow, deep breathing, as though he slept, he didn't mean anything by it. Might not know he'd done it.

He felt good there, though. Dangerously good. I should gently disengage.

In a minute. There was no hurry.

The next thing I knew, morning light filtered into the room. I was alone in bed, but someone was moving around the room. Faintly disappointed, I lifted my head. "Jack?"

"Good morning, madam," Petunia said briskly.

I shouldn't have expected him to stick around, especially when I needed to dress. We'd decided last night that we'd pay a call on Jones-Demerest and use our quarrel as an excuse for him to talk us into moving in. Still, I foolishly wished he was there. I pushed my hair out of my face and sat up.

Behind Petunia, the housekeeper arranged a coffee pot and a basket of croissants on the table by the leather sofa. "Will there be anything else, madam?"

"No. Thanks, Mrs. Bolton."

"My pleasure, madam." With a smile, she slipped out through the dressing room.

Bainbridge strode through the doorway a moment later in his Horse Lord outfit. He must've been riding this morning. I suppressed a pang of regret that he hadn't asked me to go.

"We're in," he said. "Pack your things."

The words were English, but they had no meaning. "What're we into, and why am I packing?"

On the hunch I wasn't going to like what came next, I slid out of the bed. I prefer to face challenges on my feet.

"I rode over to Simply Yorkshire," he said as though it were obvious. His hard expression dared me to object. "Having heard us quarrel, Jones-Demerest left a note inviting me to visit. When I did, he fairly oozed sympathy. He'll have a cottage ready this afternoon."

We'd agreed, but he'd changed plans without consulting me. *Make nice with MI5*, I reminded myself, compressing my lips to stop a hot retort about partnership. I suspected last night's reckless abandon had made him want to assert control in some way.

Besides, we were in. That was the important part.

"Simon rang during the dinner party." Petunia broke the tension. "He and his team are established as holiday campers in a farmer's field overlooking the lab."

Gravely, she looked from me to Bainbridge. "The World Health Organization has also been busy. Flu cases have broken out in Bonn with additional cases in Paris and Rouen. Paris now has casualties, a quarter of those infected."

Bainbridge and I exchanged an appalled glance. That was an abnormally high fatality rate. Jones-Demerest—or someone, though my money was on the rat-bastard—had unleashed one hell of a flu bug.

CHAPTER THIRTEEN

Moving into the Simply Yorkshire community that afternoon not only saved me from the foxhunting gig but gave me an adrenaline rush, a sense our case was finally rolling. I didn't have to worry about what Aunt Busy Bee might do to bother Bainbridge because she'd gone back to London.

Which also may have prevented me from shooting her.

The cottage had a small, glassed-in entry area in front of the main door—for winter insulation, I guessed. Sort of like an airlock. I'd never seen anything like it except here in Yorkshire.

Bainbridge and I stood to one side of the parlor while movers hauled our furniture, dark wood in heavy, Early Baronial styles to further our aristocratic image, through the airlock. As the three burly men wrestled the bed frame into the bedroom, I turned to him. "These guys would probably rather we'd chosen something a little lighter."

"I dare say," he murmured, "but we've an image to uphold." He lightly stroked my back, and heat flashed through my body and into my face. Good for appearances, bad for self-control.

The guys finished setting up the bed and trudged, looking relieved, back into the parlor.

"That's it, then, sir," their grizzled, slightly stooped leader said.

I smiled at them as Bainbridge pressed a wad of ten-pound notes into the lead guy's hand.

"Let us buy you fellows lunch," he said.

The movers looked startled but stammered out thanks. Tipping wasn't part of the culture the way it was in America. I really had to give him credit for a generous spirit, no matter how narrowly he might define our working options.

And even if he'd done it to appear loose with his money, it was still a nice thing to do.

The door shut behind them, and I frowned around the room. Our suitcases stood in one corner, out of the movers' way, behind the dining table. A low bookcase separated the dining room from the living room area, both looking crowded with all that Early Baronial.

"I still think we should've brought your silver plate," I said. His family owned an elaborate Baroque service for twenty that gleamed like starlight. "For show, of course."

He grimaced. "Too much trouble and too little effect."

Having grown up eating off a plastic bonus-with-purchase set from the grocery store, I disagreed, but I'd finally realized I couldn't budge him.

Moving had kept us from going over information on the new outbreaks. We hung out our *privacy, please* sign, which felt vaguely like hanging a tie on the door of a dorm room, and swept the cottage for bugs. Every time both of us had been gone and every time the maids came, we'd have to do that again. We'd also have to disable the ubiquitous outside cameras anytime we went snooping. For now, assured we had privacy, we sat down to watch the messages his laptop had stored.

When the last bulletin ended, we looked at each other.

"If we add Madrid to the list," I said, "that makes four cities, more than three hundred cases, and forty casualties, with more expected, in just a few days. Can't we just get a takedown order on Jones-Demerest and then toss his place?"

Frowning at his terminal, he answered absently. "I wish we could, if by *toss* you mean search."

"From top to bottom."

He clicked through the screens, looking back for something.

"What is it?" I asked.

"I saw a pattern," he muttered. He saved a screen, spliced it with another, and added one more. The resulting images were small. He turned it toward me. "Ever been to Paris?"

"Sure." I stared at the map, and he waited. MI5 had put a blip on the map for each affected address. Some areas had so many that they changed color.

I glanced at Madrid, another city I knew fairly well, and got a sinking feeling in my chest. I pointed at the reddest area of Paris. "You know who lives in these neighborhoods?"

"The city's wealthiest citizens."

His confirmation of my assessment made me queasy. "Can you superimpose the Metro map?"

"Hang on." He typed in a few commands and pressed *Enter*.

The Metro map appeared in blue. The line where passengers suffered the initial outbreaks had scattered dots along its route, which ran through working class neighborhoods.

"I don't think they had an aerosol weapon," I said slowly, wishing I didn't see this pattern, wishing my gut weren't confirming it with vigorous churning. "The hardest delivery system to stop is an infected but symptom-free carrier. I think that's what they had. Still have, in other cities."

"Because the people who live along the affected Metro line work in the homes of those in the most affected areas." He paused, staring at the screen. "Christ, Claire."

"Yeah." I took a breath that did nothing to settle my insides. "Our agencies will have reached the same conclusion by nightfall, I'm almost certain."

"No *almost* about it, though we must report it anyway." He pulled up the maps of Bonn and Madrid again. "Working class, scattered cases in poor areas. Upper classes, the ones who invariably have domestic staff, stricken in great numbers. It can't be coincidence. And it will open holes in the power structure."

He frowned at me. "If Jones-Demerest is responsible, he probably isn't working alone. I hope we're not chasing our tails here."

"I hope so, too. At least if we can nail him, we can uncover his cohorts." On that optimistic thought, I hurried back into the bedroom to find my scrambled phone.

For once, Martin put me through with no bullshit. I laid out our conclusions for Arachne.

A moment of appalled silence, and then she said, "Miss Billings, if you are correct, there is something much more insidious at work here than terrorism alone."

"Like someone trying to thin out the governing elites of Europe, maybe shift the balance of control by getting some of their own people in? That's what we thought."

"Hold the line while I speak with an analyst." After a couple of minutes, she picked up again. "Our analysts concur with your conclusion. They were testing other possibilities when you phoned. You must infiltrate that compound without delay."

"We just moved in."

She made approving noises.

As I signed off, Bainbridge tapped on the door and entered. He looked grim. "Nothing on Jones-Demerest's phone taps ties him to these outbreaks. Regardless, headquarters agrees with us. We are on condition Red, which means—"

"I know. Expedite without delay. In other words, cut to the chase."

His cell phone rang, and I wandered into the living area while he answered it. We needed to unpack our stuff, but that required conferring about where to put the secret things. Maybe I should roam around and meet the other residents.

We had a large living-dining area with a small kitchenette in one corner, a bathroom diagonally opposite that connected to the bedroom, and a bedroom with a sitting area. Some people might call this simple, but it was bigger than my apartment.

Behind me, Bainbridge spoke sharply. "We've only just moved in, Robin."

Ah, the *responsible* brother. I swallowed a grimace and turned to see my partner frowning in the bedroom doorway.

"No....That depends."

I edged closer, but he waved me off.

"Of course that's important," he said tersely. A pause. "Perhaps we could come just for a bit."

Another pause, longer.

"My wife has a right to be present for discussions of family business." His eyes flashed, and his frown deepened to a scowl, but he seemed to be carefully not looking at me.

"Of course she can deal with it," he said curtly. "The Bishop's Mitre, right." He snapped the phone shut.

Finally, he glanced at me. "Robin wants me to meet him and discuss this damnable investment deal."

What was Robin trying to pull? "I guess you're going." Which meant I had some time to follow my own path since the maids weren't due to help unpack our boxes for about an hour.

"Soonest tended, soonest ended," Bainbridge said grudgingly. "We're meeting in York, but I should return in time for dinner." He marched toward the door.

"Right. Go off drinking and leave me the fun job of unpacking." I quirked up one side of my mouth to show that I didn't mind.

"Woman's work, you know." Despite his light tone, his eyes were grim. He grabbed his car keys from the table by the door and stalked out.

The car wasn't near the cottage. To preserve the supposedly bucolic atmosphere, which the sight of all those Bentleys and Mercedes and Beamers and Rovers would mar, the complex had only one car park, near the front gate. The stone wall that ran all along the front of the property —built recently, its cost a testament to Jones-Demerest's wealth—kept the cars from being visible to those on the grounds. I watched Bainbridge until a slight rise hid him from view.

He had a damned sight too much tolerance for his pushy family. Why he couldn't take as firm a stand with them as he did with me, I couldn't grasp, but he didn't. And that meant he couldn't entirely be trusted. Hell's hatbox, as my granny used to say, but I knew what I had to do. I hated it, but I'd do it.

I grabbed my cell phone and punched in Petunia's mobile, scrambled number. When she answered, I explained what was happening.

Thoughtful silence came back over the wire to me. At last, she said, "You want a tail."

"'Fraid so."

"Give me half an hour. Then it'll be circuit two on your mobile."

I shut my own phone off. She'd call Arachnid's York office, which would send some nondescript soul to the pub before Bainbridge arrived. With the right equipment, I'd have as good a seat as the tail.

Yet I felt like crap for doing it. I had no choice, considering Bainbridge's tendency to shrug off the threat to his family business, which looked entirely real to me. I didn't like spying on my partner, though. I had enough deception in my life without that.

The cottage phone rang, a shrill, jangling noise that made me jump. I stretched full-length down the overstuffed sofa, still couldn't reach it, and finally hitched myself over the rolled, ornate, upholstered arm to grab the phone. "H'lo?"

"Lady Bainbridge, this the front gate. You've a visitor."

"Like who?" Please, not another unexpected Bainbridge relation.

"Lady Beatrice Devereaux."

Not just another relation, the relation from Hell, which must have frozen over. She was supposed to be in London. And wasn't this a nice little coincidence?

"Lady Bainbridge? Are you there?"

"Yeah, but Honeykins isn't." Did I want to see her? Could I afford not to see her and maybe find out what angle she was working?

A pause, and I heard him relaying the message. Someone in the background said something indistinguishable.

"She says she has come to see you, madam," the man reported in a bored tone.

Had she, indeed? Well, well. Something had to be up, and I couldn't lose the chance to find out what. "Send her along, then, but tell her I got a lot to do." I hung up without waiting for his reply.

I couldn't very well view the feed from York in her presence. I rummaged in boxes to find the phone's supposed music player accessory, plugged it in, and popped the phone into its slot. Tapping a combination of buttons shifted the phone's feed into the player, so phone's screen stayed dark.

Finished, I peered out the window. Nothing yet—oops, here she came! A white golf cart with the Simply Yorkshire cottage logo in maroon on the front appeared over the rise. Lady Beatrice sat ramrod-stiff by a driver in Simply Yorkshire livery of a blue blazer and gray slacks with a white shirt and a navy tie.

I raised my eyebrows. Not only did the livery seem too formal for staff in a *simple* place, but I'd pegged my partner's aunt as the tramp-the-countryside type, not one who'd need to ride such a short distance.

Maybe she was preserving her dignity. She had plenty of it, clad in a blue dupioni silk suit that probably cost more than my rent. A darker blue handbag sat upright up on her lap, and her face could've been carved of marble.

Good thing I'd gone with heavy black eyeliner this morning. She'd hate that.

I dug a pack of gum out of my purse. Three slices should generate a conspicuous chewing motion, not to mention noise. I popped them into my mouth before sliding the zipper on my red hoodie down farther, below the tip of my sternum. I had nothing on beneath it, so that should give her a distracting annoyance.

The golf cart disappeared from view, swinging around the cottage. I sauntered over to the door and leaned on the wall beside it. A discreet squeak of brakes came from outside, then a murmur of voices. Tires crunched on gravel, and then the doorbell rang.

I did a slow ten count before answering it. Standing in the frame, blocking her way, I looked her up and down. "Well?"

"I wish to speak with you, Claire." The words fell into the air like flint chips.

I shifted my gum. Noisily. "I got that. About what?"

"This conversation would be better conducted indoors."

I pretended to consider that, then shrugged. When I stepped aside, she marched into the room and seated herself on one of the straight chairs with blue and red figured upholstery on its seat, high back, and level arms. Of course she'd choose that. Soft furniture might wreck her posture.

"Have a seat, why don't you?" Scowling, I wandered over to the sofa. I plopped onto it and raised an eyebrow. "What's up, Bee-uh-tris?"

She didn't—quite—wince. "I hoped we might reach an understanding."

Could she possibly want to make the best of this supposed marriage? If so, Hell really had frozen over.

CHAPTER FOURTEEN

Lady Beatrice pursed her lips before straightening further, something I hadn't considered possible. "Whether you believe it or not, Claire, I care deeply about my nephew's future."

"Me, too. Listen, I got a lot to do. Get to the point."

"Surely you must see that you and Jack don't suit. His social circles must seem alien to you."

As she undoubtedly hoped I realized after that little party. "They're stuffy, but I'll manage." I waved my left hand, causing the honking big diamond in my ring to flash in the sunlight. "There are compensations."

This time, she did wince. "It's never too late to admit a mistake, Claire. To begin again, if you like. You must see that would be best for you both."

"You been smokin' funny cigarettes, babe. Honeykins and me're nuts for each other." I stretched, arching so the gap between hoodie and jeans widened. "I don't think we slept more'n an hour last night."

"That sort of thing tends to pale eventually," she said through stiff lips. "The point is, I'm prepared to sponsor you in making a new start. If you love Jack, you'll consider what's best for him."

Like Lady Daphne, perhaps? Well, that idea might sting but wasn't my concern in the long run. I pursed my lips while my mind raced. Was this really going where I thought it was? "Happiness is best for him. I make him happy."

"For now. Eventually, he must take his seat in the Lords, or better yet, stand for election in the Commons, and assume his responsibility in governing Britain."

"I got no problem with that." Though I couldn't see him enduring endless, tedious meetings and speeches. Especially given the relative toothlessness of the House of Lords.

"For God's sake, he's brilliant." Her eyes flashed. "He could go further than anyone since Churchill, but only if he recovers his ambition. You can't help him do that. You're part of this dreadful path upon which he strayed at Cambridge."

"I'm cool with that." I shrugged. Did she really care about Bainbridge, or was the family image her main concern?

"But you're not suited for it," she replied grimly. "You surely don't know how to plan a dinner party for forty, whom to seat beside whom. You cannot help him, Claire."

"I can learn." How far would she go?

"In the meantime, how many difficult evenings must you endure? How many will he find difficult because you do?" Looking hard at me, she drew something out of her bag and laid it on the coffee table. A tabloid newspaper, *The Yorkshire Watch*. Yesterday's edition.

"Publicity such as this will only hold him back," she declared. "I'm told this was on the internet the same evening it happened. Heaven knows how many people have seen it."

I peered at the paper. Under the headline "Newlywed Earl's Secret Marriage" was a picture I needed a moment to recognize as Bainbridge and me in that hot kiss in the paddock.

Oh, shit seemed a mild reaction, but I widened my eyes at her. "Hey, sweet! Bainsiekins and me look really hot together."

"But not," she said with narrowed eyes, "mature or responsible, to behave so in the open. This will rebound against him, and then what will you do?"

Rebound, as in with the shareholders she and Jones-Demerest were courting? *Double-shit* with a serious *fuck* thrown in, but I shot her a sullen look. "We'll manage."

"This marriage isn't best for either of you. Let me help you make a new life elsewhere. You give my nephew a fresh start, and I'll give you one."

"Like what?" The whole conversation embodied such a cliché that if she weren't so deadly earnest, I'd have laughed. Instead, I scowled.

"Claire, think of evenings spent amongst people whose lives are so different from yours. You can't hide here with Jack forever. He has a life to resume, and I assume you do as well."

She clearly assumed nothing of the kind. The remark represented a stab at diplomacy. I pretended to consider.

"How much?" I asked.

Her eyes lit as though I'd fulfilled her expectation. "Two hundred thousand pounds. You could make an excellent start with that, I expect."

Ten percent of her personal fortune, according to my information. Her offer amounted to about two hundred twenty-five thousand dollars at the current exchange rate. She must want Bainbridge free something fierce.

"Well," she prodded. "Shall I have a bank draft prepared?"

I frowned. "You didn't bring it with you?"

"I'm not a fool. You leave Jack, and I'll support you while you await a divorce. Then you'll receive the bulk of the funds."

"And I give up bein' a countess," I said slowly. "And Honeykins gets a sock in the face, and maybe, someday, Robin's kids inherit the title. Isn't that how things work in England?"

She looked startled. "That doesn't enter into anything."

"If Honeykins doesn't have kids to inherit the title, who does?" Robin. The *good* nephew. Jones-Demerest's toady. Considering how strongly back-stabbing ran in Bainbridge's family, I was amazed he'd turned out to have so much integrity.

"That's not your concern."

"Anything to do with Bainsiekins is my concern. Sorry, Auntie, but no deal."

Her face flushed, then paled. Slowly, she stood. "I will not renew this offer. Sooner or later, he'll tire of you. When he does, you'll be on your own."

Yeah. Me and Arachnid. I smirked at her. "Don't let the door bang your butt on your way out."

She puffed up like an aggravated toad. Her eyes narrowed in laser-bright rage, and her back stiffened. With a sniff, she stalked to the door. There, she paused to look me up and down. "You are impossibly crude," she pronounced.

Considering everything I'd done to foster that impression, I should have been delighted. Yet something deep inside me flinched. If I'd been attracted to Bainbridge on a deeper level than hormonal, I'd have explored that flinch, but I wasn't. I shoved it aside.

Did she want me gone now as a distraction so Bainbridge would forget the shipping line and, in effect, get out of the way? Was the title for Robin an incidental benefit or a major goal? Or did she really care about Bainbridge that much?

Too many questions loomed, ones that meant Aunt Bee-in-her-Bonnet wanted watching. Unfortunately, I couldn't count on Bainbridge to see that.

#

The supposed music player recording my phone's video couldn't record and play at the same time. While I waited for the light to go off, signaling the video feed's end, I plugged in the electric kettle for tea. The light blinked out and the kettle shut itself off about the same moment.

As I poured boiling water over the teabag, someone rang the doorbell. Who—oh, the maids were due to help me straighten up if I wanted. I'd have to send them away. I hurried to the door, opened it, and stepped into the airlock.

Two middle-aged, stout women in green Simply Yorkshire livery slacks and shirts stood on the step outside. Green? The gate guards wore blue. What was this, the *Andromeda Patrol* TV show's spaceship *Tempestuous*, with everyone's uniforms color-coded?

I asked them to come back in a bit, and they agreed. Of course they did, since ensuring my happiness was part of their jobs.

I curled up on the couch with the player. Whoever Arachne had sent to the Mitre, a man if the hand size held true, had a good view of Robin. He slouched at a table near the bar, a pint sitting in front of him and a sullen frown on his face. His beer or ale or whatever no longer had anything resembling a head. He must've been there a while.

I couldn't imagine Bainbridge slouching. He seemed oblivious to the many ways in which just being his brother diminished Robin, but anyone who really looked would notice them.

The watcher raised a newspaper, cutting off all view of the room except the corner where Robin sat. Judging by the angle, the camera must be in the man's eyeglasses. A moment later, Bainbridge stalked into view, bypassing the bar and a chance to order, and sat abruptly across from his brother.

"What'll you have?" Robin asked.

"The point of this discussion." Bainbridge raised an eyebrow. "What couldn't you say to Claire's face?"

His brother straightened, his expression glum. "She doesn't help you, Jack. Some on the board think she's proof your judgment isn't what it should be." He reached into the briefcase at his side for something.

I had a sick feeling I knew what, and I was right. He laid the tabloid on the table. For Bainbridge's sake, I hated that. My family didn't have much money, but we watched out for each other as his apparently did not.

Bainbridge didn't move, didn't change his expression, except that it maybe went a little stonier, but Robin fidgeted as though his brother had scowled at him.

"Go on," Bainbridge said, the words as hard as oak chips.

"Jack, I wish you happiness. We all do. Even you must admit, though, she's not precisely the model of a countess."

"Mum was the model of a countess." From oak to clipped steel. His tone didn't bode well for his brother.

And what did that mean, anyway? His mother had died in a car accident, lost control on a curve. Supposedly.

"Look, Jack—"

"The choice of Mum's successor is, as it always has been, mine alone."

"You can't deny your choice reflects your judgment. The same judgment on which you rely in obstructing this investment deal."

Bainbridge raised one eyebrow. "I chose a countess to please only myself. The shipping line, on the other hand, requires me to consider the interests of the entire family."

"I've already done that," Robin snapped. "What's more, I know what they want—what they need—far better than you can."

"You know what they *say*." Bainbridge's words rasped. "I *see* Gerry and Helena out in clubs every night and running up bills at Harrod's. I *hear* about Sarah's flights to New York to shop on Fifth Avenue and to Italy so she can visit the goldsmiths. Percy's taste in incunabulae costs a pretty penny."

Incun—? Oh, right. Antique books.

"Percy's richer than all of us," Robin grumbled.

"Perhaps he deserves to be. In point of fact, Robin, the others all spend beyond their incomes. They want an immediate infusion of funds, which they'll just as rapidly deplete."

Robin glared at him. "You spend more than anyone else. You're no room to talk."

"I have more income than anyone else," Bainbridge said mildly, "an income within which, as you well know, I stay." He paused. "What's this really about, Robin?"

He was questioning? Had he actually listened to me? Was he looking beyond the obvious at last?

Before I had a chance to sprain my arm patting myself on the back, Bainbridge continued, "You don't need money, either."

Back to the obvious. I groaned, but maybe he was just playing dumb.

"The day of the small family firm is over," Robin insisted. "We must join with someone or be swallowed."

"So long as only family own stock, no one will swallow us. You know that as well as I do."

"We've been pushed off the South Pacific route and the Newfoundland one—"

"I do read my briefings," Bainbridge reminded him.

"—while you engage us for charitable work that turns no profit."

"It garnered priceless publicity."

"Publicity doesn't pay our staff."

"Not that day, no." Bainbridge directed a quizzical look at his brother. "You approved those contracts. Don't say you resent them at this late date."

Robin snorted. "In the circumstances, I'd little choice but to approve them. But they can't help us expand."

"They bring us business."

"Not enough, Jack. If you had to cover the bills and try to turn a profit as well, you'd appreciate that."

Bainbridge studied him for a moment. "Surely you know how much I value your work," he said slowly.

"You say you do, but then something like this comes along, something that could give the firm a cushion at last, and you refuse to heed my advice. Jack, we need this."

"No. We don't." Overriding Robin's attempt to interrupt, he added, "Jones-Demerest's business model isn't ours, Robin."

No, it was far more lethal.

Bainbridge continued, "You needn't look surprised. I told you I read my reports. Hawkshead Shipping has been a family concern since Victoria's day, and so it shall remain." He stood, as though to end the discussion.

Robin's expression hardened. "You're worse than Aunt Beatrice. She doesn't like the man, but she sees his value. You stay at his playground yet scorn him as not our sort."

"Don't put words in my mouth. I've no problem with Jones-Demerest personally."

"No, only his 'business model.'" Robin gripped his pint glass, his knuckles white. "I'll fight you, Jack."

"You'll lose."

"Not this time." He glanced into his drink, then up at Bainbridge. "I have the votes."

Bainbridge's mouth went tight. He turned on his heel and disappeared behind the newspaper screen.

Robin sat still for long seconds before glancing in the direction his brother had gone. He drew a mobile phone from his pocket and entered a number. The pickup mike was better than I'd supposed—it caught the tones. Analysis probably had the number and its owner's name by now.

"Yes, hallo?" A male voice, a bit creaky, maybe with age.

"He wouldn't listen," Robin said to whoever answered. "We should proceed."

His listener said nothing for a few seconds, then, quietly, "Very well. On both fronts, I should think."

Robin paused. "I agree," he said slowly.

As he cut the connection and stowed his phone, I mulled things over. One front would obviously be the shipping line's family board and its irresponsible, spendthrift members. They'd probably never allied themselves with Mr. Responsible before. Having them on his side probably felt weird to him. The unusual alliance, if I was right about it, might also be vulnerable.

So what was the second front? Auntie Busybody and me? Or something about Bainbridge's poor supposed choice of countesses, something more difficult to handle?

#

I puttered around the little cottage, thinking, while the maids came and went. Having maids tidy up after a move-in didn't feel *simple* to me. Why would Jones-Demerest set up a community for wealthy business owners? He couldn't be making all that much money from it, so why bother? Was it that great as a cover for making bioweapons?

Or was he insinuating the bioweapons business into his guests' legitimate ones, a truly sickening thought?

I wandered to the bedroom. My leathers, a sleek jacket and pants supposedly for riding motorcycles but actually reinforced with carbon nanotube fibers, hung neatly in the closet. They couldn't stop a bullet but would offer some resistance to a blade if necessary.

I fingered the jacket's zipper line. The leather felt supple and only a little heavy. If the maids looked at it, they wouldn't notice anything.

Someone from Arachnid would call Petunia with the scoop on Robin's phone buddy. She would then call me. Not much I could do in the detective line until then. An even bigger, more immediate question was whether I should tell Bainbridge I'd spied on him.

A faint, rhythmic crunching sound reached the bedroom—Bainbridge's footsteps on the gravel path outside. Dithering hadn't given me an excuse to avoid doing what I knew I should. He was my partner. I had to come clean.

I walked into the parlor to meet him. As he opened the door, I said, "How'd it go?"

"As expected." He dropped his keys on the table. "Any news here?"

"The maids came. Your aunt stopped by for a chat."

He frowned, walking slowly into the room. "That doesn't sound like her."

"We had an intriguing visit." I lowered myself onto a corner of the massive sofa.

"You shouldn't have seen her, especially without me." His frown deepened. "She plays no role in our plans."

Right. Blame me. "So you would've turned her away if you'd been here?" Maybe when pigs flew.

"What did she want?"

Evasion. He wouldn't have refused to see her, but he couldn't admit that to me. Studying him, I stretched my bare feet out on the coffee table. "She wanted to buy me off."

His eyes widened marginally, then narrowed. "Explain."

"I thought I was speaking English, but maybe you say it differently over here. I meant she offered me money to divorce you. A lot of money. Two hundred thousand pounds."

"I don't believe you." His face metamorphosed into granite.

"So you think I'm lying?" I could do granite, too. It happens when I'm stifling a rapidly sparking temper. "Why?"

"I didn't say that," he replied in a harsh voice.

"Yeah, actually, you did. I don't know why you have this planet-sized blind spot where she's concerned, but get over it. She's in league with Jones-Demerest and your brother on this deal, and I suspect she also wants your title for Robin."

"She cannot possibly have said such an absurd thing."

"Sure, she did, in so many words." I rolled my eyes. "Of course she didn't say that." You big doofus. "But what happens to your title if you never produce legitimate offspring?"

Only the faintest hint of a wince betrayed his reaction—that and the minuscule pause before he spoke. "You must have misunderstood her."

"I have an excellent conversational memory, as I'm sure your file on me notes. Sit down, stop looming over me, and I'll tell you what she said. Then you tell me if I'm mistaken."

While I talked, his expression never even flickered. I couldn't read him at all. No wonder he was so successful at his job.

When I finished, his expression still didn't change. "Such a waste of time was annoying, of course," he said politely, "but it signifies nothing except her ongoing disappointment that I'm not more what she expects the Earl of Bainbridge to be. I doubt she'll bother you again."

Resisting a fierce urge to bang my head against the sofa's high back, I revoked every point I'd ever given him. "For such a smart guy, you are incredibly dense."

He stiffened, but I kept going. "What matters is not that she bothered me. She has allied herself with Jones-Demerest's interests despite her obvious sense of superiority to him. If you're okay with her screwing around in your personal life, that's your problem. What you refuse to see is that she is inserting herself, and possibly other relatives of yours, into this investigation."

"What do you mean, other relatives?"

I took a deep breath and braced myself. "Arachnid had you watched in York."

"You mean you did," he said flatly. His jaw set.

I shrugged. "After you left the pub, Robin made a phone call. I should soon know to whom. They agreed to proceed with both fronts of some plan."

"You think my aunt's visit was part of some greater scheme?" In keeping with his skeptical tone, he raised an eyebrow.

"Maybe, but that's not the point. Multiple members of your family are conspiring to close this deal. You told Robin, and our dossier already showed, that a number of your relatives are profligate spenders. If I were you, I'd be worried about just how deeply they're involved with Jones-Demerest."

"Perhaps you would," he said calmly. "I, however, will put the mission first. Whatever happens as a result, happens."

"Are you really that cold?" I asked slowly. "Do you not care if they've been drawn innocently into this scheme?"

He directed a level stare at me. "Some time in Her Majesty's prisons would provide a salutary lesson to a great many people."

Granted, most of their family income came from investments rather than from current profits of the shipping line. It probably didn't make much difference to him if the company folded. Yet I couldn't believe he wouldn't mind.

The Hartners would rather have been horsewhipped than lose the mill. People said the buyout and subsequent off-shoring had killed Old Man Hartner. "Don't you care about the company your family has run for almost two hundred years?"

"It will survive. Or it won't. Meanwhile, we should make an appearance at dinner."

"What about your family's involvement with Jones-Demerest? We should check into that."

My mobile phone rang, and the screen switched to the desert picture indicating a scrambled line. I tapped in the correct code. "Billings."

I listened to the brief, terse report, then signed off. Phone in hand, I faced Bainbridge. "Your brother was talking to your great-uncle, Sir Percival Basingstoke."

"It doesn't matter," Bainbridge said curtly. "My family's involvement will prove marginal. We'll focus on the important issues. Your conversation with Aunt Beatrice has distracted you to no good end. Next time, avoid side trails and stick to the plan."

"Does your plan have contingencies for your family going down in disgrace?" Did he have no family loyalty? Or had he put that aside when he realized they'd written him off? The pain in his eyes a few days back, when I'd said he deserved better, argued that he did care.

"That won't happen." He glanced at his watch. "We should dress for dinner, or we'll be late."

His speech had the ironic ring of famous last words to me, but if he couldn't bother to look out for his family, they weren't my problem.

The shipping line, however, was. If Jones-Demerest cared so much about the investment, his reasons might very well be related to his new biowarfare business.

CHAPTER FIFTEEN

A certain frost still hung in the air when Bainbridge and I headed to dinner. He looked like Lord Fashion Model, sexier in a charcoal suit, white shirt, and red power tie than any man I'd ever seen, but he was acting like Lord Granite for Brains with his stubbornness about his family. Even so, his hand felt warm and comfortable around mine, damn it.

The resort community occupied a hilltop site that had once been a medieval manor. Nothing of architectural interest remained except the structure that was also of international security interest, the former stable, which we believed housed the rat-bastard's lab. In the distance, the ground sloped gently downward, the green fields broken into rough squares by stone walls and punctuated with white shapes that had to be sheep.

The dining hall, or "Great Hall," as the *simplicity*-touting brochure labeled it, stood near the front gate. To get there from the cottages scattered to the south and east of it, we crossed a green reminiscent of a college quad. Here and there, raised stone planters full of greenery dotted the area. I frowned at them. They were high enough to sit on. Or crouch behind.

The Great Hall and its adjacent club room took up most of the space in the large, central building, with administrative offices tucked in the back. When we walked in, I recognized the room from its photos. It boasted medium-brown, oak paneling and a vaulted roof fit for a medieval hall. "I guess we see where the name came from," I muttered to Bainbridge.

He directed a quelling look at me as a middle-aged hostess garbed in a modest summer dress of amber silk glided toward us. No color-coded uniform for her, at least.

"Good evening, sir, madam," she said. "Do you prefer to dine alone or in company?"

My spaghetti-strap sundress, comparatively modest except for its very short skirt, didn't draw an eye blink, so it must've satisfied the dress code. I grimaced inwardly. In my universe, *simple* life did not involve rules about dinner clothes.

"In company," Bainbridge said before I could.

At least we agreed on something.

Still gliding, the woman steered us to a table where a sixtyish, chunky couple sat in two of the four chairs. "Lord and Lady Bainbridge, I'd like you to meet Mr. and Mrs. Fletcher."

"A pleasure. I'm Jack." Bainbridge offered his hand to be shaken.

He seated me across from Mrs. Fletcher, whose cherubic features flushed slightly. Brown eyes sparkling, she leaned a little closer. "It's a pleasure to meet you, sir, madam."

The anti-monarchist American in me surged to the fore. I beamed at her. "Same here. Call me Claire."

"Why, thank you." Her face glowed. "My name is Hilda."

"Thanks." I jerked my thumb at Bainbridge. "He means it about the name thing. He doesn't like to stand on formality, do you, Bainsiekins?"

If his smile seemed forced to me, neither Hilda nor her husband—Horace, as his name turned out to be, and how much too cute was that?—seemed to notice.

"What brings you here, sir?" Horace asked. Nice of him not to point out that we were a couple or three decades younger than the other residents.

"We're on our honeymoon." Bainbridge directed a fond look at me and lifted my hand to his lips.

The resulting contact rolled white heat up my arm and down my torso, making me want to squirm. I caught my breath as my face warmed. Today, when he was being such a blockhead, I really did not appreciate my apparently incurable attraction to him.

"Darling," he murmured. His breath whispered over my knuckles, and his eyes taunted me with awareness of what he was doing to me.

"Bainsiekins, we got company." I cast the Fletchers an apologetic look.

"Of course, darling."

When I tried to lower my hand, his came with it. He covered my fingers with his and stroked the back of my hand with his thumb. Every stroke quivered in the depths between my legs.

That'd better not be satisfaction in his eyes. Smiling at him in my best Doting Babe manner, I slid my hand into his lap and squeezed his upper thigh. He'd deployed the sexual attraction weapon first, but I could use it, too.

Beaming, I said, "Later, sweetkins."

Pure lust flashed in his eyes. "Later," he echoed with a smile on his lips and a threat in his tone.

I retrieved my hand before turning to Horace. "What brings y'all here?"

His face brightened with pride. "It's our anniversary. Fortieth, actually. I promised Hilda we'd go away for a bit, let the office take care of itself."

"What kinda office?" For a holiday, I'd have picked Devon or Kent or some other place not operated by a sleazoid, but maybe they didn't feel very adventurous. Maybe they wanted a place where someone else handled all the details.

"Pharmaceuticals," Hilda said proudly. "Horace started The Corner Chemist."

He'd started the most popular brand of non-prescription medicines in Britain and the most popular pharmacy since the Boots chain. "Wow," I said, feigning ignorance. "That sounds way cool."

"Quite an achievement," Bainbridge said.

"I wouldn't know about that." But satisfaction tinged Horace's smile. "I've been pleased, though."

"He's been marvelous," Hilda proclaimed. "But he's worked very hard, as one might imagine. When we were looking for somewhere to spend some time away, Jasper told us about this place, and it seemed ideal."

"So you were previously acquainted with Jones-Demerest," Bainbridge said with just the right degree of mild interest.

"He was helpful in finding locations for the shops here in the North," Horace replied.

"It's good to have a helper." I commented

My insides, though, were shuddering. Had Jones-Demerest wheedled his way into their business—in distribution, say? If so, were they selling what they'd manufactured? Or was he using these nice people to move something very different?

With a start, I realized I'd lost track of the conversation.

"—a family firm, if I may ask?" Bainbridge was saying.

"Oh, yes," Horace said.

"Started it from nothing, he did," Hilda added.

"Then perhaps you can advise me—in confidence, of course—if it's not presumptuous of me to ask." Bainbridge looked solemn.

Horace glanced at Hilda. Really, they were very sweet.

"I'm happy to help in any way, sir," he said.

"Jack," Bainbridge corrected smoothly. "Mr. Jones-Demerest has expressed an interest in my family's shipping line." He paused. "We've owned it outright since Victoria's reign, so we naturally want to take care about bringing in anyone else. You seem to have no complaints about him."

"None." Horace shook his head decisively. "He was very helpful when I wanted to expand my distribution."

Meaning he had access to product being distributed? "How'd he do that?" I asked. "Does he have trucks?"

"He had interests in transportation at the time, but his best advice was about potential markets."

That would have helped Horace's expansion, and The Corner Chemist shops were everywhere now, so how long—

"When was this?" Bainbridge looked thoughtful.

"Oh, seven or eight years ago," Horace said.

Leaning closer to me, Hilda said softly, "Some people wouldn't help us—didn't think a little family firm started by someone without a fancy education could compete with the big chains. Jasper didn't care, though. He could see Horace had a growing business."

Or perhaps he sympathized with another man not from Britain's elite, though Horace didn't seem to hide the background he'd risen above. Or maybe Jones-Demerest wanted access to products in the distribution chain.

"That was nice," I said. "Smart, too. When I was building my business as a trainer, some people didn't want me to train 'em 'cause I don't have fancy manners. I did fine, though."

"I'm sure you did, dear." Hilda gave me a decisive nod.

I leaned in confidentially, as she had. "Some people don't think I'll be a good countess." Bainbridge raised an eyebrow, but I continued, "I'll show 'em, though."

"I'm sure you'll be marvelous," Hilda said fiercely. She emphasized the words with another sharp nod. A bond of kindred feeling had been born.

I felt a slight twinge of guilt about playing her, but I stifled it. If Horace's business was involved, he probably didn't know it. In that case, we could protect him. I'd see to it. After we figured out just what Jones-Demerest was plotting.

"Maybe you could tell Honeykins who else here has done business with Jasper?"

"We'd be happy to, of course," said Horace.

A cheerful young woman garbed in black trousers and waistcoat with a white shirt arrived to take our order. We were back to color-coded livery.

The conversation turned into more casual paths. We couldn't hurry, but I wanted the meal to end. We had a new avenue of investigation.

#

After dinner, Bainbridge suggested a stroll. We twined our fingers together and wandered around the compound.

I assumed we were trying to meet people we could pump about Jones-Demerest's involvement in their businesses. "I could use a drink," I said as cover for trip to the club room.

"I'd rather have you, in the sunset."

Which was code for snooping. I grinned at him.

He kissed me, not long enough for the brain crash to set in, and put an arm around my waist. Leaning into each other, we simultaneously turned, as though in telepathic communication, west, toward the edge of the compound and the building marked *Private* on our official welcome map.

When the path ended, my kitten-heel slides sank into the grass. I slipped them off and hooked them over my fingers, better for both silence and speed.

A stand of ash and hawthorn separated the main compound lawn from that of the lab, the former stable block for the manor. Now a chest-high stone fence encircled it, and the building's stone walls and gabled slate roof blended in with the Yorkshire architecture. It stood near the main road with an iron-gated staff car park bordering the road.

Some of the windows on the street side had been blocked off, a strange feature in a building Jones-Demerest was touting as a corporate retreat center. More likely, they were covered to conceal a pharmaceutical or weapons lab.

Petunia's limited reconnaissance had shown nothing below ground level. The place wasn't big enough for any manufacturing operation, so what were they doing here? Research?

Bainbridge drew me under the trees. "Beautiful sunset," he said, "but not as lovely as you are."

Any directional mike aimed at us should pick that up, and so the line served its purpose. Which was, emphatically, not to create a silly little ping in my heart. I squelched the feeling as he slowly lowered his head.

If we were putting on a show, it had to be good. I slid my arms around his neck and kissed his jaw. His hands moved slowly down my back to draw me even closer before his mouth caught mine. My lips parted under his. When his tongue touched mine, my blood ignited, and I fought the brain crash. He made a guttural sound in his throat. Suddenly there was no space between our bodies but also far too much. We strained against each other.

Struggling to think, I broke the kiss and nipped his neck. He groaned into my hair. As he cupped my butt, movement by the lab caught my eye. Three burly guys in suits were coming. Three? Who did they think we were, anyway? They surely couldn't know the truth.

I tugged his head down and tried to focus despite his warm, soft lips caressing my shoulder. With my mouth close to his ear, I murmured, "Three at nine o'clock."

He squeezed my waist for an instant, a silent acknowledgement. Backing me up to a tree, he lifted his head just enough to say, "I want you, darling. Here. Now."

"Oooh, Bainsiekins." I giggled and grabbed for his belt. "You're such a stud."

With admirable if unwitting timing, a man spoke behind me. "Excuse me, sir. Madam. This area isn't open to visitors." Amusement laced his words. Good.

As Bainbridge raised his head, his expression went from impassioned, lusting newlywed to arrogant snot in an eye blink. "I am the Earl of Bainbridge." With a dismissive wave of his hand, he added, "Nothing is closed to me." He drew me against his side.

Did he make that shift so easily because he really did have a superior streak inside? The thought made me uneasy, but I couldn't worry about that now.

My new position let me see a balding man, thirtyish, with his two similarly beefy friends behind him. Their balanced, ready stances proclaimed intensive training, the sort the goons at the Italian plant had lacked. All of them were smirking at us, though, which meant they didn't see us as any kind of threat.

"I'm sorry, sir, but I must ask you to leave." Despite his firm tone, the man looked apologetic.

"We were enjoying the view." Bainbridge scowled. "Jones-Demerest will hear about this."

"You're welcome to take that up with whomever you wish, of course."

Muttering under his breath, Bainbridge drew me out of the trees.

The guards stood where they were as we walked away. For good measure, I patted Bainbridge's firm butt. "Let's go home, Bainsiekins. Now."

"Straight away, darling." He kissed my shoulder.

The touch zinged into the depths of my body, and I swallowed a groan. This assignment was a continual exercise in dealing with frustration.

Wary of possible directional mikes, we more or less groped each other all the way back to the main lawn. Talking was too risky. When we reached the main area, which we knew had cameras but no microphones, Bainbridge said, "Now we can consult Jones-Demerest—"

"And see what we can draw out of him about that place. Nice." I nodded, and his eyes warmed.

Holding hands, we veered toward Jones-Demerest's house, which stood where the old manor house once had, beyond the dining hall on the far end of the compound from the lab. About 30 yards beyond it lay the six-foot stone wall that fronted entire the property, with the parking lot beyond that.

Behind the house was a stone structure about seven feet high and forty feet on a side. Made of gray Yorkshire stone, it was shaped to mimic a miniature castle, complete with towers jutting out of the corners. Our map identified it as a garden.

I poked Bainbridge. "Is that a common way to enclose a garden? Or a disguise for a defensible enclosure?"

"Not common, no. Attractive to some prospective residents, perhaps." With a slight smile, he added, "Particularly Americans." Before I could retort, true though that was, he added, "And yes, defensible. It meshes nicely with the planters."

So he'd noticed. Points to him.

As we passed the dining hall, a silver-haired, dignified couple strolled out of it.

Bainbridge's fingers tightened on mine quickly, as though in warning. "Barnet. Pamela. Good evening," he called.

"Jack," the man said. The duo looked a little reluctant but changed course to meet us.

The woman had a pinched expression reminiscent of Aunt Busy Bee. While she looked me over from head to foot, I leaned into Bainbridge and pretended not to notice. Yet her disapproval stung. Why? I'd never see her again when this was done. I didn't care. Shouldn't, anyway. Yet the desire to let the real me peep through burned in my throat.

As though sensing it, Bainbridge slid an arm around my waist. "Darling, this is Mr. Jonathan Barnet and his wife, Lady Pamela. Jon, Pamela, this is my wife, Claire."

I smiled and thrust out my right hand. "Nice to meet you." Barnet. Of Barnet Equities financial firm, one of the names Horace had mentioned. That must be why Bainbridge wanted to waylay them.

With no apparent reservation, Barnet offered me a firm, courteous handclasp, but Lady Pamela paused a telling moment before taking my hand. I pumped hers happily.

"I love meeting Honeykins's friends." Picking up on what I assumed he wanted, I added, "Let's go have a drink."

"Darling, we were to see Jones-Demerest," Bainbridge reminded me.

Since he looked mildly amused and not insistent, I figured I'd read him right. For once. "But I want to chat with your friends." I twinkled at Barnet, who looked a little pained.

His wife's pinched expression looked uncomfortable enough for an appendectomy candidate.

"Well..." Bainbridge's smile turned goofy. "If you prefer, darling. Jon, Pamela, you'll join us, I hope."

They exchanged an uncertain glance before agreeing.

#

The club room off the dining hall was all dark wood and leather, as I imagined the storied gentlemen's clubs of London must've been. Groups of leather armchairs around low tables offered convenient conversation nooks. For the less congenial, there was also a bar. In the room's far corner, a jazz quartet played soothing music. The area in front of them, uncarpeted oak parquet with no furniture, served as a dance floor.

We settled into one of the chair groups near it. A waitress in the same black and white ensemble as the dinner server hustled over to take our drink orders.

While we spoke to her, Jones-Demerest strolled into the club room and stopped to chat with the people sitting nearest to the door. The waitress hovered as Lady Pamela tried to decide what she wanted. Our genial host covered two more tables, heading toward us, before she made up her mind.

Jones-Demerest arrived as the waitress departed. Bainbridge gave me a warning look, which I interpreted as meaning he should handle the questioning. Despite planning to comply, I lifted an eyebrow at him. No harm in keeping him on his toes.

We got the courtesies out of the way before Bainbridge said, "Oh, by the way, Jones-Demerest, some of your employees insisted Claire and I leave the woods near the western wall. They were rather curt."

With a grin, he added, "One might think you were up to something illicit."

CHAPTER SIXTEEN

Bainbridge's question all but accused the murdering rat-bastard to his face. I was surprised Bainbridge would push.

Jones-Demerest tensed but smiled. "Nothing so interesting as that, Lord Bainbridge. The corporate tenant is developing a new product line and values privacy above all. Security, you know. Industrial espionage has become so unfortunately common."

"I don't see any harm being in the woods," I said, pouting. "Me and Honeykins were just fooling around. What're they making in there, anyway, some kind of secret weapon?"

Though Bainbridge chuckled, the stern look he tossed me said I'd gone far enough. Our companions looked startled.

For a moment, so did the rat-bastard. Then he laughed. "If only it were that important, Lady Bainbridge. I'm afraid his business is quite prosaic." He glanced around the room. "I should tend to the other guests. Do let me know if you need anything." He strolled to the next group.

Lady Pamela directed a curious look at me. "I understand you're from America, Claire?"

"Yep." Did she know that from my accent or from gossip?

I slipped off my shoes. Our closely placed chairs made propping my bare feet on Bainbridge's thigh easy.

He gave me his moony look and gently rubbed my foot. To his scandalized-looking friends, he said, "Our evening ritual."

I gave him double points for going with my improvisation despite his plan-based brain and tried to ignore the warmth streaking up my leg as his thumb caressed my sole. "Anyway, Pam, how'd you hear about me?"

Her smile continued her apparent theme of gastric distress. "I'm acquainted with Lady Beatrice, Jack's aunt. And it's Lady Pamela."

"Oh, sure. So Aunt Bee told you about us! How cool!" Just as I'd guessed.

"Jack, I don't believe we've congratulated you and wished the two of you well," Barnet said. "Wonderful news."

He, at least, could feign polite enthusiasm.

Sighing, I gave Bainbridge an adoring look. "We can still hardly believe it."

We made a few more minutes of idle small talk, mostly about the weather and some about people they knew. I suspected Bainbridge was trying to get them to raise the subject of Jones-Demerest.

Meanwhile, Bainbridge's hands on my feet continued to feel like some kind of sorcery—slow, gentle caresses of the tops, down to the toes, alternating with firm, deep strokes along the soles. I soon felt a strong need to squirm, but I smiled and stifled my sighs and knew I absolutely could not share a bed with him that night. I had my standards of restraint to uphold.

Barnet said, "I understand Jasper wants to invest in Hawkshead Shipping."

Bainbridge frowned down at my feet. "I'm not in favor of taking anyone in. I understand you know him."

"Your aunt introduced us," Lady Pamela allowed.

For someone who didn't consider Jones-Demerest her *sort,* Aunt Busy Bee was awfully chummy with him.

Bainbridge's hands never paused, and his expression remained idly curious, but I detected a new tension in his touch. "A pleasant social acquaintance, even a successful businessman, doesn't always make a good colleague."

The waitress brought drinks for each of us. Barnet sipped his Scotch before saying, "Jasper and I raise money for some of his charities, the research laboratories. The man understands investment strategy."

"That's your field," Bainbridge said.

I couldn't tell what he meant by that. I'd seen Barnet Equities listed as a partner in Jones-Demerest's charity work, but I didn't see how that would involve—oh, yeah. Money laundering. Had to be.

Barnet said, "I handle the investments and funnel them into various accounts. Jasper has very firm ideas about investing it." He frowned into his drink. "Look, Jack—I wouldn't like this widely known, but we had a cash flow problem last year. Jasper helped me out with it. Very discreetly. You can trust him, if that's your concern."

"Of course."

Barnet turned to his wife and asked her to dance.

Bainbridge held out a hand to me. "Shall we, darling?"

I thought we were done here, but he obviously had something in mind. With his hands off my feet, my frustration level started to drop. I slid my shoes on and let him lead me onto the dance floor. Besides our party, two other couples moved slowly across the parquet.

Bainbridge drew me close, creating all sorts of unfortunate tingles inside me. At least, judging by the way his body felt in the embrace, he shared my frustration. That was some comfort. I ordered my hormones to take a seat and laid my right hand in his left, resting the other on his shoulder.

When I glanced up at him, he smiled. A warm, friendly, almost tender smile. Hesitantly, I returned it, and his hand slid up my back, pressing me closer.

I slipped my free arm around his neck. Despite my residual thwarted desire, his arm around me felt good, and not just physically. Whether or not he had some hidden sense of superiority, he was a pretty decent guy. Solid. Dependable. If a bit narrow-minded in his adherence to plans.

In my ear, he softly said, "I'll ask Pamela to dance. See what you can find out from Barnet."

"Right." He was good at not rushing, at laying the groundwork so his carefully planned moves seemed spontaneous.

The music ended. We applauded the quartet, and Bainbridge turned to his friends. "Pamela, if I may?"

Jonathan turned politely to me. I assumed my Clueless Babe smile as I stepped into his arms.

#

An hour later, Bainbridge and I returned to our cottage arm in arm. Letting go of him was a relief. The walk back had stirred the hormonal chorus again, possibly because the back of my brain knew there was a bed here.

"Learn anything?" Bainbridge followed me into the bedroom.

I gave him a pointed look. "Not much besides how great Jasper is to help out his buddies. I'm changing clothes now, by the way."

"Why?" Frowning, he ignored the hint to leave and leaned on the door frame.

"Because I'm going snooping. You can come if you like." Anything would beat getting into a bed with him, considering the agreed-upon limits for using it.

He threw me a teasing grin that made my insides annoyingly squishy. "I had that scheduled for tomorrow, but I'm flexible."

Yeah. About like granite was flexible. I pulled my black leather, carbon nano-reinforced pants and jacket out of the closet. "Did you know Barnet was probably laundering Jones-Demerest's money?"

"We considered it." He unbuttoned his shirt.

I hastily averted my eyes from his well-toned bod. I was trying to turn the heat down, not rev it up.

Bainbridge continued, "Following the trail, we determined Jones-Demerest launders the money in Switzerland."

The corners of my eyes refused to ignore him. Instead, they admired the sleek line of his back and the bunching of his muscles as he took black jeans and a black sweater that looked soft as cashmere from his dresser.

I shrugged. "If you're sure. Jonathan did tell me he helped Jones-Demerest buy lab supplies at discounted rates. Some people even made donations, all in the name of research."

"Hard to see where the advantage is in that," Bainbridge said through the sweater as he pulled it over his head.

"There was one thing." I waited for his face to emerge before I added, "Jonathan hired a protégé of Jasper's as an account manager last year. He handles all Jasper's accounts. And others besides."

"Skimming?" He lifted his suitcase onto the bed to take his weapon and holster out of the concealed compartment. "I'll put someone on it."

"Great. Now turn around while I change, huh?"

"If you insist," he answered cheerfully. Hands at his trouser fastenings, he wheeled. I turned my back on him and shucked my dress.

#

After temporarily disabling the grounds camera, we found a concealed spot in the woods by the lab. Since no guards showed, we figured we were temporarily safe. Face blacking was out. It didn't fit with our cover as amorous newlyweds enjoying each other outdoors.

Simon and his team were doing overwatch on the lab from a neighboring farm. He said there was only a single guard on duty. Taking a quick look should be safe enough. We hoped to sneak in there when it was empty and see what was on the computers. With more people getting sick every day, we needed as much info as we could get, and fast. Whether or not we could get it in the form of admissible evidence.

We crouched together behind a yew shrub and watched the building. Bainbridge signed to me that he would take point. Since I'd figured he would, I didn't bother to argue, just lifted two fingers, a reminder the jammer would only cover him for that long, at most, from the security cameras.

We had to get this the first time. Repeated use of the jammer would cause a faint flicker on the monitors, not much but enough to imply tampering to any guard with more than a minimal attention span.

I pressed the button. "Go," I breathed.

He ran to the stone wall, vaulted it smoothly, and raced across the open space to the building. The scanner in his hand would detect underground wires. We needed to see if we could tap their communications or power grid, not a strong bet but worth checking.

We'd set our watches to vibrate for a couple of beats every fifteen seconds. Mine gave the first warning just as he reached the building.

Much as I wanted to follow him, I had to keep an eye on the door instead. And stay alert in case of guards from the rear.

My watch vibrated again. Bainbridge was halfway down the building. Still no sign of pursuit—and no indication he'd found the conduits we wanted. Damn it, they should be on this side, to hook into the ones for the main compound.

At forty-five seconds, he made it around the back.

Wind rustled the trees and bushes. An owl hooted in the distance. *Come on, Jack*, I thought. *One fifteen gone.*

He appeared at the building's corner, a shadowy figure in the darkness. To his left, a slatted rectangle of light coming through the window blinds brightened the grass.

The building's door suddenly opened. Silhouetted against the light from inside, a man stepped out.

My heart jetted into my throat. Bainbridge disappeared around the corner. If they caught him with that equipment, we were so busted.

Hell, Britain was so busted.

I longed to grab the Walther even though I couldn't use it. Killing a guard would blow the whole operation. Still, my hand would feel better holding it.

The man let the door shut and fished something from his pocket. His relaxed stance didn't look as though he were on alert for an intruder. A moment later, he lifted something to his mouth. Light flared—from a lighter, for a cigarette.

Shit. This was not break time. He wasn't supposed to be here.

My watch buzzed a minute thirty. *Go back inside,* I mentally sent to the guard. *It's cold out here.*

My thought-beaming didn't work any better with him than it had with Lady Daphne. The guy was enjoying his cigarette. Taking his damn time with it.

Vibration on my wrist signaled fifteen seconds of cover left, the amount of time my partner needed to run across the clearing. David's dead face flashed into my head.

Jack, please, I thought. *Please don't get caught.*

My watch vibrated again. Two minutes. The jammer loop ended.

Jack's safe window was up.

CHAPTER SEVENTEEN

A sudden chill rolled through me. Jack would expect me to head for the cottage, as planned, to preserve my cover if he was spotted. Common sense ordered me to go. Fear for him held me in place.

Maybe Jones-Demerest's goons wouldn't hurt him, but that was a big, threatening *maybe* in my book. Could I draw that guard off somehow? Even if I did, that wouldn't stop the cameras and whoever was watching them inside from seeing Jack.

Could he have found cover somewhere? Below camera range on the side of the hill? Behind the opposite stone wall? There wasn't any other possibility near that building.

Dammit, where was he?

The guard continued to smoke, which had to be a good sign. Aside from his cigarette getting shorter, nothing changed. No alarms, no blaze of exterior lights.

But also no Jack.

My watch vibrated again—the time lapse that would let me activate the jammer for another interval. I immediately did.

Another two minutes went by. And another. And another.

Maybe he'd found a blind spot on the cameras. But if he came back around the building, the guard was still there. Jack couldn't reach me without going by him.

Seven minutes since time ran out. Either he was safe or there were morons watching the monitors. Since the guards had demonstrated alertness in our earlier encounter, Jack was probably safe.

I'd thought David would be okay when I'd left him. Ten minutes later, he'd been dead.

I shook off the memory. That was then. This was different.

I hoped.

Using the jammer again would be pushing our luck. Without the jammer, I could do nothing. I had to go.

The guard tossed his cigarette aside. When he stepped back through the door, I crept out of the bushes and hurried to the main compound. Using the jammer here shouldn't affect the lab's system, so I activated it as I passed through the area.

No one was stirring, and few lights showed in cottage windows. Most people were probably in bed. I pulled out my phone, turned it on, and called Simon. When he answered, I asked, "Where's Bainbridge?"

"We lost sight of him behind the rear wall. Sorry." He didn't sound especially concerned, but I wasn't reassured. Anything could've happened.

I picked up my pace, still not running even though I longed to, when I reached the path to our cottage. *Please be there. Please, Jack.*

I rounded a curve and spotted a dark, indistinct shape under the trees ahead. Heart pounding, I instinctively moved deeper into the shadows.

If anyone stopped me, I'd claim "Bainsiekins" and I'd had a fight. Which we were probably about to since I hadn't followed his plan. As long as he was safe, I didn't care.

A worrisome thought, but I couldn't examine it right now. The shape, man-sized, moved toward me. The path's turns brought it to a point where the compound lighting lay behind it, creating a silhouette.

Jack's silhouette. Moving with Jack's smooth, predatory stride. Oh, thank God!

Suddenly weak in the knees, I stumbled and clapped a hand to my mouth to stifle a gasp.

"Claire?" He ran toward me.

He must've seen me stumble. *Get it together,* I told myself frantically. *Handle yourself.*

Shit, those were tears stinging my eyes. I hastily blinked them clear.

Catching my arm, he said, "Are you all right?"

I drew a long, shuddering breath. "Yeah," I choked.

He tipped my face up—gently despite the frown now visible in the faint light under the trees. His thumb slid upward, toward the moisture on my cheek, and I jerked free.

"What the hell?" Despite his soft tone, his frown deepened.

"I'm fine," I insisted. "Let's go home." I stepped around him and hurried toward the cottage.

He didn't say anything as we returned to our little base. My thoughts, however, churned. Of course he was safe, as my common sense had said. He'd followed the plan. As I should've.

Instead, I'd let fear paralyze me. What if he'd been in trouble and needed a thinking, functioning partner? Maybe I didn't belong in the field, at least not with a partner. Or was my unacceptable reaction part of my attraction to him?

I didn't think so. I'd seen him in David's place, which meant I had more potent ghosts than I'd known. Maybe I really didn't have the inner steel to live with my job.

We reached our cottage. I fumbled for my key, but he had the door open before I found it. Politely, he stood aside for me to enter first. I sucked in a deep breath.

I had to distract him from my freaky reaction, at least until I could figure it out. Maybe a good offense... "What happened out there?"

"You tell me," he said mildly. Settling onto the couch, he narrowed his eyes.

By some miracle, I kept my face together as I took off my jacket. "I mean, how did you escape when time ran out?"

"I went over the back wall," he replied, still studying me. "Then I came here, per the plan, but you didn't." He paused. His gaze turned speculative. Concerned, almost. "Why?"

To avoid looking at him, I filled the kettle. "Aren't you going to blast me for not following the plan?"

"Doesn't seem necessary." Still that quiet, thoughtful tone.

Hell, did he suspect I'd frozen? How much did he know about David's death?

"Claire." He leaned forward, his elbows on his knees. "Why didn't you come back here?"

"You know me." I rummaged in the cabinet for tea. Scooping the loose leaves into the mesh brewing ball would take a minute. It also let me avoid looking at him. "I decided to stay as backup in case you needed me."

If he had, he'd have needed me at my best. This was not it, damn it.

Shame clogged my throat, and I blinked back tears.

Patient and persistent as a cat waiting to pounce, he quietly asked, "What made you decide to stay?"

"Geez, you're beginning to sound like a three-year-old, asking *why* to everything." I flashed him a quick grin but focused on the tea. "Do I need a reason?"

"You usually have one. Of questionable merit, perhaps, but you have one. Tell me what it was."

"Or you'll keep saying 'why,' I suppose," I said quietly.

He didn't reply, just sat there watching me, his eyes the solemn gray of a winter sky.

I put the ball into the china pot and filled the electric kettle. As my partner, he was entitled to an answer. Even one I hated and feared giving him. He deserved a partner in top form, and this mission was too important to risk on me if I couldn't stand firm.

Wishing I knew how much of my file he'd read, I turned slowly to face him. "I lost a partner."

His considering expression didn't change. "If that were your fault, you wouldn't be in the field."

"It feels like my fault." That admission would probably land me back in the psych sessions when this was over. If not sooner. Confessing it felt good, though. As did his neutral, considering look in lieu of the dismay I'd expected on his face.

Bracing myself, I added, "We were following our plan. My plan."

A light flickered in his eyes, too fast for me to read. He stood and walked toward me.

I stiffened my spine. He didn't seem like the huggy sort, but my control danced on the edge. If he touched me, I might crumble and lose the little dignity I'd managed to salvage.

He walked past me to the counter, and disappointment zinged me an instant before relief. Wryly, he said, "You forgot to plug in the kettle." He corrected the error.

Leaning against the counter with his arms crossed, he studied me, his gaze more concerned than assessing. "We'll probably have to work separately when the time comes to finish this mission. Tell me honestly —can you focus on your part, leaving mine to me, or should I arrange for another operative to help?"

Though the question burned, he was not only entitled but duty-bound to ask it. By leaving the call to me, he was granting me more leeway than I had any right to expect. Trusting me, which meant more than I could've said. I kept my eyes steady on his and tried to decide how to respond.

Finally, late but better than never, I felt the answer settle in my core. "I'll do my part. Tonight was—tonight took me by surprise."

"Fair enough." He nodded slowly.

Gracious of him not to point out that handling surprises was part of our job. "Hey, wait a minute. Why were you coming to look for me instead of waiting here? Per the plan?"

That flicker around his mouth might've signaled a grimace forming, but he stopped it. "Knowing the situation is part of my job, and you hadn't come back."

Of course, he couldn't phone me any more than I could him. A vibrating phone was a distraction. Maybe I wasn't the only one with partner anxiety, but I wouldn't press him after he'd been so reasonable about my little freakout.

When he reached into the cabinet for a mug, I figured this part of our chat was over. And I was still on the case. "What did you find?" I asked.

"Nothing." He shot me a grim look. "There are no utility lines detectable. They must be masked somehow. We need another way to find out what they're doing."

#

The next morning, I reported for my voluntary support job in purchasing, in the wing jutting out behind the dining hall. Bainbridge kissed me at the door of the low, stone building and strolled off to drive a forklift in the brewery, which stood just below the top of the hill opposite the main gate. And not too far from the lab, but we hadn't found any connection so far.

A trim, brisk woman with a shoulder-length bob and yet another livery outfit—gray pantsuit with the Simply Yorkshire logo on the jacket pocket—greeted me when I entered. "Good morning, Lady Bainbridge. I'm Susan Welford, the head of purchasing. I understand you'll be helping us."

"Yeah, sure. Call me Claire."

My snug low-riders and cropped hoodie, along with the spikey, reddish-purple hair and garish makeup, probably appalled her, but she didn't show it.

"Right this way, then, Claire." She ushered me to a computer table in the corner. A black flat-screen model adorned the top, as expected. Perfect for my plan.

"You'll be entering these invoices into the database. I've already logged you in. Mr. Jones-Demerest says you know Excel?"

"I had to, for my business. Say, you don't care if I play my music, do you? I got earbuds."

"Well...I'm sure that will be fine."

Much finer than upsetting the residents, no doubt. I pulled my smartphone from my bag and slid it into the docking station on the desk. Heavy metal crashed through the room.

Susan whirled, horror supplanting the bland expression on her face.

"Oops." I shot her an apologetic look and plugged my earbuds into the phone. Now that I'd established the device's harmless, if annoying, nature, she'd most likely ignore it and me.

I slid onto the chair before tapping the keyboard combination that triggered the wireless worm hidden under the music. By the time I finished my shift ninety minutes later, it should not only have masked my initiating keystrokes but uncovered every company with which Jones-Demerest did business.

Meanwhile, Petunia was on the trail of information about Sir Percival Basingstoke and, as a precaution, Bainbridge's mother. That terse exchange with Robin in the bar implied Bainbridge's family was in this case up to their collective necks, whether he wanted to admit it or not. I needed all the information I could get.

One of the jobs that paid my way through school involved data entry in a university office. I could do that job on autopilot, and I did. I boogied in my chair to the strident chords of the Car Crushers, tapped my fingers in rhythm and generally got both my jobs done.

I had to slow down to make the work last until the music shifted into a minor key for "Junkyard Dirge," a sign the worm had finished its work. Once it did, I typed the last entries with a flourish, removed the earbuds, and detached the smartphone.

"Susan? I'm done."

She looked up from her own desk. "You managed that rather quickly. Thank you, madam—ah, Claire."

"Sure. No prob. See you Friday." If I didn't now have grounds for Jasper's arrest hidden on my smartphone.

CHAPTER EIGHTEEN

I sauntered out of the office and back to the cottage.

The magazines on the living room table lay in tidy rows. Through the open bedroom doorway, I could see the neatly made bed. Housekeeping had been here, so I did a quick bug sweep. The cottage was clean. I had privacy until Bainbridge came back.

Which could be any minute. I grabbed my phone and called Petunia.

"Yes, Casey. We've turned up a bit on the late countess. Nothing we'd call reliable, but she's rumored to have been rather a free spirit. Hippie sort. May even have used illegal drugs."

"LSD?" That could cause lingering after-effects.

"Uncertain."

"Any sign she crashed her car on purpose?"

"Nothing but some hints that she suffered from episodic depression. Why do you ask?"

"I'm not sure. Just a hunch. Oh, by the way, Bainbridge's aunt came to visit." Running water into the kettle and putting out things for tea, I filled Petunia in.

When I finished, she said, "Lady Beatrice has become something of a champion for Robert Basingstoke. Staff gossip says she thinks he 'bred true,' while Jack didn't."

"Does she have any kids of her own to annoy?" I packed loose tea into the wire mesh ball.

"No, and she apparently sees herself, not Jack, as the true head of the family."

His home life must be hell. If he didn't care, that would be okay, but his reactions betrayed that he did mind what his family thought of him,

149

no matter how much he tried not to.

In the long run, though, not my problem. "I need you to see if Robert Basingstoke has invested either his own funds or Hawkshead Shipping's in any of the JJD holdings."

"You think he might?"

"He and Jones-Demerest are way too chummy, so I want to be sure we cover all the bases."

"I'll put the research team on it when I check in today."

Even if Robin hadn't gone that far, he'd made grave errors in judgment. Bainbridge would always stand far above the rest of his family. "Speaking of research, what about Sir Percival?"

"Ah, he's a canny one." Satisfaction vibrated in her voice.

Steam hissed from the kettle, and it clicked off. I poured the boiling water over the ball in the pot. "Tell, tell."

"Everyone knows he was knighted for his work at Bletchley Park."

"The Enigma Project, breaking the German codes."

"Right. He joined them at sixteen, a real prodigy. When the war ended, he was only eighteen, but he stepped into running Hawkshead Shipping, much as Robert Basingstoke does now. Retired to make way for Robert. Not before time, according to some, but he upheld the family tradition that the company be run by the earl's younger brother. Since then, he's spent his time down in Leicester, collecting ancient books."

"So why would he want an outsider involved in Hawkshead Shipping?"

"Perhaps he doesn't." She sounded positively smug. "Perhaps he's running a blind. Rumor has it, only rumor, mind you, that Sir Percival is angling for his own best deal."

"What does that mean?"

"I'm still digging."

"Right. Well, keep me posted."

She rang off. I inhaled the fragrance of steeping tea, my thoughts roiling. Did Sir Percival resent the secondary role reserved for Robin, a fellow second son? Did he think Bainbridge too irresponsible to make the final call about Jones-Demerest's investment?

Or were both of them running a blind on me? If Sir Percival really had been MI5, possibly a big *if*, though it seemed to fit, he was as capable of it as Bainbridge.

Bainbridge's tread crunched on the gravel walk outside. I stuffed the phone in my bag and grabbed an equestrian magazine.

When he opened the door, I asked, "How'd it go?"

Frowning, he closed the door and walked into the room. "Quite a few people work at every stage of the process. If the beer is tainted, it doesn't happen in the brewery. Unless it's in the filtration system. I'll have to manage a closer look." He dropped into a chair opposite me. "Anything turn up in the office?"

"I don't know yet. I just got back." Although I hated deceiving him, his intransigence about his family left me no choice.

I pulled the smartphone out of my bag while he booted his laptop. He sat next to me, bringing an intriguing whiff of cedar and sandalwood and an irritating awareness of his solid, masculine presence.

I jacked the phone into his machine, and we leaned close together to read the display. His arm brushed mine unexpectedly. Lightning flashed into my belly, and I caught my breath.

"All right?" His voice sounded gruff.

"Fine." I peeked at his lap and found his trousers reassuringly tight. I might be suffering, but misery had company.

Information flowed onto the screen, letters appearing in sequence and forming words with speed that would've done Superman justice. I skimmed them. "Nothing here stands out. None of the purchases that seemed odd to my shop or yours."

"Let's make certain." He tapped a combination of keys, and yellow dots spiraled into a changing pattern in the screen's center.

Movement at the window caught my eye, just a flicker that could be nothing. I straightened.

He snapped the computer shut. "The hell with work, darling," he said, louder than necessary when I was sitting right by him.

He chucked the laptop to the side and grabbed me. My brain had just worked out the fact that someone must be watching when his mouth covered mine.

I've never stuck a finger in a live electrical socket, but I imagine the sensation must be something like the one I had in that moment. Electricity crackled through me and ignited pulsing fire between my legs.

I moaned as I opened my mouth. His tongue speared into it, stroking and exploring. I sucked on him, earning a growl as he nudged me onto my back. His soft, thick hair felt like silk under my fingers. His hard chest flattened my breasts, and somehow, he was lying between my legs.

He shifted. His erection pressed into my crotch. I gasped as he groaned. My hips lifted to meet his rocking thrust and earned another lightning flash. I slid my hand down his solid, cashmere-covered back and into his pants. Under my fingers, his butt flexed, hard and warm.

He tore his mouth from mine to trail hot, tongue-flicking kisses down my neck. Through the hoodie, his hand cupped my breast, and a flash of wicked, sizzling pleasure blinded me. Reveling in our closeness, I nuzzled his ear, then flicked it with my tongue. Drew a choked sound from him.

The tiny corner of my brain still dimly functioning knew where this was going, and at light speed. I forced my eyes open, only to find one of Jones-Demerest's goons watching through the window.

I mustered enough breath to shriek. Sort of feebly, but Bainbridge's head jerked up. He pushed himself off the couch and wheeled to the now-empty window.

Someone knocked at the door. He cast a rueful look at me and walked over to the entry, straightening his clothes on the way.

I tugged mine into place quickly. Too bad I couldn't banish the hot-and-wanting sensations as fast. I took a slow, deep breath and let it out gradually. Which might've helped if I hadn't been watching his taut butt as he moved.

Bainbridge walked through the airlock, leaving the main door open. I caught snatches of conversation.

"...terribly sorry, sir." Must be the goon.

"What is it?

"Mr. Jones-Demerest sent me to invite...dinner....not sure...home."

"Well, ring the bloody doorbell in future. You frightened my wife."

Which reminded me, in the weird way of associational thought, that he might well be gaming his *wife*.

He came back inside and shut the door. In his left hand, he held a thick packet of vellum.

"That's a dinner invitation?" I asked.

He stalked to the windows and drew the curtains before answering. "Jones-Demerest does things the old-fashioned way."

"The old-fashioned, *simple* way."

"Umm." Oblivious to sarcasm, he ripped open the envelope.

I could've read over his shoulder, but even minimal contact didn't seem like a good idea until our—or my, at least—raging hormones settled a bit. Why the hell did Lord Impossible have to feel so damn good?

He passed me the note sheet, which bore the cottage logo of the Simply Yorkshire retreat in raised, gilt printing.

I scanned it. "Thursday. Why not? I vote we answer by phone or email. Unless—did Bozo wait for a response?"

"Not openly. We can call the gate if we need a messenger."

"This is such a simple lifestyle. Messengers and gold-embossed stationery."

He grinned, crinkling the corners of his eyes and warming his expression in a way that made my insides do quivery, unwelcome wiggles. "All things are relative."

"Yeah." I mentally squashed my unflattering pun about his relatives. "Your laptop should have finished whatever it was doing."

"Right." He retrieved it, sat a careful six inches from me, and popped it open. He angled the screen so I could see it.

A dialog box in the center of the screen read "0 matches. 0 anomalies. 0 unusual items."

I scowled at it. "Great. I listened to ninety minutes of The Car Crushers for this."

"You don't like The Car Crushers?"

"Do you?"

He grinned again, but his eyes didn't light this time. He closed the laptop. "I'll ask more questions at the brewery."

"I guess I'll go back to purchasing, though I can't see why. I'd rather become petulant and bored, then quit."

"Not straight away. It would look odd."

"I hope this investigation doesn't take long enough to make it look reasonable."

"That's a point."

His phone rang. He fished it from his pocket.

A moment later, mine chimed from my purse. I dug it out and tapped the screen. An ocean scene appeared, signaling a scrambled call. I entered the authorization code. "Billings."

"The first case," Petunia said, "has broken out in Dover."

Hell. "The Chunnel?" I asked.

"Hard to know. The patient's a customs officer."

Naturally. They'd have first contact with anyone coming in. "Anything else?"

"The National Health Service is monitoring, but this is deemed low impact at present."

"Got it." Low impact generally involved isolated cases, so things could be worse, but the flu could spread very, very fast. Double hell. I blew out a frustrated breath. "Thanks."

She signed off. I glanced at Bainbridge, who was pocketing his phone.

I told him what she'd just shared. "I'm thinking we bump things up. Do some more snooping after dinner."

Bainbridge nodded, his face reflecting my frustration. "We'd better find something. If this escalates, we can expect major outbreaks within the next two weeks."

And fatalities all too soon after that.

CHAPTER NINETEEN

Since I couldn't blow holes in anything while I waited for nightfall, I decided to go hit something instead. By the time I changed clothes and reached the gym, I had my frustration under better control. Heavy bags hung enticingly at one end of the mats, but I didn't dare use them, no matter how much I wanted to. My cover as a personal trainer wouldn't explain the ability to throw a solid right hook, let alone a roundhouse kick. I'd have to content myself with the weights.

Since my knee seemed fully recovered, I ran a few laps to warm up, but running in a circle bores me. Jumping in place, on the other hand, lets me zone out and think. I pulled my jump rope out of my bag, shook out the kinks, and started jumping. Not too fast but fast enough to show the proficiency a trainer should possess.

I hadn't mentioned Sir Percy to Bainbridge. If he was running a scam with his relative, he didn't want me to know. Otherwise, he'd have told me. If he was being scammed, blindly trusting where he shouldn't, could I push him into looking more closely?

Arachnid was investigating, of course, but without his inside knowledge of the players. That line of inquiry would move so much faster if he'd cooperate. He had a ludicrous blind spot about the whole Hawkshead Shipping issue. Why?

I picked up my pace. The rope made a whipping noise that alternated with the muffled thud of my feet hitting the mats between jumps.

Zen had deserted me. I needed something more strenuous.

I put the rope away, toweled off my face, and took a drink of water. At least I could set the weight machines high enough to look reasonable, though not as high as I liked.

I made the adjustments and started chest presses. This wouldn't qualify as a fabulous workout, but it beat doing nothing.

The door at the end of the room opened. Hilda peeked inside.

Arms extended against the weight, I panted, "Hi."

"Hello, Claire." She took a tentative step into the gym. Judging from the curious way she looked around, she'd never been in a gym before. Or not recently, anyway.

I let the weights clank back into place. "You can come on in, y'know." Though she wasn't dressed for it, in beige slacks, a dark green cardigan, and sturdy Oxfords that looked well suited to wandering the countryside.

"What brings you in, Hilda? Thinking of starting a workout program?" If she did, could I turn that to my advantage?

"Um…perhaps…" She looked nervous, and her inflection rose on the last word as if in a question.

"Perhaps what?" I summoned a friendly smile and strolled over to her. "It's never too late to start, you know." I'd heard trainers say that a zillion times.

"Horace works a bit each day, and I try to give him quiet."

"So you're looking for something to do while he works."

She nodded eagerly. "Our friends the Nevilles like a good soak in the hot tub in the late afternoons, and Horace swims sometimes."

Neville. They ran a lorry, or trucking, company, one Horace said Jones-Demerest had helped them set up. We should check them out.

Hilda continued, "I don't like sitting in hot water, though, and I don't swim well. Been a long time since I splashed about in the water."

"I'm sure you'd improve quickly. If you're looking for something else, though, weight training and aerobics are great for a person. If your heart's healthy."

"Oh, yes. I had an examination just a few months ago." She hesitated. "The thing is, I wouldn't know where to begin."

"I could help you with that." And pump her for information while she pumped iron.

Her brow furrowed. "I don't want to impose, Claire."

"It's no problem. I like helping people get in shape. Horace might even like to join us."

She blinked as if startled. "I hadn't supposed—but he might."

Frowning at the mats, she added, "I do wish he'd do something. He's seemed so out of sorts recently."

As in, mood shifts? Chemically induced? "How long has this been going on, Hilda?"

"A few weeks. It's almost as though—well, I suppose it's silly, but— as though he doesn't like being away from the office."

I started to say something reassuring, but her deepening frown stopped me.

"It's worse since we've been here," she said slowly. "He just seems sad. He should be enjoying himself now that we have what we worked so hard all these years to earn."

"Did you help him in the business?"

"I kept the books," she said proudly. "Ran the office. It was just him and me, starting out."

"So it's a family business in every sense."

"Oh, yes. Indeed, yes."

"We'll see if we can do anything to brighten up Horace. Meantime, d'you have any workout gear?"

She looked doubtful, so I added, "Anything you don't mind sweating in?"

"I think so."

"Then you go change into it, and I'll keep busy until you get back."

She bustled away looking much more confident, and I went back to the weights. I was getting a great idea.

If I could just make Lord Control Freak see its value.

#

I waited until I'd showered and changed to broach my idea with Bainbridge. I also made tea, that ubiquitous English beverage. He sat at the massive desk in one corner, laptop open to a website.

"I'm fixing tea," I said. "Would you like a cup?"

He glanced up at me, his eyes wary. "What do you want?"

"Nothing. I offered you tea." As a prelude to what I wanted. "Would you like a cup or not?"

"Yes, thank you. Along with whatever information or question you're delaying." His raised eyebrow stopped my defensive reaction. "You're not the subservient sort."

"I hope I'm a good enough partner to offer tea when I'm having some." He'd paid me a compliment. Why didn't it feel like one?

I made the tea and set his mug on the desk. Holding mine, I leaned against the corner of the desktop. Its carvings hurt my butt. I wouldn't move, though. This position had the strategic merit of letting me look down on him. "I did have an idea I wanted to discuss with you."

He smiled his *I thought so* and said only, "Let's have it, then."

I told him about my encounter with Hilda. "I could take a few clients. People talk to their trainers, Jack, just as they do to hairdressers and bartenders. If Hilda and Horace have let Jones-Demerest creep into their business, what's the chance someone else here has? He hasn't exactly advertised this place, but it's jumping."

He frowned. "It's not part of the plan."

"How predictable." Despite his glare, I rushed on. "Talking to people is way more likely to turn up leads than running that worm through the same computer, with the same records, again and again."

"You're supposed to be in purchasing. It was chosen for you specifically. As we discussed earlier."

"I'm flighty, remember? Anyone would believe I'd switch to something more fun."

He shook his head.

Before he could smack down the idea, I added, "If we can get a lead on even one of Jones-Demerest's illegal businesses, anything that ties him to the epidemic, you can hold him for questioning under the terrorism statutes."

Turning back to his computer, he said, "An exercise class will draw too much attention to you."

"That's the beauty of the ditz routine. No one will particularly notice, let alone care, what I do. And my cover is as a trainer, remember?"

His scathing look said his memory worked fine, thanks. After a moment, he said, "I'll think about it. Meanwhile, stay with purchasing."

Expressing my irritation would do no good. No matter much I missed the give-and-take David and I had shared, it was gone. Bainbridge had a right to make the decision. Which didn't mean I wouldn't push back later. Or that I couldn't work out with just Hilda.

Thinking of her reminded me I had news. Pushing my annoyance aside, I said, "Anyway, Hilda gave me a new lead."

He agreed we should pursue it by hanging out in the hot tub later. Which meant I'd have to deal with him in a bathing suit, buff, wet and skimpily dressed. A pleasure, but I'd pay for it in frustration.

#

Our grand strategy of soaking in steamy water while prying into the Nevilles' affairs hit a snag as soon as we reached the pool. The Nevilles weren't there. One couple, a gray-haired, balding man and a woman whose graying brown hair was pulled up in a loose topknot splashed around in the shallows looking like Mr. and Mrs. Jack Spratt in bathing suits.

Bainbridge and I glanced at each other. "We may as well wait a bit," he suggested. He carefully kept his eyes on the hot tub as he headed for it, in the corner by the glass wall looking out on the countryside below the compound.

Feeling very much on display, I followed him. On the other side of the pool, also behind a glass wall except for the stone stretch hiding the locker rooms, stood the gym.

I'd worn thong bikinis before, but I felt very self-conscious in this one. With him. His swim trunks confirmed all my prior guesses about his body, which made my problem worse. The urge to pull my shoulders back and suck in my tummy kept tweaking me, though I knew, rationally, I had nothing to suck in and not much chest to display.

Not looking at him, which would too easily become lusting after him, I stepped down into the tub. Out of the corner of my eye, I watched him sink waist-deep into the hot, frothy water. Unfortunately, it did nothing to blur his muscular shoulders, upper arms, and chest.

A moment later, Jones-Demerest entered behind Bainbridge and headed straight for us. As though he'd known we were there, a troublesome thought.

He liked to ogle, so maybe I could distract him. I sank farther into the water and yanked at my top strings despite my partner's glare and his terse, whispered, "Do not—"

"Oh, hi, Jasper," I called in the brightest tone I could muster. "We were just talkin' about you."

Hell, he was probably here to badger Bainbridge about the shipping company. I slid toward the heaviest bubbles and shoved my top at Bainbridge.

He stuck it behind him with one hand while the other gripped my right shoulder and tugged me toward him. "More bubbles over here, darling." His sweet tone belied the steely-eyed, murderous expression on his face. As he morphed it into a goofily infatuated look, I settled against the bench by his leg.

He was right. The jets made the water foamier here than in the middle, where I'd been. Much better for tantalizing, and thus distracting, Jones-Demerest.

"Good day to you both," he said with his usual ingratiating smile. His glance flicked to the frothy water over my chest. "Lord Bainbridge, I'd hoped we might have a few moments to discuss the investment your brother mentioned."

"This isn't the best time." Bainbridge sounded bored. His fingers stroked my shoulder lightly before gliding up to my ear. He traced its outline, and sudden heat that owed nothing to the warm water flooded me.

"Of course." Jones-Demerest again glanced into the tub.

How much could he really see? I'd banked on the foam for cover.

Behind him, the couple who'd been in the pool climbed out. They headed for the locker room.

"I wouldn't like to interrupt," Jones-Demerest said. "If we might arrange a better time, perhaps over dinner?"

Bainbridge's fingers caressed my neck and ear. "We received your invitation. Sorry we haven't had time to respond."

Bainbridge's low, husky voice sent new ripples of desire through me. Under the water, I draped an arm across his hard thigh. It tensed, and I exulted.

Enjoying the texture of his firm muscles and the light dusting of dark hair on his leg under my arm, I leaned back to look up at him. "I'd like that, Sweetie-buns." I'd intended a cheery tone, but the words sounded breathless, just the way I felt. I stroked his knee.

His molten silver gaze pinned me in place. He looked as though he knew exactly what the water concealed. I suddenly wished he did.

"How is tomorrow?" Jones-Demerest asked.

"We'll let you know. Right, darling?" Bainbridge toyed with the damp hair at my nape, and delight shot into my breasts and on down through me.

Biting my lip to stay focused, I nodded.

"Yes, very well," Jones-Demerest said, his own voice tight. His throat worked in a swallow as I turned even more toward Bainbridge, my hand sliding up his leg.

"Now you'll have to excuse us." Bainbridge leaned toward me. His hand cupped the back of my head, and mine tightened on his hard thigh.

His lips brushed mine—more tantalizing than pleasurable—before he straightened. His suddenly stern eyes glanced around the pool area, and he released me. "Don't ever do that again. I don't want you undressed in front of him."

"First, the bubbles concealed me. Second, there are lives at stake, and I'd take a Lady Godiva ride through Trafalgar Square at noon to stop this scumbag."

Bainbridge's eyes softened but remained intent. "Why?"

How much of my file had he seen? Regardless, my debt to David and his family was my private business. "Because he's a pustule on the face of humanity."

Bainbridge's expression didn't change. He didn't buy that as the reason. I braced myself for more questions, but he said only, "Regardless, I don't want you exposed, in part or in whole, in front of him. It isn't necessary."

"Is that the only reason?"

He opened his mouth as though to speak, then shut it and glanced out the window. "It's reason enough."

That glance softened my disappointment. His evasion meant he wasn't telling me everything. "I'm trying to help you, you know. I don't like him pestering you about the Hawkshead deal."

"I can handle him." Despite his dismissive tone, his brows drew together.

"I know, but I want to help you."

"Why?" His narrow-eyed gaze probed my eyes.

Because keeping the company clean was part of our mission brief. Because he was my partner. Because—"You deserve it," I blurted.

He looked as surprised as I felt, and then vulnerable, and then his eyes heated to silver again. My breasts felt suddenly heavy, and the frothy water brushing the puckered nipples felt like exquisite torture. I stopped breathing as we stared at each other.

He was the family black sheep, so no one helped him. Listened to him. Did he resent that? Was that why—

His eyes darkened. He shifted toward me, and I rose on my knees, my hands sliding up his thighs. His arms whipped around me while his mouth swooped down on mine.

His grip tightened. My sensitized breasts sank into the wet, silky hair on his chest and flattened against his solid muscles. I reveled in the sensation, and his tongue speared into my mouth.

CHAPTER TWENTY

Jack groaned. Withdrew his tongue and thrust it in again. His mouth left mine, exploring my ear and neck, and I trembled with greedy pleasure. My body arched into his, his erection prodding my waist.

Kissing his shoulder, I saw the windows. The hillside across the way.

"Jack—" I gasped for air. "My top—windows—"

"No one will see anything," he muttered, way more coherent than I was. His right arm tightened, reminding me his heavy biceps blocked any view of my breast from outside. He caught my mouth again, and I forgot about the windows as my hands explored his sleek chest and back. He palmed my breast, stroking it, and my insides turned to liquid heat.

My thumb brushed the top of his erection, hot and hard under the thin layer of his swim shorts. Too much—too tempting, but he made a choked noise and thrust toward my hand. I couldn't resist cupping him.

With a groan, he jerked free, leaving me wishing he hadn't. He gripped my shoulders and directed a level, flinty stare at me. "No more stripping off your kit in front of him. That's an order."

With a lithe, powerful movement, he surged out of the water. He snatched a towel from the rack by the pool and held it in front of him.

I watched him grab his shirt, slide on his shower shoes, and stalk to the door. Several comebacks occurred to me, but I swallowed them. Was he making a mission call as an operative? Or a chivalrous one as a man? Or a jealous—no. Couldn't be. Could it?

Did I want it to be?

Later, I reminded myself, retrieving my swimsuit top. We'd tabled that subject. For now, only the mission counted. And time was running out.

#

"Where's my phone?" I'd left it on the nightstand when we went to the pool, but it wasn't there or on the floor. I turned slowly to face Bainbridge across the bed.

He tugged a V-neck sweater over his head, a black one since we were preparing for another run at the lab. Grim-faced, he answered, "I took it, as I'm sure you deduced, and scanned it. We've a few issues to settle."

Just when I was starting to like him, he had to pull a high-handed stunt. I set my feet and put a fist on my hip.

"You and Arachnid have investigated my family. That stops immediately. I have the Hawkshead Shipping problem under control."

I'd worry later about how he knew that. "First, I take orders from Arachne, who wants that deal stopped. Second, I need that phone. Third, that's theft. Give it back."

He pulled it from his jeans pocket, the one place I wouldn't have searched. "Everyone wants that deal stopped. I told you I'll handle it."

"If only." I stalked around the bed to confront him. "Either you don't take the threat seriously or you want your family to screw up big-time. I don't care which, but that company's going to stay clean. As MI5 agrees it must."

"They leave the problem to me." He stared down his nose at me, his eyes hard as slate. "So will you."

"If you don't want me to call you lordly, don't act that way." With an effort, I kept my voice level.

His eyes flashed, but he handed me the phone. "Push this, and you're off this case." He turned to his nightstand for his watch, dismissing me.

I clenched my fist to keep from yanking him back to face me. "I can't let this go as long as that investment deal is moving forward. You shouldn't expect me to."

He buckled his watch and stepped around me. "Are you coming or not?"

Maybe the time had come to shoot my own bolt. I waited until he reached the bedroom door. "Are you and Sir Percival running a blind?"

"What?" Looking shocked, he wheeled.

Was he shocked because I knew? Or because the idea was so far off the mark?

"Are you and Sir Percival working together to make everyone think he's helping Robin when he really plans to vote with you?"

"What makes you think we are?" He scowled at me. His expression gave nothing away.

"One, that would explain your insistence that everything's under control. Two, he would then have a reason to communicate so cozily with your brother. Three, you both have at least some experience with deception for a good cause. Answer my question."

Turning back to the door, he shook his head. "We don't have time for this."

"I'll make you a deal. You tell me what's going on with Sir Percival, have him come for tea, and talk to him frankly about the shipping company. I won't follow up that line further until after that."

Bainbridge leaned against the door frame, his face bland. "If I'm running a blind, telling anyone about it wrecks it."

"I'm your partner, you know," I said, lifting my chin. "Last night, for the sake of the mission, I told you something I don't tell anybody. You can at least let me know what's going on around us."

He looked at me for a long moment, and conflict shadowed his eyes. At last, he straightened. "That's the best argument you've used. You are my partner, something I'm not accustomed to having."

Frowning, he rubbed a hand over his face. "Percy and I were supposed to do just as you said. Or I thought we were. Nothing explicit was said. However, I've wondered lately whether he's also playing a double game."

"For whose benefit?" I hurried toward him.

"I don't know." He stepped aside for me. "I'll ask him to tea. Now, though, let's hurry."

#

Three hours later, my left thigh cramped from kneeling in the bushes. So far, one guard was still in the lab. Granted, our overwatch team said the place was rarely empty, but rarely wasn't never.

"He has to quit sometime," I whispered.

Bainbridge shot me a *you wish* look. Glancing at his watch, he frowned.

I checked mine. Three in the morning. We had maybe another hour of full darkness left. Tonight, as every night, infected people were spreading the disease. We didn't have time to diddle around.

Keeping my voice as low as I could, I said, "I vote for plan B."

When he nodded, I pulled the jammer out of my bag. We stood, flexed our legs, and exchanged nods of readiness.

"Go," I breathed as I hit the jammer button.

We ran for the stone wall. He vaulted it again, thanks to his height, while I sort of half vaulted and half scrambled across. I made it to the front door just after the fifteen-second vibration from my watch.

From my pocket, I drew an electronic reader. Pressing it to the card-key lock would let it read the access codes. We could then pick one or, if they weren't individualized, use the only one to create a key.

Judging by the time the reader was taking, there were lots of codes. *Come on*, I thought silently to it. All we needed right now was another unscheduled smoking break.

Thirty seconds. No sign of Bainbridge, who'd run toward the back to get the specs on the generator.

Forty-five seconds. At least there weren't footfalls coming toward me from inside, not that I was sure I'd hear them through a steel door anyway. Still no Bainbridge.

One minute. How many codes did this thing hold? At this rate—

The indicator light turned green. Hooray. I let out a breath of silent relief and pocketed the scanner.

Still no Bainbridge. I would, however, do as planned this time. I would control myself, or I'd quit.

I ran for the wall again. Just after a minute-fifteen, I cleared it and kept going to the spot where we'd left my bag.

One thirty. I shouldered the bag, thinking, *Hurry, Jack.*

As though summoned by the thought—don't I wish I had that power for real?—he rounded the building at a run.

One forty-five. He reached the fence. Vaulted it. Gained the trees as the two-minute vibration thrummed in my wrist.

Holding hands in case any early-rising employee spotted us, we strolled back to the main compound. I unzipped my jacket to reveal my electric blue push-up bra, the better to look as though we'd been rolling in the grass all night.

As we neared the dining hall, footsteps crunched on gravel behind the building. Coming toward us.

We stopped together, turning to face each other. Bainbridge set his hands at my waist and lowered his head. Perhaps to avoid the brain crash problem, which I so hoped was mutual, he only brushed his mouth over mine. His warm, soft breath hinted at the coffee he'd had earlier.

I slid my arms around his neck and giggled. "That was so great, Sweet Buns. You're even more of a stud under the stars."

"Ta, darling." He chuckled and drew me close. "Now let's see how the bed compares."

The mental image shot heat through my nipples and into my belly. Worse, into my heart. Stunned, I stared up at him. I felt him harden as his teasing expression vanished like ice in a fire.

Hot and demanding, his mouth slanted over mine. A moan parted my lips, and his tongue plunged inside to fence with mine. When I gasped, he cupped my butt with one hand to press me tightly to him. His erection rubbed me in all the best places. I whimpered while my hands roamed his warm back under the sweater.

I strained closer to him. Not close enough. Not nearly.

With a groan, he jerked his head up. "Home, darling," he ground out. "Now."

"Oh. Yes," I panted, and I wasn't faking the shortness of breath. I didn't want him to stop, and the reluctance wasn't just physical. All this foreplay was building serious yearnings I mostly managed not to think about.

I wanted to know him in that intimate way, something I couldn't risk with a man so incompatible. Life with him would be one long tug of war. Maybe by the time we reached the cottage, we'd be more in control.

We stumbled back to it without meeting anyone else. As soon as Bainbridge closed the door, we headed for separate chairs. I dropped into mine and put my head in my hands. The opposite chair creaked as he sat.

After a minute or so, breathing in to a count of four, then out to four helped. I risked trusting my voice. "Got the codes. How about you?" I sounded mostly normal. *Whew!*

"I have the generator model information. For all that's worth." He sounded grim.

I straightened to find him scowling out at the dawn. "What's wrong?"

"This model has safeguards built into it. Disabling it by the usual means won't start a fire."

"Which means that unless those guards actually take a night off, forcing them out so we can search will require a traceable method," I said slowly. "Something identifiable as arson, maybe, or even going in and overpowering them." Except that the overpowering option would render a subsequent search blatantly illegal. "We need something that can't be detected."

"Exactly. There's an air conditioning unit. If we can find a time with a single guard there, we could use sleeping gas. With a group, though, it won't work fast enough to keep someone from catching on."

"Arachnid has some. I'll have Petunia get it for us."

"Good." Stone-faced, he paced to the window. "If we have to resort to force, we're done. They'll double or triple the guard or move the operation. If we don't find what we need, this will all have been for nothing."

#

That night, half an hour after leaving Bainbridge to after-dinner brandy with Jones-Demerest, I was bored silly in the club room. Also antsy about Bainbridge handling the Hawkshead Shipping angle on his own, but he had a point about being able to draw Jones-Demerest out better by himself.

I sipped a half-pint serving of cider and wished there were someone in here I could pump for info until Bainbridge came for me. It was only ten p.m., just barely dark outside, but the room was clearing. The Simply Yorkshire community did not attract night owls.

A sturdily built, blond man, thirtyish and moderately good-looking, approached with a drink in hand. He smiled at me. "Do you mind if I join you?"

"Room's thin on company. Have a seat." Who was he? I didn't recognize him from the surveillance photos of residents, but the help surely didn't drink with the clientele.

"John Wrenthorpe." He offered his hand.

I took it. "Claire Bas—Bainbridge." I twinkled at him. "I just got married. I'm not used to this titles and names business."

"Very confusing, I'm sure." His smile didn't reach his eyes. Maybe he was a pickup artist.

"We're honeymooning here. Do you live here, too?"

"Yes, actually. I moved in a few days ago."

So far, I hadn't seen anyone else who really passed for young in this place. Fifty seemed to be the floor age, except for Bainbridge and me. Of course, most young people lacked the money to live in such an expensive hideaway, and the dot-com millionaires, who could, generally wanted a more stimulating environment. So what brought this guy here?

A waiter stopped outside the circle of chairs. "May I bring anything for you?"

I peered at my empty glass. "Sure. Another half cider, house brew."

"On my slate," Wrenthorpe said smoothly.

Only a resident could run a slate, or tab, so he must live here. I frowned at him. "My Hubbykins might not like that." And where the hell was he, anyway?

Wrenthorpe smiled, just a shade of smarmy in his face. "In gratitude for the company. No ulterior motives." That smile was probably meant to be charming. "My cottage becomes a bit dull of an evening."

"There isn't much to do here, definitely."

"Surely honeymooners can find ways to occupy the time." He winked at me.

Ick. He'd crossed a line with that one, but I didn't want to scare him off. Yet. He seemed like a sleazoid, so what was he doing here? Friend of dear Jasper? If so, I needed to make his acquaintance. Instead of the glare he deserved, I gave him a confused look.

My cider arrived. I sipped it carefully. Where the hell was Bainbridge? Odd, that I should be missing him. I might learn more in his absence. "So what d'you do, John?"

"Electronics. My company makes microprocessors." From there, he launched into a discussion of marketing campaigns. Finally, he asked, "What do you do, Claire?"

"I'm a trainer. Or I was." I beamed at him. "Now I'm a countess."

"From trainer to countess. That must be quite a change."

"It's kinda weird." I giggled, more effectively than usual. Goody for me. "I liked bein' a trainer, had my own business."

"Where was that?" He finished his drink and signaled for another.

"New York, but before that, Richmond. Virginia, not the one you got here. Richmond's a very old city, you know. Oh, not like any of yours, but old for us."

"Of course," he said politely.

"It was a big center of fighting in the Civil War," I announced. If the history monologue didn't bore him into leaving, he was after something. "Everybody thinks Atlanta was the most important because of that movie, you know? *Gone With the Wind*?"

"I don't know it, I'm afraid," he murmured.

"Why should you?" I beamed at him. His face lost focus for a second. Cider, which comes hard in England, on top of the wine at dinner, must not have been a good idea. But I hadn't had that much, had I?

"Anyway, Atlanta was important, but Richmond was the capital of the Confederacy. So the Yankees wanted to capture it." I peered at him. "You know about General Sherman? He burned Atlanta."

"Indeed. Do go on."

Yep. Definitely...something. "Where was I?"

"Richmond." His face blurred, then came back into focus.

"Yeah. Virginia, it's the mother of...lots of presidents from there.... But Ohio...had a lot of 'em too, lots of..."

I lost track of time. Seconds or minutes could've passed before he said, "Let me escort you home, Claire. Your husband's probably waiting."

"Bainsiekins. Right." Should've been here by now. Maybe he'd changed his mind. I blinked at my companion. "Home."

I was far too woozy. I hadn't had that much to drink. Something was wrong, probably because of this guy, though how he'd spike my drink, I couldn't figure. Regardless, I wouldn't find out what his goal was by sitting here. I'd play along and see where this went. And reach the cottage while my brain still worked.

I got my feet under me, though my balance wasn't so great. Balance. Needed that for something.

"'s not far," I muttered.

"We'll manage." He offered me his arm. I accepted it but managed not to lean on him.

We walked outside, where the chilly night air smacked me in the face without waking me up. Bad news. "I should...go in," I decided.

"Home isn't far. I'll help you, and you'll be fine in the morning."

Why had I come outside with him? Oh, yeah. He was up to something. I was playing along. Yet I felt very conscious of his body brushing mine. Too conscious. And...restless?

What the hell?

The dew had fallen. The grass shone in the faint lights around the green. My high heels were unsteady on the gravel, and I grew more tottery with every step. Damn. Must be drunk.

"Wait." I staggered to a halt. "I want Honeykins."

He'd be pissed. I couldn't remember why. Fog wafted through my brain.

"He's waiting for you at home, Claire."

"How—you—don't know where it is."

"I saw you move in. It's not much farther."

Hell, it wasn't this way. We'd come the wrong direction. "We're lost. Got to turn around." The copse of trees ahead blurred. So did his face.

He caught me in a tight embrace. "You don't really want to go in, do you? I like you, Claire, and we're both lonely."

He lowered his head, aiming to kiss me. His erection bumped my crotch with a lightning zing. I gasped but jerked my head aside from his kiss. He sucked on my neck, and even that felt good.

Which was all very, very wrong.

Alarm momentarily cleared my head. My arms were pinned between us. I pushed but couldn't break free. He squeezed my breast, generating another faintly icky heat rush.

A light flashed somewhere. Strobes? Was I that drunk? I clawed at his wrist. "Ugh. Leggo."

I shoved at him again, then remembered. Shoes. Heels. Instep. I stomped on his, and he jerked backward.

I staggered. Lost one shoe. Kicked off the other for better footing.

He grabbed for my arm and got the wrist. I slapped my free hand around his wrist, jerked the other back against his thumb to break the grip and stepped in to punch him in the nose.

He cried out. Grabbed his nose with one hand, then lunged for me.

The trees were blurring again. The adrenaline rush was wearing off. I gathered my reeling wits and side-kicked him in the solar plexus.

With a choked sound, he doubled, then fell. I fled. The cold, wet grass made for slippery footing.

Wrong way. I was heading away from the lights. I doubled back in an arc I hoped would miss Octopus Hands. Where the hell was Bainbridge? Why hadn't he come to the bar?

By a miracle, I had my bag. I fumbled the cell phone out, but the screen was a blur. I never used voice activation, lest it come on at the wrong time. Panic chilled me and tightened my throat. What if that creep was following me? How long could I last? I had to find Jack.

I reached the green. Now there were two of the path. *Hell.* Somehow I'd been drugged, and that sonofabitch knew it. I stumbled and fell headlong. My clumsy effort to break the fall earned me scraped elbows, but I kept the phone.

I hauled myself up. No sign of pursuit. Jack must be at Jones-Demerest's house. I hoped Petunia was watching the compound, that she'd call my partner if Octopus Arms pursued me.

The dining hall loomed ahead. I passed it. My side hurt, and there seemed to be an excellent chance I'd throw up. I could see Jones-Demerest's house ahead. Two of it, in fact.

Lackeys ran to intercept me. I gathered what breath I could to shriek, "Jack! Jaaack!" My stomach churned. I tasted bile. Any second now, I'd hurl.

I dodged one lackey. Another, a tall, burly guy in a guard outfit, caught me. "Calm down, Lady Bainbridge. You've had a busy evening." He leered at me, so I punched him in the side.

"You little—" His grip tightened painfully.

I couldn't draw breath to shriek now if I had to. I shoved his jaw upward as hard as I could. There was a reason I shouldn't break his nose. I knew there was. Couldn't remember why.

"Take your bloody hands off my wife." Bainbridge's baritone cut through the chaos like a sword.

The lackeys stepped back as if electro-prodded.

I dropped to my knees. I couldn't help it. They'd turned to rubber.

Three of Bainbridge ran toward me. "Claire! Darling!"

In the path's overhead lighting, his face looked pale and furious. His arms closed around me in time to stop me crumpling on the gravel. Trembling, I burrowed into his warm, solid chest.

Safe. I was finally safe.

He might be arrogant and anal, but he was my partner. He'd take care of things. He'd have to, 'cause my world was spinning like a dryer tub. Before I could hurl, it spun me into oblivion.

CHAPTER TWENTY-ONE

I came slowly awake to the sound of pacing footsteps. Familiar. Bainbridge's. A faint scent of antiseptic tickled my nose. I opened my eyes.

Dim, yellow light came from somewhere near my feet. The world had stopped whirling, giving me a view of a low, beamed ceiling overhead. One ceiling, not several. Progress, but my gut felt as if it'd been pounded. Wincing, I slid one hand up under a soft, faded green blanket to rub the ache.

Bainbridge's footsteps sped up. He popped into my field of vision on the left, his face grave, and brushed my bangs out of my eyes. "How do you feel?"

"Like somebody's trampoline." My voice rasped, and I swallowed.

"Have some water." He reached to his right.

Turning my head let me see the carafe and tumbler on the dark wooden table by the bed. It also made my head throb like tympani.

"Ah-ah, not yet, I'm afraid," a deep, gravelly voice said from somewhere behind him. A thin, middle-aged man with a grave face and a narrow, graying mustache entered the room. The casual tone of his dark trousers, open-collared shirt and blue pullover also implied we weren't in a hospital.

With a reproachful glance at Bainbridge, he said, "You should have called me, Jack."

Bainbridge gave him a hard look but said nothing. Interesting. It'd be more so if my head stopped pounding.

The newcomer leaned over me to shine a penlight in my eye. I winced but managed to hold still.

"Hmm," he said. "I'm Dr. Solomon. How many of me are there?"

"One. Could you move the light?" He had it in my other eye now.

He clicked it off. "How many of Jack?"

"One," I said irritably. "Of course. Where are we?"

"No *of course* about it, I'm afraid. What do you remember?"

"Nothing." I shot a glance at Bainbridge, and the concern on his face surprised and warmed me.

I thought hard, and fragmented memories popped up. A frantic car ride. Me hurling on the roadside while—*oh crap!*—Bainbridge held my head. No wonder my stomach hurt. Stumbling on the walk to a low, stone cottage. Him scooping me up in his arms.

"Well, not much," I amended. Nothing I wanted to retain, though the carrying bit would've been nice in other circumstances.

"Claire," Bainbridge said, "this is Dr. Mordecai Solomon. We're in the surgery at the rear of his house. Outside Middleham. You can speak freely to him."

Mordecai and I nodded at each other. I let out a breath of relief. We weren't at Simply Yorkshire. Jack and I were safe, for now, and able to relax our guard. I told them about the encounter with Wrenthorpe, a name I doubted he truly owned.

Bainbridge hadn't said my full name. He'd given me partner status, though, not subordinate, and he stood by my shoulder like a guard dog. This little episode must've scared him.

I'd enjoy that idea more if I felt quasi-human. I tried to gather my thoughts. "Blood sample. We need—"

"Already taken one." Mordecai nodded at Bainbridge, who offered me the water glass.

"The cider must've been drugged," I said, ignoring him. "I should've had the sense to realize it sooner." Shit, hell and fuck all rolled into one. "How could I have been so stupid?"

I desperately needed to blow holes in something. Preferably with a rocket-propelled grenade. I'd often trained on launchers but used one only once in the field. I loved the very cathartic boom they made.

"None of that," Bainbridge said. "The whole point of a drug is to fog your thinking."

"The whole point of training is to resist it."

"As you did in time." He wrapped my fingers around the glass. "Or we wouldn't be here now. Let it go, and drink some water. You need fluids."

My hand shook, and he steadied it, his fingers warm and firm around mine. He slid an arm behind me to help me sit up. Though I could've managed alone, his closeness felt reassuring, so I leaned against him while I sipped.

A counter of dark wood ran along one wall, cabinets above it. A low, old-fashioned armchair occupied the corner opposite the bed. This wasn't really a surgery so much as an elevated care room.

"Any idea why you were drugged?" Bainbridge asked.

Remembering my weird reactions to Wrenthorpe's mauling, I grimaced. "Maybe, but I don't see what pawing me gains."

Bainbridge muttered something short and emphatic, and his fingers tightened almost imperceptibly around my hand. I heard and felt him take a slow, deep breath. The sudden tension in his jaw gave me an odd sense of comfort.

He let out the breath. "Your colleague," he said grimly, "has delivered a rather scathing after-action assessment."

Stunned, I stared at him across the glass. Petunia had ripped up at him? Or had she been pissed at me?

"Yes, well," Mordecai interrupted. "You may be interested to know, Miss Partner-of-Jack, your tests showed only an elevated alcohol content."

I pushed the glass away. "That's impossible. I was, emphatically, not drunk."

"Perhaps, but your labs claim otherwise." He held up a hand to stop the protest he must've seen in my face. With a glance at Bainbridge, he added, "Hard to trace, hard to stop."

A chill ran down my neck. "Great," I muttered.

Bainbridge kept his arm conveniently close to my back. "We drank the same wine at dinner," he said. "She took only a glass or two. Claire, do you recall what you had at the club room?"

"Cider. One half pint and a few sips of the second." I rubbed my throbbing forehead. It didn't help. "Something in the cider could've reacted with something in the wine."

"A compound," Bainbridge said slowly.

Nodding set off thunder behind my eyes. I winced.

"I'd suggest a date rape drug," Mordecai said slowly, "but that would show up in your blood. As for the nausea, that's probably from inexact dosage or a side effect of delivery via the cider."

Bainbridge directed a solemn, worried look at me. "Did he try to rape you?"

"He was headed that way," I said slowly. "What he did felt— irrationally good. In a sick, scary way." I closed my eyes, reaching for memory. It came, and they flew open. "I think there was someone else there. Watching. There was a flash."

"Like a camera's flash?" Jack's eyes locked on mine.

Oh, shit. "Exactly like," I said. "Unless I'm not remembering it right."

Anger flared in his eyes before they turned to slate. "Blackmail." He ground the word out. "You were attacked because of my family company."

If that made him take his family's plotting more seriously, it was worth it, but I hated the guilt forming in his eyes. I took his hand. "We don't know that."

"Perhaps you don't," he said. "The alternative is that our cover's blown, and we've been too careful for that."

"I'll leave you two to hash this out," Mordecai said. "Good night." He went through a door into what appeared to be an office, switched out the light, and exited through a door on the other side.

"Maybe Wrenthorpe is just a sleaze." Not that I thought for a second that was the answer.

I leaned into Bainbridge's sturdy shoulder, a vantage point that let me see shadows under his eyes and notice the stubble on his jaw. A wave of tenderness swamped my heart. "Attacks are an occupational hazard, Jack. I'm fine now."

"When you reached Jones-Demerest's house, I was leaving." He hesitated, his eyes grave. "I felt as though he were stalling, which made me concerned about you. I was coming to look for you."

"I'm glad you did." I'd had a much narrower escape than I'd realized. Suddenly cold, I twined my fingers through his warm, strong ones. "I guess we'll see if any pictures turn up."

He squeezed my hand. "From what you've said, I doubt there's anything scandalous, though I'd wager your bar bill shows a great deal more than two halves."

I glanced at the high window above the bed. Dark outside. "How long have I been here?"

"Since last night," he said grimly. "You should lie down again."

If I'd slept the clock around, that drug had packed a serious punch, but another thought intruded. "You stayed," I said, gently brushing a fingertip along his stubbled jaw.

Our eyes connected, his soft and tender, and my pulse sped up. I felt as though words hovered between us, but I couldn't put any on the strange emotions roiling in my chest.

His gaze suddenly shuttered. Before I had time to feel disappointed, he drew me closer and kissed my temple. The caress twisted my heart, though I didn't know why.

"Lie down and rest," he urged me, drawing away.

"I think better upright." Not exactly true, but I felt more in control. "We'll have serious explanations to make."

"Not difficult. There are many secluded spots where we might've stopped for a tryst."

His wry tone reassured me. He was doing what a partner should, picking up the ball when I couldn't quite hold it. I'd missed that feeling. I couldn't go there now, though, not in my shaky condition.

I braced myself. "What did Petunia say?"

That stony expression usually meant he was hiding his reactions, but his eyes darkened. "Rather a lot, the gist being 'A proper partner wouldn't have let that happen.' Nor should I have. I'm dreadfully sorry, Claire. I should have foreseen something like this."

"Planned for it, you mean." Looking as earnest as I could, I added, "You couldn't have. Not your fault, Jack."

"It's my job to anticipate." A muscle worked in his jaw.

I studied him. "I know we have a deal, but I have to ask. If a photographer was there, who wants the pictures? Your aunt and brother have thrown tabloids and internet scandal at us before."

"This is worse," he bit out. "And aimed at you alone."

Since he seemed pissed off on my behalf, rather than at me, which was a change where his family was concerned, I dared to ask, "Could they—or Sir Percival—be involved?"

He stared at me for long moments. Finally, he said, "I can't see them doing such a thing. Jones-Demerest might."

"And," I said slowly, remembering, "Wrenthorpe ran a tab at the bar, a resident privilege. And one of the lackeys at Jones-Demerest's house said I'd had a busy night. How would he know?"

"How, indeed?" Bainbridge's lips tightened.

I hated to ask, but I had to. "Did anyone in your family know we were going to dinner at Jasper's?"

Dismay shadowed his eyes, and lines of strain bit into his face, but he didn't flinch. "Percy." That single, curt word held a lot of pain. "Percy knew. But he wouldn't—surely not."

"Sir Percival worked at Bletchley Park during the war. Did he work for MI5 after that?"

Bainbridge hesitated. "I don't know."

"Does he know you work for them?"

"I didn't tell him."

Now I wasn't certain what to say, how to voice the certainty in my pounding head. Since Bainbridge had gone this far down the family issue road, maybe he'd go farther. "An old Cold War spy would gladly throw me, you, and pretty much anyone else to the wolves to protect his cover. That's how they survived."

"Yes."

At least he hadn't freaked, but he wasn't stupid. The thought must have occurred to him. Sometimes, though, we don't like hearing someone else voice thoughts that trouble us.

An awkward silence fell. I wanted to burrow into his shoulder, but that wasn't a good idea for a lot of reasons. "My head's drumming again," I announced. I shooed him off the bed and lay back.

"Go to sleep," he said. "Mordecai's home has the latest security, not that we'll need it. We can decide what to do in the morning."

"What about you?"

"I'll take the chair." He smiled. "It served well enough last night."

Now that he mentioned it, he didn't look as if he'd slept much lately. I didn't argue, though. I pulled the blanket up, and he turned out the light.

He stood by the bed, in the dark. So gently that the gesture brought tears to my eyes, he brushed my hair off my brow. "I'm glad you're all right," he said quietly.

"Me, too. Thanks. For everything."

He stepped away, a shadowy form in the faint moonlight the window admitted. A few seconds later, the chair cushions *shushed* under his weight.

I closed my eyes and tried to sleep. Irrationally, I missed having him next to me. He was a good partner. Or could be, if he remained willing to be less rigid. He didn't deserve to have his uncle betray him. I didn't want to believe Sir Percival would be involved in causing a flu pandemic, but stranger things had happened.

#

After a detour by the manor for a change of clothes, we drove back to the Simply Yorkshire community around noon. While Bainbridge went to have a word with Jones-Demerest about the attack on me, I met Hilda in the gym. If I could learn who else had ties to Jasper, maybe I could get my mind off last night's stupidity. Bainbridge could be as nice about it as he liked, but damn! I should have known.

Hilda applied herself with a will. As she finished her twenty-fifth triceps extension—okay, with a two-kilogram weight, less than five pounds, and a couple of breaks, but that's good for a sixty-plus former couch potato—I smiled at her. "That's great, Hilda. Really."

"Thank you, Claire." Her smile flickered, then vanished. She wiped sweat from her face carefully.

"You don't seem real pleased." Should I push? I had to if I wanted to know the cause.

"I'm fine, dear. Oh—I beg pardon, Claire."

"*Dear* is fine." I smiled at her. "Ready to start the shoulders again?"

"I think...I believe I'd best see to Horace's tea." She hesitated. "He tends to forget it, you see."

"He doesn't like tea?" I grabbed the weights to put them back in the rack.

Her lip trembled.

I straightened. "Hilda? What is it?"

"Nothing, it's—I don't think he's happy here."

"Why not?" I set the weights down so I could hand her a water bottle. Sometimes people talk more if they have something to do, to distract them from what they're saying.

Looking uncertain, she uncapped the bottle and sipped. She lowered it slowly. "It's...I suppose he misses his work." Her sigh threatened to break my heart. "We worked so long, so we could have a bit of time for ourselves. We've earned it, you see."

"You don't have to explain, Hilda. I know from hard work."

"I suppose you do, dear." She shrugged into her warmup jacket. "I don't know what to do for him. On top of that, we're all so worried about friends and relatives in London and other stricken areas."

"I know," I said softly. "We can't do anything about that, but maybe we can figure out something for Horace. Some people have to learn to relax. Work becomes a habit." I stowed the weights. When I turned from the rack, she stood where I'd left her, frowning.

"Dear Jasper has been very helpful, of course, and Horace seemed to enjoy tramping about the hills. At first."

"How's Jasper helping?" I summoned my best Curious Innocent expression, eyes wide and face blank.

"Oh, he's quite concerned." Another shrug. "He makes staying in touch with the company as easy as one could ask."

"Maybe that's the problem." I watched her sidelong as I packed up my gear. "Maybe Horace isn't far enough away from the office to let it go. I had to leave my business completely. Referred out my clients when I moved here, but I've been restless, kinda. Y'know?"

"It's your honeymoon, dear."

"Oh, Bainsiekins is great." I blew out a moonstruck sigh. "He's the best. I'm just...not used to havin' nothing to do, now that I've done it a while." I wrinkled my nose. "And his friends are not so nuts about me."

"I'm so sorry." She patted my arm. "I know what that's like, feeling out of place. But they'll change their minds once they know you, Claire. You're quite sweet." She hesitated, then blurted, "I don't care what that nasty paper insinuated."

My gut clenched anew. "Paper?"

The one with the paddock picture, please. The one Aunt Busybody'd shown me. Please, *please.*

Bristling with righteous indignation, Hilda said, "The woman in that photo, in that man's arms, didn't even look like you. And anyone with eyes can see that you and Jack adore each other. The very idea that you'd

—you'd—"

"I wouldn't," I assured her around a sick feeling. Stupid, stupid, stupid, I'd been incredibly stupid. At least we'd maintained our roles effectively until now, and the little voice that wanted to do handsprings about the mutual admiration bit needed to remember that it was truly part of our roles.

"Thanks, Hilda. Thanks a lot. You ready?"

We grabbed our gear. Hilda still looked unhappy. Over Horace? Or was she concerned over rumors about me?

"Countess" or not, I grabbed the door for her. I figured it was in character.

She sighed. "I thought it would help, knowing so many other couples here. Jasper has introduced us to everyone he knows, but Horace doesn't seem interested."

She and Horace had told us earlier about the rat-bastard's connections to some of his guests. Quite a few, in fact. My old idea surged forth. If I didn't pursue it quickly, the moment would pass. Bainbridge would just have to understand.

"You know, Hilda, we could do a workout class. If the women all became involved together, the men would have to rely on each other. Maybe push Horace into making friends."

She looked doubtful but didn't shake her head.

"You could make more friends, too," I pressed. "There's nothing like shared aches for bonding." Which would, in turn, earn confidences for me.

We walked down the gravel path from the gym. A group of people played croquet in the field to our left. In the distance, a man and woman strode down the hill, obviously accomplished roamers of the countryside. No one else was around. The golfers were probably at the nearby course.

This lifestyle might seem simple to some of these people, but I'd bet it didn't to Hilda, any more than it did to me.

"It's worth a try," she said with sudden decisiveness. "Such a class would do us all good, I imagine."

"Great. I'll talk to Jasper."

I beamed at her, but I was far from happy. Jasper would agree to anything that won me to his side about Hawkshead, and even Bainbridge had admitted the idea had merit, but despite the happy face I'd put on for

Hilda, my latest publicity couldn't help any aspect of this situation.

#

Bainbridge and I decided to ignore the nasty publicity. Doing anything else would only give it more currency.

Besides, we had more important concerns, like trying out our new card key. Unfortunately, there were guards on duty, and the lab was occupied. Despite my black leathers, the chill night air gave me goose bumps. Yorkshire might boast temperate June days, but its nights resembled those of Hartner Falls in November.

After three hours of crouching in the shrubbery, Bainbridge softly said, "It'll be light soon. I'm going for a look."

"That's right, have all the fun," I muttered, hitting the jammer as he broke cover and ran for the building. Since looking didn't require us both, I'd watch his back.

His back, not the play of moonlight on black denim covering a very nicely sculpted butt. Forcing myself to focus, I scanned the moonlit grounds. Nothing moved.

Meanwhile, Bainbridge crouched beneath a side window. He extended a snakescope with quick competence and eased it toward the window sill. I'm a sucker for competence. Pair it with confidence, and I'm in trouble. Lucky for me, arrogance like Bainbridge's gives me a safety valve.

Minute turns of his hand told me he was swiveling the little scope, taking a good look inside. He eased the scope down again, collapsed it with that same deft speed, and dashed back to me in under ninety seconds.

Wind rustled the tree limbs, and moonlight coming through them cast a flickering silver pattern on his face. The resulting lines and craggy shadows made my heart do a quick skip-hop. I told it to behave. His looks mattered way less than his attitude.

With his lips close to my ear, his breath flickered over it, generating bubbly, unwelcome heat deep within me and making me too damned aware of his broad shoulders and muscular body so close.

As I told my hormones to stuff themselves, he spoke softly. "Front room's a security office with monitors. There're two guards in the office, as Simon predicted, and a man in the lab. We'll try another night." He stepped clear of the bushes, then offered me a hand.

I took it reluctantly, and he drew me close. Our cover story, as usual, called for us to pretend we'd been out having steamy sex under the stars if we met anyone.

Despite the little hop in my pulse and the rush of warmth through my body, this wasn't personal, and I suddenly, sharply regretted that it wasn't. It couldn't be. We'd kill each other in no time. Still, when he put his arm around me, I stuck my hand in his back pocket.

As we walked, his firm butt muscles moved under my palm. Corresponding ripples of heat rolled through me. I set my jaw and withdrew my hand. When this was over, I really had to get a life.

"It's good that we didn't set a fire," he said, grim-faced. "On the security monitors, I saw signs posted outside the lab door. That room is spark-free."

"So we could've blown up everything we're hoping to find." Great. Just great.

"It looks as though sleeping gas in the air conditioning unit is our best chance," he commented. "We need to search those computers soon. They may hold information key to fighting the pandemic."

"We have the gas. Now all we need is a night with only one guard."

"True," he conceded, "but I'd rather go when the place is empty if we can manage it. Though Simon reports that as rare, it would eliminate having to worry about the guard waking up too soon."

We walked a few steps in silence. I looked around at all the very elegant cottages. The people in them depended on Jasper's good will more than they knew.

"I can't believe Jasper wasn't more solicitous," I murmured, wanting to think of anything other than Bainbridge's body. "A guest being assaulted is terrible publicity."

Jones-Demerest had tut-tutted and produced a bar bill showing I'd had four sherries. He'd also claimed Wrenthorpe was a stranger who'd slipped in and out unnoticed, that letting him run a tab was a mistake by the bartender.

"We expected as much," Bainbridge reminded me.

"That doesn't make it any better." I kicked the grass edging the walk. "Crap. I can't believe I fell for that."

"Stop it." He halted and turned me to face him. His gaze level, he said, "Playing along made sense. You had no way to know that drug would hit you so hard, so suddenly. You realized something was wrong and fought him off. That's what matters. Only that."

His mouth quirked up at one corner as he brushed a lock of hair off my face. "You saved me from having to fight a duel over your honor."

"I guess that's some comfort," I said dryly, though the words gave me a silly rush of pleasure. I wasn't the kind of woman men fought for and had never wanted to be, but he made me feel, for an intoxicating moment, as though I were.

His gaze sharpened. "Don't think I wouldn't."

After a moment, compelled by the honesty, and maybe even tenderness, in his eyes, I nodded. This giddiness must've been normal to Cleopatra, but I couldn't afford to let it carry me away.

I'd been there, done that with a guy from the social elite, and I'd fit in about as well as overalls at a presidential inaugural ball. Even so, the breakup had been painful for us both.

To lighten the moment, I cocked an eyebrow at my partner. "I've seen you with a pistol. What if your opponent chose swords?"

"With either, I win." He spoke with breezy confidence, and I had to squelch the desire to see him in action.

I let him tuck me against his side, but I so did not need the breathtaking image of him wielding a sword. I was in enough trouble already.

We reached our cottage without incident and stowed our gear in its secret drawers. He wandered back into the living area. After shrugging into a short, green silk robe, the most decent one the wardrobe crew had provided, I stuck my head in there. "I'll flip you for the shower."

"That's all right. After you." He stared, frowning, at his cell phone. "Robin called."

"I guess you have to call him back." And let him blather on about the investment deal again.

Still very uncomfortable in a frustrated, hormonal way, I stalked toward the bathroom. Faint tones sounded behind me as Bainbridge cued voice mail.

In the doorway, I glanced back. He stood still, staring at his phone as though he'd never seen it before. His face had gone grim and ashen.

We had trouble, then. "What is it?"

No answer.

I padded back to him. "Jack, what's wrong?"

At last he glanced at me. His stricken eyes stabbed me to the heart, and I put a hand on his arm.

"Aunt Beatrice," he said numbly, as if in disbelief. "She has the flu."

CHAPTER TWENTY-TWO

"Your aunt?" It didn't seem possible, even to me, that something as measly as a virus could fell her.

He nodded, his gaze unfocused again. Numbly, he said, "Robin says she's in hospital, under quarantine. There are rather many outbreaks in London. And across the South. Severe cases. This likely means the National Health Service will upgrade to high impact."

"We're doing what we can about that." I still didn't see why he was so devastated. She was meddling and outright mean.

Regardless, he was upset, and I, as his partner, had to pull him together. Concern for him gave me sincerity when I said, "I'm sorry she's ill."

From a tactical standpoint, this was probably a good thing. She couldn't meddle with Hawkshead Shipping. Still, I'd rather gain my tactical advantages without having innocent people, however annoying, face death for them. Bainbridge had to know as well as I did that any strand of flu hits the elderly hardest. They're the first to fall ill and the most likely to die, often from complications like pneumonia.

"Sit down." I tugged him onto the sofa, more to have something to do than because I thought he'd notice. "I'll put the kettle on." Tea, the great English restorative, should help if anything would.

Starting the kettle and setting out mugs took only a few moments. When I finished, he still sat there, blind. "Should be ready in a bit," I said.

"Ta." He answered me absently.

I could try to snap him out of it, bring his mind back to work, or I could go with the flow. Considering that he was usually Lord Control

Freak but had lost focus altogether, the flow seemed dominant.

I sat down next to him and laid my hand over his larger, calloused one. "What are you thinking?"

His hand turned over to grip mine. "It's only...She was always there. Whenever we needed her."

"You mean, helping out? Around the...uh, house?" However unlikely that image felt to me and however little that mansion seemed like a home where one middle-aged woman could make a difference.

"Mum wasn't well." Old pain darkened his eyes, and I felt guilty for causing it, as if I'd stepped into a room I wasn't supposed to enter. "Dad was often gone. With her. Robin and I..." His voice trailed into silence.

Just when I thought I'd have to prod him, he added, "Aunt Beatrice was always there."

"That must have been difficult for all of you."

"We coped, but it would've been a good bit harder without her. Riding competitions—like that Middleham meet, you noticed the photo in my bedroom—school programs. To have no one there...one feels neglected. Despite understanding why."

"But you had her." The image still felt out of focus, unlikely. Other pieces were falling into place, though. No wonder he'd put up with so much from her.

"She even came to Eton to see us, took us out on days that was allowed." He exhaled, a heavy sound laden with pain. "Set her own life aside."

For the first time, he looked at me. Despair shadowed his eyes, and his hand tightened on mine. "She had such hopes for me."

Only to see him become, as far as most people knew, an idler and a wastrel and a dilettante. "Despite your best efforts, I think she believes in you."

"She has no reason to." His head dropped back against the high cushions.

"She thinks the right wife would do wonders for you if that's any consolation." She hadn't used those words, but her actions implied as much.

The shadows in his eyes lightened for a moment before he shook his head. "She wants me to go into the House of Lords, perhaps even stand for the Commons, marry well, and live as she thinks my father should've. The life her father lived or, even better, the life her grandfather had. He owned thirty thousand acres."

"Wow." I couldn't imagine figuring out what to do with that much land.

"Quite so. Until the land transfer tax and the estate taxes diminished the power of the nobility." He glanced at me with a wry expression that didn't relieve the gloom in his eyes. "Aunt Beatrice believes in the traditions, privileges, and responsibilities of noble birth."

"I'm guessing you don't." At least he was talking in comprehensible sentences.

"The responsibilities," he said wearily. "Taking the tremendous advantages I've been given and using them for something bigger. Only that justifies having them when so many other people struggle. The imbalance never seemed right to me—privilege and traditions that're all hollow but are used to justify living in ease while others can't, making mistakes or reckless choices that hurt others and never—" His lips tightened, stopping the cascading words.

Birth and privilege certainly hadn't done his mother much good. And it sounded as though they were a burden to him. Was that what had sent him out to risk his neck time and again, a need to justify his privileged upbringing? Was this why he was a control freak?

I wanted to tell him he'd more than proved himself, that his family wasn't worth the dragging weight they placed on his shoulders, but with his face lined with worry over his aunt, that'd be like shouting into a hurricane.

He stared at the ceiling again. If not for his death grip on my hand, I would've felt dismissed.

I laced my fingers through his and laid my head on his shoulder. No wonder he seemed so rocked. His domineering aunt had been his surrogate mother—a good one, in his view. Now, thanks to her age, she well might die, and he couldn't even go see her. With the quarantine, not even an MI5 credential would allow him into her hospital room.

He also had a mission to complete. Responsibilities and all that.

The kettle clicked off. As I stood, he released my hand.

I watched him covertly as I poured the hot water over the tea ball and into the pot. He stood, ran a hand through his hair, and paced to the window. The rising sun sent a shaft of reddish light into the room, giving the blues, reds, and golds in the Axminster rug sudden brilliance. He didn't seem to notice, just stared out at the dawn.

Since he seemed to be focusing, I left him alone while the tea steeped. I had a feeling our little moment of sharing was over. Besides, I had concerns of my own. The Atlantic Ocean might separate home from the current sources of contagion, but that wouldn't last forever, especially if Jones-Demerest's tentacles latched onto transport companies.

I drew the tea ball out of the pot. "How do you take it?"

He crossed the room with slow, even strides. "I'll fix it, thanks."

His shoulders still looked taut, but his face had lost its haunted look. He'd put his personal issues into their own tightly locked slot for now.

I handed him the cup. "Careful."

"I know. It's hot." He threw me a wry look and reached for the sugar. Spooning some into his tea, he abruptly said, "Teach your exercise class. We need everything we can use. But don't quit purchasing."

If only he'd agreed because I'd suggested it instead of because of his aunt, but I'd take the victory. "By the way," I asked casually, "who holds your aunt's proxies for the Hawkshead Shipping board?"

"Percy." The clipped, curt tone said he shared my concern over that answer.

"And Percy's on Robin's side?"

"That, as Hamlet would say, is the question. We'll see what we can get out of Percy over tea tomorrow."

#

Percy arrived punctually at four. In honor of his visit, I'd gone a little less tarty by topping my low-riders with a snug t-shirt decorated in a bright, abstract print. This was our chance to see where he stood. I didn't want my clothes to distract or offend him.

He walked slowly into the parlor area, glancing about him. His slight nods here and there might have meant he recognized the furniture, or they might have signified approval.

Or they might have been signs of senility, though that seemed unlikely.

Bainbridge draped an arm around my shoulders. "Darling, this is my great-uncle, Sir Percival Basingstoke. Uncle Percy, my wife, Claire."

"Pleased to meet you, Lady Bainbridge." Percy twinkled and bowed over my hand. He appeared to be more relaxed than Lady Beatrice. Was he really, or was the amiable gentleman an act, right down to his brown tweed jacket?

"Call me Claire." I beamed at him.

"Please sit, Uncle Percy." Bainbridge ushered him to the massive armchair.

Percy sank into it with a small sigh. "This is quite nice. Quite nice. I like these old pieces, you know."

If he'd said *they don't make 'em like they used to,* I would've been hard pressed not to gag. Thank goodness he didn't.

"I'll get the tea." I hurried over to the kitchen.

"Have you any word on Beatrice?" Percy asked.

"Not today," Bainbridge said.

Relying on Petunia's advice, I'd assembled a creditable tea layout on a silver tray. Delicate bone china cups and saucers, matching teapot, sugar bowl, cream pitcher, and silver spoons completed the set, with Irish linen napkins.

"Dreadful business, dreadful," Sir Percival said.

A heavy silence fell. Maybe the little cucumber and watercress sandwiches, minus crusts because I'd read they were supposed to be, lemon bars, and ginger cookies spiraling around the Waterford crystal plate on my tray would introduce a lighter note. Unfortunately, I did not have the traditional tiered cake stand on hand.

The business of fixing tea took a few minutes. When we'd all settled in, Bainbridge directed an earnest look at Sir Percy.

"I didn't ask you here only to meet Claire," Bainbridge said. "I'd like to hear what you have to say about this investment deal Robin's so keen to bring about. I thought you opposed it, but Robin says not."

"Ah, Jones-Demerest's offer." Sir Percy's blue eyes looked bland above the rim of his teacup. "My opinion is fluid."

Fluid. Like for sale?

"So you're for it? How come?" I leaned forward to pass the plate. "Have a sandwich." Ignoring Bainbridge's hard look, I did Clueless Babe for Sir Percy.

"I see its advantages." Another bland look, this time across the sandwich plate as he chose a cucumber one.

Around a mouthful of watercress, I asked, "Like?"

"Shared risk, primarily." Percy's blandness gave way to an annoyed frown. "Robin has all the details, you know."

"Claire was asking what you think, Percy. You ran the company for fifty years."

"Yes, and I'm glad to have retired. Robin manages the business nicely. In my view, that earns him the primary opinion."

"As he intends to argue," Bainbridge said flatly, his eyes narrowing, "at the shareholders meeting next week."

I frowned at him. He hadn't mentioned that to me.

Percy shook his head. "Can't be helped. Now I really must go. I've an appointment in York to see about purchasing a sixteenth-century edition of *The Canterbury Tales*."

"You haven't said whether you're for this deal or not," I said. "Jack's the head of the family. He's got a right to know."

Rising, Percy sighed. "I haven't decided, but I'm inclined toward it." He smiled. "At least for today."

He now voted his own shares as well as Beatrice's. According to Petunia's research, the subject of the vote, whether Bainbridge was arbitrary or capricious, automatically limited Bainbridge's votes to forty-nine percent. He needed one other shareholder to carry the day.

"Jones-Demerest is a corporate raider," Bainbridge said, his face hard. The shadow in the depths of his eyes might've been the pain of disappointment as he continued, "He builds businesses, but he also tears them down."

Percy stood. "I'm sure you can inject some safeguards. Thank you for tea, Jack, Claire. A pleasure."

We said our goodbyes. Bainbridge walked him to the door. We were no better off than we had been. If Percy was MI5, years and years ago, he'd lost whatever compunction he might've had about dealing with the enemy.

"Maybe he doesn't know what Jones-Demerest truly is," I said as Bainbridge shut the door.

"He can't be told." Bainbridge stalked back into the room. "No one can unless we prove our case."

"There has to be a way. But I'm late for work in purchasing." I'd planned my shift for today to give Bainbridge and his uncle a chance to talk privately. That plan was now busted. I'd have to hope my next idea worked out better. Whatever it was.

#

Expecting to waste a great deal of time being tortured by heavy metal, I bopped into the accounts office, smartphone clipped to my belt and buds in my ears. The obliging Susan put me to work.

I sat at my keyboard, thinking. If only there were some way to get a look at her machine. I could see spreadsheets coming up from time to time, ones I knew weren't on my desktop.

The Rioting Gazelles screeched in my ear about love and sex and loss, all to an acid, metallic beat. A girl group from Liverpool, they had, I thought, a lot of enthusiasm and marginal talent. They made for good cover, though. I'd chosen them today for consistency's sake.

Susan's phone rang. I tuned out the gazelles to eavesdrop.

"Yes," she said. "Yes, of course I'll check that for you, madam."

Keys clicked behind me, barely audible over my music. What with the worried conversation at meals yesterday about the London outbreak, fears of a general quarantine here, and concern for friends and relatives in general, I'd bet serious money that she and the other staffers had a lot of phone calls to handle these days.

"Yes, madam." She paused. "No, that's correct. Yes, I'm quite certain." A longer pause ensued.

I sneaked a peek.

Her tense shoulders belied her cool tones. "Yes, madam...Of course...Certainly." She hung up with a little more force than necessary.

I pretended not to see her approach my desk. For good measure, I bounced in my seat in time to the music, which she couldn't miss hearing at this range, earbuds or no earbuds.

"Lady Bainbridge."

I bopped faster.

"Lady Bainbridge." She tried again, louder.

I looked up at her. "Oh. Wait a sec." I tugged out the left earbud. "Did you need something?"

"I must go and see about a guest." She hesitated.

I couldn't let her kick me out. Her absence could provide a unique opportunity. "No problem. I'll be done in a few."

"Well...if you'll just shut the door when you leave."

"Sure. No problem." As soon as she turned away, I hit a quick key combination, chose what would seem to be a heavy metal track on the smartphone, and triggered its drive killer signal. My screen went dark.

"What?" I yelped. "Wait! No! Oh, shit!"

Susan spun back to me. "Lady Bainbridge?"

"Look," I wailed. "It's dead. Freakin' dead."

"Oh, dear. I'll have someone from tech support come and see about it. I'm afraid—"

"I was almost done, too! Shit, and Honeykins was so proud of me for being efficient! Isn't there some way I can finish? It won't take me long."

"Well, no, I'm afraid."

"I could wait for tech support. I thought this stuff was important." I scowled at her. "Or is it just make-work crap?"

She bit her lip. "Well, I suppose tech support will be here soon. I'll ring them before I go."

"Whatever, just so I can finish." I replaced my earbud and resumed bopping.

She hung up the phone. "They'll be here soon," she shouted at me. "I'll just be going."

"Yeah. Sweet." I waved to her.

She looked dubious but gathered a couple of files and a laptop. A wave to me, and she departed.

As soon as the door shut behind her, I jumped over to her chair. Tech support might, indeed, come quickly. I didn't have much time.

CHAPTER TWENTY-THREE

I pulled a thumb drive out my bag and jacked it into Susan's machine. "I Need You" by Alex and the Artists wailed from the speakers. I grabbed the phone and punched in the extension for our cottage. *Come on, come on,* I urged Bainbridge. He'd better be there.

On the third ring, he answered.

"No time to explain." I tapped in the combination to recapture, then enter, Susan's password. "You have a computer emergency, and you need tech support right now."

Silence filled the line for a beat. "Claire, what—"

"Gotta go." I was in.

I banged down the phone, then tapped the key combination to search for financial info. *Please let there be just one techie on duty at a time. Please, please. And please let Bainbridge just cooperate.*

If anyone came in, I could blank the screen, so it'd look as if I'd just been trying to play a music track, but I'd still have to scramble to explain.

Minutes ticked by. Alex and his pals screamed in a major key, not the minor strains that would signal completion of the drive search. Footsteps crunched on the gravel outside, faint but coming nearer. Shit. The program was still searching.

Where the hell was—

"Hello," Bainbridge's voice called. "Any chance you're tech support?"

The affirmative answer came from just outside the door. I held my breath.

"No wonder I missed you," Bainbridge said, nearer now. "My drive is frozen, and I can't seem to fix it. Have you a moment?"

"I'm due on a call here," a gruff, male voice said.

"I'm stuck until it goes back up," Bainbridge replied. "I was just coming to fetch my wife."

To run an intercept. Two points to his lordship for going with my brainstorm.

"Well...I can have a look, I suppose."

The footsteps moved away. I breathed. Bainbridge had bought me time. Saved my ass, maybe. Unless he wanted it for my deviation from his precious plan. This had better pay off.

#

An hour later, after watching the computer guy pronounce the first machine I'd used dead, I strolled back to the bungalow. Closing the door behind me left me with neither relief nor sanctuary. Bainbridge would be pissed over my improvisation.

He lounged on the sofa, a pot of tea in front of him and his laptop on the table. "Well?"

"Let's see." No explosion yet. Good. I pulled the thumb drive out of my bag and slid it into his computer's port.

The loading bar appeared on the screen. When it reached 100 percent, a password box replaced it.

Bainbridge tapped in the code.

A selection of spreadsheets appeared on the desktop. We sat down to go through them.

Half an hour later, I frowned at the screen. "Jones-Demerest has quite a few holding companies. More than my report said."

"Mine as well. He may not own them all, just shares in them." He frowned down at the page. "Including this one, the Camlann Fund."

"What about it?"

"Robin owns it." Bainbridge spoke slowly, as though dragging the words out of his mouth. "He uses it for his own investments. Bloody hell, how deeply is he into this thing?"

"Maybe not too badly." At least Bainbridge finally seemed to care. Maybe Percy's defection was waking him up to the danger his family faced. "He may have sold Jones-Demerest a piece of his company to sweeten the pot with Hawkshead Shipping. You know, a gesture of trust to make up for your stubbornness."

"Miss McIntosh can research this further." He scowled.

"She's fast. Should have news by tomorrow." I eyed him warily. "By the way, that was quick thinking, intercepting tech support. Thanks."

"You gave me little enough to go on." He cocked an eyebrow at me. "Good thing I studied at Cambridge."

"Right." His light, joking tone signaled acceptance. I should let it go, drop it while I was ahead. I couldn't resist going further, though, like a kid picking at a scab. "You're not unhappy I improvised?"

He raised an eyebrow. "Why do you think I wanted you to keep going back? I hoped such a chance might arise."

"It's in your plan?" I gave him my best skeptical look.

"Of course." He reached for the computer. "So was the exercise class, though farther down the list. Would you care to see it?"

"I'll take your word for it." If I looked at that plan of his, with all its purported branches, my brain might go *tilt*.

"Let's call Miss McIntosh, then, and start her working. The overwatch team confirms that Jones-Demerest usually stays in the club room as long as it's open. That gives us time to search his house. Meanwhile, I'd best have a word with my brother."

I didn't envy him that job. I picked up my phone to call Petunia. Still, that plan of his nagged at me. "You've plotted out every contingency?"

"Tried to." Staring at the screen, he tapped keys on his laptop.

"What's the ultimate one, the all-else-has-failed scenario?"

His hands stilled. Looking up at me, he said, "Fall on the grenade and save the cause. Let's hope it won't come to that."

#

Bainbridge and I circled Jones-Demerest's house. A wide expanse of yard separated it from the nearest landscaping. We crouched in the shadow of a big tree. Just in case we met anyone out late, I'd chosen dark jeans and a black sweater, matching Bainbridge's usual garb, instead of leathers.

A cool wind blew over the countryside. Moonlight cast ghostly shadows under the trees and along the uneven ground. I didn't consider nine thirty p.m. late, but no one else was stirring. No one but Jones-Demerest had a reason to come this way. We hoped.

If we waited until the club room closed, he might return before we had a chance to make our search. He'd kept a file on bioweapons research in his desk in Italy. Maybe he had one here somewhere. With people dying faster every day all over Europe, we couldn't overlook any possibility.

Finding something here that could lead us to concrete evidence of criminal wrongdoing would let us proceed without searching the problematic lab first. Since I didn't work for the British government, I could serve as a confidential informant—shaky, but it would hold—and send a tip that would lead to a search warrant. If we found the good stuff, of course.

We could then move in with a team, lock the compound down, and search it at our leisure. Surely he had a hidey-hole in his house. He wasn't the type to keep incriminating info where other people had access to it.

Bainbridge pulled a thermal scanner out of his jacket. Even through walls, it would register the body heat of anyone inside the house. He clicked it on, the switch soundless, to check the front of the house.

I peered over his shoulder at the ghostly view of room outlines. No warm bodies appeared.

We hurried across the open, grassy expanse of lawn, now silvery in the moonlight, to the rear door. Bainbridge checked the scanner. Again, nothing. He pocketed it silently.

I stuck an alarm dampener on the door. Even though our information said the house had no alarm, we weren't taking chances.

Bainbridge picked the lock. Once it clicked, we pulled on black leather gloves. I opened the door a couple of inches, slid one hand inside, and did a quick sweep with my own pocket scanner. No alarm sensors. No vibration consistent with a silent alarm.

Quietly, I stepped inside. Bainbridge followed, closing the door behind him. He hurried toward the stairs, as we'd planned, while I started for the kitchen. He'd look upstairs, I'd look down, and we'd meet on the ground floor. Despite our personality differences, I felt as though we were in sync when we were working, as David and I had been. I'd missed that feeling.

I had my hand on the knob of the cellar door when a faint sound came from beyond it. Voices. A television. Oh, hell!

Muffling my steps as best I could, I hurried back to the hall. "Psst," I hissed up the stairs. "Hey."

Bainbridge appeared at the top of the stairs, a ghostly shape in the gloom.

"Toss me the scanner," I whispered.

He pitched it down without question. I held up a hand, indicating he should wait, and stepped back to the kitchen doorway. From there, I could aim the scanner at the basement.

Where it registered a reclining human form.

Hell's bells. Someone was home, someone the scanner hadn't picked up before because he was below ground level.

I sped back to Bainbridge. "One downstairs," I whispered.

Moonlight coming in the windows upstairs showed me the faint outline of his scowl. "I'll hurry," he said softly. "Keep watch."

He must consider half a search better than none. I agreed. I aimed the scanner at the kitchen floor and waited.

Minutes dragged by. My eyes started playing their usual tricks on me. When I stare at anything electronic for a long time, the colors go funny. I had to blink periodically to keep my eyes clear.

The figure downstairs moved off the bed. I tensed. Was he coming up?

He moved toward the stairs. If we'd alerted him, though, surely he'd have come up sooner. I eased myself backward, creeping toward the main stairs. The guy probably just wanted a drink. Silently, I shifted my weight onto the bottom step.

I tilted my face upward. "Psst!"

Two heartbeats, and Bainbridge appeared at the top of the steps. Climbing quietly, I shifted the scanner so he could see it and pantomimed drinking, the goal I guessed the guy had in mind.

Calm but alert, Bainbridge's eyes met mine in the faint light. After a brief, agonizing moment, he nodded. We'd wait it out. I shifted silently upward in case I needed to join him.

Just as my scanner showed the figure at the top of the stairs, the basement door creaked open. Footsteps crossed the linoleum. The faint *kthwlp* sound of a refrigerator door opening heralded a beam of light across the kitchen floor.

Glass clinked. The light narrowed. A moment later, the door closed. Again, footsteps crossed the linoleum—going toward the basement, according to the scanner. The basement door shut, and the figure descended out of sight.

Only then did I realize I'd been holding my breath.

Bainbridge tapped me on the shoulder. His hand moved past my face, pointing toward the door. I nodded hastily, and we beat a quick retreat.

Once we'd reached the safety of the yard, we circled toward the club room. He reached out for my hand, as per our cover story. We twined our fingers together. Warmth stroked my heart, but I tried to ignore it.

"Anything?" I asked softly.

"Appointment diary. He's meeting the Home Secretary on Tuesday. Nothing else." In the moonlight, Bainbridge frowned.

"The meeting could be about anything," I said slowly, thinking.

"Or something very big. Perhaps he's about to develop a cure."

"There's an idea." I paused, then shook my head. "Doesn't feel right, but maybe he has a vaccine, maybe something for early treatment, something that would make carriers quicker to volunteer. Why unleash a disease that could take you down, too?"

"He could also have something worse ready to unleash," Bainbridge said grimly. "We're running out of time. If we can't search the house in the next few days, we'll have to find a way into the lab."

Risking everything if we didn't find the proof we needed. "We have a few days," I said. But he was right. That interval was all we could afford to give ourselves.

#

The next afternoon, my workout class threw themselves into the drill, maybe trying to forget their worries over friends in afflicted areas. The mood in the whole compound was down because of such concerns.

I ended the class on a sort of endorphin boost, myself. I hadn't done a measured, orderly lifting sequence in a while. Since everyone seemed to be in a good mood, maybe I could take advantage.

We put our gear away and walked out together. "Anyone want to stop by the club for an energy drink?" I asked.

"We're not very presentable." Hilda looked doubtful.

A blonde whose husband ran a computer telecom operation nodded agreement. So did several others.

"It won't be busy this time of day." I shrugged. "Guys walk around however they like." Not strictly true about CEOs, but I'm willing to stretch. "Why shouldn't we?"

Hilda nodded. "I'll join you, Claire."

The chunky, blonde—Janet, I thought—fell in with us. We wandered into the club room and headed for the bar.

Seated halfway down the room, Bainbridge and his brother scowled at each other across glasses of what looked to be whisky, neat. Neither of them looked my way. Why had Robin come?

My pals and I ordered smoothies with protein supplements. I'd have preferred water, but we didn't need the club or each other for that.

As the bartender departed, I turned to Janet. "So how long have you been in the phone business?"

"Roger's spent our whole marriage, thirty years or so, at it. He designed a mobile receiver, digital when everything was analog." Pride shone in her smile. "From that, he built the company."

"Sweet." I nodded.

The waiter set smoothies in front of us. I stirred mine and angled my head to sneak a peek at Bainbridge. Judging by his glower, things weren't going well.

The bartender retreated a discreet distance. Although he wiped and racked glasses with a distracted expression on his face, I couldn't help wondering how much he generally overheard. His job could make him a valuable set of ears.

"Do you know the difference, Janet?" Hilda frowned slightly. "Digital or analog, that is? Terms like that confuse me dreadfully."

"No." Janet chuckled, shaking her head. "I know digital has a clearer signal. Of course, miniaturization of electronics has helped business. That, I do understand."

"I bet you know all about trucks, Hilda," I said.

"I know more about routes," she said. "I planned them all. Horace says I'm his detail person. His memory, if you will."

Janet sighed. "That's wonderful. I wish I understood that much about what Roger does."

"Oh." Hilda looked down the room. "Isn't that your husband, Claire?"

"Yeah. And his brother." Grateful for an excuse to watch, I swiveled farther on my stool. "I didn't know Robin was coming today." I shook my head. "He and Bainsiekins are butting heads over some business deal. Something to do with Jasper. It sounds good to me, but what do I know?"

Bainbridge set his glass down with a snap. He stalked toward the door. Robin followed. Considering the thunderstorm expressions they wore, I half expected ozone to crackle as they passed.

"He doesn't look happy." Janet demonstrated a gift for noting the obvious.

"No." A bad feeling was gnawing at me. "'Scuse me. I'll be right back." Sliding off my stool, I gestured to the bartender. "My tab—er, slate."

"Yes, madam." He nodded without pausing in his glass-wiping procedure.

I hurried outside. I'd come in part to play the concerned spouse but also because I'd never seen Bainbridge look so enraged. I might need to intercede.

Besides, I was worried about him. Lord Cool and Controlled had become Lord Hot and Glaring.

"...owe this to her," Robin ground out as I pushed through the door.

"Don't go there," Bainbridge said.

"Your entire life has disappointed her. Now you've a chance to give her something she wants, and—"

Bainbridge slugged him. Straight from the shoulder into his brother's jaw. So fast, I barely saw it coming.

Robin dropped like a sandbag, and Bainbridge stood over him, unrepentant and hot-eyed.

I ran to Bainbridge. "What the hell's the matter with you?"

His murderous stare swiveled to me. "Stay out of this, damn it."

"The hell I will. Have you gone nuts?" *Remember what's at stake,* I silently urged him. *Remember where we are, that we're surrounded, and by whom.* "An argument shouldn't—"

"Shut up!" he roared. That was not in his role, and he had given Robin grounds to have him arrested.

I had a moment of surprise, chagrin, and even hurt before my own anger erupted. "Shut yourself up," I said in the low, tight voice that signals danger to people who have sense. "Shut up and think."

The door whooshed open behind us. The yelling must have attracted people. Now we really had an audience. Great, just great. I risked touching his arm. "You hear me, Jack?"

The fury in his eyes ebbed. He stared at me and then, as though just noticing him, down at Robin. "Claire—"

Robin groaned and pushed himself upright.

Two burly guys in maroon security livery jackets hustled up to us. "Everything all right, Lord Bainbridge?"

Anger ignited in Bainbridge's eyes again. "Show my brother off the premises." He ground the words out as though his teeth hurt. "Claire, I'll see you at home."

He turned on his heel and stalked away, toward the open countryside.

One of the security men leaned over Robin, then helped him stand.

"Wait, Jack!" I took one step after him. "Where are you going?"

"For a walk," he roared. Fists still clenched, he stomped away.

He'd never bellowed at me. Anger made him soft-spoken and icy-controlled, not belligerent and hot-headed. What the hell had gotten into him?

Gotten into him...

Oh, shit. Had he been drugged? I hurried after him. "I'll go, too."

He wheeled. "You will go home. For once, do as I say."

I hesitated, but making him angrier wouldn't help. Since he'd been so emphatic about my not going, I'd call Simon and Petunia and ask them to watch him.

"This isn't over," Robin shouted. "I have the votes."

I turned to him. His sorry, gullible ambition had created the whole family mess. "Oh, shut up," I told him. To the guards, I added, "Mr. Basingstoke is leaving."

"You don't have to tell me twice." Robin stalked away, the set of his shoulders remarkably like his brother's.

I blew out a deep breath, raised my chin, and turned back to the crowd to smooth over this disaster. The family squabble excuse might be trite, but that's because it's so often true. Good thing I'm adept at improvising.

Yet worry churned inside me. Nothing I'd seen in Bainbridge or read about him implied that he could snap so suddenly. People who do generally don't earn decorations like the George Cross, and I couldn't help thinking of a night I'd left this very building behaving totally unlike myself. What if he got sick out there alone?

"Sorry about that, everyone," I said brightly. "Brotherly spat and all that." I located my companions in the crowd. "Sorry, ladies. I think I better go home so I'm there when Honeykins comes back."

They nodded understanding, and I took my leave. Despite my bright, if fake, demeanor, I felt far from calm as I pulled out my phone and punched the scrambler.

#

At seven o'clock, Bainbridge still hadn't come back. I peeked out the window. People strolled across the compound, going to or from the dining hall or maybe just taking a walk. No sign of my partner.

He'd been gone three hours. Since no one had reported his having problems or dropping off the radar, I assumed he was okay. I picked up my phone and tapped his speed-dial.

No answer. Damn it, he knew protocol. Considering his control freak streak, I normally would've expected him to answer on the first ring. I could take advantage of his absence to improve the hell out of his precious plan.

Was he too sick to care? Too enraged to remember procedure?

Spurred by uneasiness, I phoned Petunia. "Where's Bainbridge?"

"Coming up the north slope and heading your way. Simon watched over him while he marched over the hills at a mad pace, though judging by the way he's walking, I'd say he more likely stomped."

"But he's not sick or obviously impaired?"

Ordinarily I wouldn't be so worried, but I couldn't help remembering what a nasty cider had done to me. If he was out there retching, I wanted to be there helping him.

Because he was my partner, of course, and my being with him fit our cover story. Not for any other reason.

"I'd have called you," she said. "He's just pissed off. According to Simon, though, he never pouts, rants, or lashes out." She hesitated. "You be careful."

"Yeah. Talk to you later." I cut the connection.

Should I adopt nonchalance or concern? Either way, he'd likely tell me to butt out. Nonchalance, though, seemed less apt to further piss him off. And maybe he'd calmed down some. Choosing a magazine at random, I settled myself on the big couch.

The only problem with nonchalance, I soon found, was its lack of space for clock watching. Where the hell was he?

As if the thought had summoned him, a key clicked in the door. Bainbridge came in, locking the door behind him.

Grim-faced and ramrod straight, he dropped his keys on the table by the door and stalked into the room.

I smoothed my face into bland unconcern. "Hey." Good tone, even pleasant. I flipped a page.

"'Hey?' That's all you have to say?" He glared at me.

I stifled the urge to return the favor. "Jack, how do you feel?"

He waved that aside with an abrupt gesture. "You interfered in a family matter."

"Actually, I didn't." All I'd done was try to talk to him.

"I've told you. Stay out of my family's affairs." He pointed at me. Pointed!

Resenting that but worried for him, I shut the magazine very carefully. "Think about it, Jack. Do you really want people to see you in an angry confrontation with Robin?"

Unfortunately, he didn't look any calmer than he had earlier as he stalked toward me. I stood. Damn if I'd cede the height advantage altogether.

"You," he said, still pointing, "do as I say." He stopped with his finger about an inch from my nose.

I drew back just enough to see it. I would've shoved his hand aside, but avoiding aggressive moves seemed wise with someone so angry.

Slowly, I raised my gaze to meet his. I took a deep breath to keep my voice calm and slow. "Don't point at me, Jack."

"I'll do as I bloody well please." His eyes narrowed, but he lowered his hand. A bit too slowly for comfort.

My fists balled, fingernails digging into my palms. I forced my fingers to relax. Fighting for an even tone, I said, "Maybe we should take a walk together."

"Don't tell me what to do," he ground out.

I didn't see the man I knew anywhere in that blazing stare. Whatever they'd given him, as I was now sure they had, was in control. I counted three slowly.

"Something's going on here," I said quietly. "We need to figure out what it is."

"Don't make excuses," he rapped out, glaring.

"Think about this," I coaxed. "Jack, your reaction—"

He grabbed both my arms. Shook me, dammit. "You don't tell me—"

Hell with that. I stomped on his foot and broke free. Off-balance, I backpedaled.

He stepped forward, his right fist driving for my face.

CHAPTER TWENTY-FOUR

Sonofabitch! Even as my fists rose to counter, I couldn't believe he'd swung at me.

I parried his blow hard to my right, pushing his arm across his body and leaving his right side open. He missed my head by less than an inch. To avoid antagonizing him more, I held my counter-punch and jumped back. I couldn't afford to close with someone so much bigger, not when I didn't want to hurt him.

Spinning, I put a chair between us. "Jack, listen."

He grabbed the chair and hurled it aside. I retreated.

When he reached for me, I ducked under his arm. Quickly side-stepped farther out of reach. "Jack—"

Nothing. No expression but anger.

"Jack, wait!"

No answer.

If talking wouldn't work, maybe I needed to take him down. I let him come closer, then pivoted to slam a sidekick into his gut. It knocked him on his back.

He should've seen it coming. Should've parried or dodged. Clearly, he was off-form.

I jumped behind the coffee table. "Jack, let's talk."

With a roar, he rolled to his feet and lunged. I kicked the table into his path. Against a foe who's out to inflict pain, fighting to avoid damage sucks, but he wasn't responsible for this mood.

He jumped the table. I wheeled around the other chair. Tripped on the fallen one.

He dived at me. I scrambled to my feet, off-balance, in time for him to land on all fours. Whatever he had in mind, I wouldn't like it.

We circled the furniture and glared at each other. In an old cartoon, the scene would've been funny. In real life, it was scary as hell. I was going to have to knock him out, or else lock him out. If I reached the bedroom, would the door hold against him?

He caught my arm. Yanked me closer. I slammed my free palm over his ear canal. Air ramming into his eardrum jarred him enough to loosen his grip. I stepped in to clock him with a right cross.

He staggered. I wheeled into a roundhouse kick. If I cracked a rib, he'd just have to deal.

Bad idea. He caught my leg. Swept the other one, taking me down, and landed on top of me with murder in his eyes. Shit.

He had a serious mass and strength advantage. He pinned my wrists and ruled out both scratching him or going for his eyes—a last resort anyway since I didn't want to hurt him. At least he hadn't gone for my throat. Yet.

I could get enough leverage to buck him up, then twist my hips so his balls landed on bone when he came back down. That might hurt enough for me to break his grip. Or not. And it was a guaranteed piss-off, though that wasn't why I felt strangely reluctant to try it.

A wild idea screamed through my brain. If I could channel that aggression...

I raised my head and kissed him.

For an instant, he froze. Then his tongue thrust into my mouth, hot and velvety and exciting. I sucked it, and he groaned. Catching my wrists in one hand, he slid the other down to cup my breast. Electric heat shot through me. I gasped into his mouth.

He freed my hands, yanked up my t-shirt and palmed both breasts. Arching upward on a wave of pure pleasure, I whimpered and wrapped my arms around him.

He trailed hot, tongue-flicking kisses down my neck. A haze of pleasure fogged my brain. Dimly, I realized some part of Jack's mind remained true to itself. This was rough for my taste, but it was give and take. If Jack were completely submerged, we would already have done the slam-bam-thankee-ma'am bit. Maybe a couple of times. The warm, sweet realization wrapped around my heart.

I kissed his ear. Licked it, and he shuddered.

His mouth reached my breast. Warm and wet and soft, his tongue circled the nipple and sent spirals of hot need through me. He nipped gently, then did the same to the other breast.

He raised his head. Dazed, I looked up at him.

Torment shadowed his eyes. Rage still burned there, but I could see him fight it.

"No," he gritted out. "Not. This. Way."

His fine cotton shirt rasped over my sensitized breasts, and his erection dug into my jeans seam, exquisite torture. Despite his misgivings, he hadn't moved off me.

"Can you—what if we don't?" I panted. Would he lose control again if we stopped? To keep from caressing his back, I fisted my hands at his waist. I wanted him now, with an ache that verged on pain, but not if this would haunt him.

"Don't—want—" Frustration flared in his eyes. He made an inarticulate, angry noise, and his head dropped toward mine. His tongue plunged into my mouth, swirling and demanding.

I yanked his shirt up, palms flattening on his sleek, muscular back. Sliding one hand down into his jeans, under his briefs, I gripped his firm butt.

He groaned. Muscles flexed under my hand, an intoxicating sensation, and his hips thrust against mine.

Moaning, I rocked upward to meet him.

He straightened, unsnapped my jeans and yanked off jeans and bikini panties in a quick, efficient rush of motion.

I reached for his snap. It popped easily, but the jeans stuck on the hard bulge in front. With an impatient sound, his eyes blazing, he shoved them down and leaned over me.

His arms and shoulders shook with tension. He looked at me, waiting despite the wildness in his eyes, and my heart swelled with affection.

"Sweetheart," he said. "I don't—" His lips tightened. Averting his gaze, he shook his head.

Unexpected longing jabbed my heart at the endearment. I gently touched his cheek. "I'm offering, Jack."

Our gazes met, and heat that wasn't anger burned in his. With a groan, he surged into me in a swift, sizzling thrust that took my breath away. It returned in a long, deep gasp.

My back arched, settling him deeper as he stretched and filled me. "You feel so good," I managed.

The heat in his eyes became possessive, then tender. He lowered his head beside mine, withdrew, thrust again, and the world became a blur of sensation—warm, firm muscles under my hands, hard, delicious weight pressing me down, and sweet, solid lightning thrusting inside me.

I'd never been so aware of a man, of the way his entire body caressed mine with every thrust, of the small sounds of pleasure he made. I locked my legs around him and moved faster. Pleasure became need became building, pushing tension.

Raising his head, he gave me a fierce look. "Mine," he gritted out before he plunged in again. "*My* partner." Another deep, electric thrust, and I whimpered but couldn't look away from those demanding eyes. "My lover," he said on a slow, emphatic slide into me. "*Mine.*"

"Yes, Jack," I panted, moving with him. "I'm yours."

Shit, I meant it. Where had that come from?

With an inarticulate sound, he lowered his head again and thrust faster. Harder. I stopped thinking. Every part of me was feeling too much for thought.

"I'm going to—" he gasped. He slid a hand down to touch me where our bodies joined, stroking.

My breath caught. My back arched again, and the tension burst into crashing wave of pleasure. I vaguely felt him shudder.

When my head cleared, he lay on top of me, our bodies still joined. We were both breathing hard, hearts pounding wildly together, and his shirt front against my chest was damp with sweat. More of it pooled, slick and warm, under my fingers at the small of his back.

I kissed his shoulder and sighed. Despite the way that coupling began, I wouldn't trade it for anything.

Which was a really scary thought.

On its heels came a strange realization. Jack was still hard. Worse, his back muscles felt tense.

I stroked his hair gently. "Jack?"

"It'll—be—all right." He didn't raise his head, though. He didn't relax.

Hellfire, what'd they given him? Only a powerful drug would so snap the controls in such a disciplined man.

If only I had that excuse. Now that we weren't fighting, he felt wonderful inside me. The selfish, too-long-celibate part of me didn't want this to end. *Down*, I told it.

"Bloody bollocks," he snapped. He pulled his body free of mine and directed an angry, tormented look at me. "You know I want you, but not like this. Never like this."

Hurting for him, I stopped his shift to the side with a slight tightening of my hands at his waist. That earned me a surprised frown, but he stayed where he was. Turmoil again roiled in his eyes.

"Jack," I said, groping for words, "the desire for this has been there between us at least since the party at your house. I'm okay, really."

Seizing my courage in both hands, I said, "Leaving aside the way this started, I like the way you feel—" deep breath, bigger risk—"and the things you said."

His frown deepened. "What did I say?"

If he didn't remember, he probably didn't mean it. Damn. I swallowed hard and forced a smile. "Sweet nothings. It's fine."

Dark gray with worry, his eyes searched my face. "Claire..."

Someone knocked on the door. We ignored the sound.

It came again. "Lord Bainbridge? Madam?" a man's voice called. The knocking rose to pounding. "Are you all right?"

"Bloody hell," Jack muttered. He lifted his head. "We're busy," he shouted.

I chuckled at his word choice. I couldn't help it. If only he looked amused.

The pounding recurred. "One of the men heard crashing sounds. Yelling. Are you sure? Is Lady—"

"I'm fine," I yelled, not hiding the fact that I was pissed. Doubly so because a nasty suspicion was forming in my brain. "Hang on."

To Jack, I added quietly, "Take off your shirt."

He rolled off me, muttering things I didn't doubt were vile Brit epithets. He still looked crazy-eyed. This might be the eye of the hurricane. We had to ditch these "helpful" snoops fast.

I shucked my top and grabbed the throw from the sofa. While I wrapped it loosely around me, he rolled to his feet. The room was a wreck we had no time to straighten.

He somehow forced his jeans to fasten, which had to hurt in his condition. "Christ's balls," he muttered.

We made our way, a bit clumsily, to the door. When he opened it, I made sure the throw drooped to reveal one naked leg and hip as well as both bare shoulders.

"What the hell do you want?" Jack demanded.

Two—a number stinking of setup!—heavyset security men stood on the step. They looked nonplussed for an instant before their faces went rock-bland. "Sorry to disturb you, sir," the front one said hastily. "Must have been a mistake."

"Whose mistake?" I demanded.

"A groundskeeper." He very carefully did not look at my little exhibition. "The man heard crashes, as I said, madam. Shouting. So sorry—"

"Sod off," Bainbridge roared. He slammed the door in their faces. Apparently, the interruption, and the setup he'd probably deduced the same as I had, had pissed him off again.

With an angry, wordless sound, he slammed the butt of his fist into the wall and rested his head on his forearm.

I touched his rigid shoulder. Except for the muscle working in his jaw, his face had gone stony again.

"Jack," I said quietly. "It's okay."

"Not yet." He looked at me with guilt and pain in his eyes.

That look told me what he needed and was doing his best not to take. "I'm your partner," I said, remembering with a pang the way he'd insisted that, the precious words he didn't recall. Not at all sure I was doing the right thing for either of us, I slid my arms around his neck. "I'm here for you."

Giving him time to pull away, I stretched up to kiss him gently. He hesitated a long moment. I was about to draw back when his lips parted. Relieved, I flicked my tongue into his mouth. He growled and yanked me to him, my naked breasts flat against his warm, hard chest.

I tore my mouth free to press kisses on his neck, running my fingers through his thick, silky chest hair. When I touched his stubby nipple, he made a choked noise and cupped my butt, pulling me against his erection. I gasped at the sudden rush of pleasure, and his tongue invaded my mouth again. He rolled my nipple between his thumb and one finger.

My back arched. Moaning with pleasure, I tugged at his pants. The snap opened. He backed up half an inch to force the zipper down, and I pulled his briefs and jeans after it. He cupped my buttocks again, lifting me to bring my breast to his mouth.

He sucked, and delight speared through me. I cried out with it. My head fell back, my hips rocking in time to the waves his suckling created. Until my back met the wall, I didn't realize we were moving.

Gasping, I opened my eyes to see the fierce need in his. Answering need rose within me. He lowered me slowly, giving me time to say no, I guessed, until his erection touched my cleft. I kissed him hard, and he thrust upward.

Again, that sizzling pleasure. I'd never had sex against a wall. Never wanted to, but I wanted him any way I could have him. Another thrust of his hips pushed the frightening thought away. I locked my legs around Jack's waist and rode him hard as he pressed his face into my neck.

He lowered his head, licked my nipple, and came with a driving, shuddering thrust. The sight of his face tight with pleasure I'd given him pushed me over the edge. The tension in me burst so hard it threatened to blow my head open.

I clung to him, hanging limp in his arms and panting. Our hearts again pounded together, no clothes between them now.

Nothing between us at all. Maybe in more ways than one.

I started to lower my legs.

"Shh." Jack kissed my neck. "Wait."

He carried me to the bed, and we collapsed on it, side by side. I missed him inside me. Wanted him again.

Attraction or not, this had started out as a fuck in the line of duty, a new experience for me. I hadn't considered it as anything else at first. I certainly hadn't expected it to leave me yearning. I've had sex a couple of times to ease a momentary urge, but that never left me wanting more.

Not even with my unfortunately incompatible fiancé, Trey, had I felt bereft when our bodies parted after sex. I was in serious trouble.

I glanced at Jack. He stared at the ceiling, his face tense and his eyes dark with an emotion I couldn't read. I brushed my knuckles over his cheek. "Jack? What is it?"

His eyes closed. His mouth tightened, and he pushed himself up on an elbow. When his eyes opened, pain shadowed their depths.

"Oh, Jack..." I reached out to him. The guilt and pain in his eyes stabbed into my soul, and I wanted to kill whoever'd done this to him. Who'd tainted what should've been only a joy between us.

He caught my hand. Pressing it to his heart, he said, "Claire, I'm so very sorry. I would never—" He stopped abruptly, as though he couldn't finish, but the words *assault a woman* hung, unsaid, in the air.

"Jack, I know that." Smiling at him, I freed my hand to brush an errant lock of soft, inky hair off his brow. "I know."

"How can you possibly?" Bitterness laced his words, and disbelief churned like storm clouds in his eyes.

"Because you're a kind man—a hardass operative, the most reliable sort—but a kind man. A gentleman in the old-school sense of the word. You help your staff, even though you really don't have to, you're genuinely nice to Horace and Hilda in ways our roles don't require, and you have a kind-hearted ex-girlfriend, one who wouldn't put up with a brute."

When he looked startled, I added, "I did overhear that bit between you and Lady Daphne, you know."

"That was years back," he muttered.

Neither his history nor the fact he'd bothered to clarify it were my business, so that little happy rush could just stifle itself. It didn't, though.

He pushed himself off the bed. "Blood and urine samples," he said. "By the way, that was quick thinking. At the door."

"Thanks." This wasn't the time to rub in the value of improvisation.

I'd have asked if he needed help, but he seemed in control of himself. I watched him take the kit out of a hidden compartment in one of his suitcases. Kneeling, he laid out the equipment on the closed bag.

"You were set up, you know," I said quietly. Not wanting to raise any barrier between us, I deliberately didn't cover myself before rolling onto my side to face him.

He said nothing as he knotted rubber tubing around his upper arm. With enviable unconcern, he used his teeth to uncap the needle, then slid it into the vein.

"We need to think about why," I told him.

Watching his blood fill the sample tube, he said, "Either they know who we are, which still seems unlikely, or it's about Hawkshead." His lips tightened. He withdrew the syringe and pressed a square of cotton into the crook of his elbow.

"If you're in jail, you can't attend the meeting." A fact that made me wonder if Robin had refrained from calling the police earlier because he knew this explosion was coming. Jack was in no frame of mind to hear that now, though. Admitting the possibility this was aimed at his company had taken a lot.

He packed away the blood kit and took the vial he'd filled into the kitchen. A *kthwlp* signaled the refrigerator opening. A moment later, it closed. "We need to sneak Miss McIntosh in so she can pick this up."

"I'll call her, but in a little while, after everyone's gone to bed."

Putting the suitcase away, he said, "Maybe you were right and my family wants closer watching."

That was a huge concession. It even implied that he realized Robin could be involved.

Not looking at me, he stalked toward the bathroom with a specimen vial in hand, leaving me wondering how to help him. How to put us back on a comfortable footing. How to make him understand that I really, truly, had wanted him tonight.

He came back into the room after putting the specimen bottle in the refrigerator, too. Still not looking at me, he turned to the bed.

"Just so you know," I said off-handedly, "I'm on the pill, and I have STD tests every six months." I paused but made myself be honest. "And I haven't been with anyone in over a year."

I hoped that was light in his eyes when he added, "Nor have I." At last, he looked at me, hesitantly. "I also have twice-yearly tests."

"Come to bed, Jack." Letting him take that however he wanted, I held out a hand to him. We needed to search the bar area, see if we could find a sample of whatever he'd been given, but we couldn't do that until the club room closed.

He gripped my hand. When he sat on the edge of the bed, his eyes searched mine. "Someday," he said slowly, "I hope you'll let me show you how I would've preferred to seduce you."

Did that mean he'd hoped to follow through on our attraction, that he felt it when we weren't in its immediate grip? Or...I narrowed my eyes at him. "That offer wouldn't be by way of an apology, would it?"

"One could take it that way." He hesitated. "I meant—I care what you think." The last words sounded fast and harsh, as though they'd been ripped out of him.

"Good," I said, "because I don't do apology fucks."

If he wanted my good opinion as a lover, we were on new, risky ground. The happy little rush deepened, but I bit my lip. Maybe he just wanted me to respect him as a man. Either way, I wanted him. Wondering how he'd use that brilliant mind and athletic, disciplined body when he had full control of himself created restless heat deep inside me.

"That's no, then." He stared at me with a furrow between his brows and tension in his shoulders.

"It's yes." I smoothed the crease between his brows and let my hand drift down his temple and cheek in a caress. Bracing myself, I admitted, "I care what you think, too."

Surprise flickered in his eyes. Smiling, he raised my hand to his mouth and kissed my palm.

I smiled, too. "So what's wrong with now?"

"You're not sore?" Hope laced the words and lit his eyes.

"No." I pushed myself up to kiss him.

With a groan, he kissed me back. His arms slid around me. My heart soared. I tugged him down beside me. We'd have one time, at least, for its own sake.

He pressed quick, hot kisses along my cheek to my ear. His breath sliding into the opening sent warm prickles through me and tightened my nipples. "You're sure?" he said.

"Yes." I rolled above him, kissing his chest and stroking his flat, ripped stomach with one hand while the other gently squeezed his erection. "I love your abs."

Smiling into his intense face, I licked the washboard divisions. He shuddered, eyes closing, as I added, "I've wanted to do that for days."

His eyes opened as his fingers slid into my hair. Watching his face and his hot, possessive eyes, I kissed his penis.

He groaned, "Don't, love. Not now."

Unsure what that endearment meant or what I wanted it to mean, I let him press me back into the mattress. Cradling my head in the crook of his arm, he stroked my hair away from my face. The tenderness in his eyes pierced my heart with longing, and I caressed his broad, solid shoulders.

"You've a wonderful face," he said softly. "Strong." Leaning down, he kissed my left eyelid. "Intelligent." Kissed the right one. "Beautiful." Brushed his lips down my nose.

His breath whispered over my mouth as he murmured, "Not in a magazine cover way." He nudged my head back to kiss the underside of my jaw, and sweet shivers rippled through me. "In the way that lasts," he finished, and his mouth covered mine.

Slow and long and deep, the kiss went on and on. I ached for him to touch me, but he didn't until I arched my back and tugged on his wrist. Kneading my breast, he kissed his way to my ear and licked it. Pleasure shot through me like lightning. I writhed in his arms.

From there, he trailed slow kisses down my neck, between my breasts, and over to one nipple. Gripping his nape, I tried to tug him upward, over me, but he kept going, kissing and nipping his way down my belly, taking his time exploring and tasting but moving inexorably lower.

"You're so strong but so soft," he murmured, stroking my breasts. "You show the world such a hard face, but your skin's quite soft here." A kiss on my belly, and he added, "and here."

His hot, tender eyes locked on my face as he dipped his head toward my cleft. Nuzzled it, sending quick heat through me, and said, "And especially, here." Holding my gaze with his smoky one, he lightly tongued me.

I gasped, my back arching. He slid his hands up my sides to massage my breasts. My fingers tangled in his thick, soft hair.

"Mmm," he said, and his breath tickled my clit. I made a choked noise and clutched at him. He stroked his tongue over the sensitive flesh, teasing and arousing until I writhed with pleasure and bucked against his mouth, panting. Nothing existed but his hands and mouth on my body, and the pleasure built in wonderful, tightening spirals.

The spirals tightened until I couldn't stand any more. Tightened again. Exploded into hot pinwheels of pleasure.

Again and again he pushed me to the brink and beyond, but I wanted more. On the edge again, I choked, "I need you in me. Jack, please!"

"Ah, sweetheart," he groaned, wrenching my heart with wanting. As he sheathed himself in me, his warm, possessive gaze roamed my face. I hadn't thought I could feel anything stronger, but that thrust echoed through my entire body. I gripped his shoulders. Rocked my hips up to meet his next thrust.

He shuddered, and the world convulsed with him. I think I may have screamed.

A long time later, I realized I was lying in his arms. I nestled closer. His embrace tightened, and he kissed my temple. Lying there like that, with him, felt so good.

So right.

We fell asleep in a warm, intimate tangle of arms and legs.

I woke up alone. In darkness that was too quiet.

CHAPTER TWENTY-FIVE

I didn't see anything unusual, but I lay still except for inching my left hand toward the Walther on my night table. Aside from the faint sounds of wind outside, the living room clock ticking and the refrigerator humming, the cottage was silent. And I had no sense of a presence at my back.

My fingers closed around the Walther's grip. I peeked over my shoulder for Jack, and my heart twisted. He wasn't there. Probably wasn't in the cottage. Somebody'd turned out the lights, and nothing hinted at an intruder.

Hurt and a little worried, I sat up. A twinge between my legs startled me. So did the covers sliding over my naked body and the musky smell of sex wafting from them.

Naked. Sex. With Jack, who'd gone out—to work, I hoped—without me. Damn it, we were a team. We were lovers, at least for now. Why the hell had he sneaked out? Had the drug they'd given him flared again, or was he working without me?

I slid out of bed and dressed quickly in jeans and a sweater, with the Walther in its shoulder holster concealed by my leather jacket. Waking up alone after tempestuous lovemaking is never a good sign.

Of course, it probably wasn't lovemaking for him.

I froze on the thought. Had it been for me?

I'd have to worry about that later. Now I needed to find my partner.

Maybe he'd gone to search the café. That seemed like the most optimistic bet, so I went with it. He'd been pretty shaken. My own drugging episode had driven home the pain of losing control, and I hadn't even done anything violent, except to defend myself. Someone as controlled as Jack would probably have even more trouble coming to terms with his behavior. Maybe he wanted some time alone, but he should've told me, let me stand guard.

The bedside clock read three seventeen. No one should be around now, so I slipped out of the cottage and walked toward the club room. If I met anyone, I'd claim Jack and I'd had a fight and I was looking for him. That had the merit of partial truth.

I didn't see anyone as I walked through the cool, breezy night. Although I tried, I couldn't quite compartmentalize what had happened between us. That last time had been just us, no drugs involved. It had felt as though he were claiming me. And I had wanted him to, I realized with a jolt of anxiety. Had claimed him in return without consciously realizing it.

Had I been a moonstruck idiot, mistaken in seeing the tender possessiveness in his eyes as more than fleeting passion?

At the tree line, I paused to survey the green area in front of the club room and Great Hall. A figure slid around the edge of the building, and I froze. Then he stepped into the light. Jack, with a face like granite.

Shit.

I squared my shoulders and walked out of the trees. Waiting, I stood with my feet braced. I knew when he spotted me because his head rose slightly. His stride looked as smooth as usual, so maybe he wasn't having physical after-effects. The emotional ones had to be hell, though.

When he came within arm's reach, he said curtly, "You should've slept in. I've handled it. I also passed off the blood and urine samples to Miss McIntosh."

I took a deep breath to gentle my voice. "We're a team. I was worried. Did you find anything?"

"No." He kept walking. I fell into step with him.

Grim-faced, he asked, "Did I hurt you?"

"Nothing to speak of." I'd had worse in the gym. Physically. Emotionally might turn out to be a doozy. "Jack—"

He shook his head once, hard, to stop me. "My behavior was inexcusable. I apologize for my lapse in control."

He was calling passionate, tender, earth-shattering sex a *lapse in control*? Even his phrasing, so formal and cold, set me at a distance. Worse, it hurt.

He'd seemed fine earlier. What had set off this change?

"We covered this before—" I bit back the words *before you made love to me as though you meant it* and took a slow breath.

"You were drugged," I said gently. "As you told me, 'not your fault.'" I took a deep breath. "Besides, the sex was my idea."

"You had little choice." We reached our cottage. He opened the door and stood back for me to enter the living room wreckage.

"If you think that, you don't know me very well."

He shot me a skeptical glance as he locked the door. Heading for the kitchenette, he added, "I should have been more careful."

I flipped the lights on and followed him. "That's not what you said to me when they gave me that nympho drug or whatever it was. You can't chemically test everything put in front of you. Even if you could, the test might not show whatever was there. They've developed some sneaky stuff."

"Regardless, I failed in my duty. I do apologize. I assure you, it won't happen again." He filled the kettle and turned it on. "I'll put the furniture straight."

Maybe I should let the subject go at that, but I couldn't. I, too, needed my partner functioning and not moping. I leaned back against the counter beside him. "So it was no biggie that I swallowed a funny cocktail, but you're not allowed? Come off it, Jack. Give yourself a break."

His shoulders tensed, and his expression turned wooden. "That sort of thinking drove the nobility into uselessness."

"Well, sure, if you're King Serial-Wife-Murderer Henry Whatever or some effete ass like that prince guy in Regency novels. Jack, you've already proved—"

"Resting on laurels is for old age. With all the advantages I've had, I have no excuse for failing in anything."

Was he just being hard on himself, or did he truly think his background had given him such an edge that he had to live up to, and maybe even deserved, a higher standard? My heart beating fast, I asked, "So your making exactly the same mistake you excused when I made it isn't okay because you're the Earl of Bainbridge, *et cetera, et cetera*, is that it?"

Was the gap between us that wide, that bolstered by a superiority complex, albeit of a sort I'd never seen before? My throat tightened, something in it burning.

"Leave it." He jerked the cabinet open and pulled out the tea canister. The deep breath I drew made my chest hurt. "Sorry, but I have to know." I needed a different kind of answer. Needed it desperately. Like air. Or hope.

He slammed the canister down on the counter. His eyes hardened. "I am, as you note," he said, spacing the words carefully in a cold, lethal voice, "the Earl of Bainbridge and holder of numerous other titles. My ancestors arrived with the Conqueror. I am a product of England's finest university and of one of your country's best. I am, in short, trained not to make simple, careless mistakes."

Unlike me, apparently. He was closing the subject. Closing me out, and it hurt more than I could've imagined.

"So you're above us other mortals." Us lintheads. The shadow of Jimbo Hartner rose in my mind, but I wouldn't take the words back.

Bainbridge stared hard at me. "I said, leave it."

He didn't deny it. My heart broke.

I took a deep, painful breath. Stupid idiot, I should've known better than to fall for such an arrogant jackass. "I'm going for a walk. You and your lineage can work this out between you."

I turned on my heel. I couldn't stay here with him another minute.

"Claire." Out of the corner of my eye, I saw him wheel, but I kept going. Damn if I was going to belabor my lunacy.

"Claire, I didn't mean—"

Someone knocked on the door. I glanced at Bainbridge, who frowned.

"Who's there?" I called.

"Claire, it's Janet. I'm so very sorry to disturb you at this hour, but I was just on my way home and saw the light."

Janet? Oh, right. The chunky blonde from my workout class. I opened the door.

Her eyes were puffy and swollen. "I thought you should know. Horace has died, I'm afraid. Cut his wrists in the men's dressing room shower. Hilda wants to see you as soon as is convenient."

Bainbridge hurried to stand at my shoulder but didn't touch me. Though I ached for him to, I didn't touch him, either.

"If she's awake, we can go now," he said.

#

Bainbridge and I hurried over to the bungalow Horace and Hilda had shared. When we knocked on the door, Susan, from the purchasing office, ushered us inside. Hilda sat primly, in true Anglo-Saxon, stiff-upper-lip style, on a flowered divan. A teapot sat on the low table in front of her.

She stood when we entered. "So very good of you to come." Her voice sounded thin but resolute. "Susan has been a great help, of course—"

Hilda pressed her lips together. Her chest rose in a deep, audible breath, and her shoulders straightened. "Susan, I've kept you long enough. Lady Bainbridge will stay for a bit, I hope."

"Of course. Hilda, we're so very sorry." I'd do whatever I could for her, with the unfortunate caveat that the mission had to come first.

She acknowledged our condolences with a brief nod. "Will you have some tea?" she asked.

"White, please, with sugar." I didn't really want the tea, but I felt as though she needed something to do.

Bainbridge also agreed to tea, with sugar.

As Hilda passed us tea, Susan lingered by the door. "Are you certain you don't need me to do anything else, Mrs. Fletcher? Mr. Jones-Demerest said looking after you is to be my first priority."

"No, dear, thank you. All I need is the company of our family. You've kindly called them, and they're on their way. I'm sure you need your rest for work tomorrow."

Maybe her work was keeping an eye on Hilda as much as helping her. I made a note to check on that somehow.

The door clicked shut behind Susan. Hilda didn't look up at the sound but continued fixing tea.

"I know you've had Susan," I said, "but we'd be glad to help if you need anything."

"As a matter of fact, I do. I appreciate your coming so late. Or early." She hesitated, her eyes grave. "I asked you here, Jack, for a bit of a presumptuous reason, I'm afraid. I believe you must know a great many people, perhaps some in the government. Or the CID."

The CID? As in the Criminal Investigation Department? For a wild moment, I feared she was about to confess that she'd killed Horace.

She set her cup down, precisely and carefully, in the center of the tray. Solemnly, she regarded us. "I don't imagine you've heard, Horace supposedly committed suicide."

"Supposedly?" Bainbridge asked, his face and voice neutral.

"I don't believe he killed himself." Hilda raised her chin. "I'll never believe it. I'm certain Horace was murdered."

I very carefully didn't look at Bainbridge, though I'm sure the same memories of drug-induced behavior that ran through my mind also touched his. "Why do you think that, Hilda?" I asked.

"Horace hated violence. He disapproved of suicide as cowardly."

Bainbridge leaned forward slightly. "You said he'd been depressed. We didn't notice that, but of course we only just met him."

"Not that low." She hesitated. "I don't wish to cast aspersions on someone who has been very kind, but Jasper seems a bit too ready to step in at the company."

"In what way?" I asked.

"He's offered to have someone supervise our office manager." Hilda's eyes flashed. "I know every detail of that office. If anyone supervises, I will."

"Of course," I said. "Do you have any other reason to feel, uh, bothered?"

Hilda's brow furrowed. "I've been a bit low, myself. And Josephine, dear William Barrow's wife, took an overdose of pills."

I didn't remember her. I glanced at Bainbridge, who supplied, "Barrow Chemicals, I assume."

Hilda nodded. "That was a few days after we arrived. At the time, when Jasper offered office staff to run things for William while she recovered, it seemed so kind. But now it feels, well, convenient." She bit off the last word.

I didn't know anyone who could admit to being in law enforcement. Maybe Bainbridge did.

After a moment, he said, "It may be that Jones-Demerest is merely being kind, but I've a few friends who could ask discreet questions about him. If that would put your mind at rest."

"It would, indeed. Thank you." She sighed loudly. "I don't wish to seem like a—an overly suspicious person or one who can't accept the truth. It's only, it feels wrong. It's one thing to offer advice about markets and such, another altogether to take a hand in management."

"I'll make some enquiries," he said, quietly proving my much earlier point about his kindness. "Horace deserves that."

Her shoulders squared. "Yes. He does. Thank you, Jack."

She was handling all this about as well as anyone could expect. Bainbridge and I exchanged a glance. His eyes echoed my regret we could do so little for her.

On the table behind me, her phone rang. At a nod from her, I picked it up. "Mrs. Fletcher's cottage."

"A Mr. and Mrs. Harris from Leeds to see Mrs. Fletcher," a gruff voice said.

I relayed the information.

"That'll be Tom and Vivian. Thank you, Claire. Tell them it's all right, if you would."

I did as she asked. Bainbridge and I took our leave.

Outside, I looked around to be sure we were alone. "Well?"

"*Convenient* is a very good word," he said. "We need to know who else has suffered unfortunate problems."

"Petunia should have that list of holding companies by now. I'll check with her."

"Right. We should try again for the lab."

He hesitated. The focus in his eyes blurred into uncertainty. "Claire…"

"Yes?"

He shook his head, and the focus was back. "It will keep. Let's go back and make our plans."

On the surface, we were back in harness. Anything deeper, though, was impossible. Bainbridge was a decent, solid guy. His superiority complex was a burden to him, an obligation, not an ego boost like nasty Jimbo Hartner's had been, but the bottom line was the same. Neither of them could respect me as an equal.

We passed the bulletin board in front of the club. A tiny roof, more like eaves overhanging each side, sheltered it. Out of habit, I looked at it. A new piece of paper occupied the exact middle, neatly tacked down on all four corners. I skimmed it quickly.

"Here's something useful. There's a bonfire and a moonlight sing next Tuesday, with everyone to be there. This notice says that includes staff. Jones-Demerest's house will be empty."

"That's four days. God knows what else could happen between now and then." Bainbridge frowned at the notice. "I'll convince Jones-Demerest to move it up, combine it with a memorial service for Horace."

Considering Jones-Demerest's desire to buy into Hawkshead Shipping, Bainbridge could probably succeed.

"You'll take the house, and I'll take the lab," he continued, his face hard. "Whether or not it's empty. We can't waste any more time waiting for a break that may never come."

CHAPTER TWENTY-SIX

Fighting the water in the pool held little appeal when I didn't know what chemicals besides the usual might be in it. Horace had liked to swim. I went to the gym to relieve my frustration. I had no idea what Bainbridge was doing and resolved not to ask.

When I returned to the cottage, he had the television on. The BBC was broadcasting news about the pandemic, which had been officially classified as high impact in most of the larger urban areas. It had spread up the M1 as far as Newcastle, and some of the initial cases from Dover and London had died. Outbreaks—luckily, still sparse—were also reported in Liverpool and Manchester. All working-class neighborhoods, so far, in the northern cities.

Bainbridge looked as grim as I felt. The flu had spread from the lower-income neighborhoods where domestic workers lived to those of their employers with devastating speed on the Continent and in the South.

Staring at the screen, I said, "Jones-Demerest comes from nothing, right? Lost a sister in a flu outbreak and had to battle for acceptance because of his gypsy blood." I was feeling my way. "If we're right, and he's planning to build a new power structure, why hasn't he moved against more of the people here? Lots of them are rolling in money."

"Perhaps he's going after those he considers snobs. Or those he sees as dangerous." Bainbridge nodded at the TV, which showed a family walking down a street, the woman wearing long skirt, long sleeves and hijab. "Some of the areas affected have high Muslim populations. Remember what Aunt Beatrice said about Jasper and his Muslim employees."

"You can't target a germ, or virus, or whatever that specifically, though," I grumbled.

My phone rang. I swiped it to connect and pressed the scrambler.

"Jackpot, as you Yanks like to say," Petunia informed me. "Jones-Demerest has bought shares in holding companies where many of his guests are majority shareholders."

"That doesn't explain why he'd eliminate Horace Fletcher, though."

I beckoned to Bainbridge, who leaned close to listen. I caught a whiff of cedar, and my heart twisted. Damn. I'd gotten over guys before, though. I'd get over him as soon as we didn't have to share such close quarters.

"It might," Petunia said. "Shaw Freight Haulers, which Corner Chemist owns, is one of the largest such concerns in the country. If he could gain control of that, he could move whatever he liked."

"He can do that now, with his own trucks. Uh, lorries."

"Think who's in his company structure," Bainbridge said. "Up-and-comers from various parts of the old Empire, ones who've assimilated."

"If he could put them into these other concerns," I said, "replacing people like Horace, that would elevate his protégés in that community." I held up a finger to stop Bainbridge, who'd opened his mouth as though to speak. "Horace might've come from modest stock, but he'd polished himself up as tidy and polite as any—pardon the expression—earl."

Bainbridge directed an annoyed look at me. "Ask Miss McIntosh. To people like my aunt, birth determines all. No matter how much refinement someone like Horace or Hilda acquires, it won't matter."

"Not to her, maybe," I said. "Petunia, I'll call you back." I disconnected. "Think about it. Jones-Demerest must know that, but he also knows money talks. If you've shed your roots, you can't rise above them. You've hidden them instead. Just as he had to."

"That doesn't make sense."

"Not to you, maybe." I hated saying something that skated so close to our quarrel, but it was important. I continued, "Not to anyone to the manor born. But to the outsider with his nose pressed to the window, who thinks he's there precisely because he's not from that set, it might make all the difference. If you can't get into the power structure, knock it down and make a new one."

He cocked an eyebrow at me. "The old American adage of pulling oneself up by the bootstraps but to a lethal degree."

"People used to have to change their names for that to work—look at any list of old Hollywood stars—but not anymore. Jones-Demerest changed his anyway. Money can buy him a voice but never respect."

Bainbridge looked unconvinced.

"We'll see," I said.

"Claire." He glanced away, then back at me, a wary look in his eyes. "This morning, I didn't mean to imply—didn't intend to say birth determines destiny. Or anything of the sort. I know that's rubbish."

My heart took a painful jerk. My throat felt suddenly tight. "You're not a snob, Jack. That's plain. But you do think your birth sets you apart, even if you see it as a demand rather than an entitlement. I can't deal with that."

"Judge me as I am. That's fair." His eyes dark and pained, he said, "But don't, please, confuse me with anyone in your past."

"I'm not." Was I? Surely not. Maybe he cared for me after all, but caring wasn't enough if he set himself above me.

"I hope not." He rubbed a hand over his chin, his expression skeptical. "We're two rather different people, obviously, and perhaps everything between us comes down to that."

"Maybe so." I pushed the words out around the block in my chest. I'd told myself that since I'd met him. Why did hearing him say it hurt?

If he believed what he'd said, why did he look so strained?

His phone rang. He grabbed it from the table, tapped the screen, and scowled. "Yes." A pause. "People are being encouraged to stay home, in case you haven't noticed." His mouth tightened, and anger darkened his eyes as he listened.

"It'll be whatever it is," he said at last. "Meanwhile, sod off."

I blinked at his hard tone. "Problem?"

"Robin. The shareholders have scheduled a vote." His grim expression said he was finally taking this seriously.

Well, that sucked. "Nothing like taking advantage of chaos. Can you stop it?"

"I don't know." Stretching as though to relieve tension, he gripped the back of his neck with one hand. "The question's never arisen."

"Then let's have Petunia email us your bylaws, or whatever you call them over here, and we'll see." Anything to avoid having more of that personal chat. As far as I could tell, we had nothing left to say. We were partners. Period.

A bitter smile twisted his mouth. "Until Robin took over, half of the governing documents were informal memoranda signed by all the shareholders. We stored them in a loose file in a room at Bainbridge Park."

"Then maybe we can hoist Robin on his own petard." If Bainbridge was accepting help on the Hawkshead question, so much the better.

Besides, I hated just waiting around. Any chance for action, even action involving tedious corporate detail, sounded great.

#

Three hours later, we sat together in the living room. I straightened my stiff back and glared at my laptop. The tiny print of the verbose, endlessly detailed bylaws of Hawkshead Shipping filled the screen. "There's nothing about teleconferencing. Unless you have something I don't."

"Robin wants that on the agenda for next year's board meeting." Bainbridge looked thoughtful. "There's no provision for it now."

"Then if people can't travel through the quarantine, maybe he can't assemble a quorum."

"There's also nothing that forbids video or telephone conferencing."

"You can claim people have to show up with proxies. If Robin argues otherwise, can't you get some high-priced barristers or solicitors, or whatever, to tie him up in court?"

"I can try." Frowning, he stood. "Meanwhile, I'll have a go at Percy. He's my best chance of winning other votes. Even if he votes Aunt Beatrice's shares her way, I can win if he votes his with me." He grabbed his phone and headed for the bedroom.

I pulled up the National Health Service quarantine page and the shareholder list. Cross-checking should let us know where Bainbridge stood.

Which seemed to be up Shit Creek, I decided shortly. Assuming all the shareholders were currently at their primary residences, which might not be a safe assumption, enough of them could travel to constitute a quorum. If I'd counted right.

I frowned at the bedroom door. I couldn't approach Percy myself without breaking my cover. I could, however, adapt to the needs of the moment. Since my partner wouldn't likely appreciate improvisation, it could just be my little secret. I turned on my phone, speed-dialed Petunia, and stepped outside.

#

After teaching my exercise class the next morning, I reluctantly headed back to the cottage. The tension between Bainbridge and me was growing unbearable. At least we wouldn't have to endure it much longer. He'd talked Jones-Demerest into moving up the moonlight sing and combining it with a memorial service for community morale.

Hilda had gone back to her home, so she wouldn't be there. Bainbridge and I would duck out early and take an all-or-nothing shot at accomplishing our mission.

Steeling myself, I opened the door. Bainbridge sat on the sofa with his laptop open and a lined notepad beside him. He flicked a glance at me before going back to his reading.

"How did class go?" he asked.

"I didn't learn anything new. What're you doing?"

"Studying formulas. Refreshing my memory for raiding the computer files." He paused but didn't look up. "You're welcome to join me."

"I did that already. Around two a.m." Because I couldn't lie next to him and listen to him breathe and not think of might-have-beens. Damn if I wasn't turning into a sappy idiot.

His head jerked up, a startled expression on his face. "I'm sorry," he said quietly.

"Occupational hazard." I set my gear bag in the closet. "I need a shower. Then I'll..." Do anything but sit here with him. I suddenly couldn't take that, and I'd done my prep already.

Heading for the bathroom, I said, "I don't know—maybe I'll take a riding lesson or something."

I should've chosen any other activity. I knew it as soon as the words left my mouth.

"I could teach you. I owe you another lesson." Jack looked up, keeping a white-knuckled grip on his pen. The vulnerability in his eyes tore at my heart. "I'd like to teach you."

Clearing my tight throat, I swallowed hard. "I can't, Jack." My lips trembled, so I pressed them together as his face fell. "I can't do Moony Newlyweds with you. Not right now." I sucked in a shaky breath.

"I'll be fine tonight," I promised us both. "It'll be game on, and I'll have my head in it. Just—not now."

His outline blurred, and I fled to the shower, cursing silently. I'd known sex with him would be a game changer. I just hadn't realized the game was Battleship and I'd be sunk.

#

That evening, we prepared carefully. I eyed Bainbridge as we gathered our gear. My black leathers might blend, thanks to my punk-girl look, but he didn't seem to have any protective clothing. I'd be happier when I could zip my jacket and cover the bright pink bustier I'd worn to draw attention from all that black leather.

Bainbridge looked fierce. He'd never said how his call to Percy had gone, which I gathered meant it went badly. The shareholders meeting had been today. I should've stuck around to buck him up instead of wandering around the hills all afternoon. Unfortunately, I appeared to have some limits on my partnership account.

"I assume you expect me to thank you," he said curtly.

"For what?" I opened the shallow false bottom on my suitcase. Inside lay two headsets. I tossed one to him and tucked the other in my jacket lining.

"My cousin Isabel had, apparently, sugar in her petrol tank. A very expensive petrol tank, in a Mercedes. Robin backed out of his driveway over a police-issue spike net that flattened all his tires."

"So they missed the meeting." Hah!

"For now. It's only a temporary respite, of course."

"Of course." I looked blandly up at him.

His gaze had dropped to the bustier. He averted his eyes hastily and another burst of regret lashed at me.

At least he'd refrained from lecturing me about meddling in his family affairs. Or improvising. Or illicit shadow organizations.

With a sudden lump in my throat, I went back to what I'd been doing, tugging my jacket sleeves down to cover the knives on my forearms. I'd miss those lectures. For a little while.

"So we're going to sneak away from the bonfire, ostensibly to neck, search Jones-Demerest's house and the lab, and sneak back," I said.

"That's the plan," he agreed. "Let's go."

CHAPTER TWENTY-SEVEN

The gathering took place in a circle of benches set into the hillside about halfway down. As the light faded, we had a spectacular view of the dale below. Everyone sat in a ring, singing folk songs around the bonfire. Jones-Demerest sang loudest of all, a big drink in one hand. I had nasty visions of Jonestown and lethal soft drinks, but not even he would be so stupid as to bring his evil out of the closet. Surely.

Still, Bainbridge and I didn't actually drink anything. His blood test had shown elevated levels of testosterone and adrenaline along with a chemical the scientists hadn't yet pegged. Better to play it safe, so we carried our cups around and pretended to sip.

Eventually, we wandered to the fire but snuggled together on a bench at the back. He hooked an arm around my waist to draw me close. I laid my arm along his thigh, stroking lightly and trying not to remember the precise texture of skin and hair and muscle beneath his jeans.

I remembered all too well.

He nuzzled my ear. Although I kissed him then, smiling, the act wrenched at my heart. Best to find how he really felt before I made a complete ass of myself, but it still hurt.

His touch felt tender, as though he truly cared. Maybe he did, but not enough in the way I needed him to see me, as his true partner and equal.

He laced his fingers through mine and stood. We walked out into the darkness. Climbing the hill put us out of view. I zipped my jacket to cover the godawful bustier.

Farther out, away from all the lights, we stepped behind decorative shrubbery and opened my fashionably huge purse. Pulling out the packages—suppressors for our concealed weapons, various gadgets, headsets, scanners, and flashlights, took only a few moments.

"Meet you at the lab," he said softly.

"Right." I resisted the urge to say *be careful*. Simon had reported only one guard and no researchers at the lab. But that could change before Jack finished. As he knew well.

Also, saying it would sound goopy. Like I cared too much.

He hesitated. "Good luck," he said at last, and slid into the darkness.

If there was only the one guard, he would use the sleeping gas and his duplicate key to get in. If there were researchers or additional guards, he would have to use more gas and hope it kept them out long enough for him to finish. If it didn't, he'd have problems. The spark-free room restricted weapon choices. Taking out guards would be more of a challenge with the collapsible baton tucked into his jacket than it would've been with his suppressed Glock.

Really, just shooting the rat-bastard would've been so much easier.

I headed back to Jones-Demerest's house to finish searching it. I hoped.

I plucked the flexible headset from my pocket and slipped it on. It resembled an extremely miniaturized Bluetooth earpiece with a thin microphone lying along my cheek. I tapped it twice. "Check," I whispered.

Back to me came two taps and a "Check" from each of our team members, Bainbridge, Petunia, who led the team watching the residential area, and Simon, whose crew was watching the lab. Just as I'd wanted my regular backup on duty tonight, so had Bainbridge. We'd maintain radio silence now unless something hit the fan.

#

Jones-Demerest's house looked deserted. A lamp burned in the front parlor, revealing its emptiness, but no other light showed inside. Of course, that didn't apply to the basement. I pulled the infrared scanner from my pocket.

No one on the ground floor or upstairs. Drawing on leather gloves, I silently mounted the back stairs. From my left sleeve, I drew my lock picks. I had the door open in a couple of seconds.

Aiming the scanner at the basement produced no hits. No one there, at least for now. Bainbridge wasn't the only one who should hurry.

A wide quadrangle of light fell on the kitchen floor from the parlor lamp. Taking care to avoid the bright area, I edged toward the basement stairs. I had my night vision eyepatch, so I could see in the almost-total darkness down there without using a flashlight.

No light came from the bottom of the stairs. No sound. Stepping on the edges of the risers to avoid creaks, I silently descended the plain, wooden stairs. At the bottom, a wide room opened out. The television I'd seen on the scanner during my last trip should lie somewhere off to the left and behind the stairs.

I reached the bottom. No one had shot at me, so I probably didn't have any superbly concealed foes to worry about.

A large room paneled in dark wood stretched back behind the stairs. I moved farther into it. Walls partitioned off an area that now lay to my right, probably the room with the TV. Ahead stood a couch in front of the end wall. A seascape hung above the couch. I stared at it. The wall was too close. The basement should be larger.

A glance upward didn't help. Exposed rafters might've given me a clue, but sheetrock covered the ceiling.

I checked the room on the right. As I'd expected, a bedroom with a TV, wardrobe, and nightstand. Probably the lair of Jones-Demerest's personal security. And the rear wall was farther back than the one in the outer room.

I went back out to check it. The seams in paneling make it useful for concealing hidden rooms. I saw nothing irregular through the eyepatch or, closing that eye, by using my flashlight.

The passage of time felt like a prickle on the back of my neck. Purely psychosomatic, but it expressed my antsy urges. Tamping them, I ran my fingers up the seams in the paneling as high as I could reach. The process seemed to take forever.

It yielded nothing. Shit. But the wardrobe in the room to the right had backed up to the side wall. It stood in the corner in the area where that room was longer than this one. I hurried in. Yep, the wardrobe stood farther in than I would've expected after looking at the other room. I checked again, poking my head out the door and then in, to be sure. Definite space discrepancy.

As a child, I'd loved C. S. Lewis's *The Lion, the Witch, and the*

Wardrobe. Had Jones-Demerest?

I stalked to the wardrobe, yanked the door open, and examined the back. Nothing. Crap. I closed it and peered behind the wardrobe. At the outline of a doorway.

Jackpot!

Now I just had to move the freakin' thing. Rather than slide it sideways, I focused on walking one side forward, rocking it, to make room for me to open the door. It had a recessed handle, probably pocket-panel construction.

I wedged myself into the tight space I'd created and grabbed the handle. When I pushed, the door slid silently aside. My heart pounded as I stared into into the room beyond.

I blinked. Did I really see—? Yes, I did. Weaponry. Instead of hiding an enchanted world, this wardrobe concealed a den of death. AK-47s hung on one wall. A .50-calibre machine gun leaned against a wall in a corner all by itself. Racks holding about 30 of the new FN 5.7 pistols, complete with tactical lights and night sights, with one shelf dedicated to loaded magazines, rounded out the arsenal. Shit. Jones-Demerest was prepared for a war, and I could finally prove it. His hide was mine.

He might also be keeping important secrets in here. Grunting and trying to breathe, I wiggled inside. More stacked boxes, probably of more ammunition and guns, circled the walls. Moving all that stuff would take an hour, time I didn't have. Any minute, Jones-Demerest might decide to return.

This arsenal gave us more than enough reason to haul the sonofabitch in under England's antiterrorism statute. I snapped a series of photos with my phone and sent them off to MI5. My anonymous tip, with the photos to back it up, would set the necessary wheels, which were already primed before the investigation started, in motion.

Once we had him in custody, we could search all his properties. Who knew what else he'd concealed at his many holdings?

I slithered out and rocked the wardrobe back into place. I didn't have time to worry about tidying the contents. On the way to the stairs, I scanned the floor above to be sure no one had come in, but I still had the place to myself.

Since I had relative privacy, I tapped my headset as I mounted the stairs. "Petunia." When she answered, I told her what I'd found. "It's time to call the cavalry."

"Right. I'll alert the team."

"I'm in," Bainbridge reported from the lab. "The guard is asleep, and I'm starting the downloads. There are refrigerated cabinets full of nasty stuff—plague, smallpox, and such. Simon, see whether the Home Office wants heavier forces."

By that last, he meant SAS. I wouldn't mind having them show up to deal with that stuff.

I slipped out of the house, keeping to the shadows in the empty yard. "I've sent my anonymous tip, so things should break any minute. You could wait for the raid."

"The guard won't sleep very long. Besides, once this breaks, they'll likely try to destroy the hard drives, so—"

"You! Step away from the board," a hard voice ordered him. "Hands in the air."

My heart pounded into my throat, and I broke into a run. Jack wouldn't have overlooked a guard. "Simon! Where did that guy come from?"

The smack of flesh striking flesh cracked over the pickup. More blows. Grunts. Heavy breathing. Scuffling feet. There had to be more than one foe—many more, or Jack would've won quickly.

Simon's answer came back, hard and frustrated. "No one entered the lab, Casey. No one. Bloody hell."

Then how the hell—a hiss, as though gas deployed, coughing, and then "Christ," strangled-sounding, but in Jack's voice, and then more hoarse coughing.

I jumped a fallen log and ducked a branch. Twigs cracked under my feet. Speed mattered more now than stealth.

A furious, male voice demanded, "Who sent you?"

A smack like a blow striking a face. Jack's face, and the sound twisted my heart in knots. I stumbled. Tripped on a juniper bush but recovered to run on.

Oh, God. How had this happened?

Over more harsh coughing, the questioner pressed, "Tell me or lose a knee."

"No," another voice, a cooler one, said. "We'll test the new drug. With that knifing through his blood, he'll beg to tell us anything. If he survives long enough—"

"Wait. His radio."

A click. And then nothing.

I swallowed a cry. If something happened to him—but I wouldn't let it.

I touched the sending stud on my earpiece. "Simon. I'm going after him, but the guards will call backup, probably from that glorified dormitory. Don't let them reach the lab. And take out the grounds camera system."

"Roger. We're inbound, en route to the dormitories to mop up there," he said. "We have your back."

I should have had Jack's.

Somehow, I had to save him. I couldn't bear to lose another partner. Especially not this one, no matter what lay between us.

Only a fool would run straight to the lab. Circling toward it, I resisted the temptation despite the memory of David's dead face urging me to throw caution to the winds and just *get there*. My racing into a trap wouldn't help Jack.

Covering the short distance seemed to take forever. When I reached the lab, all the lights blazed beacon-bright. The exterior ones cast a brilliant perimeter thirty feet wide around the entire building. And Jack was in there. Damn, damn, damn.

His precious plan hadn't allowed for this. Yanking off my eyepatch, I retreated into the shadows. At least no reinforcements from security appeared anywhere around. Neither did the MI5 contingent. What the hell was keeping them?

Floodlights blazed suddenly around the compound. An amplified voice came from over by the gate, but I was too far away to make out the words.

"Petunia, what's up?" I asked.

"Our MI5 friends, in the guise of the North Yorkshire Police, are at the gate. They just told the guards they had a warrant and ordered them to open up, or they would break in the gate."

Shouts rang in the woods over by the gate. Weapons fire. With our side using suppressors and subsonic ammo, any shots we fired would make only clicks, no bangs, so the audible gunfire was coming from the bad guys. Jones-Demerest's goons had fired on law enforcement with weapons they couldn't legally possess. It was hard to believe they were that stupid, but it was a good thing the rat-bastard had been busy with the singalong. He might've tried to brazen the whole thing out, but now he was well and truly trapped.

No sound came from the amphitheater or the bonfire crowd. They'd probably scrambled home to hide, with Jones-Demerest running for whatever bolt-hole he'd planned. And speaking of that, the gate was blocked off. Going across the countryside would involve crossing open country and getting around stone fencing. If he couldn't leave by car...

I switched frequencies to the private Arachnid one and pinged Petunia. A moment later, she said, "Yes, Casey?"

"Do we have anything that would take out a helicopter?" I knew she had an arsenal with her. I just wasn't entirely sure what was in it.

"RPG launcher and three grenades for it," she answered. "You want them?"

"Not yet. Stand by. Unless you see a non-SAS helicopter anywhere. In that case, come quickly."

"Roger that."

So that possibility was covered. I'd reached the lab. Where Jack was —he had to be—alive and holding out for rescue.

I approached the lab on the side away from the luxury compound. Crouching in the shrubbery, I directed the thermal scanner over the stone wall at the building. It showed me one person near the main door. Closer to me, in the lab, three people stood. One held something in his fist, maybe some kind of sparkless weapon. Flanked by the other two standing figures, one form lay on the floor, jerking convulsively.

Jack—Panic whirred in my brain. With an effort, I forced it back. I had to focus, or he was screwed.

Unless the guard was totally worthless, the door was locked. I couldn't use my card key, either. The lock would whir, alerting the guard. Even if I could kick it in and shoot him—tough with a steel door—his buddy could then bash Jack's head in before I reached the inner room.

If a frontal assault was out, I'd have to rely on subtlety. Improvisation. So very Not Jack's Favorite Thing. If this worked, maybe he'd change his mind.

Petunia told me SAS were deploying and would take command on arrival. The news made me move faster. The elite British commandos would mop up anything Jones-Demerest had, but saving Jack wouldn't be their priority. The lab guys, on the other hand, might want to eliminate him as a witness.

Cold with adrenaline, my heart hammering, I jammed the closed-circuit camera transmissions and scrambled over the wall. Simon had said he would take out the cameras on the grounds of the residential area, but these might be on a separate circuit. The front room with windows, on the far side, held the guard station. I hurried to kneel under the window and peered up through the blind slats.

A stocky, blond man sat watching the video screens. Beyond him, across the hall, a slice of what looked like a lab was visible. One screen offered a wider view of it with cabinets and racks of vials lining the walls. A bank of computers sat along the counter on one side. I couldn't see the corner below the camera. Since Jack wouldn't have mistaken flammable gasses, they must be in that corner.

In a space at the back, between two of the three black-topped lab tables, Jack shuddered on the floor. He had his eyes and jaw clenched shut in his strained, paper-white face. Cuffs held his hands behind his back, and sweat beaded his face. His gear lay on the nearest table.

If he died—but I wouldn't let him die. At least this view showed me what I was up against.

The guard standing over him didn't have a truncheon. He had a tactical baton, collapsible, sparkless, and deadly. I'd trained with them but rarely used one since a suppressed firearm was quicker and actually quieter overall than the baton. For all I knew, though, the guy also had a firearm.

Two men in white lab coats flanked Jack, one tall and gaunt and young-looking, with shaggy brown hair, and the other of medium build, bald and wearing glasses.

No one else in sight.

Chewing my lip, I scrambled back over the wall before the jammer loop ran out. "Simon," I said into the mike. "You there?"

A brief delay before he answered. "Roger."

"I'm behind the stone wall, west side of the lab, about halfway down.

I need a diversion. Also, did you capture a lab coat, anything white? Any Simply Yorkshire livery?"

"Nothing white. Whatever sort of livery you want. We're in the dormitory." That meant they were east of the dining hall, just beyond Jones-Demerest's house. They would need a few minutes to get here.

"Bring me one of the maroon jackets security wears and a towel." To get rid of the punkish look. "And some C4."

"We're coming. Anything else?"

"Detonator of choice. The explosives are for you."

"Why, thank you," he said.

While I waited for him, I unscrewed the suppressor from the Walther and stuck it in my bag. The gun went back into its shoulder holster.

Simon's voice in my ear warned me of his approach a moment before he ran out of the trees with two other men in black fatigues and *Police* vests. They crouched beside me.

I took off my leather jacket and donned the livery one Simon handed me. Buttoned, it covered the bustier, the holster, and the throwing knives on my forearms.

"I'm going right up to the front door," I told him, wiping off my heavy makeup with the towel.

"Here, let me." Simon took the towel and held it in front of my mouth. "Spit." At my questioning look, he said, "I have a two-year-old. Keep talking."

I spat, then held still so he could scrub while I finished explaining. "As soon as I'm inside, the instant the door shuts, I want serious boom out here, something to distract them long enough for me to grab my Walther."

"Casey," he said, frowning, "If you fire a shot in there—"

"In the lab or clean room, yes, but the hallway's safe." I hoped. Gripping his shoulder, I stared into his eyes without trying to hide my own fear for Jack. "I need only one bullet, point-blank. I won't risk discharging it into the lab. I promise, Simon."

Although if everything blew, at least I wouldn't be the one who came back. No one would. But that wouldn't save Jack.

"Your face is clean." Simon tipped my chin to the light. "Detonator's rigged. We're ready when you are."

CHAPTER TWENTY-EIGHT

I circled through the woods so I could approach on the side with the gate, by the road. Hurrying fit the tale I had to tell, so I ran across the parking lot, swiped my card key in the iron gate's lock, and raced around to the end door.

Looking up at the camera, I said, "Mr. Jones-Demerest sent me. It's urgent," and swiped the key.

The lock whirred. Scowling, the big guy I'd seen through the window stood in the security station doorway with—hallelujah!—a tactical baton, collapsed, in his hand. If all went well, it would be my nice, spark-free weapon in a few minutes.

"I don't know you," he said slowly, squinting as though trying to place me. "Show me your identification."

I rolled my eyes but fumbled in the jacket. My fingers touched the gun butt.

Behind me, the door clicked shut. I braced myself in the heartbeat's delay that followed, and then a massive boom shook the building. Simon apparently loved his explosives. Ready for the shock wave, I drew the Walther as I fell against the wall.

Security Guy bounced off the doorframe, flicking the baton out to full extension and aiming a slashing strike at my head in one move. Ducking, I fired point-blank, into his forehead in case he was wearing a vest. He toppled backward. I holstered the Walther, popped my left knife into my hand and scooped up his baton with my right.

As I cocked my left arm to throw, the guys in the lab were climbing back to their feet. Their positions made a loose V with Jack on the floor on the end opposite Baton Guy, another guard.

The guard was taller than I was and heavy-set. Facing me, he drew his arm back as though to hit Jack. "Stop," he barked at me, "or—"

With an agonized groan, Jack swept one leg into the backs of the guy's knees. He crumpled backward with a grunt but caught himself on a table.

The tall, thin man in a white lab coat reached for Jack. I threw. As Baton Guy raised the baton to strike Jack, my knife buried itself in Tall Scientist's shoulder. With a gurgle, he rocked back, then fell forward. His fall knocked the strike at Jack askew. I charged the guard with my captured baton.

Wheeling to face me, he shoved the wailing scientist aside. He struck down at me hard. My baton blocked the blow. Barely. I was no match for his strength. Grinning, he used another overhand strike.

I blocked it, then ducked a strike aimed at my head. With his baton still in motion from the missed blow, his weight was all forward, leaving him vulnerable. I slammed my baton into the nerve running down the outside of his left leg. The leg twisted. Caved.

As he fell, I went for the outside of his knee. Roaring, he fell on his right side. My next slashing strike took out his ankle.

He swung feebly at me across his body. I wheeled behind his strike to slam my baton across his forehead. The impact made a sickening *thunk*, and he went still.

The guy with my knife in his shoulder lay on the floor, holding his arm and cursing. I took a good look at Baton Guy, not a pretty sight but obviously a dead one. And no longer a problem.

The older researcher fell to his knees. "Please don't hurt me!"

His companion moaned. "Please. Help."

"You're lucky I don't kill you both for what you did to my partner." Watching the two men, I asked, "Jack, where's the key to your cuffs?"

"This one's...chest pocket," he ground out, nodding at the dead guard. "Claire—tunnel. Back office—" Leaning on a table, he hauled himself to his feet. "To—brewery."

Well, shit. Building that had been one very secret project. The utility lines we couldn't locate probably ran through there, and it had been very effectively masked.

"Is that how they caught you?" I asked, crouching to check the designated pocket.

He gave me a curt nod. My gran would've said he looked like death warmed over. I doubted he could walk, much less run, but his leg sweep had bought me the time I needed to reach him.

"Simon, we need backup and a medic for a prisoner." My fingers closed around the key. I unlocked Jack's cuffs quickly, handed him the baton, and edged into the hall. There, I drew the Walther to watch that back office.

"Coming in," Simon announced.

Still watching, I opened the door for him. He passed me my bag and helped me change my jacket while I filled him in. He sent two men to guard the tunnel entrance.

He'd acquired a few more since I'd left him. Two came with me, one to examine the scientist I'd knifed and one to take charge of the other prisoners.

Hurrying back into the lab, I noted tanks of oxygen and hydrogen racked in the corner, as I'd suspected. "Get up," I said to the older, uninjured scientist, resisting the strong urge to kick him. People shouldn't play high-stakes games if they can't handle the risk.

I popped my remaining knife into my right hand and glared at him. "Give him the antidote. If you give him anything else, you're dead."

Shaking, he nodded.

"Get up," I snapped again.

Jack jerked his head toward the nearest rack of vials. "Based on— what they gave me—this is it."

He was the one with the biochemistry degree, and he'd seen where they stored the stuff. Assuming his eyes were focusing properly.

"Is that it?" I demanded of the trembling researcher. "If it doesn't work, you're dead, too."

"They...showed me," Jack rasped, passing me the baton.

With shaky hands, the scientist grabbed a syringe and the vial Jack indicated. He had trouble sticking the needle through the stopper.

"Be sure you draw the right dosage," I said softly.

No noise from outside. Had Jones-Demerest decided to bail? Where the hell was SAS, anyway? I hadn't figured they were coming all the way from London.

The short man pulled the syringe free, tapped it, and squirted out some of the contents. "P-please," he whispered. "This—"

Jack grabbed the syringe, stabbed himself in the arm, and pushed the plunger. His eyes closed. Shuddering, he clenched his jaw. An inarticulate sound escaped him.

My heart froze.

At last, his eyes opened and turned to mine. The look held for a long moment, full of gratitude and warmth I could so easily misread. I couldn't sort out my tangled feelings to speak. He was alive. That would have to be enough.

"Ta." He pushed away from the table. "Let's go. Simon, you'll need to finish those downloads. I'll leave the thumb drives."

The scientist I'd knifed glared at me. I returned a stony look. Jack was clearly recovering, but I still wanted the guy's head.

"We're secure. We'll watch that tunnel," Simon vowed.

"Can you make it?" I asked Jack.

He nodded grimly. We gathered his gear and hurried into the night. Despite a staggering gait and hunched posture, he did better than I'd feared he might. We scrambled over the stone wall together.

Bainbridge's breath rasped. Putting on his holster and jacket looked like a struggle, but I knew better than to comment.

I tapped my headset. "Petunia? Where's Jones-Demerest?"

"He broke from the campfire and headed for his house with two of his bodyguards. When the shots rang out, he made motions that they should go with him and the others should keep singing. As though that would happen." She snorted. "The guests' concerns delayed him, or he would've reached the house by now. His bodyguards are armed, remember. Heavily."

Also illegally, but no one ever would've known in the ordinary course of things. Now, compared to what we'd found in the basement and the lab, those guns were minor.

"Roger," I said. "We'll keep our heads down."

Bainbridge had himself back in order. He'd stopped sweating. In the moonlight, I couldn't judge his color.

Guys in Simply Yorkshire's maroon security livery were running across the green toward Jones-Demerest's house.

Bainbridge and I looked at each other, and I allowed myself one brief tremor of relief that he was safe.

"Thanks," he said, eyes dropping to his weapon as he chambered a round. "I knew you'd come for me."

"Because I don't follow procedure." My voice sounded flat. I wanted to throw myself at him, feel his arms close around me and hold his living, breathing body against mine, but we weren't lovers anymore. Maybe we weren't really even friends.

"Because you'd never abandon a partner," he corrected simply, a half-smile tugging at his mouth.

There was so much I wanted to say to him, but none of it would change anything. "Are you good to go?" I asked.

He gripped his Glock. "Ready and eager."

We stood, and he touched my arm. "When this is done, give me five minutes." His tone made the words a command, but the look in his eyes made them a plea.

Nothing he could say would make a difference, but I couldn't refuse him. I nodded. "Let's go."

We ran toward Jones-Demerest's house. "Remember," Bainbridge said. "We need him alive."

"I don't like it, but I'll do it." If the murdering scumball gave me reason to shoot him somewhere not fatal, on the other hand, I wouldn't hesitate.

On the day of David's funeral, I'd found myself alone with his wife in their kitchen. "I'm jealous of you, you know," she'd said abruptly.

Shaken, I stammered, "Amelia, David loved you—there was never— I swear—"

"That's not what I mean." She squeezed my hands, her brown eyes fierce. "I accepted your sharing part of his life I never could, but this...Casey, I want so much to avenge him, to bring that bastard to justice, and I know I can't. But you can."

"I will," I'd promised her. "I swear by all that's holy, Amelia, I will." Then my partner's widow had wept on my shoulder, every tear acid on my heart because I'd let him die.

Now I was about to keep my promise, if not quite in the way she and I had hoped. My lips tightened in frustration. Maybe Jones-Demerest would resist us and give me that excuse.

In my ear, Petunia added, "SAS helos inbound, ETA four minutes."

"Copy," I said. "We're on it."

Ahead, a trio of men rushed through the trees. They hurried into a patch of moonlight that made Jones-Demerest clearly visible. If the rat-bastard was heading for the house, he might have transport on the way. Helicopter or not, an RPG would stop it, so I shouldn't delay getting my hands on one. Though I would have to use it carefully to ensure that we took him alive.

"Petunia, leave one set of eyes there and bring us the stuff I asked for."

"On my way," she replied.

"We'll flank them," Bainbridge said, echoing my thought. "Wait for my signal."

His calling the play was not part of my plan, but I nodded as he veered away without slowing.

A few strides later, he called, "Jasper, a word if you please." Barely breathing hard, Bainbridge stepped into view. His right hand hung at his side, his weapon and its suppressor concealed behind his trouser leg.

Jones-Demerest didn't pause. "No time," he panted. "Emergency."

If he bothered with that kind of reply instead of a volley from his goons, Bainbridge's cover was safe.

Bainbridge took a step nearer, and the bodyguards drew Glocks. My fear for him threw everything into slow motion, but his gun rose even faster than mine. It clicked twice and double-tapped the guard nearest to him in the head as I did the same to the other one.

The two men toppled. Time accelerated to normal. Jones-Demerest made a squeaky noise and froze, hands rising. "For Christ's sake, Lord Bainbridge," he gasped. "If you want the investment deal dropped, you needn't go to such lengths."

Keeping a weather eye out for other guards, I circled toward Bainbridge.

"The investment deal is dead," Bainbridge agreed. "If you move, so are you."

Jones-Demerest couldn't know we needed him alive.

"If it's money you want—"

"Sod your money," Bainbridge's cold, hard tone could've chipped steel. "On your knees. The police want to talk to you about terrorism and the flu epidemic."

I slipped into the little clearing but stopped about ten feet from Bainbridge, facing him, to watch his back.

Our prisoner glanced at me. "Not quite what you appeared, either."

"There's a lot of that going around." Finally free to glare at the rat-bastard, I leveled the Walther at him. "On your knees. If you don't, I'd really love to shoot you."

Bainbridge threw me a warning glance but said nothing.

Jones-Demerest stared at me. "What are you, a mercenary? Scotland Yard?"

"Let's just say we're both protecting family interests," Bainbridge said. Fishing cuffs out of his jacket with his free hand, he stepped forward. "Knees, Jones-Demerest. Now."

If Jones-Demerest didn't cooperate, Bainbridge would make him. I'd have seriously, deeply preferred just shooting him. In the gut, like David. But I guessed I could grudgingly settle for Bainbridge knocking him around a little. Maybe humiliation and ruin would be worse than death for him, considering how much value he'd placed on prestige.

"Damn it, you asshole," I said. "You had everything—respect, money, social standing, and you pissed it all away."

He glared at me. "How d'you think I became rich? I didn't inherit my money. Worked my arse off for it. You call me 'asshole?' Try gypo, pikey, jidder, the terms that persecuted my family. Cost my sister her life. Damned doctor wouldn't treat a gypo girl."

Try *linthead*, I thought. "I know all about labels, and they're no excuse. Because of you, someone I cared about is dead."

Killing him wouldn't satisfy me, I suddenly realized. I doubted anything ever would, but nothing said I couldn't make him suffer. Leveling the Walther, I added, "I think I'll shoot you after all. Bainbridge, stand back."

Suddenly hard, his gaze caught mine. "I can't let you do that." He paused, then added, with a slight nod, "Not without cause."

Whew. He knew *good cop, bad cop* and was willing to play along. I narrowed my eyes. "He isn't cooperating. He doesn't need both kneecaps."

He was, however, sweating, and I gave him a grim smile over the gun barrel.

"Down," Bainbridge snapped, staring past me. His gun rose.

Wheeling, I went into a crouch as a bullet buzzed by my face. His shot zinged past my ear with a sound like a pencil snapping in two.

Another shot barked out of darkness broken by a muzzle flash. Then Bainbridge slammed into me. The sound of his Glock firing so close was still only a loud *click* in my ear. The attacker fired again as Bainbridge locked an arm around me and bore us both down, into a roll.

I came to rest prone, with him half over me, and aimed my weapon the way his faced. No more shots came toward us.

"I think you got him," I said softly.

Bainbridge grunted and rolled off me.

I rose cautiously, without drawing fire. "Thanks, Jack."

But Jones-Demerest was gone.

"Hell. Come on," I said. "Let's catch that bastard."

My headset crackled. "I'm coming with identifying vests," Petunia's voice said. "Don't shoot me."

Through the trees, lights flared around Jones-Demerest's helipad. Bainbridge stared at it but didn't move.

"Jack, let's go."

He shook his head. "You go." He sounded breathless, probably from the fall. Looking strained, he clutched his left shoulder. "Stop that sodding bastard."

My brain froze, not computing. "Jack?"

"I'm hit," he ground out. "You must stop him for us both."

CHAPTER TWENTY-NINE

No. He couldn't be hit.

I dropped to my knees beside him. "Jack, let me see."

"Go." He gritted his teeth.

I tugged his hand off his left shoulder. A dark, coppery-smelling fluid stained his upper chest and palm. Blood.

Part of my brain registered a black helicopter coming in beyond the trees, heading for the dining hall. Another flew toward the lab. They must be SAS. Good. They could handle Jones-Demerest, and I didn't need to leave Jack.

Operating on autopilot, I tapped my earpiece. "Officer down. Chest wound." My voice shook. I tried to steady it. "I need a medic about one hundred yards south of Target One's house."

"Roger that," someone said. "Dispatching medics."

"Incoming," a familiar voice called.

Gun rising, I swung toward the sound. Petunia sped out of the darkness, her face streaked with blacking and her hair covered by a black watch cap. The long case slung over her shoulder had to be the grenade launcher. She thrust a vest at me that read *Police*.

I stared at it. "Jack's hit." Saying the words felt like a kick in the heart. "Hell, I don't have anything to use for a bandage." Damn leather!

"Go." His face hard, Jack gripped my hand. "You must."

I'd left David, and he'd died.

I hadn't loved David. I did love Jack.

Time froze. My heart stopped for the space of a breath. When it and time resumed, the universe had tipped on its axis.

I stared down at Jack's strained, irreplaceable face. "I can't leave you. Jack, there're soldiers and agents all over." The din of automatic weapons fire reinforced my words. "They can handle it from here."

"It's our—job," he choked. Holding my gaze with his, he drew my hand to his mouth and kissed my knuckles. "I'm—not David." His quiet, thready voice carried straight to my heart despite the din around us. "I'll be here when you return." The words ended in a wheeze.

I tightened my grip on his hand. I'd never told him my partner's name, but I should've expected him to know. He was MI5, after all.

"Down," Petunia snapped. She fired at something toward our right.

I dropped to cover Jack. Wounded though he was, he tried to tug me behind him, and my heart twisted. Through a film of tears, I stared down at him. "Promise me. Promise you'll be here."

"I promise." He drew a wheezing, scary breath, but his intent eyes never left mine. "I love you, Casey."

Even in these circumstances, the words gave me a rush of joy and relief. "I love you, too, Jack. Always." I kissed him hard and fast, then flung myself upright.

Casey. For the first time, he'd called me by the name I'd chosen. There had better be a second time.

I looked hard at Petunia. "I'm leaving him with you."

A thunderous crash shook the ground, throwing me off my feet. I managed to fall so I covered Jack. Although he groaned at the movement, he tucked my head against his good shoulder, shielding it with his arms.

Petunia gasped, "Christ, no." With an agonized look at me, she added, "One of the SAS helos crashed."

#

I hurtled through the darkness, darting from structure to structure, and tried to form a plan. Jones-Demerest would likely make for his house, so I headed there, too. Even if he didn't have a helo coming, there were weapons there and, from the sound of gunfire, guards not hesitant to use them.

An explosion rocked the night. Light flared in the direction of Jones-Demerest's house. Keeping the dining hall between me and it, I ran toward the sound. The pungent, smoky scents of hot brass and burned powder filled the air.

At the corner of the stone dining hall, facing Jones-Demerest's house, four guys in SAS black kit used the building for cover as they fired on the house. Half a dozen men sat or lay on the ground between the dining hall and the wreckage of a helicopter, with two others, probably medics, working on them. At least the bird had gone down where it wouldn't take fire from the guards defending the house.

Despite wearing the vest Petunia had given me, I had her notify the commandos that I was approaching. When one of the medics looked toward me, I jogged up to him. We did fast introductions, and I asked, "Where's the target?"

He jerked his head toward the house. "We can't break through to reach him until our backups arrive. Bastard had a quick reaction force nearby. Brought down our bird with a .50-calibre."

Machine gun, he meant.

With a grim smile, he continued, "We took that out. Now there's a hole in the bloody garden wall, but we can't get to it. Our CO is injured. Master Sgt. Beckwith, over there, is in command."

He jerked his head toward the corner where his comrades fired on the house. I ran toward it. The four men standing there weren't enough to rush the garden, but they'd taken out bits of the wall, maybe with a standard grenade launcher. My launcher carried a bigger boom.

The medic must've said something into his radio because one of the black-clad figures turned to meet me. "I'm Sgt. Beckwith, Agent Billings."

I nodded. As we watched, a small helo came out of the night and descended in the middle of the garden. The wall blocked it from view. Damn it, Jones-Demerest was not getting away.

"Can you take that chopper out?" I asked

"No. We're a quick reaction force, too. And we can't get through that field of fire until our reinforcements arrive."

Surrounded by men in combat gear and body armor, Jones-Demerest hustled out of his house. He clutched a box to his chest as if it were gold. I'd have bet anything it held the formula for the flu virus. The ring of defenders tightened, leaving the house open, as he and his escort edged toward the helipad.

"I have something that will do it," I told him. "Hang on."

He resumed firing on the garden while I dropped to the ground, took the RPG launcher from its case, and loaded it. I stood, shouldering the launcher, and tapped his arm.

"We need Jones-Demerest alive," I told him. The rat-bastard was probably scrambling aboard the chopper now. If I hit it directly, everyone on it was dead. If I could get it while it was on the ground, that was ideal. "I need a good angle. While I get it, I can help you with the garden wall. Can you give me covering fire?"

He nodded. "On three," he said.

His team let out a fierce, concentrated volley. I popped out of hiding and fired the grenade at the stone wall hiding the helicopter.

As I ducked back, an explosion and cries of pain filled the air. My ears rang as I loaded the second grenade.

"Bastard's taking off," Beckwith warned.

I shouldered the launcher. "I'm ready." I had to get the helo while it was low, or the crash wouldn't be survivable.

"Now," the sergeant snapped. He and his comrades unleashed a deafening fusillade of fire.

I stepped out. Both the tail and the missile would rise, so I fired just above the tail. I ducked back again but peeked around the SAS team.

Trailing smoke, the grenade hissed into flight. It struck the chopper just forward of the tail rotor, and triumph surged through my veins. Spinning, mowing down Jones-Demerest's lackeys like hay, it crashed with the scream of tearing metal and the cries of the injured.

That's for you, Jack, I thought, a hard smile curving my mouth. *You, too, David. At last.*

Whirring rotors overhead heralded another pair of black helicopters. They landed behind the dining hall, and commandos in black poured out. The proverbial cavalry had arrived.

I wanted to run back to Jack. I couldn't, though, not until I could report complete success to him.

Meeting little resistance, the newcomers charged the wall. Sergeant Beckwith and I followed with those of his squad who were still functional.

The rat-bastard's helicopter was burning. The soldiers dragged out Jones-Demerest, who lay limply in their hold. I hoped his bloodied face and arms hurt like hell. He still held fast to his box, though. One of the commandos yanked it free and carried it to Beckwith, who flipped it open.

He favored me with a little nod and a grin. "Very nice, indeed." He showed me a file marked *poena summa*, the name I'd seen in Jones-Demerest's safe in Italy, though on a different folder.

I flipped through it hastily. Was there—oh, please—yes! A listing of warehouses with vaccines and antivirals. Jones-Demerest must've planned to play the hero when he decided enough damage had been done.

With a nod of thanks at Beckwith, I tapped the sending stud on my earpiece. "Jack, mission accomplished. I'm on my way back." He didn't reply, and cold gripped the center of my chest. "Jack—"

"Casey, they couldn't wait," Petunia said in a carefully neutral voice. "He tried, but he didn't have the breath to fight them. They're flying him to a hospital in Edinburgh."

They couldn't wait.

I couldn't breathe. Hot tears stung my eyes, and my brain wasn't cycling. I wheeled, putting my back to the commandos. SAS was the model for the world's toughest, ablest warriors. I wasn't about go weepy in front of them.

"Casey." Petunia sounded worried. "Did you copy? Casey?"

She knew about David and cared about me, and now I was scaring her. Drawing a deep, shaky breath, I gathered myself. "Roger that. He tried—"

A boulder in my throat blocked the rest. He hadn't been able to resist. Strong, domineering, protective Jack, who loved me, knew about David, and thus had to know how scared I'd be, hadn't been able to stop them from taking him away.

No. Oh, no. Please...

Petunia was still talking, fast, as though to make up for what she'd had to tell me, filling me in. Despite the sob threatening to burst out of my chest like a vicious little alien, I tried to focus. Set my jaw and took a harsh breath through my nose.

"MI5 officers and local police are calming the residents. Everything's under control." She paused. "Do you copy?"

"Copy," I choked. "Wait one."

I took another deep breath and told myself, *Suck. It. Up.* Jack had a hole in his shoulder, really in his upper chest. He belonged on the fastest possible route to an operating room, not hanging around to reassure his adult, supposedly rational partner.

Partner. *My partner*, he'd said. *My lover. Mine.*

Oh, God, he'd meant those words after all. Why hadn't he wanted me to know? Would I ever have the chance to ask him?

David's face flashed into my mind, and I shuddered. Gritting my teeth, I pushed the memory away for a better one, of Jack holding me after we made love. Jack. This was about him now, not David and definitely not me.

I swallowed hard. "Anything else, Petunia?"

"He pressed his keys into my hand." Probably because I was functioning, relief echoed in her voice. Wryly, she added, "I assume they're for you."

But he hadn't been able to say so. Keys... "Is there one for the Triumph?"

A pause. Jingling. "Looks like."

I swallowed hard. He might've had some other reason for the gesture, but I chose to take it as what I hoped it was, a request for me to come to him.

As if I wouldn't anyway.

But having the car key would make it easier. I also wouldn't be tempted to hot-wire his classic car, a thought he'd probably known would occur to me. Good. *I'm coming, Jack. You be there. Please be there.*

I turned to Sergeant Beckwith and nodded at the file box he held. "You'll see that the right people get that?"

"Of course. Is there a problem?"

"My partner was hit. He's on his way to Edinburgh, and I have to go."

"Bruce Hospital." Beckwith nodded sagely. "A fine facility. We use it."

"Thanks." I glanced around at the ambulance pulling up for Jones-Demerest and his crew and the commandos fanning out to sweep up any stray rats. "I'm glad you were here. It was a close thing."

"Too close." He shook his head. "I hope to hell they can distribute the vaccines quickly."

So did I, but that wasn't my job. I packed up the launcher and ran to meet Petunia.

#

Roaring up the A68 in Jack's style, which is to say, as fast as I dared on such a curvy, hilly road, I had the top down and heavy metal blaring. I wanted wind in my face, noise on the radio, anything to distract me, but I couldn't stop thinking about him. About us, to the extent there was an *us*.

I was still a linthead's kid, one who'd gone far beyond anyone's expectations. Jack was still a nobleman of distinguished lineage who thought that put him a cut above everyone else. Which I still couldn't accept.

As he'd said, we were very different. Could we somehow move past that? Would love be enough to bridge the gap for us?

Love.

With a sick wrench, I remembered our cover story. We were supposed to split up when this was over. I was supposed to disappear from his world. Never see him again.

Tears welled in my eyes. My lips trembled, and my throat closed. Angrily, I dashed a hand over my eyes. I was not giving him up. Not for anything except his own choice.

He'd been right about one thing. I'd seen more of Jimbo Hartner in him than Jack deserved. *Judge me as I am*, he'd said. And so I would. Damn it, I'd drag him past that whole superior-burden-and-lineage thing if I had to.

Unless he decided, when he'd had time to think, that we really were not right for each other. That we should amicably part after all. Which would truly break my heart.

Still, we came from different worlds. Just as Trey and I had. Love hadn't been enough for us. Maybe Jack and I would prove equally incompatible outside the strictures of a working partnership.

Scrubbing at my eyes with the heel of one hand, I set my jaw. Making myself crazy with *what-if* scenarios wouldn't help me or Jack.

My phone rang, and I jumped before remembering I'd phoned the London office to ask for a report on him. I shut off the radio before tapping my wireless headset to take the call. "Billings."

"Congratulations, Miss Billings," Arachne said, "on your success.

Well done, indeed." Before I could thank her, she added, "You may be interested to know that Jones-Demerest died shortly after going into hospital. The files you and the SAS recovered, however, contain the information we need."

"Then I don't guess anyone will lose sleep over the rat—er, Jones-Demerest's loss."

"No," she agreed, her voice dry. "I requested a report on Lord Bainbridge's condition. Unfortunately, MI5 doesn't believe we 'need to know' that information."

My grip on the wheel tightened painfully. MI5 needed to take the sticks out of their butts, but she wouldn't appreciate that language. "Petunia said he had pneumo-something? A collapsed lung and air in the chest cavity. The medics put in a tube."

Just saying that made me faintly ill, but I continued. "Surgeons will fix the wound and reinflate the lung. That much, I know already. She said the medics called it routine."

"Pneumothorax," Arachne supplied. "For a gunshot wound, it probably is routine. It might've been much worse."

"Yeah." I nodded, my gaze focused on the narrow ribbon of asphalt the headlights illuminated. Even the simplest procedure could go wrong. Unsuspected complications, later blood clots, damage they couldn't detect in the field—but I couldn't let myself go there. "What's MI5's problem? Assuming they have a particular one."

"Lord Bainbridge checked the lab even after he could've waited for backup and apparently allowed you to threaten a prisoner in violation of field regulations." Her dry voice added, "They attribute this 'erratic' thinking to your influence."

"They don't know him very well, then." Checking the lab was in Jack's plan, and for a good reason. We needed to get any useful info in it before anyone had a chance to destroy it. Therefore he would check it, no matter what. As for the rest, I couldn't deny he'd done that for me, knowing I'd needed to do it even if it wouldn't bring David back, and I loved him all the more for it.

"Perhaps they don't," she said. "I do have other contacts, however. Lord Bainbridge is in surgery now."

He'd reached the hospital alive, then. And he would be fine. He would be.

A pause, and then she added, "The corpsmen who brought him in put you on the visitor list at his request."

"Thus stealing a march on MI5." He'd probably anticipated their pissy reaction. He'd also been alert enough to think ahead when he reached Edinburgh. I grinned into the wind. "I like it."

"I thought you would," she said dryly. "We've also found records indicating that Jones-Demerest had you and Lord Bainbridge followed in York and after. So we can acquit Robert Basingstoke of any involvement in that."

"That will please Ja—his brother."

"Yes." She paused. "Miss McIntosh has briefed me fully. I assume you'll want a few days leave."

"Yes, please." I had two coming to me because of the mission I'd finished, but Jack would be hospitalized longer than that. I swallowed hard against new fear. I was so not ready for this chat, but putting it off wouldn't help. "Then you know we need a new cover story."

"Miss McIntosh thinks Lord Bainbridge would agree."

I gathered my courage. "So shall I come up with something, or will you?"

"Lord Bainbridge's shop must also agree." She paused, and I held my breath. "What if they or we insist you stay with the original story?"

I hesitated. Despite my misgivings, I wanted my chance with Jack. To get it, I had to sound far more sure than I felt. Drawing a deep breath, I said, "Then I'd have to make a choice I'd rather avoid."

Assuming Jack wanted me badly enough to make it with me, and that was by no means certain.

CHAPTER THIRTY

I don't like hospitals. I don't like the way they smell, and I don't like what they signify, serious illness. Maybe even death. The tube running out of Jack's chest to a vacuum bottle seemed particularly ominous. The bottle would suck air from his chest cavity so the lung could reinflate.

He slid in and out of consciousness for all the next day and night. He should've awakened much sooner, but the doctors blamed the pain inducer that scum had given him. I stayed by his bed and waited for improvement. I wouldn't believe he would recover until he talked coherently to me.

I was grateful, though, for the kind efficiency of the staff. And for Petunia, who brought me fresh clothes and the rinse to make my hair its normal deep brown again, insisting I take a shower and use both.

She'd also told me Jones-Demerest had given his security team orders that to hold off the cops at the gate, using any necessary force, so he could make his getaway. He must've known that if there was enough evidence for a warrant, and the police arrived in large numbers, his luck had run out. In his jacket, the SAS had found all the necessary documents for starting a new identity in Venezuela. With her various errands handled, she tactfully left me alone with Jack.

On the second morning, I awoke slowly to the sensation of someone stroking my hair. I jerked upright in my chair. I'd laid my head on Jack's bed, for just moment, I thought. I must've dozed off.

I caught his hand and turned my head to look at him.

He smiled. "Casey." His voice sounded hoarse but steady.

"Good morning." Sitting up, I kissed his hand. He was awake and calling me by name, great signs. "Do you want some water?"

"In a bit." He tugged at my hand, drawing me up toward the head of the bed. His lips brushed my knuckles, sending frissons of delight up my arm, into my breasts and farther down. Holding my fingers to his mouth, his eyes warm, he said, "I love you."

"I love you, too." I almost added, *always*, but now that we were both safe, I wasn't sure we should go there. I'd never been good at relationships, and I'd failed spectacularly in my only attempt at one with someone from a background similar to his. Reaching across him, I rang to tell the nurse he was awake.

He smiled. "I'll take that water now, if you please."

"Absolutely." I pushed the button to raise his head, then poured a cup for him. "Take it slowly at first."

His hand shook only a little when he accepted the cup. Cautiously, he lifted it to his mouth. I decided not to help unless he asked. Better to respect his pride.

"You saved my life," I said quietly. "That bullet would've hit me in the face."

He wrapped both hands carefully around the cup, his gaze steady on mine. "But I didn't keep my word. I'm sorry, love."

"What?" I couldn't think what he meant for a moment. Then it registered. "You were here when I arrived. You're here now. That's good enough."

"Not in fighting trim, perhaps." He grinned.

My heart did its little kick-thump, and I grinned back. "You'll get there soon enough."

"No, actually, I won't." His eyes heated. Surveying me, he set his cup on the bedstand and reached for me. "Not soon enough. I'd rather be there now."

I kissed him carefully. He slid his IV-free hand into my hair and deepened the kiss. His tongue brushed my lips. I started to relax onto him but remembered his chest tube and stopped myself.

"Too soon," I said against his mouth. Reluctantly, I straightened.

With a tender look, he stroked his thumb over my hand. "The medics told me you caught Jones-Demerest. Avenged David. Not that you had any fault there, you know."

Maybe I did know it, finally, and I took some comfort that Jones-Demerest had died of his injuries. But..."If you'd died, it would have been because you saved me."

"Worth it," he said, smiling. He still sounded a little short of breath, as the doctors had warned. "I would do anything for you."

If we both felt that way, the future was worth fighting Arachnid and MI5 for and confronting the very real differences in our backgrounds and civilian lifestyles.

Holding his hand, I asked, "Did you really not remember calling me your partner and lover, that time on the floor?"

His fingers tightened on mine. His gaze level, he said, "I didn't know how you felt, and I'd sworn not to complicate our mission with personal issues. Not like—" His jaw tightened, and he stared at the ceiling.

Holding my breath, I waited to see if he'd trust me.

At last, he looked gravely back at me. "Like Mum. She loved us, but her crises often arose at important times. And they always came first."

Instead of her sons. He didn't need to say it, and my heart ached for him. No wonder he was such a control freak. And no wonder his aunt's steady affection had become so important to him. "Petunia says your aunt's holding her own."

"That's good." A sudden, stiff breath betrayed his relief. As his throat worked in a swallow, he turned his hand to cup my cheek. "After attacking you, I didn't want to make any personal claim. Didn't dare hope you could forgive me. When I awoke after we made love, then while I searched the club room, all I could think about was how badly I'd failed you."

"You're doing it again. Don't hold yourself to superhero standards, Jack. Even they make mistakes, despite their powers."

Jack lifted a brow. "They're imaginary, love."

"Exactly my point. You're not a superhero, either. And I wouldn't want to live with one."

The doctor chose that moment to bustle in. I liked this petite woman and her brisk, confident air. "Good morning, Lord Bainbridge." She stopped by his bed. "You're awake at last."

"How long was I out?" He directed a quizzical look at me.

My fingers tightened on his.

"The better part of two days," the doctor said before I could. "I'm Dr. Grantham. How do you feel?"

"As though someone shot me." Dry, if a bit slurred, his tone reassured me as to his mood.

"That's as it should be, then." She checked his dressing with brisk efficiency, made clucking noises of approval, and replaced his covers. "We'll likely remove the chest tube this afternoon, then keep you a few days. You may have more water if you like and work your way up from there. You'll still need to recuperate somewhere quiet for a couple of weeks." When he opened his mouth, as though to protest, she added, "That's if all goes well, of course. Complications will prolong your stay. Any questions?"

He raised an eyebrow at her. "Are you expecting complications?"

"Not if you follow instructions."

"Right, then." His head dropped back as though the effort of talking had exhausted him.

She nodded. "Good day to you, sir. Miss Billings."

"Thank you," I said.

"Ta," Jack added. He probably didn't have the breath for the full thank-you routine. Although his color had improved, it had a way to go before it hit normal. His dark stubble highlighted the pallor in his face, which looked tired and strained.

Dr. Grantham strolled out.

Jack reached for his water again. "What's been happening while I slept?"

Caring had to count as a good sign. I smiled. "Simon checked your voicemail. Before all the shooting started, Percy left a message saying he planned to vote his shares your way. He didn't say why."

Jack grunted. "He might've spared us all that trouble."

"Somehow, I don't think that's Percy's way."

With a nod, he asked, "What's the situation?"

"Lots of people are improving, thanks to a stock of drugs in Jones-Demerest's Dorset warehouse. He had vaccine and a store of antivirals. We found the formulas for everything there as well."

Of course, even with a formula, creating more vaccine isn't fast. "Jones-Demerest died of his injuries, but his records show no sign that he slipped his goods into those of the companies he pretended to help. The assistance must've been to build social capital. Trust."

Jack grimaced, and I continued, "Our guess about his goal was correct. His records led us to his allies on the Continent, other wealthy men who'd immigrated to their countries but weren't accepted socially. They planned to kill off those they saw as the ruling elites and replace them with smart, ambitious immigrants. Who would, of course, be loyal to them."

"Of course." Jack scowled into his cup. "Do we know what the mood-altering chemicals were for?"

"Products for sale. You could sow a lot of social disorder with any of them, making it easier to stage a coup. Especially in countries where the social order is already weak."

I paused, disgusted anew by what I had to say next. "They'd apparently used that tunnel from the brewery to move supplies and test subjects into and out of the lab, by the way. When they caught you, four guards were returning from the brewery. They'd just delivered a dead homeless man to go out in a keg."

"Bastards." Grimacing, he asked, "Anything about Horace?"

His caring about Horace and Hilda was one of the reasons I'd fallen in love with him. "There are indications that Horace may have been drugged, that any midlife crisis was exacerbated by one of the drugs Jones-Demerest was testing. There's no way to know for sure, but that could've caused his death. I don't see why Hilda shouldn't believe that if it comforts her."

"Nor do I."

"When you're feeling up to it," I said, "maybe we should call Hilda and see how she's doing. Maybe, if our agencies agree, tell her a cover story. She was so sweet and has had such a rough time, I'd like her to know we care about her. What do you think?"

"I'd like that, too." His eyes rose to mine, warm and rueful. "Your improvisation at the lab was rather clever. They told me the drug they'd given me would eventually have proved fatal. You saved my life."

"And my ancestors didn't even come over with the Conqueror." The words popped out before I thought. "I didn't mean that the way it sounded. Jack—"

"No, you're right." He reached for my hand. His was warm and solid, just as it should be. I gripped it tightly.

"Casey. Sweetheart." His gaze searched mine. "My father was like Aunt Beatrice, wanting the good old days back, when the nobility owned most of England and answered to almost no one. He lived to ride in the hunt, drive fast cars, and drink at his club. My mother..."

He sighed and shook his head. "She was a free spirit, an artistic, Bohemian person who thought her wealth should always be there."

"It wasn't?" I asked carefully.

"Oh, it was. Hawkshead Shipping is sound, but Mum was bored, I think. She always looked for the new thing." His thumb rubbed over the back of my hand, and he stared down at it. "She took LSD, but it didn't open her mind. It gave her a bad trip, left her with chronic, suicidal depression." He looked up, watching me. "When I was ten, she wrapped her MG around a tree."

"I'm so sorry, Jack." He seemed totally composed, but I now knew he was good at faking that. Hesitantly, thinking of Petunia's report on his mother, I asked, "Do you think it was suicide?"

"I'd like to think not, but I fear so." He shook his head.

"Then your Aunt Beatrice came to take care of you."

Jack took a deep breath and winced. "Bloody tube," he muttered. Holding my gaze, he said, "Old habits die hard, but I'll try to, as you put it, give myself a break."

"I hope so. Don't judge yourself harder than you do others." *Like me.* "And I have to admit I made assumptions I shouldn't have—based on my past, as you suspected."

I hesitated, hating to think of those days, but I owed him the same candor he'd given me. "Not every mill town was like Hartner Falls. Some mill owners actually cared about their people. But the Hartners didn't. They owned all the businesses in town, fired anyone who defied them. There was no other mill close by, and the skills aren't exactly transferable."

"I've read about such things." His hand tightened on mine.

"The worst time for me was when I was eight, the first time I crossed one of them. I made the mistake of beating Jimbo Hartner, who was my age, in a spelling bee. The teacher threw it his way anyway, probably fearing for her job. I protested. I shouldn't have." I took a deep, heavy breath. Weird, how the pain could come back after so long.

"Love, you needn't—"

"Yes, I do need to. You should know why I'm so hyper about class and fairness." The sympathy in his soft, gray eyes tore at my heart. I looked at the trees outside the window instead of at him.

"There was a holiday program the next week. I was supposed to read an essay, so I wrote one about my grandfather. Unlike the Hartners, who sat out World War II in their nice, cozy house, he served in the navy in the Pacific. He came home and stayed, worked in the mill, because my gran was afraid to live anywhere else, afraid of the city."

"Afraid to risk hope," Jack said quietly.

"Yes." He did understand. Maybe I should've known he would. "By the time I started school, he had brown lung disease, and he was so, so sick. Anyway, Jimbo's daddy went to the teacher just before the program and told her I wasn't reading, that I'd copied my essay."

"What a bastard." Despite Jack's shortness of breath, anger crackled in his words.

"Yes, but that's how life was in that town. Not just for my family, either. I could tell you lots, but this isn't about that. PawPaw had come to see me read, come in a wheelchair, and I so wanted to show him how proud I was of him."

Even now, I had to blink back tears, remembering the disappointment that sweet man had tried so hard to hide. "He didn't know my essay was about him, and I read it for him later, but that...tainted the whole thing. My dad was furious, but if he'd argued, Hartner would've fired him on the spot, and my mom, too."

"That's when you resolved to get out."

"Fuck, yes. There were other things, too, along the way, but—Jack, PawPaw had a heart attack the next day. He never regained consciousness and died a week later. He had no business being there, but he'd come for me, and that son of a bitch—"

I tightened my lips to stifle a flood of bitterness.

Jack tugged me toward his good shoulder.

I resisted. "I'll hurt you."

"Sod that, come here." He tugged harder, and I gave in.

I kept my weight off him, bracing myself on my elbow and barely touching my forehead to his shoulder, but I had to admit having his arm around me helped.

"Part of me expected the worst from you all along," I said. "But you're not that way, and it wasn't fair of me. I'm sorry for that, and I won't do it anymore."

He pressed his lips to my temple. "Holding myself to a high standard doesn't mean I think I'm better than you. I swear it. You're the first woman I've known who's so regrettably often two steps ahead of me."

"My preferred position." I sat up again and smiled to cover my teary relief.

Someone tapped on the door. I scrubbed my eyes quickly as Robin walked in, his face anxious. My spasm of fury wouldn't do. I tamped it into blandness. "Good morning, Mr. Basingstoke."

"Miss Billings. Jack, how are you?" He hurried to his brother's bedside.

Jack shrugged, then winced again. "Well enough. Have you spoken to Aunt Beatrice?"

"Not yet." Robin shot a contrite look at him. "Jack, if only you'd told me you were working with the Security Service. You weren't named, Miss Billings, but I knew whom the article meant. We're all very grateful."

Jack and I traded confused glances. Article? What did Robin mean? How could he have learned about the roles we'd played in catching Jones-Demerest?

"It was all over the news services and in all the papers," Robin said. "I suppose you haven't seen them."

A tap on the door heralded Petunia. What was this, Kings Cross Station at rush hour?

"Oh, good, you're here," she said to me, as though she hadn't known perfectly well that I was. "I overheard that last, Mr. Basingstoke. Miss Billings is a colleague of mine. Our firm specializes in discretion, so I must ask you not to reveal her identity."

MI5 must've agreed to a new cover story. Had even spread it. My heart gave a sudden leap. Jack and I smiled at each other.

"Of course, of course," Robin said hastily. "Not a word."

This was a great chance to make a point, so I added, "We had specific orders from MI5 not to reveal that we were working with them, but you might have trusted your brother's judgment."

Jack glared, but I'd already said what I needed to. I answered him with an arched eyebrow.

"Yes, I might." Robin shook his head. "You may've been sent down, but you did rather well at Cambridge before that."

That Jack had won a spot there in the first place spoke volumes, I thought, but I didn't say so. I supposed I'd overstepped, since this qualified as their business, most definitely not mine, but speaking up had felt good. Maybe it would also help Jack with his family down the road.

"I misjudged you as well, Miss Billings," Robin said. "I would never have guessed you were a corporate finance investigator."

"Part of the plan," I told him.

"The investment deal is dead, of course." Robin looked worried. "Jack, when you're recovered, we might discuss some ways to strengthen the company."

"If you like." Jack's voice was definitely fading, and he looked even more tired than he had before.

"You should probably rest, Jack," I said.

The comment earned me another glare from him, but I didn't care. Robin hadn't shown any skill at picking up subtleties.

"One last thing." Robin squared his shoulders. "My remark about Aunt Beatrice's opinion of you, at Simply Yorkshire, was ill advised. I'm certain it was also wrong. I was angry, but I shouldn't have said it."

Jack raised an eyebrow. "Is that why you didn't call the police when I hit you?"

As I'd guessed, the possibility his brother had set him up hadn't occurred only to me. Unless maybe Jack just wondered.

Robin shook his head. "After provoking you, I'd have been ashamed to do so. Besides, you're my brother."

So he hadn't been part of setting his brother up. I gave him points for class, for the apology and the restraint.

Jack's face relaxed. "Sorry for the punch as well."

They smiled at each other.

"I'll be going, then." Robin drew an envelope from his jacket. "Percy sent you this." He wished us both a good day and hurried out.

With a wink and a wave, Petunia followed him. I stared after her. She could've told me about our new cover on the phone. Could she have wanted to see my face when she shared the news? Regardless, it seemed that I now had official clearance to be part of Jack's world. No matter how I felt about some parts of it.

And I'd have to get over those feelings if I wanted to be with him. Could I?

Jack opened the envelope. "A letter." He removed it. As he scanned the paper, his curiosity became a frown, then deepened to a scowl.

"Jack? What is it?"

"That old bastard." He handed me the letter. "He never intended to vote for the buy-in. All his nonsense about it was designed to test my response—to see if I was the 'frippery fool' I seemed to be, especially after my odd marriage."

Glancing at the paper, I smiled. "But you 'proved your mettle' to the entire family. Well, of course you did."

He took the letter back and tossed it aside.

I sank onto the bed again. As I smoothed back Jack's hair, he caught my hand. "Robin's arrival interrupted me. I want you in my life, Casey, but I know you don't trust those of us from privileged backgrounds."

And there it was, the elephant in the room. How like him to haul it into the center of things.

"I was engaged once, to a guy whose world was kinda like yours."

"I suppose it didn't go so well," he said gently.

"You could say." Really, I wouldn't have been surprised if his mother'd shot off fireworks when she learned I'd given back his ring. "I didn't fit in the world of cocktail parties and charity luncheons and country clubs. Your world includes some of that. But I'm willing to try."

Even though just the thought of it was calling up memories of the various subtle and not-so-subtle snubs I'd endured. I also had a strong feeling that, even without purple hair, someone like me would not be what his aunt would want for him. She would certainly not be shy about making her feelings known. If we were together, that wouldn't only be his problem.

As though Jack sensed my misgivings, he added, "I want a partner, not a hostess or a social prop."

"I hope so, Jack. But life has a way of—"

His headshake stopped me. Wrapping his hand around mine, he looked at me as though weighing his words. "We fight for what we want, the two of us. The story you shared about your grandfather confirms the info in your dossier, that you come from what Americans like to call the *wrong side of the tracks*."

"Yeah. So?"

"So people who escape such settings—even resourceful, quick-thinking people like you—often fear they lucked out, they don't really deserve what they've attained." He hesitated, his fingers tight on mine. "That they're just...I believe *lintheads* is the term."

He'd laid bare my deepest secret. I couldn't deny it, not to him. "How did you know that? How could you?"

"Because I love you. Because I admire what you've done with your life. You completely deserve everything you've gained. And because I sometimes fear the over-privileged aristocrat in my blood will take control at a bad time, one that might be fatal for someone else."

I stroked his cheek, my fingers rasping over two days' beard growth. "That's what you meant, that morning at Simply Yorkshire. You just didn't say it that way."

He rubbed his thumb over my hand. "I was angry. Disappointed. I'd wanted you ever since I walked into Arachne's office and saw you standing there. Your hair was vile, and your clothes were baggy, but you had your chin up and a look in your eyes that said you could take anything anyone dished out."

I blinked back sudden, stinging tears. "Jack—"

His grip on my hand tightened. "I should've said something sooner, told you how I felt, but I'd vowed never to let personal issues come before my duty."

Because of the way his parents' self-centeredness had affected him, I guessed.

He continued, "Instead, I waited. Let myself hope, for when the mission was over. I wanted champagne and roses in the bed of my London flat for us, not violence and desperation on the floor of a criminal's rented house."

I cupped his cheek with my free hand. "Thank you for that, but please stop regretting that night. I don't."

"I hope not." His eyes bored into mine. "We have official sanction to be seen together. Will you come to Yorkshire with me when they let me out of here?"

Crunch time. If this thing between us fell apart, it was going to be really bad. I'd fought for Trey, and I'd failed. I hadn't had the right weapons for that arena. Panic flared inside me, but not as strongly as when I'd realized Jack was shot.

If only he'd come from a background more like mine, or even like David's solid middle-class one. But then he might not have become the man I loved.

I'd waited for him my whole life, a scary thought. I'd be crazy to just walk away.

I took a deep breath. "Sure."

"I can't wait to show you everything." Tender warmth softened his eyes as he added, "It will be good to be together without having to play roles."

I leaned close to kiss him, and the sweet, gentle touch wrapped warmth around my heart.

He closed his eyes, lowering our joined hands onto the bed. "I'll just rest for a bit."

"I'll be here," I said, but he didn't react. He was already asleep.

I held his hand and watched him. I'd do anything he asked, almost. Another scary thought. He came with a mansion—several of them, really —a household staff, and a mean, domineering aunt. Not to mention MI5 rules and a social set where I fit in about as well as a donkey at Churchill Downs.

What had I gotten myself into?

THE END FOR NOW
Casey and Jack return in *The Runway Murder Affair.*
To read an excerpt, turn to page 273.

Author's Note

Thank you for reading *The Deathbrew Affair*. I hope you enjoyed it.

During the time I worked on this book, the World Health Organization and the United Kingdom's National Health Service revised their guidelines for classifying and addressing pandemic flu several times. I chose the features that worked best for this story from the various sets of guidelines.

Anyone familiar with the Yorkshire Museum and York Museum Gardens will recognize some aspects of my fictional Abbey Museum. I love Museum Gardens and the museum itself but adapted them to my story's needs and changed the museum's name. While much of my museum is directly borrowed, some important features are entirely fictional. No one who reads this book and then visits Museum Gardens should expect it to be the same.

If you're inclined to leave a review of this book on an online vendor site, I would appreciate it.

There's information on my website (www.nancynorthcott.com) about how to obtain signed cards showing the covers of my books and short stories. I don't keep addresses, so asking for a cover card won't get you on any mailing list. If you're interested, you can go to http://www.nancynorthcott.com/for-e-book-readers/

If you'd like me to keep you posted about new releases, you can sign up for my newsletter on the right-hand sidebar of my homepage. Just go to www.nancynorthcott.com. I never share your email. Newsletters come out only when I have a new release or other important news, so you'll hear from me just a few times a year.

Thanks again!

The Runway Murder Affair

Note: Because *The Runway Murder Affair* is still being edited, this excerpt is subject to change.

Chapter 1

My fellow agents and I wanted the day to start with a bang, just not the kind that would result if any of our group happened to step on a mine. I especially didn't want the report to say, *The task force lost the element of surprise because the Arachnid agent, Katherine "Casey" Billings, didn't watch where she put her feet.* Not only did I hate the idea of turning up dead before my twenty-eighth birthday, but Arachnid took enough flak from national intelligence agencies as it was.

As we crept through the quiet woods, I kept a wary eye out for the little yellow flags the explosive ordnance team had used to mark mine locations. The task force consisting of French counter-terrorism (GIGN) agents, assorted others, and me wore full assault gear. The flat gray fatigues, body armor, helmets, and gloves, and even the gas masks strapped to our left thighs, were haute couture for raiding smuggling dens, but none of that made us invulnerable. If only.

One team had already neutralized the lookouts. With dawn just breaking over the French countryside, the jihadi smugglers occupying the two-story, stone farmhouse we surrounded should still be sleeping. We should take them by surprise. *Should* being the operative word.

We reached the edge of the trees. My teammate, Gaston Monsengwo, looked at the two guys with us, then at me. We all nodded that we were set.

"Team two ready," his voice said in my earpiece. Even with his face shield flipped up, I couldn't see his mouth move because of the black Nomex hood he wore under the Kevlar helmet.

At five eight, I topped the wiry Congolese security officer by a couple of inches, but he had a reputation for toughness.

Still no signs of activity in the farmhouse. With its slate roof, rustic shrubbery in the clear area around it, and matching garden shed, it could've graced a postcard with "Visit Central France" emblazoned over it. In French, of course.

The other teams checked in, one by one. Waiting, I let my thoughts drift to Jack, who was probably still asleep in London. Tall, dark-haired, and gray-eyed, at age thirty-four he had the skill and rugged good looks of a pirate and the soul of a knight, all wrapped up in a package that was Earl of Bainbridge, MI5 agent, and—maybe—love of my life.

Unless he turned out to be my most painful mistake. We came from very different worlds, and I wasn't at all sure we could bridge them.

With a sigh, I shook my head. I wasn't usually distractible at times like this, but knowing Lord Heartthrob waited for me gave me a new stake in my own safety, one I hadn't expected to feel and wasn't entirely sure how to handle. Regardless, I couldn't let it distract me.

I took a better grip on the HK416 I carried, both for its firepower and because it helped me blend with the GIGN operators, who all carried them. I liked it fine but missed the lighter weight and easy familiarity of my favored Walther PPK.

The last team was checking in. Any moment, we'd roll.

Faint light streaked the gray eastern sky. Except for leaves rustling in the breeze, everything was silent. Poised. Even the birds, which should've been rousing, kept their peace, probably uneasy about all the strange, gray figures in their domain. My heart hammered just a little faster than usual, thanks to adrenaline pumping through me. This raid was the culmination of weeks of joint work by Arachnid, GIGN, and others. If it didn't go well, all that effort was wasted.

"*Et bien*," the tenor voice of Etienne Vacher, GIGN agent and task force leader, said in my earpiece. "*Avaçons.*" Advance, he meant, so we hurried across the clearing to our positions by the house like a dozen drone ants converging on a picnic hamper—but an armed and deadly one.

Monsengwo, our two burly companions, and I plastered ourselves against the stone walls flanking the back door. I have a certain fondness for making things go boom. However, because this was Monsengwo's first major op, I'd take the lead inside, so Vacher and I had agreed the newbie could have the door-blowing fun. Monsengwo and I would attack up the rear stairs. The other two on our team would take the cellar.

Silently, Monsengwo stuck a C4 door opener against the lock. Then he informed Vacher the charge was set. A similar message from the front door team whispered in my headset.

"Still clear," the thermal imaging team reported in French. Which meant our targets were still horizontal in the rooms upstairs, not showing signs of rousing. Perfect. Looking good on the surprise front so far.

His voice now don't-screw-with-me hard, Vacher announced us in French on a loudspeaker, then demanded the occupants' surrender. That was the signal for a couple of guys somewhere out of sight to cut the phone and electrical lines. The loudspeaker's off switch clicked over the command net as Vacher snapped, without pausing, "*Attaquons.*"

Monsengwo triggered the explosive, which made a hard, fast *bang* and knocked the door in. We charged through the smoke. We swept our weapons across the empty kitchen and reported it clear. Through the parlor door, we could see the front team doing the same. We rushed toward the stairs. A pair of muffled *bang* noises, in quick sequence, behind me and the vibration in the wooden floor signaled the cellar team's flash-bangs detonating. A series of blasts outside shook the ground as the explosives team detonated the perimeter mines. That should rattle our targets nicely.

Hitting the landing, I aimed my weapon up the stairs. Monsengwo lobbed a chemical smoke grenade up to the next floor as breaking glass heralded others crashing in through the windows. Coughing, curses in French and Arabic, and sounds of scrambling came from above. My heart kicked into a faster pace, and I set my jaw because, dammit, I did want to make it home.

A door above and to the right burst open. Monsengwo and I fired together, the barrage taking down four guys, whose weapons sent streams of bullets over our heads to crash into the walls behind us. When the firing stopped, we started upward again.

I'd almost gained the top when a scruffy, bearded man popped out of a room across from the stairway, Beretta in hand. As I squeezed the 416's trigger, his weapon fired. Lightning spiked into my side, turning my vision to streaky black. The impact knocked me backward. My head and shoulders hit hard. Streaky black became midnight with purple pinwheels, and then everything went dark.

#

I surfaced lying on my back. Breathing hurt, and someone tugging at my shirt didn't help. Pressure on my side sent a hot knife of pain through my gut. "Ow, shit," I snapped, forcing my eyes open. I was outside, lying on grass. "Watch—the hands—Vacher."

Etienne Vacher leaned over me, pale blue sky above him. Framed by his combat helmet, his narrow face and dark eyes held worry, but his lips curved up. "You always say that," he commented in his lightly accented English, and I realized I'd automatically used my native tongue, complete with original North Carolina inflections.

"Be still," he added.

If Vacher had time to poke at me, the fun must be over. And I'd missed most of it. Damn.

I'd lost my vest and headgear, and a sweat-dampened lock of dark brown hair blocked part of my vision. Shoving it back with reassuringly minimal pain, I heard the familiar mopping-up sounds around us—voices giving orders, making comments. I sucked in a painful breath and ground out, "What—"

"Your armor stopped the rounds," he said, "but you'll have a couple of nasty, hand-sized bruises. They're going to hurt. The medic checked you for any rounds we missed. She'll take a more thorough look after she tends to those who're bleeding."

At my questioning look, he added, "Minor wounds, not serious. I don't think your bruises signal anything grim, but we'll have her check. We took four of the enemy alive, recovered all their cargo and records. When we finish searching, we'll see what we have." He straightened my shirt and gave me a wry smile.

Four out of ten. Not what we'd hoped. We needed all the information we could wring out of them about their plans. Chatter said they planned something huge for September, which started day after tomorrow. "The one who shot you had the worse of your exchange," Etienne added. "You killed him. Head shot. Very neat. Monsengwo is impressed."

"Like—you're not." Breathing felt marginally easier, which meant talking was.

"You always impress me, *m'amie*." He grinned. "You're probably fit for that romantic celebration I keep offering. Perhaps this time?"

I rolled my eyes. With a wink, he rose and departed. His amiable, easy manner when suggesting horizontal celebrations made the offers flattering rather than offensive. Even though I suspected he'd proposition pretty much anyone with female plumbing. Vacher had that kind of light, flirtatious charm.

Jack did not, which was one thing I loved about him. Thinking of the bruising, which would become extremely colorful in the twenty-four to forty-eight hours before I saw him again, I grimaced. Monsengwo might be impressed. Jack definitely would not be.

#

Thirty-six hours later, I strolled into the Tube station at Heathrow. This mission didn't have the urgency to rate a car and driver, so I'd take the Underground to Arachnid headquarters in South Wimbledon. I had work to do, but after that I wanted to see Jack.

Unfortunately, his protective instincts would react very badly to the bruise that had developed rather disgusting shades of purple and green. I'd save that little tidbit for a face-to-face explanation, but I could certainly let him know I was back. I tugged out my phone and hit his speed-dial number.

His phone rolled to voicemail, and his strong, deep voice said, in its Oxbridge accent, "This is Jack. Sorry I can't take your call. You're welcome to leave a message." Polite but to the point, like the man himself.

The message tone beeped.

"Hey, Lord Hot Stuff." Wishing I could see his reaction to that, I smiled. "I'm back, heading to work to tie up some loose ends. Give me a call when you're free." I waited a beat, softening my voice. "I missed you. And I love you."

Snapping the phone closed, I dropped it into my tan leather shoulder bag. I'd worn nice, cream-colored slacks and a lilac, short-sleeved V-neck sweater, dressier than my usual jeans and knit pullover, in the now vain hope he'd be free. At least I wouldn't have to change before meeting him.

Coming home to someone, even though we didn't live together, felt odd. Last time I'd left England, no one outside of work had kept track of whether or when I returned. Now I had someone who not only kept track but was eager to have me back.

If that eagerness didn't last, losing it was going to be agony.

I waved my card at the turnstile scanner and pushed through. My train was at the platform. Hurrying aboard, I pondered Jack and our hypothetical future. His title gave him entree to London's elite social circles. As part of his cover, he moved through those circles often. He would naturally want me to go with him as the fall social calendar geared up, especially to events benefitting charities his family supported. I wasn't sure I could deal with that lifestyle for the long haul. Or with his relatives and old friends, who all reveled in their social standing.

I'd been engaged to a guy from a wealthy, socially prominent family back in North Carolina. They were very new money compared to most of the people in Jack's circle but were definitely the big fishes in the local pond. Raised in a mill town by parents with little money, I hadn't mixed well with that set. In fact, it would be fair to call the engagement a disaster.

Now here I was, facing the same task but at a much higher level. And not feeling any more confident about my chances of succeeding.

As if that weren't enough, Jack and I worked for agencies that cordially disliked each other. MI5 and many of its counterparts resented Arachnid's ability to skirt the rules binding them, while we didn't appreciate having them receive credit for our accomplishments because our existence was secret.

Despite all that, Jack and I had fallen in love when we worked together earlier in the summer. We'd been inseparable during his recovery from a chest wound he'd taken shielding me, but we had spent that time secluded in Yorkshire, with minimal family interaction and no social obligations. Then we'd gone back to work.

Thinking of work reminded me of the mission I'd just finished. Along with the expected munitions and wads of cash in dollars, euros, and various other currencies, we'd recovered miscellaneous other bits, including a pouch of gems and high-grade fakes. That last seemed off-kilter, not in the usual line for these people. And why mix gems and fakes? Money laundering?

Coming out of the Tube in Wimbledon, I stepped onto a street full of mundane businesses—estate agent, florist shop, tea room, book shop, and so forth—that helped conceal Arachnid's presence in the neighborhood. I opened my phone to check messages. Just like the

Queen of the Lovesick. Really, I should get a grip on—

The phone rang in my hand, chiming "Rule Britannia," which I'd assigned exclusively to Jack. My heart skipped a beat, then picked up its pace—so moony, but what could I do?—as I punched the button to receive. "Hey."

"'Lord Hot Stuff?'" Jack's wry baritone sent fresh tingles through me.

"It fits you." I was grinning, so happy just to hear his voice. And that was a sobering reminder of all I stood to lose if we couldn't make this work.

"You cannot possibly expect me to agree with that," he responded.

I managed to keep my voice light. "So don't. Your modesty's great, but we both know it's true." His modesty was also sincere, and one of the things I admired about him. He'd been on track for a first, or top honors, at Cambridge until he'd deliberately washed out as part of his cover, had earned a Ph.D. in biochemistry from MIT under an alias, and secretly received the George Cross from Her Majesty the Queen for deeds of valor, but he never boasted about anything.

A heavy sigh came back to me. "I'm glad I please you," he said politely.

"You do more than please me," I told him, gentling my voice, "and you know it." Sent me into orbit was more like it, and that also was scary. Losing Trey, my former fiancé, had been painful. Losing Jack would be devastating.

Bottom line, though, I loved him, so I would try my best to make this work.

I pushed the unsettling thoughts aside. "Where are you, and how's your shoulder?

"Fine. As it was when you left." The hint of impatience in his voice reassured me. The high chest wound had hampered his shoulder movement for a while, but he seemed over that.

"I'm at work," he continued. "Where are you?"

"About to go into work. Dinner tonight?"

"Daphne's cocktail party is tonight, remember? We could have a late dinner after."

I didn't remember, probably because I preferred to block all things Daphne-related from my brain. Jack's childhood friend and onetime love, the aristocratic, blonde Lady Daphne Archibald, shared things with him I never could. Things like noble blood, family wealth, and social cachet. Mill workers' kids like me come equipped with none of the above. But I was trying to make nice for his sake, so—

"Casey?"

"Sorry. I'm almost at the door. I remember the party, Jack. I'll meet you there." And hide my reluctance behind a smile as sincere as I suspected Daphne's was. My radar pinged on her every time she came near Jack, giving me a strong hunch she didn't define *past* quite the same way he did.

Jack and I signed off. For now, at least, I could forget about Daphne and wrap up my own business, which carried considerably more importance to very many more people, even if they never knew about it.

I pushed through the front door of the unassuming brick office building, swiped my ID, and palmed the scanner. The guard on duty flicked her eyes over the readouts. With a nod, she said, "Welcome back, Agent Billings. Arachne wants to see you."

A call to the boss's office after a mission usually means one of two things. Either an agent screwed up big time, or the mission requires sensitive follow-up. Since I hadn't come anywhere close to screwing up, I should've greeted the summons with pleasure. Instead, reluctance dogged my steps as I walked to the elevator and punched the button for level one, the most secure part of our underground complex. If my case needed more action, I wasn't handing it off. But I wanted my two days of standard post-mission leave to spend with Jack.

Frowning, I watched the floor readout change. How had he gotten so deeply under my skin, and so quickly? Was I that deeply under his?

The elevator stopped with a *ding*, and the doors opened. I took about a score of steps over unremarkable indoor/outdoor carpeting—easy to clean when people bled on it—in British Blue to the faux oak, steel door of Arachne's office.

When I opened it, the motherly receptionist, Lucy, gave me her cheery smile. "Go straight in, Agent Billings. She's expecting you."

I thanked her. From a desk in the corner, Arachne's blond assistant, Martin, glanced at me through his gold-rimmed glasses. "I see you returned whole, not trailing blood or other fluids." He sniffed. "Congratulations."

Striding past him to the inner door, I smiled in a sweet way calculated to annoy him and wondered why the hell he sounded disapproving at my lack of injury. If I'd come in bleeding, he would've expressed concern for the carpet.

I tapped on Arachne's door and walked in.

She looked up over half-moon glasses and waved me to a seat. We had no idea what her real name was. The head of our European operations went only by that single title, Arachne. Stylish as always in a rose silk suit, she gave me a quick nod of approval. "Very nicely done, Miss Billings."

No too-modern *Ms.* for her. "Thank you, ma'am."

She closed the folder in front of her, set it aside for a moment, and regarded me gravely. "The Security Service has taken an interest in your smuggling case."

That was the other name for MI5, Jack's agency, which probably didn't bode well. "I assume that's not good," I said, not wanting to leap to a nasty conclusion.

"No. In fact, they have warned us off it."

"The hell they—sorry, ma'am." But damn it, I'd done good work on that case, as had several of my colleagues. I blew out a breath. "Do they realize all signs point to something big coming? Why the f—why wouldn't they want all possible eyes and ears open for it?"

"Precisely my own questions." She studied me for a moment. "According to the latest report from France, the interrogations point to one of two events as a target. The first, London Fashion Week, begins in two weeks, which you may not realize if you haven't followed fashion news." A tactful way to inform me since she knew I paid little attention to Fashion Anything. "The second is the prime minister's wedding the week after that."

I pursed my lips in a silent, dismayed whistle. Either of those would involve hundreds of people, with thousands more on the streets. The prime minister's wedding guests included a veritable Who's Who of the Industrialized World. "Knowing that, MI5 and MI6 wanting to take this alone makes even less sense."

Watching me closely, she said, "I have reliable information that the order comes at the suggestion of Lord Bainbridge. What do you know about that?"

Jack. For a moment, I couldn't believe it, but her grim expression convinced me. Damn it, how could he? Why would he? If she said her info was reliable, though, it was.

I met her stare with my own most direct one. "I know nothing about it, ma'am."

But I for-damned-sure would before today was over.

Acknowledgments

I worked on this book in fits and starts for a long time. Various writers generously shared their time and perspectives as I tried to get the story just the way I wanted it. I'm indebted to Marcia Abercrombie, Caren Crane, Suzanne Church, Claudia Dain, Jeannie Dees, Merle Finch, Scott Hancock, Louise Herring-Jones, Terry Hoover, Nancy Knight, Dianna Love, Laura Klink-Maldonado, Rebecca Moore, Angie Narron, Kathleen O'Reilly, Berta Platas, Patricia Rice, Jo Robertson, Michele Roper, Gerri Russell, Judith Stanton, Anna Sugden, and Ann Wicker for their input.

Jeanne Adams, PJ Ausdenmore, Van Garrison, Cassondra Murray, and Wendy Felker read drafts and offered detailed, invaluable critiques. Steve Doyle and John Robinson offered advice on various aspects of action sequences.

Laurie Dunn, Joan Kayse, and Suzanne Ferrell advised me on how best to have Jack shot and still keep the story on the track I wanted.

Anna Sugden answered numerous questions for me about British expressions and customs and hunted up photos she thought I might use as references. She also wandered through York twice with me while we played "what if" for the scenes set there. If I got something wrong, it's because I didn't think to ask her about it.

Rob Rundle and Hass Yusuf helped me with questions about London.

I toured Wensleydale, the area where much of the story is set, with Yorkshires True Tours. Judy Horwell helped me arrange dates and itineraries, making great suggestions in the process. My excellent guide, Alan Rowley, tailored the day to my interests and cheerfully answered my many questions about customs and geography, both for this book and the ones to come.

Jeanne Adams, Suzanne Ferrell, Dianna Love, and Gina Robinson have been generous with promotional assistance.

Lyndsey Lewellen created the covers and branding for the series. Ann Wicker kept the prose clean, and Mitchell Rhodes of Libris in Caps designed the layouts and formatted the text.

The Romance Bandits, as always, offered encouragement, support, and advice. My home chapter, Carolina Romance Writers, and my home away from home chapters, Heart of Carolina Romance Writers and Georgia Romance Writers, gave me ongoing support.

My agent, Beth Miller, steadily supports all my efforts with this book and others. Her input was invaluable.

My husband and son, Mark and Gavin, always encouraged me move forward with *The Deathbrew Affair* and to keep writing. Knowing they're always in my corner keeps me going.

Thanks, everyone!

About the Author

Nancy Northcott's childhood ambition was to grow up and become Wonder Woman. Around fourth grade, she realized it was too late to acquire Amazon genes, but she still loved comic books, science fiction, fantasy, history and YA romance. A highlight of her college years was the summer she spent studying Tudor and Stuart Britain at Oxford University.

Nancy has written freelance articles and taught at the college level. Her most popular course was on science fiction, fantasy, and society. A sucker for fast action and wrenching emotion, Nancy combines the magic, romance and high stakes she loves in the books she writes.

Her debut novel, *Renegade*, received a starred review from *Library Journal*. The reviewer called it "genre fiction at its best." Nancy is a three-time RWA Golden Heart finalist and has won the Maggie, the Molly, the Emerald City Opener, and Put Your Heart in a Book.

Married since 1987, Nancy and her husband have one son, a bossy dog, and a house full of books.

For more information about Nancy and her books, check out

http://www.nancynorthcott.com.

You can also connect with Nancy on social media:
Facebook: https://www.facebook.com/nancynorthcottauthor
Twitter: https://twitter.com/NancyNorthcott
Goodreads: https://www.goodreads.com/Nancy_Northcott
Pinterest: http://www.pinterest.com/nancynorthcott/

Also by Nancy Northcott

Romantic Suspense
Danger's Edge, an Arachnid Files novella in the anthology *Capitol Danger*
Danger's Dance (a novella, forthcoming

The Lethal Webs

The Deathbrew Affair

Paranormal Romance

The Light Mage Wars encompasses three books published under the series label The Protectors. Each book or short story contains a stand-alone romance but is also part of one longer story arc.

Sentinel is a prequel to the both The Protectors and The Light Mage Wars. For readers who want to read the parts of that longer arc in order, this is the sequence:

Sentinel (an extended-length novella)
Renegade
Protector (a novella)
Guardian
Warrior
"Magic & Mistletoe" (short story)
"The Magic Christmas Guy" (forthcoming)
Nemesis (forthcoming)

Free Light Mages Stories

"The Solstice Ball" in *Tiny Treats: A Holiday Collection*
(expanded to become "Magic & Mistletoe")
"Green Beer" in *Tiny Treats 2: A St. Patrick's Day Collection*

Fantasy

The Boar King's Honor Trilogy:
The Herald of Day
The Steel Rose (forthcoming)
The King's Champion (forthcoming)

Science Fiction

The New Badge, a novella in the *Welcome to Outcast Station* anthology

www.ingramcontent.com/pod-product-compliance
Lightning Source LLC
Chambersburg PA
CBHW070850260626
47170CB00007B/2571